TO RESCUE A ROGUE

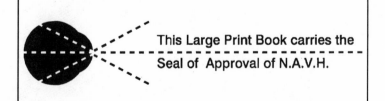

This Large Print Book carries the
Seal of Approval of N.A.V.H.

To Rescue a Rogue

Jo Beverley

THORNDIKE PRESS

An imprint of Thomson Gale, a part of The Thomson Corporation

THOMSON

™

GALE

Detroit • New York • San Francisco • New Haven, Conn. • Waterville, Maine • London

THOMSON
GALE
™

LIBRARY OF CONGRESS CATALOGING-IN-PUBLICATION DATA

Beverley, Jo.
   To rescue a rogue / by Jo Beverley.
     p. cm. — (Thorndike Press large print basic)
    ISBN 0-7862-9101-X (hardcover : alk. paper) 1. Large type books. I. Title.
  PR9199.3.B424T6 2006
  813'.54—dc22
                                         2006029854

U.S. Hardcover:
ISBN 13: 978-0-7862-9101-4
ISBN 10: 0-7862-9101-X

Published in 2006 by arrangement with NAL Signet,
a member of Penguin Group (USA) Inc.

Printed in the United States of America on permanent paper
10 9 8 7 6 5 4 3 2 1

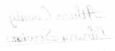

ACKNOWLEDGMENTS

Thanks as always to my agent, Meg Ruley; my editor, Claire Zion; and everyone working at New American Library who make the interface between crazy creativity and the business of publishing work.

To my many writer friends, who are always willing to help.

To my family, who put up with someone whose head is often in another world.

To Nancy Mayer, who sent me a photocopy of *A Visit to London,* and to Jen Pazzotti, who made the original copy.

To Nan Gao, who helped me to bring Feng Ruyuan to life.

And in particular to the anonymous man who shared with me his withdrawal from oxycontin, an opium-derived modern drug. I've done my best to deal with that subject honestly.

And to all the readers who make

writing these novels so rewarding. Without you, none of this would be possible.

To the Company of Rogues. I've piled problems and challenges on you over the years, but you've remained gentlemen to the end.

CHAPTER 1

London
May 1817

A London night is full of sounds, but the barefoot young woman had not let any of them halt her flight until she heard the rattle of a carriage. Hoofbeats pounded along the street toward her and lamps threw light onto the dark pavement.

Lady Mara St. Bride froze. The coach could hold members of the fashionable elite. People like her. She could ask for help.

No. What use would safety be if the price was ruin? She could survive this. She could.

Mara turned away, praying that the occupants of the carriage were dozing. That even if they were looking out they'd see only a barefoot wretch huddled in a blanket. Two-a-penny in London, and no concern of theirs.

With her present luck, the passengers were

charitable saints inspired to rescue the unfortunate.

The vehicle rolled by, however, its lamplight gilding stones and railings to her left, then to her right, then moving on, leaving her in the unquiet, dangerous dark.

Mara longed to stay in hiding, but she forced herself on. The pause made her newly aware of rough flagstones shredding her silk stockings, of stones bruising her feet, and worst of all, of the occasional something that squished between her toes.

Even though it wasn't particularly cold, she shivered, trembling with a new awareness that London after midnight was not asleep, but full of life. She heard the yowl of a cat, a rustle and scurry that was probably rats, and most dangerous of all — distant human sounds, the music and voices that had to be from some sort of tavern.

In the last century this area close to St. James's Palace had been the most fashionable part of London. There were still many fine streets, but woven among them, like wormholes in fruit, lay warrens of decay, vice, and violence.

Oh, to be in Mayfair, where gaslights triumphed over gloom. Here the only light came from the lamps kept lit outside the doors of responsible householders. They were enough to break the blackness, but not enough to tell what scurried in front of her and then away.

Her sister Ella's Mayfair house was simply too far away. A mile at least. If Mara's sore feet were capable of it, her nerves weren't. But she could make it to nearby Great Charles Street, to the Duke of Yeovil's house, where she might have a friend.

Then she heard voices. Male voices and coarse laughter. Coming this way.

She couldn't be caught like this — stripped down to shift and corset beneath the blanket! She looked frantically for a hiding place. She should have seized the chance of rescue at any price.

The terrace of tall houses stretched unbroken left and right, the doorways too shallow to offer a hiding place, but the railings at the front guarded a stairwell down to the basement door. She grabbed the nearest gate, but as she'd feared, it was locked. The men had turned onto the street. Four of them.

She backed, blessing shadows now, wondering if she could climb over the spiked top without killing herself. Not with shift and blanket and trembling hands. She shook the next gate hard and almost tumbled into the well when it swung inward. Thank you,

God! She stumbled down the steep steps into the deepest shadow.

A stink made her gag. There was a dead animal here somewhere, giving off that particular sweet-and-foul odor. She turned her head away and breathed as little as she must as the booted feet and voices came closer, closer, closer. She couldn't understand a word they were saying, so strong their accent was, but another burst of sniggering laughter melted her bones with terror.

Panting, leaning against the gritty stone wall, she waited until all sound of the men faded. Why had she been such a fool? Why had she sneaked out of her sister's house at night?

Despite the stink, she longed to stay in the dark, but daylight would make exposure more likely and her maid was waiting to let her back in. If she didn't return soon, Ruth would panic. She'd tell Ella and George and they'd tell her family, and her family would drag her home to Brideswell. The very thought of Brideswell felt like heaven, but she didn't want any of them to know how stupid she'd been.

She could escape this with few the wiser. She *could.*

Mara made herself move and climb the

rough steps back to the blessedly deserted street. She scurried to a corner and peered up at the writing on the house. Upper Ely Street! She knew where she was.

She wasn't far from St. James's Square and King Street, where Almack's Assembly Rooms were situated, and Dare was in the next street.

Lord Darius Debenham, the Duke of Yeovil's younger son, was a close friend of Mara's brother Simon from their school days at Harrow. Dare had spent many summer weeks at Brideswell.

Mara and Ella had met him in St. James's Park the other day and he'd said he was living at Yeovil House. He'd even said that his parents were away, visiting somewhere. Oatlands? Chiswick?

She shook her head. What did that matter? Dare was nearby and he was as good as a brother to her. Like a brother he'd never let her forget her folly, but he'd get her out of this pickle and safely home and might even agree not to tattle to Ella and George.

She hurried on, keeping to the shadows until she reached the next corner. Great Charles Street. Thank the Lord!

Two solid ranks of identical four-story houses stretched before her. She knew Yeovil House was a mansion, taking up the center of one side, but that wasn't obvious. Which side was it on? She scurried along, anxious about sounds of life from some of the houses. What if someone came out?

The mansion should be obvious, but in the dim light her panicked mind could make no sense of anything.

Then she saw it — the stretch of facade with only the one central door.

She ran across the road toward it, but then the flare of relief faded. Yeovil House loomed dark and quiet.

She clutched the gilded railings, strength draining away. Dare had probably gone to bed hours ago. He wasn't completely recovered from his Waterloo wounds and then there was the other problem. Didn't opium make people sleep a lot?

Even if he was awake, how did she get in?

By day, even alone, Lady Mara St. Bride could simply knock. Now, if she managed to rouse a servant, they'd slam the door in her ragamuffin face.

She couldn't go on. The soles of her feet felt raw, her legs wobbled, and her heart raced with panic. She tested the gate in the railings, but of course, it was locked.

She looked up at four daunting floors of windows. Even if she knew which one was Dare's bedroom, she doubted she could throw a stone high enough to hit it. Throwing things had never been one of her skills, much to her brothers' disgust.

Overcome, she slumped on the lowest step, half hoping someone would see her, as long as they were respectable enough to get her back to Grosvenor Square. Her family would be shocked and disappointed, but that would be that. Except that it would reinforce her father's opinion that London was a nasty, unhealthy place and he'd never let her visit Town again.

It *was* a nasty, unhealthy place. It was crowded, dirty, and noisy, but she'd never expected it to be boring. She mopped tears with the scratchy blanket, knowing that wasn't precisely true. Life with her sister was boring, but it wasn't Ella's fault that she was at the stage of pregnancy when she felt sick most of the day and exhausted the rest so that they never went anywhere.

If Mara had stayed home at Brideswell, this wouldn't be happening. There was no novelty there, but at home she had friends, family, and constant activity. There, she'd never have pitched herself into such a disastrous situation, but if she had, every house would have held a friend. What's more, the whole area could know her folly and never let a word of it out to the wider world.

She sighed and made herself stand. She'd tossed herself into this broth and she would get herself out of it. If she had to walk to Grosvenor Square, she would.

Then she heard booted footsteps — coming down the street from her right. No hope of refuge in the stairwell here, but the door was deeper set. She ducked in and huddled down.

The booted feet came closer — then stopped.

Move on. Move on!

The steps turned toward her.

Mara squeezed her eyes shut as if that might help.

"Are you in need of help?" a gentle voice said.

Mara peeped up over the edge of her blanket, and then threw herself into the tall man's arms.

"Dare! Oh, thank God. Dare, I'm in such a pickle! You have to help me. . . ." She was sobbing now and couldn't help it.

"Mara? No, don't talk. Not here. Let's get you inside."

She heard the click of key in lock and the door opening, but was hardly sure how she came to be in the elegant hall. A glass-guarded candle shed faint light on the gleaming floor, a grand staircase, and Dare locking the front door. He was in jacket, breeches, and boots. Casual clothes. Not evening wear.

Her mind was spinning, and she was clutching the blanket around her as if that would help her stay upright, but she was safe. Dare would save her.

When he turned to look at her, she said, "This is like the bullfighting, isn't it?"

"What?" He looked as if he doubted his senses.

"Remember? I decided to try to fight a bull as the Spanish do. You rescued me. I felt the same giddy relief to be alive."

He shook his head, but said, "And I'll rescue you again." He frowned at her feet, picked her up and carried her upstairs. "It'll have to be my bedroom. Don't worry about that. Whatever mad start you've fallen into this time, Imp, I'll sort it out."

Imp.

The teasing name comforted her even more. That's what he'd called her in those past golden days when she'd been a child and he'd been the merriest young man she'd known.

She turned her face into his jacket and worked at not crying anymore. She was safe.

As safe as if she'd found refuge with one of her brothers. Safer. Dare wouldn't rip up at her the way Simon or Rupert would. And surely he wouldn't tell her father.

He opened a door, then carried her to sit sideways on the high bed. "Take off the remains of your stockings and we'll clean you up." He went to the washstand.

He'd spoken so coldly, as if he were disgusted with her. Of course he was. She was disgusted with herself. She was eighteen, not twelve. Too old for such a foolish start. He must think her a crazy hoyden, and this time it hadn't been a bull, but a more dangerous male — a man.

She sighed and carefully rolled down her silk stockings, but they no longer warranted care. They were embroidered with flowers and had cost a shameful amount, but now they were ruined. As she had almost been.

"They're off," she said, pulling the blanket back around herself, her voice squeaking. "But I have to get home, Dare. Now. Can you —"

"Not before I've checked your feet." He turned, bearing a bowl of water, a washcloth, and a towel, which he spread on the coverlet. "Put your feet up on this."

She obeyed the impersonal order, her filthy, ruined stockings still clutched in her hand. She'd rather he rip up at her as Simon would. Too late, she realized that she wanted Dare Debenham to see her as a young lady now, an adult. Respectable.

He held out his hand and she reluctantly put the stockings into it. He tossed them in the fire, then sat by her feet and raised each to study it.

"No blood, I don't think." He looked up, blue eyes steady. "All right. What happened, Imp?"

Again the name shook her. He'd started to call her Imp because she had the same dark hair shot with red that Simon had. Or because she'd been an impish child. From the perspective of a six-year-old, a fourteen-year-old lord had seemed awe-inspiring. She'd reacted with some bit of cheek and he'd called her "an imp from hell."

With his usual grin, which had always stolen her heart.

"Mara, what happened?"

She focused and realized what the dark concern in his eyes meant.

"Oh! Nothing like *that,* Dare. I ran away."

She saw him relax. "So where did you have to run away from? And," he added, looking down to dab at the sole of her right foot with a soapy cloth, "why were you there in the first place?"

It stung and she squirmed, or perhaps that was because of his tone. "You don't need to do that. Wash my feet."

"Stop trying to avoid the confession. What bull did you wave a red cloth at this time?"

"It wasn't my fault," she protested, but then grimaced. "I suppose it was. I sneaked out of Ella's to go with Major Berkstead to a gaming hell."

He paused to stare. "In God's name, why?"

She looked down and saw how grubby her hands were. One fingernail was broken. Not a lady's hands at all. "I've been asking myself that. I suppose I was bored."

Surprisingly, he laughed. There wasn't a lot of humor in it, but it was a better re-action than she'd expected. "Your family should know better than to let a devil-hair have time on her hands."

"They probably never will again."

Devil-hair. That's what her family called the dark hair with red lights, and it wasn't a welcome sight on a St. Bride baby. It pre-dicted a taste for adventure at best, disaster at worst. It was said to be an inheritance from a medieval ancestor known as Black Ademar.

Devil-hair was rare, but her parents had two afflicted offspring. The first was Simon.

When a second had appeared, they'd stared down the devil and called her Ademara. She'd much rather have been Lucy, or Sarah, or Mary, and have the typical St. Bride brown hair and comfortable nature. Look where the hair had brought her now.

Dare rinsed the dirty cloth and resumed bathing her foot. "So who is this Berkstead? Not, I assume, an approved suitor."

"But he is! I mean, not precisely a suitor, but I've met him at Ella's house on a number of occasions. He's an MP. From Northumberland."

"Never trust a politician," he remarked, shifting his attention to her other foot. "You escaped from the gaming hell?"

She didn't want to answer, but must. "No. From his rooms."

His look was brief, cool and scathing.

"I know, I know! I can't imagine now why I went there except that I hadn't been playing in the hell, only watching. I wanted to try some of the games."

"Who saw you there?"

"At the hell? Many, but I was masked and Berkstead didn't use my name. He called me 'my queen of hearts,' which should have been enough to turn me off card games for life."

She'd tried for a lighter tone, but Dare

didn't smile.

"What about the hair?" he asked.

"Turban."

He nodded and returned his attention to her foot, for which she was grateful. She'd never have thought Dare could be so profoundly disapproving. She wanted to protest that once he'd have thought this a jape, but perhaps that wasn't true, and in any case that merry madcap clearly no longer existed.

"Continue," he said. "Tell me everything."

"Berkstead had been a perfect gentleman all night. I *liked* him. He's a military hero and a great deal more amusing than the rest of George's associates. I usually have a good instinct for people — you know I do."

"And?" He was relentless.

She scowled at him even though he couldn't see it. In fact, she probably wouldn't have done it if he could see. She was, she realized, nervous of him. Not for her safety, exactly, but just nervous.

"We played for a while," she said. "He was drinking and encouraged me to drink, but when I wouldn't, he didn't press me. I know all about sharps getting flats drunk in order to fleece them."

He glanced up, brow raised. "Do you? But no suspicion of your greater danger?"

"No. He must be nearly forty!"

Perhaps at last he showed a glimmer of humor. "I assume he acted as if unaware of his advanced years."

"Men do, don't they? He proposed to me."

Now she had his full, astonished attention. "What?"

"He did. He asked me to marry him. No — he said we'd be married. That my being in his rooms didn't matter because we'd soon be married. Of course I turned him down. Politely," she added.

His eyes were cold again. "Which he didn't, I assume, take well."

"He didn't take it at all. I've never known such a blockhead. He treated my every word as if I was playing a game."

"In the cur's defense, you had gone willingly to his rooms at night."

"That's no common indication that a lady wishes to *marry* a man."

As usual, her quick tongue had raced ahead of sense, and his dry "No" said volumes.

She tried to pull her left foot out of his hands, but he tightened his grip and parted her toes to clean between them. It suddenly looked and felt shockingly intimate.

"You really shouldn't be doing that."

"I can hardly summon a servant. What happened next?"

"I can't remember." In part because her mind was slipping into misty distraction of a different sort. "It all became very foolish, then very unpleasant."

"Ah. Tell me about the unpleasant part. I do note that you seem to be undressed."

A wave of heat passed over her. It was probably turning even her toes red.

"He didn't," she assured him. "We didn't. He simply wouldn't *believe* me. He knelt and protested that he adored me. That he'd cherish and take care of me. I didn't know what to do, so I told him that I couldn't marry him because my parents would never let me move far from Brideswell. That's true — you know it is — and I'd never do it anyway. Instead of giving up, he took that as a challenge and declared that we must . . . go to bed to force their hand."

He looked at her, a steady question in his eyes.

"Of course we didn't! I keep telling you that, and I certainly told him. He was pleased, would you believe? Said it proved I was a virtuous lady despite my wild behavior. Then he decided that my staying there for the night would work just as well. In the early hours, he'd send a message to say that we wished to marry and had spent the night together. I told him my maid was waiting up and she'd set off the alarm before then. It didn't shake him. Nothing I said could move him. This is all," she said with a scowl, "a consequence of Father becoming the Earl of Marlowe. No one would act so idiotically with plain Miss St. Bride of Brideswell."

"You underestimate your charms."

It was a dry statement, but Mara's spirits perked. "Really? I have had many suitors — but none has lost his wits over me."

"Not a single madman? No pale corpse laid to your account? How dreadful. So what then? How do you come to be without your gown?"

She supposed she'd never had a hope of passing that by.

"He took it off. I made an error and said I'd escape. I don't think he believed me, but he insisted I take off my gown and shoes to, as he put it, prevent my putting myself in danger. I couldn't fight or scream without being discovered. You see that, don't you?"

"Yes. What happened next?"

Mara decided to skip over the way Berkstead had looked at her corset, then kissed her in a slobbering way, before thrusting her into his bedroom.

"He locked me in his bedroom," she said.

"How many floors up?"

"Only one. And there were sheets for a rope."

"As you said, a blockhead."

"For not realizing I'd escape, even shoeless and undressed?"

"For not realizing that someone would kill him."

Mara sat up straight. "No duel!"

"You have no say in this."

"Oh, yes, I do." She dragged her foot out of his grasp. "When I heard Simon had fought a duel and almost died I knew they were an invention of the devil. I won't have it, Dare. I *won't!* I couldn't bear to have you or Simon hurt because of my stupidity. I don't even want Berkstead killed. It was at least half my fault."

"He's a louse."

She looked at his set face and wanted to scream with frustration. Instead, being an experienced sister, she tried piteous. "*Please,* Dare."

He briefly closed his eyes. "Very well. You won't mind, I assume, if I warn him away from making further trouble?"

"I'd be very grateful. And," she added, "no one else need know? You won't tell Simon?"

Or Father, she thought.

"If you don't want Berkstead dead, I most

definitely won't tell your devil-haired brother. But I probably should tell your father. Perhaps he'd whip some sense into you."

"You know he wouldn't, but please don't." She reached to touch his arm. "I promise I've learned my lesson. I'll never do anything like that again. I was just so *bored.*"

He moved slightly back, breaking the contact. "Didn't Johnson say that when someone is tired of London, they're tired of life?"

"I'm not tired of it. I haven't yet experienced it. Ella's expecting. To be fair, she didn't know when she offered, but apparently at this stage she's incapable of anything more than tea with friends, quiet concerts, and drives in the park. Never, of course, at a fashionable hour. Too much noise and hurley-burley."

"Which is exactly what you want."

She responded to the understanding in his eyes. "Is it so bad? We were here for the special Drawing Room on St. George's day, but that would have been absolutely too much for her."

"In fairness, it probably would have been, and a dead bore to boot."

"But it would have been something. Almack's. The theater. Something. Ella's house is quieter than Brideswell."

"Not difficult to achieve." Perhaps there was a smile in his eyes.

She smiled back, for her crowded home was all bustle and life. "No, but you know what I mean. The only guests are matrons like Ella, talking endlessly of husbands and children, and George's fellow MPs wanting to discuss the Corn Laws, sedition, or the ruinous cost of the army. All very important, I'm sure, but tedious."

"Enter this military Berkstead. I assume he's handsome and dashing."

"For a man of his age." She almost added, *He was at Waterloo,* but thought better of it. That was where Dare had been so terribly wounded. "He took me to amusing places such as the waxworks and the Egyptian Hall. And he knows all the best scandals."

He stood, dropping the washcloth in the bowl. "You need some livelier lady to chaperone you."

Clearly he did not approve of waxworks, the Egyptian Hall, and especially not of scandals. Could he really have become so prosy?

"None of my friends from Lincolnshire are in London yet. Simon and Jane are to come soon, but it keeps being put off. It is *excruciating* to be so close to a treat but have to view it from within a cage."

"Poor Mara."

Her deliberate exaggeration had been rewarded with the ghost of a smile. Suddenly she needed to revive the old Dare, to make him smile as he used to — widely, brilliantly, infectiously. She needed him to make a witty joke, or propose some outrageous piece of mischief — daring her, daring everyone, to join him.

He was only twenty-six. Surely not too old for merriment and mischief. War, wounds, and other problems may have ground down his spirits, but it must be possible to build them up again.

He carried the basin back to the washstand and then turned to study her. Something about his stance, or the candlelight, or her steadier nerves made her aware that the changes were not entirely for the worse.

He was still slim, but stronger, with broader shoulders and more muscle. There was something about his face, too. It was still a little long, the mouth a little wide, but there seemed to be more definition around his jaw and eyes, giving it a pleasing symmetry. Or perhaps the effect came from his light brown hair being fashionably cropped, not falling carelessly around his collar as he used to wear it.

Just perhaps sobriety suited him. . . .

He quirked a brow as if wondering what she was thinking. She began to scramble off the bed. "I really do need to get home, Dare. My maid will set up an alarm."

"Wait a moment. I'll find you something of Thea's to wear."

He left and Mara could breathe properly and try to gather her wits.

CHAPTER 2

Thea was Lady Theodosia Debenham, Dare's younger sister. Mara had read about her introduction to society last spring. Anything to do with Dare had been of interest, for at that time the St. Brides and the world had still mourned him. The St. Brides had learned of Dare's discovery alive in the paper, too, for with Simon still in Canada, no one had thought to tell them.

What a delirious day that had been, even though the paper had said he was grievously ill and addicted to the opium that had been given him for the pain of his wounds.

She lifted and turned her right foot so she could inspect the damage. A couple of scrapes across the ball of her foot could be sore for a while, but even if walking hurt her tomorrow, she'd be able to conceal the injury and its cause.

Dare had never had a chance of concealment. When a duke's son had been thought

31

dead at Waterloo, then spectacularly appeared alive over a year later, some explanation must be made.

Thus the papers had recounted the story in full — how his horse had been shot from under him and he'd been trampled by cavalry, resulting in broken bones and a head wound, which had deprived him of awareness of who he was for quite some time.

He'd been cared for by a kindly Belgian widow, who had given him laudanum for his excruciating pain, but so much of it for so long that he'd become addicted.

Mara could understand. How could anyone watch someone suffer when relief was at hand? Once someone was accustomed to opium, however, it was very hard to break free.

She'd asked their family doctor about Dare's chances, but Dr. Warbuthnot had shaken his head.

"On it a year? Heavy dose? Better to stay on it, m'dear. It changes the body, you see, so that the organs need it to function. Sudden abstinence can kill, and if it doesn't, it can drive the sufferer mad."

She'd been appalled. "But surely some people manage to free themselves?"

"Very few in my experience."

"But the system of gradual reduction?" she'd persisted. "That's what Lord Darius is using."

"Haven't witnessed the attempt, but I have grave doubts. Who has the strength for constant torment, and what is the point? If a person has the courage for that, they have the resolution to take only what they need to live a normal life. There are men and women of respectability, even of eminence, m'dear, in just that condition. There's no shame to it."

It hadn't been the assurance Mara had wanted, but now she wondered if Dare had settled for that path. Why else was he in London, living a normal life? He'd lived in seclusion at Long Chart, his family's Somerset estate, since his discovery. She'd been surprised to encounter him in the park the other day.

Yet he wasn't living a normal life. He wasn't taking part in the early events of the season, for that would have been noted in the papers. He'd responded to Ella's invitation to dinner with a vague comment about living quietly. No normal young lord lived quietly in London, especially not Dare, whose friends had to be legion.

He returned and she smiled, wiping away any trace of her thoughts. She had no right to be picking apart his life, but she couldn't help caring.

He passed over cotton stockings, kid slippers, and a gown of dull gray silk. "I don't think Thea will miss these."

"I'll return them."

"The stockings are darned, the slippers battered, and I'm sure she'll be glad to see the end of the dress. I assume it must have been for mourning."

For him, probably, Mara thought, wriggling into the plain gown. Lady Thea must be taller and with a more bounteous figure, but it would have to do. She turned her back. "Fasten it, please."

His hesitation brought her to her senses. What was she *doing?* Dare had been like a brother once, but he was a stranger now.

Four years ago when Simon had sailed for Canada, Dare had stopped visiting Brideswell. Since then, she'd only met him twice — two days ago in the park, and at Simon's wedding last December. She remembered how shocked she'd been by the change in him. He'd been so pale and thin, in some ways even fragile, and she'd hovered for fear he'd collapse.

He wasn't fragile now. He'd just carried her up the stairs and he was making her shivery and uncertain in all kinds of ways.

But someone had to fasten the dress.

"Please? I can't do it for myself."

She heard his footsteps, and then felt his fingers against her spine. A secret shiver heightened her sudden awareness that she was half dressed in a man's bedroom. She clutched the dress to herself at the front and sought something, anything, to say.

"It's loose. Your sister must have a good figure."

"There's nothing wrong with your figure."

"I'm almost flat in the bosom."

"Not flat."

"Well, no, but meager."

His fingers halted between her shoulder-blades. "Mara, really. Is this situation not awkward enough without discussing your bosom?" He finished and stepped back.

She turned, aware of the gown bulging empty at the front. "I'm sorry. I don't have much experience with strange men. I mean, you're not strange. But you're not a brother—"

"You discuss your bosom with your brothers?"

"They have been known to tease me about it."

"Then they're cads."

But he was smiling. He was!

As if he heard her thought, his face turned

35

blank. "Shoes and stockings," he said, indicating the items.

She pulled on the stockings, fixing them with her discarded pink satin garters. She caught him staring. He quickly looked away, but Mara smiled as she put on the shoes.

"A bit loose," she said, "but they'll do once the laces are tied." She did so and stood, but then froze. "I'm going to arrive home in different clothes! Ruth will . . . I don't know what she'll do."

"Who's Ruth?"

"My maid. She's to wait by the basement door to let me in. We couldn't leave the house unlocked. Not in London."

"Such a responsible houseguest."

"Don't sneer. Ruth has a very low opinion of men and sees it as her duty to protect me from them."

"And she permitted this exploit?"

"She's my maid, not my warder."

"Pity."

"Don't be nasty, Dare. She thinks I'm at a masquerade ball, but when she sees this gown, she'll tell Ella and Ella will tell George, who'll tell Father, who'll summon me home, and I'll never be allowed far from Brideswell again."

He took her hands. She realized she'd been fretting at the front of her dress and

— heavens! — tears were blurring her vision.

"Imp, don't try to tell me you can't wrap your maid around your little finger. When you arrive home safely and promise her you've learned your lesson, she'll do your will. But promise me, too. If you don't, I'll have to tell your father."

His hands on hers had wiped her mind blank, so she simply looked at him, blinking to try to clear her eyes.

"I mean it," he said.

"Oh. Yes. Of course. I mean, of course I've learned my lesson."

A thoroughly startling one. *That lean, long-fingered hands, warm and strong on hers, were magical. That Dare, her almost brother, was magical. That she wanted to stay here with him.*

No. Impossible.

But see him again. Soon. Tomorrow.

She met his eyes with what she hoped was innocent expectation. "It would be easier to be good if I wasn't so bored. If I had the chance to see more of London." He seemed blank, so she tried a smile. "If I had an escort."

Agree, Dare, agree!

He released her hands. "I'm not attending ton events."

"Oh, I don't mean Almack's or anything like that." She rapidly searched for an unalarming destination. "Even Hyde Park would be a treat."

He studied her as if wondering where the trick lay, but said, "Very well."

"Tomorrow?"

"At ten."

She'd hoped for the fashionable afternoon, but it would do for a first attempt.

"Thank you!" Mara focused her best, brightest smile on him. A lifetime had taught her that her best, brightest smile was a potent force. Perhaps he even blinked.

"If you're ready, let's get you back to Ella's." But then he looked at her feet and the trailing dress. "I doubt you can walk that far."

Practical concerns felt rather like being tossed into a chilly pond from a high-flying swing. "No, I'm sorry. Can you order a carriage?"

"At this hour? It'll have to be horseback. Can you walk to the stables?"

So very tempting to have him carry her, and her feet were sore, but Mara settled for truth. "Of course."

He picked up a candle, and passed her the discarded blanket. "You can hide in this in case we encounter any servants. Then we'll drop it in the street. Someone will be glad of it."

She put it around her shoulders and cast a quick glance in the mirror in passing. She wished she'd not. The gown hung like a sack and her hair was a scarecrow mess. She'd dragged her silk turban with the diamante clip off before escaping.

She accompanied him down the corridor feeling low. He probably thought of her as the ragamuffin child he'd used to tease.

When he steered her down a set of back stairs, she whispered, "The house feels so empty."

"I'm the only one of the family here at the moment, and the servants will be asleep."

The silent house felt eerie. Brideswell could never feel as empty, even in the deadest hours of the night. If the people were asleep, the dogs and cats still roamed. As if summoned, a silent dark shape slid up the stairs to brush against Dare's leg and purr.

"Shush," he said, and as if understanding, the cat went silent, but it padded with them down the stairs and along a basement corridor.

"Your cat?" Mara whispered, liking the thought.

"No."

A silly question. It was probably the kitchen mouser.

They followed corridors, turning twice, and then Dare turned a key in a door to the outside.

There was a rustle to their left. "Who's there?"

Mara dragged the blanket up over her head. In an alcove by the door, a round-faced boy sat up and blinked at them. A youthful guardian of the portal.

"Lord Darius. All's well. Go back to sleep."

The boy's eyes were closing as he lay down again.

"He'll probably not even remember," Mara whispered as they passed through the doorway into open air.

"I hope so." He closed and locked the door and Mara noticed that the cat was no longer with them.

A breeze fluttered the candle flame and then extinguished it. Mara gasped, blind now, but Dare took her hand, seeming to know the way. She went in simple trust.

There was some moon and her eyes adjusted, but she would have been stumbling and bumbling without his help. Then a golden glimmer broke the dark and she realized it was a lantern. In moments they were at the mews stable yard, surrounded by the familiar smell of horses.

Mara pulled the blanket up around her head again, but the night air had revived her and she suddenly felt almost happy. She was safe on a lovely moonlit night amid the familiar smells of a stable.

A creak told her Dare was opening a stall door, but then a sharp voice called, "Who's there?" A sturdy young man appeared, pistol pointed. Yeovil House was well-guarded.

He stared at Mara, but then said, "Oh, milord. Sorry, milord."

"Nothing to be sorry for, Adam. I'm pleased you're so alert. Perhaps you could get Normandy for me."

Mara almost spoke, for the name stirred memories. Her brother Simon had always called his favorite horse Hereward after their ancestor who'd led the resistance to the Norman invaders after 1066. Without malice, Dare had paid tribute to the fact that his family had pure Norman roots by using the name Conqueror for his. Not Conqueror now, but a related name, as William the Conqueror had been Duke of Normandy.

Was there any significance to the change?

She'd joined in the fun by calling her horse Godiva, after Hereward's mother, the famous Lady Godiva. Godiva was here in town. Perhaps they could go riding together.

Despite giving the order, Dare was helping the groom. In this setting he was an intriguing blend of strength and loose-limbed elegance, but completely at home. Not surprising. All the men she knew loved the stables more than the drawing room.

The men didn't saddle the big dark horse. Dare dismissed the groom before leaping easily onto Normandy's bare back and riding him to the mounting block. "Sit in front, my fair lady." A smile in his eyes had turned up the brightness of the stars.

Mara climbed the steps of the block, skirt clutched high. "Like in *Young Lochinvar*? How romantic."

" 'So light to the croupe the fair lady he swung/So light to the saddle before her he sprung!' " he quoted. "Being bareback, in front, seems better." He extended an arm. "Come on."

Getting onto the horse was surprisingly tricky, but Dare put his arm around her waist to hoist her into place, making her breathless. Or perhaps it was the place — nestled between his thighs, that strong arm around her. . . .

"Someone should revive this fashion of riding," she said, as they headed out at a walk. "The croupe can't be nearly as much fun."

"Mara, you're irrepressible."

"I hope so," she said. "I'd hate to be repressed."

He'd sounded amused. She could do this. She could bring light into his shadowed world. Or better, lead him into the sunshine.

Any attempt at speed could draw attention, so they ambled down the back lane and along the quiet streets, the horse swaying beneath them like a cradle. Despite her need to be home, Mara didn't want this strange journey to end.

The hooves clopped noisily on cobblestones, but the few people they passed paid them little attention. Dare didn't seem to want to talk, and that gave Mara time to think.

It was nine months since Dare had been found, desperately frail from wounds and illness and addicted to opium. From Simon, she knew his physical recovery had been slow but steady. He was healthy now, which was doubtless why he'd finally emerged from seclusion. But he wasn't his old self. There was something missing.

For fleeting moments, however, she had amused him and brought the old Dare to life. She must do more of it. Simon would probably see it as interfering, but someone had to crack the walls.

Yes. Walls. For all his health and composure she sensed that Dare was imprisoned in some way. By opium, still? Did that explain everything, or were there other problems as well?

She was a St. Bride with the fiery hair and thus driven to heal wounds and fix problems. How better than by spending more time with Dare? Lady Ademara St. Bride was going to ride to the rescue of her prince in the dark tower.

No, her rogue.

At Harrow school, Simon and Dare had been part of a group who called themselves the Company of Rogues. Simon's stories had been such fun that she'd always wanted to be a Rogue. Rescuing one was the next best thing.

She would rescue her Rogue from his dungeon and bring him into the sunshine. It was a noble enterprise suited to the descendant of Black Ademar and Hereward the Wake, and even better, it should keep her out of boredom-induced disaster.

CHAPTER 3

Half an hour later, Dare watched Mara St. Bride slip safely into her sister's Grosvenor Square house. Once he was sure all was well, he turned Normandy toward this Major Berkstead's address. Best to deal with the man now and without fuss. There must be no fuss, even though he'd like to disembowel him.

Terrorizing little Mara.

Not so terrorized, he reflected, and not so little anymore, for all that she bemoaned her lack of breasts. His lips twitched, but he was aware of a problem.

He'd thought himself dead to the appeal of women — perhaps something to do with the drug — but he'd felt a most inappropriate interest in Mara St. Bride's small breasts. And in her delicate neck, the fine dip of her spine, and her warm, indefinable perfume. Having her nestled against him during the ride had been a mistake.

He was used to thinking of Mara as Imp, as a child, but now he was aware of the difference four years made — the difference between the flat-chested tomboy of fourteen and the lovely young minx he'd encountered tonight. He even had a faint scrap of sympathy for her clumsy suitor.

She'd teased a promise from him to escort her around town.

Bad idea, Dare.

And yet he wanted to do it, like a man in a dungeon longs for sunlight on his skin.

The final battle against opium was proving harder than he'd expected. He took very little now, but he'd failed twice in attempts to cut off the drug entirely. It was as if the beast knew it risked defeat and fought all the harder. Perhaps he shouldn't have left Long Chart, but he'd chafed at its safety and thought a taste of the world could spur him to victory.

Once — before — he'd loved the world, people, London.

His physical wounds were healed and he had his strength back. He'd stoically eaten nourishing food since the day of his rescue, and once he was able, he'd found that vigorous, even violent exercise helped when the beast gnawed at him. There had been days when he'd walked from dawn to dusk, and sleepless nights he'd passed the same way.

Then Nicholas had sent Feng Ruyuan, who had given him purpose and discipline and begun the true healing. He was stronger and fitter now than he'd ever been, in body, but especially in mind. Freedom was in reach, but for the first time he wondered who he would be when he crawled out of his prison.

The old Dare was dead — and yet something was stirring, was trying painfully to break free, searing him with forgotten emotions.

His fear over Mara had cut sharp as a saber.

Fury had scorched him.

The feel of her skin, the scent of her body, the look of her bright eyes had stirred parts of him he'd thought dead.

Had he ever reveled in a woman's charms before? He knew he had, but never like that. Never in a shivering, breathless insanity that had wanted to gobble every bite of the forbidden feast. It terrified him more than opium. On the horse, she'd rested against him so trustingly when lust had growled inside him like a beast.

What to do?

A mistress?

He couldn't face the fuss and demands of

47

that, but a brothel, perhaps. A simple business proposition, and no repercussions if he failed to perform, which seemed likely enough.

How long was it since he bedded a woman?

Before Waterloo.

He didn't count Thérèse.

Yes, he should visit a whore. Otherwise, heaven alone knew what might happen. The cure, especially now, required him to live on the edge in almost constant need of opium.

His body needed the beast to function. It punished shortage with pain of mind and body and rewarded every dose with blissful ease. After each dose the beast whispered that without it, he'd never know such peace. . . .

He jerked his mind away from that pit.

He'd chosen life — desire, distress, pain, and all. He couldn't wait to be free of the three small doses he took each day. Each night, he built his strength, forcing his body to accept that it could live without the beast as it had for most of his life.

Every night his mind and body screamed. Every morning he greeted the foul dose like a drowning man gasping for air.

He could feel the need now. A shiver of discomfort, an awareness that all was not well, as if he'd eaten something rotten and would soon vomit.

It should be worse at this hour, but when he'd gone to find clothes for Mara, he'd coaxed a little more of the drug from Salter, arguing that he needed it in order to see Mara safely home and then deal with Berkstead. Salter hadn't balked him, so his reasoning must have made sense, but deep inside the beast had purred in victory.

Salter was his chosen guardian of the door to hell. From the day he'd been able to leave his bed, burly Salter had doled out his allowed amount of opium and accompanied him everywhere to prevent him from obtaining extra. He'd recently started to go out alone, testing his ability to resist the temptation available for pennies in every druggist's shop.

Laudanum for the headache and the toothache, or for calming a fretful baby. For the agony that came after being kicked in the head by a horse, then charged over by an army of others. He'd be dead if so many corpses hadn't cushioned him.

One day he'd be able to sit in a room with opium on the table and ignore it. One day. That was his Holy Grail. Now he shivered at the very thought. Any benefit from the extra dose was fading fast, but when he returned, he'd tell Salter never to let him change the pattern again, no matter what the circumstances.

No retreat. No surrender.

The horse stopped and he realized that he was back at the stables instead of in nearby Rennie Street.

Dare let Adam take the horse and then walked back down the lane, hoping the groom didn't notice he hadn't gone directly into the house. It was ridiculous to be worried about what a groom thought, especially when all the servants knew about Lord Darius's little problem.

As he walked to Rennie Street he focused his fragmenting mind on his quarry. He burned to hurt or kill this Berkstead but Ruyuan wouldn't approve. Ruyuan's Taoist philosophy said to achieve action through minimal action. Hardly the English gentleman's way of dealing with a villain, but he'd promised Mara the cur would live. If Oriental disciplines couldn't restrain him, that would.

He arrived in Rennie Street and considered the unbroken terraces of tall houses. He didn't know the number. He made out an arched tunnel built through two houses to the back and entered its pitch-dark maw. The exit looked lighter by contrast, and when he emerged, moonlight shone on something white. Mara's dangling rope of sheets.

A flicker of something stirred and he recognized the temptation to mischief.

He made his way to the rope and tugged it. Strong enough. He climbed up and then pulled himself over the sill into a dark room. It could be a coal cellar for all he could tell, but smells of dirty linen, snuff, and pomade spoke of a man's room. He pulled in the sheets, then picked his way to the facing wall to feel for the door, aware, as if of an old wound beginning to ache, of anticipation.

He found the latch. Hoping Berkstead wasn't passed out drunk, he rattled it, then tapped with his knuckles. Quick, nervous taps.

Something scraped in the next room. "What is it, my queen?" a well-bred voice slurred. The man had apparently been drowning his sorrows, or celebrating what he thought was victory all this time.

Closer, on the other side of the door, Berkstead added, "You won't do anything stupid like try to hit me over the head with the chamber pot, will you, my fiery-haired sweetheart?"

"No! Oh, no!" Dare gasped, as weakly and

breathily as he could manage.

The key turned and the door opened into candlelight.

The broad-shouldered man in pantaloons and an open-necked shirt took a second to adjust. He had to raise his blinking eyes from where he'd expected his prisoner's face to be to Dare's. They bugged out with complete befuddlement.

"Lord Darius Debenham," Dare said and slapped him so hard the drunken man stumbled sideways and sat down. "The lady in question forbids a duel, so you'll have to eat that insult. Stay there!" he snapped, when Berkstead made to move.

The man probably was handsome — well built, bold featured, dark eyed — but he was presently slack with shock.

"You are a louse, sir," Dare said, banked fury roaring free and finding a target. "A cur. A slug. The events of this night never happened. If any hint of them ever escapes, I will destroy you."

Berkstead was wriggling back, but he stopped and a sneering smile curled his lip. "Debenham. I know all about you."

It stung, but Dare hid it. "I doubt it, but if you don't fear me, fear her brother."

"A St. Bride of Brideswell?" Berkstead stopped trying to rise but looked more comfortable by the moment. "A bunch of country mice. Not one of them a soldier."

"There are St. Brides and St. Brides. Simon St. Bride will kill you by inches, but the list lining up behind him will include some of the most powerful men in England, none of them squeamish about crushing lice. I could start with the Duke of St. Raven and the Marquess of Arden."

The sneer died. Apart from being the most high-ranking of the Rogues' set, the two men Dare had named were known for being hard-riding, hard-fighting, and hot-tempered.

"I want to marry her!" Berkstead protested. "She wants to marry me. She's afraid of her family. They won't let her marry out of Lincolnshire."

Pity began to taint Dare's fury. "If Mara St. Bride wanted to marry a Hottentot, she would probably do so."

"I'll buy a house in Lincolnshire."

Mara was right. The man didn't listen.

"She considers you too old," Dare said, looking around for Mara's clothing.

A table still held scattered cards, two glasses, and an empty decanter. On a chair he saw white gloves, a pretty pink dress and a light pelerine of pale cloth. He picked them up, and the slippers from the floor, then took a candle back to the bedroom and found the turban.

When he returned Berkstead said, "Too *old?*"

"Is there anything else of hers here?"

Berkstead's mouth opened and shut but nothing came out. He pointed. Dare picked up a pale silk reticule from the floor by the table.

Behind him, Berkstead muttered, "Too *old?* I'm only forty."

Dare headed for the one other door that must lead to the stairs. Hand on handle, he looked back at the crumpled man. "Remember. None of this happened. That, sir, is your only hope of salvation."

CHAPTER 4

Mara woke the next morning when Ruth drew back the curtains with disapproving force. "Good morning and I hope you learned your lesson about men, Miss Mara."

"Oh, dear, I'm Miss Mara, now."

Ruth glared, her rather pouchy features making her look like a peevish hound. "*Lady* Mara, then. But a lady is as a lady does, and a lady does *not* come home in a different gown to the one she went out in."

Mara used her best repentant smile. "Dearest Ruth, I truly am *very* sorry, and I have learned my lesson. There'll be nothing like that again. Honor of a St. Bride."

Ruth continued to glare, but Mara could tell she'd softened.

"I know I frightened you, but nothing bad happened. Thank you for not alerting Ella and George."

"Which I should have done," Ruth retorted, turning to pour the hot water she'd brought into the washing bowl. "You give me your Christian word that you'll never sneak out with a man again?"

"Cross my heart."

"I don't know how you could! I warned you ahead of time that you can never trust a man, milady. A woman's only safety is to never be alone with them. Ravening beasts, they are. . . ."

Mara let the familiar lecture wash over her as she climbed out of bed and stripped off her nightgown. Ruth had a point, as Berkstead had proved; but a woman wasn't entirely defenseless, as she had proved. She had to admit, however, that if he'd planned worse than a forced betrothal she might have been in a pickle.

And if she hadn't found Dare . . .

But then Dare had shown that men can indeed be trusted.

"And what am I to do with that ugly gown, milady?"

"I'll find a way to return it."

"How am I to explain the disappearance of your pink — *that's* what I'd like to know."

Mara wanted to order Ruth to stop fretting, but she was owed as much of a fret as she felt inclined to take.

"Who's to notice other than us?" Mara

said. "But Lord Darius will find a way to return it."

"That one. Not a serious bone in his body."

"He's changed."

"And not for the better, I'm sure. When I think what could have happened, you alone with him like that."

"Ruth, he's like a brother."

"But he's not." Ruth was bent over a drawer. She'd apparently run out of steam, however, for she was taking out fresh underclothes.

Mara washed, probing her emotions for shame about last night. Bad girl that she was, she couldn't find any. She knew she'd been foolish, and she hoped no one other than Ruth and Dare — and Berkstead, she supposed — need ever know. But she couldn't regret something that in the end had been so *thrilling.*

Looked back on from her present safety, even her flight through the dark streets felt thrilling. And Dare — how magnificent he'd been. She wished she'd been able to see him deal with Berkstead, but she'd had to get back here before Ruth panicked.

And Dare would never have permitted it.

She brushed her teeth, considering that.

No, he wouldn't have, and that thrilled

her, too. If she chose to do something he opposed, he would be a challenge. How intriguing.

And now she had a true challenge, a perfectly acceptable one. She was going to tease, trick, or force Dare Debenham back into the world, starting today.

She rinsed and spat. "What's the weather?"

"Cool and cloudy at the moment, milady, but not likely to rain, according to Cook, who always feels it in her bones."

Mara went to the window to look for herself.

"Miss Mara, you're stark naked!"

Mara pulled the blue damask curtain in front of herself as she studied the weather. Of course she couldn't see much here — not as she could from her window at Brideswell. That looked far out over Lincolnshire countryside and she could read it like a weather almanac.

"Come away, milady, and get decent before a man sees you."

Mara had never discovered if Ruth had been harmed by a man or came by her fears some other way, but it was the one feature that pushed her patience. In her own experience, gentlemen were sometimes irritating but never truly dangerous.

She turned to put on the shift. "Ruth, really. Even if a man in the square glimpsed my body, he could hardly rush up here to ravish me, could he?"

"He could pounce on you when you go out."

"I'm never alone when I go out. I generally behave exactly as a young lady should. I even wear a corset when I hardly need one," she added, putting her arms through the holes so Ruth could lace it at the back.

"You wander about at home."

"But not in Town. Not even in Lincoln."

Ruth tugged particularly hard on the corset laces.

"I need to breathe, you know," Mara protested.

"A good tight lacing'll remind you you're a lady. You're too trusting by far!"

"Too breathless, you mean. Stop it!"

When Ruth relented and eased the laces to a natural fit, Mara said, "I admit to misjudging Major Berkstead, but even there, his main intent seemed to be to *marry* me. It was most peculiar. He seems to truly think he loves me."

"You're a very desirable bride, milady, and you need to remember that. But of course, you could never marry a man from *Northumberland.*" Ruth said that as if it were the

South Seas.

"So I said. It didn't help."

Ruth passed over the stockings and garters. "Some people won't listen to anything but what they want to hear. What dress today, milady?"

Mara pulled on the first stocking, thinking regretfully of the ruined ones, and then of Dare throwing them in the fire. For some reason that memory thrilled her, but everything about Dare last night thrilled her. The way he moved, his direct eyes, his firm mouth . . .

"Milady, what dress?"

Mara snapped out of wicked thoughts. "The brick red. I'm driving with Lord Darius this morning. You have to admit he's as safe as the Mint."

Ruth turned to get the outfit, but muttered, "Addicted, he is."

"He's better." How Dare must hate even the servants knowing.

"Driving where?" Ruth demanded, carrying the dress and spencer back.

"None of your business," Mara replied as a general reminder of who was servant here and who was mistress. But then she added, "Hyde Park. In daylight. Nothing could be tamer."

Ruth grimaced.

"We've all known Dare since he was a shaveling," Mara protested. "There's not a scrap of bad in him. Not a scrap. So we'll have no more of this."

Ruth stopped her complaining, but the way she walked to the armoire and took out the Shako-style hat that went with the outfit spoke of mutiny. Old family retainers could be a sad trial, but Mara couldn't imagine being comfortable with a stranger. Ruth had tended her in the nursery.

Mara didn't usually take great interest in her clothes once they were purchased, but today, she cared about her appearance. Because she wanted to look right for Dare. Because he'd seen her in such disorder last night.

She knew her mind was whirling in a peculiar way, but it wasn't so surprising. Yesterday she'd been smothered by tedium, but last night had plunged her into different and dangerous waters — ones she rather liked.

The dusky shade of the red outfit was practical for the often sooty London air, but it also suited her. It brought out the highlights in her dark hair and the glow in her complexion. The spencer was so ruched and braided that it added inches to her bust.

Of course Dare now knew the truth. . . .

61

"What's the matter, milady?" Ruth asked, twitching the skirt into line. "It's one of your favorites and suits you very well."

Mara turned with a shrug. "Nothing. A goose walked across my grave."

"Don't you say that, miss! Sure sign of bad news, that is. Why, just before we heard that the old earl was dead and your poor father must become Earl of Marlowe, I'd just said those exact words. A shiver took me and I said, 'A goose just walked across my grave.' I swear it's true."

"I don't doubt it," Mara said, but she wanted to roll her eyes.

Last year the knowledge that their distant relation, the Earl of Marlowe, was on his deathbed had hung around Brideswell like a cold fog, making them all shiver one way or another because the death would bring terrible changes.

It would turn her father, plain Mr. St. Bride and happy to be so, into the earl. Worse still, the Earl of Marlowe's principal seat was a mansion in Nottinghamshire that was famous around the world for its classical perfection and they would all have to live there for part of the year. It couldn't be abandoned.

Even the joy of Simon's safe return from Canada hadn't entirely dispelled gloom.

Geese must have been stampeding backward and forward across the graveyard.

Simon's return had brought the solution, however. Her father had inherited the earldom and Simon, as heir, had become Lord Austrey. Nothing could prevent that. However, Simon and his new wife had taken on the duty of living in and caring for Marlowe. The St. Bride family, great-grandparents to babies, was free to continue living in cozy, imperfect Brideswell.

Though Simon clearly loved their home, he couldn't feel as strongly about it as the rest of them. After all, he'd fought to leave, to travel, and then spent years in Canada.

Despite Black Ademar's hair, Mara shuddered at the thought of spending so much time away or, worse, living far from home. Northumberland! Berkstead was mad.

A tap on the door brought the footman with a note. Mara opened it, excited even though she knew what it must be.

From Dare, formally requesting the pleasure of her company on a drive at ten. She'd never seen his writing before and considered it. Long tops and tails, but very neat. She felt strangely sure that his writing would once have been wilder, freer. She refolded it and put it in the desk drawer.

"I suppose I must ask Ella's permission.

Go and see if she's able to see me, please."

When Ruth left, Mara put on her shoes, aware of the tenderness of her feet. How fortunate that she'd arranged a drive rather than a walk.

Her mind drifted to Dare's gentle cleaning. Did men often wash their ladies' feet? She couldn't imagine no-nonsense George washing Ella's. But Simon washing his wife, Jancy's? Yes, perhaps.

Something about Simon and Jancy had been an education, perhaps especially as Jancy was Mara's own age. The newlyweds behaved properly in public, of course, and all lovers could be caught looking at one another, or sharing secret smiles.

Simon and Jancy's connection had seemed intense, however. Almost hot. Hot enough to send a shiver through Mara, for what sense that made. Certainly her Lincolnshire suitors had seemed even more dull after that.

She tied a ribbon, thinking that perhaps she was ruled by Black Ademar's hair after all. Not into seeking travel and adventure, but in matters of the heart.

She shook herself. Simon seemed to have burned through his wanderlust. Perhaps after a bit more London mayhem, she'd happily settle down with one of her quiet, dependable neighbors. Matthew Corbin, perhaps, or Giles Gilliatt.

Or with Dare? Her heart gave a patter of warning.

But he was from Somerset — almost as far from Brideswell as Northumberland. Impossible.

She went to the dressing table to put in pearl and garnet earrings. After a hesitation, she added just a touch of rouge to her lips.

What are you doing, Mara?

Anyone would think she was trying to attract Dare.

Nonsense, but deep inside, something purred.

Ruth returned. "Lady Ella's free to see you, milady."

Mara started as if caught in a sin and hurried off to her sister's room. She entered Ella's bedchamber with her mind elsewhere — to find George and Ella kissing. Not just a peck on the cheek, either!

"Oh, I'm sorry. . . ."

Mara almost had the door shut again when Ella called, "Don't be a widgeon, dear! Come in, come in."

Mara returned to find her sister and brother-in-law apart, smiling, but blushing. "I truly am sorry. Ruth said . . ."

"George just came to say goodbye." Ella

smiled wryly up at her husband. "So many meetings and committees, then another long day in the House, he fears."

George, a robust man with high color and fleshy build, nodded. "Troubled times. Must be off. My dear. Mara."

Mara watched Ella watch him leave. "I want to marry someone like that."

Ella turned to stare. "Like George? You'd never suit."

Ella was as robust as her husband, though with a perfect cream-rose complexion and a trim waist, for now. Her soft brown hair — proper Brideswell hair — only showed as waves at the edges of a lacy cap tied beneath her chin.

"No. I'd drive him mad," Mara agreed with a laugh. "I mean someone I can adore as you do him, and who would feel the same way about me."

"Oh, but of course. It would never do to marry for less. Especially with the hair."

Ella's maid came in with a fresh chocolate pot and put it on the table by the window, where Ella had clearly been taking breakfast.

"Sit and eat," Ella said, resuming her place, and pouring chocolate for Mara. "I can't do all this justice." She nibbled at a piece of toast. "It's my observation that people have different requirements in marriage. Do have a currant bun, dear. They're always excellent and I can enjoy it through you."

Mara took one and buttered it. "You mean some people like a currant bun for breakfast, and some like dry toast?"

"I do *not* like dry toast, as you well know. Wait until your turn comes. We're all like this, but we bear well, and that's a blessing. Now where was I? Ah, yes. Some people seem to be truly content with a cool marriage — one in which their spouse means no more to them than a friend." She topped up her teacup. "Most require something warmer or they will be unhappy at best and unfaithful at worst. A few require fire. I suspect Black Ademar's hair makes that demand."

Mara sipped at her chocolate, wishing she dared ask where on this thermometer Ella placed her own marriage.

"That's why I haven't yet found a man to suit?"

"Very likely, but you're young yet."

"You married at twenty."

"*I* found George."

Ella's smug tone made Mara laugh. "Hardly a heroic achievement when he's lived not five miles from Brideswell all his life and been in and out as well. *Not* finding him would have been the miracle."

Ella pulled a humorous face. "You know what I mean. He was there waiting for me and me for him."

Ella had never shared such romantic notions before, but she was right. About four years ago she and George Verney had *recognized* each other. Suddenly they'd changed, acting like perfect fools to everyone's gentle amusement, and then announcing their plan to marry as if expecting people to be surprised.

"Did you have no idea?" Mara asked. "I know every possible young man within thirty miles of home and I can't imagine suddenly seeing any of them surrounded by a golden light."

"Oh, dear." Ella picked up another piece of toast. "Someone new may move into the area."

"Or I might meet my destiny here." She watched for horror, but instead, Ella seemed to take it as a complaint.

"I'm sorry, dearest. I do intend to take you to more lively events, but right now I'm so unpredictably queasy. And I tire so easily, especially at the end of the day."

Mara reached to squeeze her hand. "Don't distress yourself. And I have relief for you. Dare Debenham has invited me to drive out with him this morning."

Instead of showing delight, Ella's face became blank. "Are you sure that's wise, dearest?"

"Why ever not?"

Ella turned pink, waving the piece of toast. "You know."

"Opium." Mara practically growled it.

"Well, yes. Very unfortunate for him, of course, but it could make him . . . *unsafe.*"

"In what way? You think he'll froth at the mouth or try to ravish me?"

But then she wondered if Dare was avoiding society for a reason. Did he have fits? Or fall asleep? Or run amok?

"Do you have reason for concern?" she demanded.

"No."

"Then why say such a thing? You met Dare the other day. He was neither in a stupor nor a rage."

"But much changed."

"Since Simon's wedding?" Mara said, deliberately misunderstanding. "Yes, he did look more robust, didn't he? Besides, we're only going driving in Hyde Park."

"Make sure he has a groom along."

"Ella, really! I don't need a servant to be safe with Dare."

"No, but I wish Simon were here."

That reminded Mara uncomfortably that Simon seemed to regard Dare as cracked glass, to be handled with care at all times. But what could go wrong in a drive around the park?

"You give your permission?" she asked, standing. "A drive in the park, no more than that, I promise."

"With a servant in attendance."

"Of course." Mara leaned to kiss her sister's cheek, then hurried back to her room.

Once there, she stood in frowning thought, then wrote a letter to her oldest brother. She chattered of this and that, asking when Simon would arrive in London. As promised, underlined. Then she mentioned meeting Dare in the park, and that he was shortly to take her driving, and perhaps to other venues on future days.

She consulted her guide book and listed some of the most highly recommended attractions: Westminster Abbey, the Egyptian Hall, the Tower of London, the Menagerie at Exeter Change, Dubourg's cork models, Barker's Panorama.

If Simon believed that a round of activity would harm Dare that should bring him posthaste. She folded the letter, sealed it, and addressed it to *The Right Honorable, the*

Viscount Austrey, Marlowe, Notts. The horrid house was so famous she could probably have addressed it to *Marlowe, the Globe,* and have it arrive. Simon should be grateful for escape.

She gave Ruth the letter. "I won't wait for George to frank it. Have it sent to the post office. In fact, have it sent express."

Ruth's mouth pursed at such extravagance, but this issue was worth a pound or two. What else was money for but to take care of friends and family?

Ruth left on her errand, so Mara put on the tall hat unaided, fixing it in place with a couple of pins and then moving her head to be sure it would stay on. It added a foot to her height, not counting the curling feather, and she liked that.

Too impatient to wait in her room, she went downstairs. Halfway down she heard the knocker, and by the time she arrived in the hall, Dare was coming in. She paused for a moment, struck by how normal he looked. No, not normal. Remarkably handsome in a shaft of sunlight.

It occurred to her that he must be spending a fortune on clothes. Apparently he'd been emaciated when discovered, but he'd have needed clothes then. At the wedding he'd still been too thin, but his clothes had fit. Now his olive green jacket, fawn breeches, and cream waistcoat fit his strong, healthy body perfectly. But then, he was no more short of money than she was.

She continued down the stairs and gave him a cheery greeting. For the benefit of the footman, she added, "How kind of you to suggest a drive."

But then she faltered, wondering for the first time how he would treat her after last night. A wary glance showed an unreadable expression. If he mentioned it . . .

But he smiled, looking her over from half boots to feather tip. "You have some objection to a gentleman being taller than you are, my lady?"

It was all right. She cheerfully squinted up to assess her height in comparison to his. "I feel sure you're up to the challenge, my lord."

"So do I."

CHAPTER 5

As she took his offered arm and left the house, Mara decided there'd been a hint of warning in those words. How delicious. Any shadowy concerns drifted away. This was going to be delightful — a feeling confirmed when she saw the carriage.

"A high-perch phaeton! I've always longed to ride in one. I should have known you'd have the latest thing, Dare."

"Must I confess that I borrowed it from a friend? I don't keep my own vehicles in Town at the moment."

Something about "at the moment" carried shadows. Mara beamed at him to drive them away. "Then you have excellent taste in what you borrow."

She eagerly navigated the steps up to the high seat. "And excellent taste in friends," she added as he joined her. "A Rogue?"

"No. St. Raven."

"A duke's rig. Even better!"

Dare took the ribbons as the groom ran to his position at the back. If Ella was watching she'd be comforted by his attendance. She'd be comforted by Dare's appearance, too. No one could imagine him a wild man.

Perhaps he was already free of the drug. Yes. Why hadn't she thought of that? It explained his arrival in London.

"Vive la liberté!" she declared as they rolled out of the square down Upper Brook Street.

He glanced at her. "You embrace revolution?"

"Only in the rolling wheels that carry me out of Fortress Grosvenor."

"What?" A hint of laughter in his voice delighted her and she continued her nonsense.

"Don't you think the four terraces of a square are like fortress walls, designed to keep some people in and others out?"

"Quite likely. London being so full of others."

"So is Monkton St. Bride, Dare. Delightfully so."

He slowed the team to navigate a spot complicated by a large wagon. "Some of the London others are a bit too otherish, Imp."

"As in the inhabitants of the Seven Dials?" she said to show she knew something

74

of the world.

He glanced at her with a frown. "What on earth do you know about a place like that?"

"I wander there at night." She laughed at his expression. "Of course, I don't. Mind that child."

He turned his attention back to his horses and slowed them to let an urchin dash across the road. "With you, one can never quite be sure."

"I think I like that."

"You shouldn't."

"Don't be prosy. I am surprised, however, at how close such a den of thieves lies to Oxford and Bond Streets. It's less than a mile from here, even."

"And how do you know *that?*"

"From a book."

"Lord help us. What sort of book?"

"*A Guide to London's Wickedness.*" At his alarmed look, she laughed again. "It's *A Young Lady's Guide to the Educational Delights of London,* given me by my godmother, the bishop's wife. Completely respectable."

"Not if it mentions the Seven Dials."

"Only to warn young ladies away from danger. Indeed," she said in response to his groan, "such warnings are *extraordinarily* useful."

He looked at her again, but now he was

75

sharing her amusement. His smiling eyes were so much the old Dare that Mara wanted to leap down and dance.

"Don't worry," she said. "I'm not the slightest bit tempted to explore there. But another perilous enterprise does appeal." When he didn't ask what, she added, "A public masquerade."

"No." He turned the team into Hyde Park Lane.

Mara sighed, but didn't press even though Dare would be the perfect escort for such an adventure. He'd share the fun, keep her safe, and never step beyond the line.

Safe. Yet after last night, safe wasn't exactly the right word. She'd trust him with her life, but the brush of his body against hers now was sending a tingle down her spine, and even the deft action of his gloved hands on the reins seemed a wonder.

Dare?

She tore her gaze away and concentrated on the enormous park. As it lay on the edge of London, it was countryside at its limits. At this unfashionable hour, it was quiet enough to be the countryside, populated by only a few pedestrians and some children out with nursemaids.

"This is lovely," she said, enjoying the greenery and the soft clop of hooves on the earthen path. Horseshoes sounded so harsh on cobblestones. "Illogical to long for Town when in the country, then pine for country when in Town."

"Doubtless why the *haut volée* migrates between the two."

"Flying high from country nest to London mating ground?" she suggested, enjoying the whimsy.

"Such a chattering and fluttering and puffing of fine feathers."

They shared a smile at the image, but she said, "I suppose we, too, will do the same."

"I have no country nest," he said. "Nor a town perch, if it comes to that."

"You own no property?" Mara was surprised. She'd always assumed him to be rich, but he was the younger son.

"A few, all leased to long-term tenants. No place appeals to me enough to evict them."

"But you'll need a home one day."

He was not fixed in Somerset, however. She noted that.

"I'll probably take rooms in London again," he said.

"Is that why you're in London now?" she asked. "To look for a place?"

"No, just for a change of scenery. And to please Mother. She longs to see me 'out in the world,' as she puts it. Back to my old self."

His tone was wry, and Mara thanked heaven he was focused on guiding the team past some boys with a kite or he might have seen her stab of guilt. Wasn't that what she, too, was doing — trying to restore the old Dare?

Something was wrong here. He needed his friends.

"Simon should be here soon," she said, then realized she'd spoken to her thoughts, not the conversation.

He drew the carriage to a halt and said, "I wish I'd gone with him."

"With Simon? To Canada?" But then Mara understood. If Dare had gone with Simon there would have been no Waterloo, no injuries, no opium.

"There's no point in might-have-beens," she said, but then winced. "I'm sorry. That was horribly preachy."

"But true. I wasn't pining, merely reflecting. I'm an object lesson on not plunging into enthusiasms without due thought."

"Now you're preaching. I told you I'd learned my lesson. I'm going to behave with complete propriety from now on."

He seemed neither skeptical nor amused. This wasn't going as Mara had expected.

Perhaps Simon was right about Dare's fragility. Her intention to meddle was beginning to feel like tossing around a precious glass bubble.

"I'm going to be good," she promised, "but I do long to meet more Rogues. I've only ever met you. And Simon, of course." The horses shifted, and she grabbed Dare's arm for balance.

He ordered the groom to the horses' heads and Mara almost felt warned off touching him. She removed her hand and laid it in her lap.

"That shouldn't be difficult," he said. "The MPs are here to do their duty in Parliament."

"Sir Stephen Ball. I've read some of his speeches in the papers. Who else?"

"The peers. The Earl of Charrington . . ."

"Lee," she said.

"Viscount Middlethorpe."

"Francis."

"Simon has bored you with us all, hasn't he? Lord Amleigh?" he tested.

"Con."

"Indeed, but he's not arrived yet. His infant took ill."

"Not seriously, I hope."

"She's recovered, I understand."

Mara counted on her gloved fingers.

"With you and Simon, that's six. Where are the other four?"

"None of them are Members of Parliament, but Hal's in town. He's married to the actress Blanche Hardcastle. Miles, I assume, is in Ireland, and Lucien at his country place, but he'll come for part of the season. Nicholas thoroughly dislikes London, but I suspect he'll be here soon."

"Why?"

He looked at her. "Because I'm here and he's playing mother hen."

"That doesn't sound like King Rogue to me."

Nicholas Delaney had formed the Company of Rogues in his first days at Harrow, and had always been the leader even though many of the others outranked him socially. She was surprised he still took that role seriously now they were all grown men.

"Do you truly mind his concern?" Mara asked.

"No."

"I hope I meet him. I hope I meet all the Rogues."

"Simon will provide you entrée."

"Or you." It popped out before she could help it, heating her cheeks. "I mean, if Simon for some reason can't be here."

"I'm not sure that would accord with the rules."

She grasped the escape. "There are rules?"

"Better than rules, we have a blood oath. Let me see if I can remember it." He leaned back, considering. " 'I do hereby pledge myself to the service of this noble band; to defend each and every one, individually and as a group from all malicious injury, and to never cease in my endeavor to bring horrible vengeance to any who might injure one of my fellows.' "

"How thrilling! What happened if anyone broke the oath?"

" 'If I should be forsworn,' " he recited in the grand manner, and Mara saw a hint of the old Dare, " 'or if I should reveal to any person the secrets of this band, I shall be boiled in oil, devoured by worms, or inflicted with other torments too horrible to mention.' We were," he added with a smile, "about thirteen at the time."

"I think it's deliciously bloodcurdling. You said *blood* oath?"

"We cut our hands with a penknife."

"Do you still have the scar?"

He pulled off his leather glove and showed her the pale scar on the ball of his thumb, but she saw other, more recent ones. She noticed for the first time that his middle finger had healed slightly crooked. They had slid into darker matters.

Quickly, she asked, "So what are the secrets?"

He pulled the glove back on, gathered the reins in both hands, and put the horses back into motion. "Under such threat, you can hardly expect me to reveal them."

"I don't think there are any."

"That in itself would be a secret, wouldn't it?"

"Wretched man! So what are the torments too horrible to mention?"

"Lack of schoolboy imagination. Which time has amended."

That had been a stupid, stupid question.

Mara looked around for escape. "I wish I'd been here in 1814 for the victory celebrations. I remember begging Papa to bring us, but of course he detests London."

"The premature victory celebrations," he pointed out. "The victory pagoda burning down was probably an omen if anyone had paid heed."

Why did everything keep circling back to Waterloo? Mara was seeking a safe response when cries of "Papa! Papa!" startled her.

Two children were racing toward the phaeton, outpacing their alarmed maids. Instinctively, Mara reached for the reins,

82

but then the groom leapt off the carriage to stop the children and Dare brought the team to an orderly stand.

All was calm, but she was aware that she'd reacted because Dare had been a second slow to do so.

"You can handle them?" he asked her, looking pale.

"Yes."

He tossed the reins to her and climbed down to go on one knee in front of the children, perhaps scolding them. Any trace of distress lasted only a moment, and then the dark-haired little girl and the sturdy, brown-haired boy were hanging on him, chattering merrily.

Papa?

Mara could hardly breathe for the knot of pain in her chest.

The groom was at the horses' heads now, but without assistance, she was stuck in the seat. Height gave her an interesting perspective.

The two maids had retreated to watch, smiling. The two children treated Dare as if he were the sun and the stars, and though he had his back to her, she sensed he felt the same way about them.

Papa?

How could she not have known Dare was

married? She'd wring Simon's neck when she saw him!

No. Nonsense. Simon would be bound to have told the whole family. And though the girl might only be about four, the boy had to be five or six. He would have been conceived when Dare was about twenty and in and out of Brideswell all the time. He couldn't have been married then.

Bastards, then. But that didn't work either. She couldn't imagine Dare having bastards, particularly ones he clearly loved, and no one at Brideswell knowing about it. Then the answer dawned.

Stepchildren.

He'd recently married a widow with children. Of course he had! The Belgian widow who had saved his life. The ache swelled again, because he was out of reach before she'd even realized she wanted him.

Dare turned and she saw the remains of happiness on his features like sunlight. She had to try to be happy for him.

He hurried to her. "I'm sorry for abandoning you. Would you like to come down and meet the children?"

She made herself smile. "Yes, please."

With his help, she made the descent in dignity and went over to the two young ones — who clearly were not seeing her arrival as a treat. They were strangely unalike for brother and sister. The sturdy, brown-haired boy could be described as plain, but the girl, with a heart-shaped face, huge eyes, and dark, bubbling curls, was beautiful.

"Mara," Dare said, "permit me to introduce Delphie and Pierre. Children, this is my friend, Lady Mara St. Bride."

"I'm pleased to meet you, Delphie, Pierre."

The children, still unsmiling, gave her a perfect curtsy and bow. But then Pierre cocked his head. "Our uncle Simon, he is called St. Bride." He spoke with a strong French accent.

So Simon knew about Dare's family. Kill him, definitely.

Mara smiled. "He is my brother."

Both children relaxed. *"Ah, bon!"* said Delphie. "I very much like your hat, *madame.*"

"She thinks of nothing but clothes, ma'am," protested the boy.

Mara put aside her anger. "And what do you think of, Pierre? Horses?"

"*Oui,* and guns, *madame.* I will be a soldier when I grow up. Or perhaps a naval officer." In the same breath, he said to Dare, "I would very much like a toy boat, Papa."

"Perhaps," Dare said, but in the way that suggested a toy boat would be forthcoming.

"I had a splendid one when I was young. I wonder what became of it."

"Might it be in Yeovil House, Papa? May we search?"

The children *lived* with him? Of course they did. They were his stepchildren. But last night Mara had been in Yeovil House, including Dare's bedroom. Even though his wife would have a bedroom of her own, she couldn't make the facts fit.

She longed to cut through her confusion with a few straight questions, but this was a situation without any etiquette that she knew. A touch on her skirt made her look down. Delphie was fingering the silk braid down the front. *"C'est joli."*

"Merci beaucoup."

The girl's huge eyes shone. *"Vous parlez francais, madame! Papa, il le parle avec nous, et Janine aussi, mais tous les autres, c'est anglais, anglais, anglais."*

She chattered on and Mara gave thanks for her French tutor, which she'd thought a waste of time when travel to France had been blocked by the war for most of her life.

Then Delphie demanded her papa's attention and both children urged him down to the Serpentine to see something. He glanced at Mara for permission and she smiled and joined them. He had joy in his life and she must be delighted by that.

Pierre pointed out a particularly fine toy sailing ship, scudding across the water under full sail. Delphie chased ducks, shadowed by her maid, and then stopped to pick some buttercups and daisies. It was an idyllic family moment, except that Mara was the outsider.

The little girl ran back to present half her flowers to Dare and half to Mara. Dare fixed his through his buttonhole, as any good papa would. Mara tucked hers through a loop of braid on her bodice.

Delphie fixed her with a look. "My papa is well now," she said in French.

"I hope so."

"He will not die."

"No, of course not."

The girl nodded as if a truth had been established, then turned back to her harvest of flowers. Of course, the child would have known Dare when he'd been deathly ill. Mara swallowed tears, smiled, and wanted to rush back home and nurse her grief.

Eventually Dare led Mara back toward the phaeton. She felt sure that he would much rather have stayed by the river with them, and if she'd seen any way to return home alone, she'd have allowed him to.

"They're delightful," she said as the carriage moved off.

"When not being imps." He smiled at her, inviting amusement over the name.

She tried to respond. "Belgian, I assume."

"Possibly. It's not clear."

"Not clear?"

He glanced at her. "Didn't Simon tell you? They're the children of the woman who nursed me after Waterloo."

"So I supposed, but I presume *she* knows their nationality." It came out tartly for many reasons, not the least of which was that the children were so unalike that they'd probably had different fathers.

"If so, she can't tell. She's dead."

"Oh, Dare, I'm sorry." But Mara wasn't. It was as if the sun had suddenly come out from behind heavy clouds.

"Sorry?" he said. "Simon really hasn't told you anything, has he?"

"I thought you must have married her. Out of gratitude."

Even though she could only see his profile, she saw his mouth tense. "Hardly."

Mara was suddenly afraid of blundering. "But the children call you papa."

"They fell into the habit, and I will be their father unless anyone proves a better claim." As if compelled, he added, "They've experienced unpleasant things."

"The death of their mother."

When Dare didn't respond, Mara tried to read his expression.

He was looking fixedly at the road ahead even though it hardly seemed necessary. There were few other vehicles around and the horses were placid. Remarkably so for such fine animals, she realized. Had St. Raven's servants taken the edge off them before entrusting them to Dare? He'd been a fine whip — before Waterloo.

Something was terribly wrong. "What sort of woman was she?" Mara asked.

"Evil." But then he shook his head. "I'm sorry. I can't talk about that now."

Mara looked down at her gloved hands. Something dark lurked and the truth of it was now crucial to her. Her reaction to the thought that Dare was married had been like the ripping of a curtain, revealing truth.

She wanted to be married to him herself.

She supposed that meant she loved him, but her emotions were too tumultuous for that sweet label. He was hers. For better or worse, for richer or poorer, till death do them part. No wonder men had seized women through the ages. If she could, she'd toss Dare to the croup and ride off with him.

She fought laughter at the image. She was

neither Ellen nor Lochinvar. What was more, there was no reason that she and Dare couldn't court and marry.

A startled joy turned her to him, but his tense features reminded her all was not well. She did not speak. She had time and she needed to know more.

All the same, as Dare drew the horses to a halt in front of Ella's door, Mara felt as if he were slipping away from her, as if he might drive out of her life into the hovering gloom. She'd never been given to that sort of fancy, but she could taste dark drama in the air.

"What shall we do tomorrow?" she asked brightly. "You did promise to provide entertainment."

"Like a performing monkey?" If he smiled, it was very wry.

"In a red tasseled cap," she agreed, "dancing to a hurdygurdy. I hear there are performing monkeys at the Adelphi Theater."

"A push too far, Imp." The groom was at the horses' heads, so he climbed down and came around to assist her.

Mara was feeling daunted, but she would not give up. Once she was safely on the ground, she said, "If not the theater, then perhaps Monsieur Dubourg's corks?"

She caught his interest, at least. "What on

earth are they?"

"Models of antiquities all made of cork. It's supposed to be splendid."

"Corks?" he asked doubtfully.

"Please."

She thought he was going to refuse, but then he said, "Very well."

She had to work not to let out a whoosh of breath. "Tomorrow? At ten?" Giving him no time to back out, she said, "Thank you!" and planted a kiss on his cheek, exactly as little Delphie had done.

But she wasn't little Delphie, and surely he'd not looked at Delphie with shock. Mara sent him another bright smile and escaped before she did anything else stupid. Once inside the house, she ran up to watch from her window. The phaeton was just disappearing from the square, and so she had only a glimpse of Dare.

It was enough to show her that he was no longer driving.

She'd been right. He'd taken a turn for the worse. It might simply be a headache. Did he get headaches because of his head wound? She suspected, however, that it was something to do with opium. He was not free of it. He was not well.

It had seemed only reasonable to tease Dare out of his shell, but this was all more complex than she'd imagined. He was deeply troubled and she already felt inextricably bound to him.

Heart pounding from more than a race upstairs, she wrote his name in the patch of mist created on the window glass by her breath.

Dare.

Lord Darius Debenham. Lady Darius Debenham. That would be her married title. Lady Dare.

She'd urged Simon to come to London and she wanted him here to explain and advise. His arrival would change everything, however. Dare would no longer be isolated, so she'd have no excuse to badger him for outings.

Mara moved away from the window, unpinning her hat. She wanted to be alone with Dare every day and to wave a magic wand that would restore him. All in all, however, she had to hope her brother came to London posthaste.

CHAPTER 6

Dare shuddered with relief at not being in charge of the prime bits of blood anymore, but that counted as another test failed.

Maybe not entirely, for he'd done it and survived, but where was the pleasure he'd once felt in driving, in speed, in curricle racing, even? Come to think of it, where was his custom-made racing curricle? Stored somewhere at Long Chart, he supposed.

Carefully out of sight.

For a year his parents had thought him dead, but none of his possessions had been touched. Guilt over their grief often weighed on him and he asked himself whether he could have returned sooner.

By the time he'd recovered enough from his wounds to attempt escape, opium and too little food had weakened him — as Thérèse had intended.

His strongest prison, however, had been the children. Escaping with them had seemed an impossible challenge, and leaving them to bear Thérèse's revenge unthinkable.

There was the other possibility, however — that opium had sapped his ability to form and execute any plan. Perhaps he should have realized sooner what was happening. Perhaps he could have refused the stuff, or only pretended to take it.

How, when the lack would have brought on the spasms, the agony, the sweats, and tremors? Those horrors that hovered daily, that must be faced if he was ever to be free.

He didn't close his eyes because that made the swaying motion of the high vehicle worse. He'd walk home if his control didn't feel so fragile. Icy sweat was trickling down his spine. His guts felt as if they were shuddering and soon his teeth might start to chatter. It shouldn't be so bad yet. Emotions seemed to make things worse.

They passed a druggist's shop and he felt an almost physical tug toward it, toward a few pennies' worth of ease.

"Riggs."

"Yes, milord?"

"You are not, under any circumstances, to stop before we reach the house."

"Very well, milord."

The servants knew. Everyone knew, which

was enough to make him puke without the beast tying his innards in knots. Sometimes he felt he had no privacy, no dignity left. There were days and especially nights when death called to him. But he couldn't abandon the children or cause his family such pain.

Again.

He would live, and he would be free, but he wished the path wasn't so damned painful.

Once back in the house he went straight to his room. Salter assessed him with steady eyes.

"Nothing too badly out of order." Dare tried a smile, though a sudden twitch probably made it a grimace. "I don't know what's wrong. It shouldn't be like this yet." But then he said, "I took extra last night. Is that the problem? Have I ruined the process?"

God, oh, God. He couldn't start the slow reduction all over again. That had to be nonsense. One extra dose couldn't ruin everything. But the devils deep in his mind leapt in to whisper, *What's the point? You'll never win free. Give up now. Take what you need to be comfortable. Live with us. . . .*

"Sit down, sir." Salter steered Dare into a chair, but he sprang up again.

"The staffs."

They normally only did this at night, but Dare led the way to the ballroom at a brisk pace, stripping off jacket and waistcoat as he went. Once in the room, he pulled off his boots and grabbed one of the long sticks Salter had carried, denying the chill, the shudders, the threatening sickness. He'd fight the devils to the death.

He practiced solo as Salter stripped down, then attacked.

This was his best relief, his comfort, his salvation in the worst of times — to fight, to sweat, to think of nothing but action and reaction.

Not boxing. Something about boxing revolted him, especially if there was blood. Fencing was too delicate and refined. The ancient art of the quarterstaff was strenuous and earthy, and required intense concentration.

Dare focused every sense on the staffs, until a movement to his side distracted him.

Feng Ruyuan.

Salter's staff slammed hard onto Dare's thigh and he winced before turning and bowing, hands together. What was his Taoist master doing here, sliding in as silently as mist? His time was the night.

Ruyuan had been found by Nicholas

Delaney, the person who seemed to understand his fight better than any. Dare wondered if somewhere in his travels Nicholas had tried opium and had to escape its sweet coils.

Tall and quiet, Yuan had brought many skills, including massage to soothe a tortured body and herbs to alleviate the worst symptoms. Above all he had brought the precise and physical art that burned through sleepless nights and acted like a massage for Dare's screaming mind. He did not approve of quarterstaff work, but didn't forbid it.

"You are distressed." Ruyuan spoke softly as always, his speech heavily accented but clear.

"Too many unusual events," Dare replied.

"You came to London for unusual events, I think?"

"Some are unusual enough to be shocking."

Like his reaction to Mara St. Bride.

"Such things will make the path harder, but it is through difficulties that we grow strong."

"Then I should be a damn Hercules."

Ruyuan smiled. "But you are, Darius. You are worthy of your name."

Dare had known he was named for a Persian king; he had not known until Yuan told him that the name meant "strong."

"I'm not strong. I tremble for the beast."

"But are not huddled, whimpering. Or fighting Salter to seize it."

Dare laughed shortly. "I wouldn't win."

"I believe you could. Now you are your only guard."

Dare inhaled. "You terrify me."

Yuan smiled again, as if to say, What else am I here for?

"It is past your time," Yuan reproved.

The words sang through Dare as if he were a harp string plucked. Past time for his midday dose, and his regimen said he must take it, just as he must not take it early.

"Perhaps I can do without." All except a tiny fragment of strength screamed in rejection.

"That is not the way."

"Why not? Isn't that the golden chalice? The time when I can refuse the beast and survive? Why not now? Today?"

"Impetuous rejection is as weak as impetuous submission."

Yuan bowed again and left, his smooth, silent tread masking amazing physical power.

"What does that mean?" Dare complained, restlessly jiggling the staff. "Why do I have to follow the path? The aim is to free me from opium, but when I say I want to do it, he says I'm not allowed. What sense is there in that? Why can't I? If I want to. I'm a lord. I can do what I want. . . ."

Salter's hand on his arm stopped him. Damn, he was babbling. Much longer and he'd be spewing every thought in his head as his brain jangled along with the rest of him.

"Come and eat, sir." Salter took the staff and guided him back to his bedroom, where cold ham, bread, and fruit were laid out.

Dare didn't want it. Sometimes he had cravings for food, but never for normal foods like these. He'd grab pickles, and he had once eaten three lemons, skin and all. Mostly he had no appetite at all.

This, too, was part of the discipline, however, the rules Ruyuan had brought, that were bringing him toward his goal. He must take his dose of opium exactly on time. He must eat before taking it to dull its immediate effect and slow its absorption. He must eat everything set before him.

He forced himself through the contents of his plate, then contemplated the glass of dark liquid Salter placed before him. He tried to tell himself he was reaching for it because that was the rule. But if Salter tried to snatch it back he might kill him.

Damn. His hand was shaking.

Thérèse Bellaire's poisonous heritage, he thought, picking up the glass. The thing he loathed above all but could not live without. He downed the bitter liquid. For a little while, the world would seem serene, without strife, without pain, without suffering of any sort. And that illusion would be very hard to leave behind.

CHAPTER 7

Mara woke early the next day, aware only that she'd soon see Dare again. Who could have imagined that a visit to the cork exhibit would shine like sunrise?

To stop herself mooning about Dare all morning, she wrote a letter to a friend, though it felt false because she couldn't say anything about him. Not yet, at least. She was past the age of confessing impetuous loves.

Impetuous?

She sat staring into space. Rather, it felt predestined, as if her lack of interest in her suitors had been because she'd been already committed to Dare. She could envision their wedding at the church in Monkton St. Brides. She could see friends and family celebrating.

She shook herself and returned to her letter to write a dull account of political dinners and a drive in the park "with an old friend of Simon's."

Ruth came in with the washing water. "Nice day again, milady. What will you be wearing?"

"I'm going out with Lord Darius again. We'll be walking to the cork exhibition." She mentally riffled through her walking dresses and discarded practicality in favor of prettiness. "I'll wear the Nile green with the flounced hem and the bronze pelisse."

Ruth pursed her lips as if she'd prefer to send Mara out in a nun's habit, but she didn't openly protest.

Once dressed, Mara visited Ella again and played with little Amy, thinking for the first time of children of her own. Dare's children. When he was announced, she raced to add gloves, pelisse, and bonnet, but then went downstairs in careful dignity.

She paused at first sight of him, to absorb a special thrill that came from knowing he was her beloved. When she took his proffered arm, the simple action excited her like a kiss. She managed a dignified good morning, but then babbled as they went out into an overcast day.

"I hope this is interesting, but I have little faith. Cork, after all."

"I've seen clever models out of paper, plaster, and even bone," he said.

"I remember our governess setting us all to making an Egyptian scene with pyramids of papier-mâché. It also involved a lot of sand. We were brushing it out of clothes and carpets for weeks."

"I can imagine. Did you all take lessons together?"

"Much of the time. Though Benji went to school eventually, of course." Mara wanted to cut her own throat. He was going to die of boredom with such dull talk. "When did you go to school?" she tried.

"I had tutors until I went to Harrow at thirteen."

"Did you mind leaving home?"

"Not at all. It was an adventure."

She lured him to tell stories of the Rogues, including some about Simon that her brother had concealed. By the time they arrived at the exhibition in Lower Grosvenor Street, she almost had her head back on straight.

The building seemed like any other house, but once Dare had paid, they were ushered into a large chamber at the rear, well lit by windows up near the ceiling. Tables around the walls held ancient monuments in miniature, but in the middle of the room stood the pièce de résistance.

"Oh, my," Mara said, approaching a

craggy rock crowned with the ruins of a temple. Water trickled down to gather in a pool at the base. "No wonder these are famous. Apart from the scale, it could be real."

"Very cleverly done," Dare agreed.

"Is it truly all from cork?" Mara longed to reach out and touch and glanced around. She could only see six other visitors, but an attendant was already hurrying over.

"Indeed, yes, madam," he answered. "Monsieur Dubourg discovered entirely by accident that cork, in texture and color, is ideal for the representation of ancient structures."

He chattered on, but Mara simply looked, enjoying the trick played on her senses. Silence fell and she saw that Dare had given the attendant a coin and he was now approaching another couple.

"I half expect people to emerge from the temple at any moment," she said, "but it doesn't bother me that none do."

"Perhaps because it's a ruin. We expect ruins to be deserted."

She looked at him. "Have you seen real ruins? I mean, in Greece?"

"No, but one day I will."

He intended to wander? She couldn't imagine sharing a life like that. Brideswell

St. Brides stayed close to home. It was their nature.

"Where else would you like to go?" she asked, hoping her concern wasn't obvious.

"All Europe lies open to the traveler now. Wouldn't you enjoy travel?"

"Short trips, perhaps," she said, not adding the essential, *With you.*

"Despite being a Brideswell St. Bride, you would be an enthusiastic traveler, I think."

"You were once full of enthusiasm, Dare."

He looked at the model. "As that was once whole and full of worshipers. Come, let's admire the Tomb of Virgil."

"No tombs," Mara said firmly. "According to my guide book there's a model of Vesuvius that actually erupts. I wonder where that is."

Dare shook his head, but summoned the guide.

"Indeed, sir, madam. It is in that curtained area over there for darkness, but it erupts only at certain hours."

"How very convenient," Dare commented. "Would that some people were like that."

His eyes were twinkling and it was as if an eruption threatened inside Mara. She deliberately plunged into enthusiasm. "I *long* to see it explode, Dare."

"Of course you do, but I admit, so do I.

Natural darkness seems more appropriate than curtains. May I bring you this evening?"

"Yes! No. Bother, I can't. We're going to the theater. At last. Covent Garden. Some new piece called *The Lady's Choice.* But we must see this soon. Promise? And *don't* come without me."

"I promise. My time is almost entirely free, so you must set the day."

"Like a wedding," she said — then wanted to strangle herself. "Oh, look. Pyramids!" She towed him to the side tables. "Smaller than the ones we made at home, but much more believable."

They contemplated pyramids, and then strolled past an amphitheater and an obelisk. These models were quite small, but still exquisitely realistic.

" 'The Temple of the Sibyls at Tivoli,' " she read from the next label. "What exactly is a sibyl?"

"An oracle?"

"They can't be the same thing."

"Perhaps a sibyl is a type of oracle. Or an oracle a type of sibyl. Just as a minx is a type of young lady, but not all young ladies are minxes."

She wrinkled her nose at him. "This minx knows something about a sibyl."

"What?"

"One of them — I can't remember which — had twelve books of prophesies. She offered them to a king — I can't remember which —"

"*Not* an attentive student," he remarked.

"Were you?"

"No." He was still smiling, so she continued to amuse.

"This Sibyl offered her books to the king for an enormous price. He tried to haggle, so she burned three and offered the nine for the same price. When he refused to pay, she burned three more. By the time he gave in, there were only three left and he paid her original price for them. I like her."

"You would. But think of all the wisdom lost."

"That was the king's fault for being miserly. He probably thought a woman would buckle to his demands."

"One would think a king would have greater wisdom."

"Why?"

He laughed. "An excellent question, especially as ours is mad. What do we have next? The Grotto of Egeria. Who was Egeria? We need Nicholas or Lucien."

"We do?" Mara was treasuring that laughter.

He glanced at her. "Nicholas Delaney and Lucien, Lord Arden."

"I know that. Why do we need them here?"

"Nicholas has a magpie mind and Lucien — never tell the world — was a brilliant scholar."

"Shocking!" she declared, moving on to some sort of medieval square.

Their guide reappeared at their side.

"Ah, Verona! Site of the touching story of the star-crossed lovers. Behold the model of Juliet's house, the Casa di Giulietta. That is the true name in Italian, ma'am," he kindly explained. "And here you see the very balcony upon which fair Juliet stood to be admired by Signor Romeo. Beside it we have her tomb. . . ."

"No tombs," Dare said and steered Mara firmly onward. "With Black Ademar's hair it would be fatal to encourage tragic love."

"I'm a St. Bride of Brideswell," she protested, laughing. "I'm incapable of it."

". . . the Coliseum, where Christian martyrs were fed to wild beasts," the guide orated with determination.

"And can you really imagine the St. Bride family involved in a blood feud with anyone?" Mara asked.

"In Simon's case, yes." Dare thanked the frustrated guide and dispatched him with another coin.

"He's going to make a fortune by pestering us," Mara pointed out. "I think Simon's burned away that sort of fury, and Jancy is the epitome of calm practicality."

"Thus, a perfect match."

Mara ignored antiquities. "Opposites make an ideal couple? Ella and George are very alike, and Rupert and Mary, and father and mother —"

"But none of them have Black Ademar's thatch."

"So," Mara asked, "what would my opposite be?"

"Dull."

"A compliment, I think."

"I suspect many pray for a dull spouse." He turned her toward the display. "Pay attention to the ruins."

"The Parthenon," Mara said, considering the famous temple. "Father might enjoy this, you know. He hates travel, but is interested in antiquities. He thinks there's some sort of ancient temple beneath Brideswell, but can't think how to explore for it."

"I wouldn't be surprised."

At his tone, she glanced at him. "Why?"

"There's something special about the place."

"It's a rambling hodgepodge of a house."

"I don't mean Brideswell itself, though that has a sort of magic, but the house, the church, the village. It's all built within the grounds of the old monastery. If that had been built on some pagan site, it would explain why it feels . . . good," he completed, obviously dissatisfied with the word.

Mara's heart was beating fast. "You'd always be welcome there, Dare. We think of you as one of the family."

Would you like to live there? Marry me, and it can be done. Father's already built a wing for Edmund and Mary. He'd build one for us.

But he was looking around the room. "Pierre might enjoy this. The volcano especially."

Mara let the moment slip away. There would be other times. "Boys being boys," she said, "and liking noisy explosions."

He smiled at her. "I seem to remember a lady expressing enthusiasm."

She wrinkled her nose. "As you say, it's the hair."

They strolled past the last models and left the house. Mara eyed the clouds, praying it wouldn't rain. Rain wouldn't dampen her spirits, but they'd have to hurry home.

"Buy a souvenir for your lady, sir?"

The harshly accented cry drew Mara's attention to a woman selling reproductions of the models. She was holding one out to tempt Dare. *Your lady.* Mara cherished that as they strolled over.

The copies were crudely made, but Mara picked up one of the volcano. "I wonder if this could be made to erupt. It could be filled with gunpowder."

"No," Dare said firmly, taking it from her, "but Pierre would probably like it and not have such notions." He purchased it, and a Casa di Giulietta for Delphie.

"You'll encourage her toward tragic love," Mara teased.

He picked up a Juliet's Tomb. "For you," he said, "as warning against unruly love."

Mara protested his words, but took her package with delight. Her first gift from Dare! They turned to walk the short distance back to Ella's house, but Mara couldn't bear this excursion to end.

"Would you mind if we visited the bookshop in the next street?" she asked. "It's not far out of our way and I have a copy waiting of Sarah Burney's *Tales of Fancy.*"

"Not, I assume, about boxing."

"Fancy," she said, "not 'the fancy.' How anyone can find amusement in watching two men pound each other with their fists, I don't know."

"We're vile creatures, we men. So what is the fancy in question?"

"Imaginary things. In this case, a ship-wreck."

"All too real, unfortunately."

"In this wreck," she said as they turned the corner, "a lady and her daughter are stranded on an island, just like Robinson Crusoe."

"With a Man Friday?"

"In the shape of a fine English gentleman, also a survivor of the wreck."

His lips twitched. "Definitely an imaginary thing."

"What? A fine English gentleman?" Her laughing eyes met his. A perfect moment. "It's supposed to be very adventurous. And very touching."

"So I would think."

"Dare, you're having naughty thoughts!"

"Mara, men *always* have naughty thoughts."

She winked. "So do women."

His brows rose and he propelled her into the bookshop. The bookseller hurried to bow and quickly produced *Tales of Fancy* in three volumes, the pages already cut, and gave the package to Dare.

"As I have a beast of burden," Mara said,

"I think I'll look to see what else is on the shelves."

Dare followed, protesting, "Three volumes won't keep you occupied for at least a month?"

"I lead such a quiet life at Ella's." She slid him a look. "Except when a dashing hero rescues me."

"Simon will be here soon."

"A brother can never be a dashing hero to a sister."

"But when he arrives, won't you move to Marlowe House with him and Jancy?"

"Yes, and life's bound to be more lively then, especially as it will probably have Rogues."

"Which sounds rather like 'have rats.' "

She laughed. "A plague of them."

She turned to the shelves. "Oh, look." She grabbed four volumes entitled *Husband Hunters!!!* "Three exclamation marks. Very promising, don't you think?"

"Of excess, especially from an author called Amelia Beauclerc. What about that one? *Barozzi, or the Venetian Sorceress.*"

"But it's by a mere Catherine Smith. Doesn't such a commonplace name threaten a commonplace book?"

"Mara, how can anything about a Venetian sorceress be commonplace?"

"You'd be surprised," she said darkly. "There are novelists, would you believe, who create the most tempting delights only to use them as a vehicle for pious homilies. It should be illegal."

"If I enter Parliament, I pledge to see to it. It occurs to me that you should pen novels."

She looked at him in surprise. "I? I struggle to write letters."

"But you have the name for it. Can't you see *The Captive Corpse of Castle Cruel* by Ademara St. Bride?"

"My goodness, yes. But how could a corpse be captive?"

"We're talking fancy. The corpse is under a spell. Or a potion, like Juliet."

"Locked away until her hero can find her? How thrilling."

"Then write it."

She gave a theatrical shudder and fluttered her lashes at him. "You could write it, dearest Dare, and I would lend my name to it."

"Simon would shoot me. Come along. You have enough literature here to last till doomsday."

"Especially if I'm writing novels at the same time." She arranged for the account to be sent to Ella's house and Dare paid for the books to be delivered, though Mara protested that he was shirking his task.

They left the shop in high spirits.

"What shall my heroine's name be?" she asked, to keep the fun going.

"Bellissima," Dare said. "Bellissima di Magnifico."

"No, no. The heroine must be an ordinary lady with a name like . . . Anne."

"Anne Brown?"

"Too dull."

"Anne Orange?"

"Stop it!" But she adored him in this playful mood.

"Anne White, then," he said. "White is suitably virginal. I assume she is a virgin."

Mara prayed not to be blushing. "Of course. Spelled with a y to give it elegance."

"Virgyn?"

"Whyte!" Mara exclaimed. "And the hero's name is . . . ?"

"Can *he* have a glorious name?"

"As long as it's not Glorioso. What about Tristan?" she suggested.

"St. Raven would strangle us both."

They paused for a sweeper to get rid of some horse droppings before crossing the street. "That's the Duke of St. Raven's Christian name?" Mara asked.

Dare tossed the lad a coin. "Yes."

"How do you know?"

"I knew him as a boy. What other name appeals?"

"Darius," she teased.

"Then *I'd* have to strangle you."

"Novel writing is a lot harder than it seems," Mara complained as they walked on. "We need a noble name. Kingly, even."

"Ethelred."

"As in Ethelred the Unready? No!"

"Halfacanute, then," he said, naming another ancient king.

"A whole Canute or nothing, sir."

"There you are, then. Your hero is Canute. Canute Or-not-to-canute," he declared, "lost Duke of Dawlish. They're always lost heirs to something, aren't they?"

Mara was laughing almost too much to talk. "You're impossible." *You're the old Dare.*

"I dare you," he said.

It was as if he'd picked up her thought. "To do what?"

"To write a novel using those names."

"If I succeed, what do you forfeit?"

"I have to write a novel myself?"

"In iambic pentameters."

He winced. "It would be a very short piece." They strolled on for a moment. Then he recited: "Canute Ornottocanute, lost

Duke of Dawlish/Was raised as a pig boy, and thus somewhat poorish."

"Those lines have only four beats. Iambic pentameters require five."

"There's a silent beat, like the silent k on knock. Wait, wait, I have more: He met pure Anne Whyte,/Which inspired him to fight,/Which he did with an elegant flourish!"

She laughed but said, "Your beat is all off, and there's not a trace of a captive corpse, never mind the castle. Be serious."

"Why?"

An excellent question. Mara felt she could almost float away on light spirits.

"Very well," Dare said with an artificial sigh. "Who is our villain? Presumably he has poisoned poor Anne and locked her in a dungeon."

"In her wedding gown," Mara suggested.

"They do tend to be, don't they? So, the villain?"

"The lord of the castle, of course. Baron Bane."

"Very good," he said as they waited for a laden coach to pass. "Savage Bane, Baron Cruel."

"Isn't that just a little heavy-handed?"

"Have done with subtlety. He probably has a squint and oozing sores."

"No one christens a baby Savage," Mara

said. "What about Caspar? That's a real name but with a savage sound to it. Caspar the Cruel lusts after virtuous Anne Whyte, innocent maiden of the village. She is the beloved of Canute Ornottocanute — that really is ridiculous! — who is striving to reclaim his title."

"Which of course has been misappropriated by Caspar, his wicked uncle."

"Who believes he killed Canute as a baby . . ."

". . . except that he was smuggled away by an honest kitchen maid . . ."

". . . called Ethel the Ready."

"Very good," Dare approved. "And Canute has been raised in the forest by rabbits!"

"Rabbits?"

"Rabbits. Which explains his timid nature."

"We can't have a timid hero," she protested.

"He must be, or how does he allow this tyranny to continue?"

"He doesn't know the truth?"

"He thinks he really is a rabbit?" Dare said, but the brightness was dimming.

"He doesn't know he's the duke. How does he find out?"

"A sibyl finds him."

But the spark of inventive fun had died, so they talked of novels they'd enjoyed. By the time they reached Ella's house, Mara was carrying most of the conversation and she wished she could pelt him with questions.

Are you still addicted? How does it affect you? How much do you take? Will you be able to fight free? What should I do to help?

When Ella's footman opened the door, however, she could only make a cheerful farewell.

She was inside the house before she realized that she'd neglected to force another appointment. She hurried to her room to write a note thanking Dare for the visit to the cork exhibition. She added an urgent desire to see the Tower of London. She did truly long to see the site of so many of England's famous events, but she chose it for another reason. The Tower was a long way from Mayfair and would require a lengthy carriage drive there and back. Hours together for inventive silliness and for learning more about his situation.

She sat nibbling the tip of her quill, dipped the nib and signed her note from *the famous novelist Ademara Saint Bride. You will note that I have lengthened St. to Saint, for names acquire importance letter by letter.*

She received his reply during lunch agreeing to the expedition and signed *the infamous Todareornottodare Debenham.*

She read this to Ella, who was amused, especially at the mere idea of Mara writing a whole book, but who seemed uncomfortable about something.

"What's the matter?" Mara demanded.

"Nothing. Only that you seem to be growing very close."

"It's only Dare," Mara protested, aware that she was lying.

Ella fiddled with a piece of bread. "I hear he has children in his house."

"The children of the Belgian widow who nursed him. Apparently she died. Delphie isn't much older than Amy. Perhaps they might like to play together."

"They aren't likely to meet often, are they?"

"Why not?"

"Yeovil House is quite a distance from here."

Mara saw her sister's pursed lips and felt her rare temper build. "You don't *want* Amy to play with Delphie."

Color touched Ella's cheeks. "Really, Mara! But who knows who the child is?"

"She's Dare's adopted daughter."

"All I know is that there's a mystery about

those children. From what I've heard, they don't look as if they had the same parents, and the Belgian widow herself is something of an enigma." Ella's lips pursed even more. "She was probably his mistress."

"If so, it was in the past and the poor woman is dead. Her children —"

Ella put a hand to her abdomen. "I really can't be upset at a time like this, Mara. It creates a fractious baby — you know it does. The world is full of waifs in situations a great deal more unpleasant. If you want to do good works, help me sew clothing for the Charing Cross Orphanage."

It was penance, but Mara agreed, and spent the afternoon hemming. Under soothing occupation, Ella relaxed into light conversation and Mara didn't try to raise the subject of the children again. By the time they left that evening for Covent Garden Theater, all was peace and harmony, and she could enjoy the experience.

CHAPTER 8

This would be Mara's first visit to a London theater, and she welcomed the opportunity to wear one of her finer dresses. She chose her ivory satin sprigged with country flowers. It suited her very well, and the low bodice and evening corset did wonders for her breasts. She wished Dare would see her like this.

"Come along, Miss Mara," Ruth protested. "They'll be waiting for you."

Mara quickly chose pearls and simple flowers for her hair. As Ruth put her green velvet cloak around her shoulders, Mara looked at the Tomb of Juliet that sat by her bed; then she ran down to join Ella and George.

As their coach drew close to Covent Garden, they encountered a stream of carriages and slowed to a dawdle, but the excitement in the air and watching the people on foot were a play in itself. Hawkers cried fruits and flowers, and Mara saw an urchin filch a handkerchief.

At last they could alight and enter the theater, where they were joined by the unfortunately named Scilly brothers and went up to the box. Reverend Scilly turned out to be the very self-satisfied vicar of a prosperous London parish. Captain Scilly was sharp-faced and sour because peace left him with no ship under his command. Both were bachelors and eyeing Mara with too much interest, but she could handle that.

She went upstairs on the vicar's arm, paying scant attention to his conversation, keyed up as she was for the moment when she would see the auditorium, which was supposed to be one of the most elegant in the world.

When she walked into the box, she paused in satisfaction. The four tiers of seating rose in gilded magnificence, the occupants glittering under brilliant gaslight. Feathers bobbed, fans waved, and jewels flashed in the light.

"What a dull duck I am," she said without great concern as she joined Ella at the front. "A fan, but no feathers. Mere flowers in my hair and only pearls. No flash at all."

Reverend Scilly leaned forward. "You are

a perfection of maidenly modesty, Lady Mara."

Mara's eyes met Ella's and laughter threatened. Mara managed, "Perfection, Vicar! How delightful."

What was truly delightful was the attention she was receiving. Some gentlemen even raised quizzing glasses to study her — the ultimate accolade — though of course she pretended not to be aware of it.

A movement below caught her eye and she looked down into the pit, expecting another admirer. It was, but a most unwelcome one.

Berkstead!

He was even standing to stare up at her, drawing the attention of those around him. Pinned by so much gawking, Mara felt furious. She frowned, trying to send a message that he desist. Instead, he put his right hand to his heart and bowed.

She looked away, but her cheeks were flaming. No one in her box seemed to have noticed; perhaps most in the theater were unaware. But how intolerable. What if the wretch was brash enough to come up to their box? He was well acquainted with George.

As the theater continued to fill, Mara surreptitiously kept an eye on her unwelcome suitor. He had sat down and stopped staring, so perhaps his nonsense was over.

Mara tried to settle to enjoy the play, but it was a sad disappointment. *The Lady's Choice* had sounded so promising, involving as it did a clandestine betrothal, but it reminded her of her complaint to Dare about novels designed to teach. This was a play written to teach a lesson, in this case that a lady should surrender her choice of husband to her father. Mara hoped it would be enlivened later by rebellion, but didn't have much hope.

At the intermission, they ignored the dancers who came onstage and left the box to promenade in the elegant gallery. Mara took the arm of Captain Scilly this time, sharing her favors.

"Not a bad piece, eh?" he said. "Free of barnacles."

Mara stared at him. "Barnacles, Captain?"

"In sound shape, Lady Mara. Seaworthy. With a well-scraped bottom."

Mara desperately fought laughter. "I don't suppose it will leak, Captain Scilly. Do you attend the theater often?"

"Now and then, now and then, Lady Mara, being stuck ashore with no hope of action."

"But you'd not want war, Captain?"

"Never," he declared, but wasn't the slightest bit convincing.

"Perhaps a noble mission, such as the Barbary campaign?"

As she'd intended, that set him off on a description of his role in that enterprise, which had forced the release of the Christians enslaved by Barbary pirates. But he reduced the exciting mission to topsails and tacking.

Mara made the appropriate comments, but her eyes wandered. In Lincoln she would be surrounded by friends and relatives at a moment like this, but here she hardly knew anyone. Her gaze paused on the back of a man's head that looked familiar.

Dare?

Her heart sped. It was. He was talking to two elegant couples. Rogues?

Paying just enough attention to heavy seas, batteries, and going to leeward, she gently steered a course toward Dare, trying to guess which Rogues the men might be.

The slender blond looked very clever. Sir Stephen Ball? Nicholas Delaney? Or the scholarly Lucien, Marquess of Arden? No, he was a prime athlete.

The dark, gentle one. Francis, she thought. Francis, Lord Middlethorpe — she was sure of it by process of elimination.

When she was within feet of her target, Captain Scilly was hailed and Mara was turned to join a Captain Macken and his wife. Naval conversation ensued. Mara ground her teeth behind her smile. She couldn't just walk away, but she sent silent pleas to Dare to rescue her.

And he did!

"Lady Mara, I hope you are enjoying the play."

She turned, a brilliant smile no effort at all. "In parts," she said, adding, "The barnacle-free bits."

His brows rose in a query, but he also looked down at her breasts and was still and silent for a moment.

Then he introduced his companions.

She'd been right about Francis, and the blond man was Sir Stephen Ball MP. Rogues. At last! But Dare's reaction to her gown was the greater thrill.

The naval party was as delighted as she was. A duke's son, a viscount, and an influential politician!

Amid general conversation, Mara studied the Rogue wives. Lady Ball was a true beauty, with lush dark curls and brilliant eyes. Mara remembered that she had been a toast during her first marriage.

Lady Middlethorpe wasn't a beauty in the same way, but her looks were remarkable. Creamy skin, heavy-lidded eyes, and startling deep red hair created an impression Mara could only think of as *sultry.*

Certainly the naval gentlemen were agog and Captain Scilly probably couldn't have reefed a topsail right then to save his life.

Lady Ball turned to Mara and said, "Serena and I plan a quest on Saturday. We have word of a fabulous emporium of Oriental silks on the borders of respectable London and mean to find it."

"With escort," Lord Middlethorpe said firmly.

"Of course, dearest," Lady Middlethorpe said. "You know I have no taste for risks."

"Unlike Mara," Dare said.

Mara flashed him a hurt look. He lightly added, "Everyone knows that a devil-haired St. Bride is born to be wild."

Lord Middlethorpe laughed. "Lord, yes. The things Simon got up to. Only to be expected that he'd start a war in Canada."

"He didn't *start* it," Mara protested.

"I'm not convinced. He certainly went raiding with some group called the Green Tigers."

"He had no choice but to defend British territory against attack," Mara said.

"But no sooner does he arrive back in England than the masses riot at Spa Fields."

Lord Middlethorpe was clearly teasing, and Mara felt as if she were with old friends.

"Simon certainly had nothing to do with that," she said. "The unrest is all to do with unemployment and the Corn Laws, which are the responsibility of you members of Parliament." But then she covered her mouth with her hand. "I can't believe it. I actually raised the subject of politics!"

Everyone laughed, including Dare, who looked so much like his old self. This was how he should be, laughing with his friends.

Their eyes met and held for an extraordinary moment, and she knew hers spoke her thoughts. His lids lowered and he turned to say something to Lady Ball just as the bell announced the next act.

Mara quickly settled the details of the silk-hunting expedition and returned to her box, wishing she could go with Dare instead.

But would he want her to? She very much feared that she'd let her heart speak in her eyes, and he'd deliberately cut the connection.

She took her seat fighting tears. She'd dallied and flirted for years, but she'd never had to try to hide her feelings before. It had never mattered before.

Oh, Lord. Was she doing to Dare what Berkstead was doing to her? She resolved to ignore Dare for the rest of the evening.

During the next intermission she expressed interest in watching some performing dogs. During the third and last, Ella wished to listen to what sounded like a pious monologue and Mara simply couldn't bear it. She would have been better off. The Scilly brothers both insisted on escorting her but talked to each other over her head, and the only people they joined were the Mackens and a dust-dry Reverend Forbes.

Mara saw Dare some distance away, but stuck to her resolve. She prayed, however, that he'd come to her again. He didn't, even though she saw him see her.

At the bell, she returned to the box feeling tragic enough for *Romeo and Juliet*. She held back for a moment outside the door to compose herself.

"Please, gentlemen, go ahead."

It was the sort of vague feminine comment men never question. They went into the box and Mara fiddled with her gown. She was nothing but a pest to Dare. She couldn't bear it.

But she achieved a smile and was turning toward the open door when a theater servant came up to her. "Lady Mara St. Bride?" he asked, holding out a folded paper.

Startled, Mara took the note. It was a slim, stiff package with only her name on the outside. The orchestra signaled the beginning of the final act, so she concealed it in her hand and took her seat.

Was the note from Dare?

Telling her to stop pursuing him?

She couldn't bear to wait. Once the play was under way again, she unfolded it as quietly as she could, then looked down, grateful for the small lamp in the box.

A blank sheet of paper enclosed the play-bill and a playing card: the queen of hearts.

Mara suppressed a nervous laugh. This package could be wildly romantic, but it didn't feel like that. It felt peculiar. Then she noticed that the play's title, *The Lady's Choice,* had been circled in black. In the margin, the sender had written: *May your choice be forgiveness, my queen.*

Forgive what? Was Dare asking forgiveness for ignoring her? Opium could play strange games with the mind, but she didn't want to think Dare had sent this.

With sudden suspicion, she looked down into the pit. Major Berkstead was looking up at her again, trying to catch her eye.

She shook her head, frowning. He clasped

his hands in prayer. The exasperating buffoon!

She longed to send a pointed message by dropping the card into the pit — torn into pieces, in fact — but someone would be sure to notice. Instead, she bent it in half and pushed it into her reticule.

The only thing to do was to ignore the wretched man, but now she felt threatened. She'd thought of him as a buffoon, but his eyes had shown a frightening intensity.

For the first time in her life, Mara felt threatened by a man. It was nonsense. Berkstead didn't want to harm her, only marry her, but she didn't know what he might do. He could cause her endless trouble. He could embarrass her with his attentions, but worse — what if he revealed her escapade with him? He'd tried to force marriage through scandal once.

She shivered. Surely if honor didn't restrain him, fear would. He'd have to know that Simon or Dare would call him out for it. All the same, her reputation would be in shreds.

She kept her eyes on the stage, but was hardly aware of the weeping and repentance followed by an unbelievable picture of domestic bliss. The play was followed by a farce about servants and mistaken identity that would have pleased Mara much better if she hadn't been so upset.

She made sure never to look in Berkstead's direction again until they rose to take their leave. Then she checked what he was up to. Thank heavens, his seat was empty and the pit audience was pushing and shoving toward the doors. Good riddance.

She breathed with relief as they all made their way along the gallery and down the stairs, and even managed some intelligent comments on the play. She kept an eye out for Dare — she couldn't help it — but it was as well she didn't see him. She was upset enough to do something stupid.

What a miserable evening this had turned out to be.

It grew worse. When they finally arrived at the bottom of the stairs, Major Berkstead walked up to them. "Sir George, Lady Verney, Lady Mara, grand play, don't you think?"

Mara wanted to cut him dead, but that could create the scandal she had to avoid.

Enough was enough, however, and once they were in the carriage, she said, "I'm sorry if this will make things difficult, George, Ella, but I must ask that I not be obliged to meet Lord Berkstead again."

"Good Lord, why?" George demanded. "Sound enough fellow."

"He has conceived a mad passion for me and will not be put off. He was staring at me tonight in the most uncomfortable manner."

"Good grief," George muttered, irritated rather than appalled.

"Are you sure, Mara?" Ella asked. "We are used to having him visit us now and then."

Mara considered producing the card, but really, she couldn't. It could raise too many questions.

"And must continue to do so," she said. "Please, I'm not asking you to alter your ways. It's only that I don't wish to be partnered with him again, at dinner, for example. Or drive out with him again. It shouldn't be for long. When Simon and Jancy arrive, I will be moving to Marlowe House."

"Very well, very well," George said, looking as if he wished women and all their foibles could be wiped off the Earth.

Mara hoped she'd repelled attack, but still felt threatened, as if Berkstead might leap on her one day and drag her off. Nonsense. Surrounded by propriety and a large, loving family, she was as safe as the Crown Jewels.

By the time she arrived in her bedchamber and threw Berkstead's package on the fire, she'd persuaded herself that he offered no real threat. That, however, left room for anxiety about Dare. Was she truly pestering him as Berkstead was pestering her?

When Ruth left, Mara contemplated Juliet's Tomb. Had that, too, been a warning? Hadn't he said something about unruly love? If only she'd not gone to that gaming hell.

But then she wouldn't have enjoyed that intimate experience with Dare, might hardly be aware he was in London. She'd not have enjoyed time with him, and might not have realized what he meant to her.

That he was the one, the only, man for her.

She suddenly felt as if she stood perilously on a high windblown peak, a breath away from disaster.

Dare truly was the only man for her.

The only man she could love.

The only one able to stir passion with a touch, even with a look. He *must* love her in return.

It all gave her a poor night's sleep, and when Ruth woke her with a reminder that she was going to the Tower, she wondered if she should cancel the outing.

No. She couldn't bear to do that, and she was no Berkstead. She'd done nothing so foolish as to send Dare embarrassing protestations of love.

She remembered their lively exchange about Anne Whyte and Canute Ornottocanute. He couldn't find her a bore or a pest, and she was able to bring out laughter in him.

Mara chose the red gown again. As Ruth fastened it at the back, Mara recalled Dare behind her, fastening her gown, speaking to her. Of breasts. She remembered the way he'd looked at her breasts last night. She imagined them alone and he, eyes intent, lowering his lips to hers —

"Stop twitching, Miss Mara!"

Mara pulled herself together, hoping a fiery blush didn't show from the back.

CHAPTER 9

When Mara went down, she couldn't help searching Dare's face for reluctance. She saw none, so she pushed her foolish worries aside and took his arm to go outside. She expected the phaeton again, but found a closed carriage.

She paused, for traveling in a closed carriage with a gentleman was not quite right.

"I made sure George didn't object," he said. "In fact, his comment was that even you couldn't get up to mischief in a drive across London."

"I could take that as a challenge," Mara retorted, continuing on.

"And I pray you'll behave."

She settled on the crimson brocade seat. "I rather like the idea of being a dangerous lady."

He laughed as he took the seat opposite her. She would rather he sit beside her, but this way she could enjoy the sight of him and he was still deliciously close in this confined space.

"So why are we in a closed carriage?" she asked as they rolled away.

"We'll be traveling through some of the rougher parts of London."

"That sounds promising."

He shook his head, but still looked amused. That was her purpose — to amuse Dare. To lighten and brighten him.

"So whose is this elegant vehicle?" she asked. "Crimson damask and polished walnut don't seem quite in a rakish duke's style."

"And what do you know of rakish dukes?"

"Rather less than I'd like to."

"Tut-tut." But he was definitely amused. "The carriage is mother's and thus unaccustomed to such talk."

"I wonder. How long will it take us to reach the Tower?"

"At least an hour."

He sounded apologetic, but Mara was delighted. An hour alone with him.

"We must decide what parts of the Tower to see," she said, pulling her guidebook out of her reticule and opening it. "We have the Bloody Tower, Traitor's Gate, the Crown Jewels, the Armory . . ."

"That's my favorite memory of my last

visit. Masses of weapons."

"Typical of a male."

"Be kind. I was a mere lad. I liked the lions and tigers, too."

She smiled at him. "Very well, we'll visit the armory and the menagerie, but then on to the footsteps of history. William the Conqueror. The poor murdered princes. Lady Jane Grey and the Princess Elizabeth."

"A somewhat grisly tour."

"History is full of it, isn't it?"

"Gristle?"

"Grim tragedy!" she said. "At least Princess Elizabeth survived to become one of our greatest monarchs. Only think of the Armada."

"Defeated by a storm rather than by military force."

"But still glorious."

"The hair, the hair," he lamented. "It is probably a blessed fate to play no part in history, you know."

He had to be thinking of his part in Waterloo. Mara looked out for distraction and found it. "Edward Street. Isn't that one of the seven that make up the Seven Dials? Can we drive down there?"

"Poverty and gloom is not a spectacle."

Stung, she protested, "I didn't mean that!"

"My apologies. I'd prefer not to hazard

damage to mama's carriage."

Mara turned back as they passed another of the seven streets. "I see what you mean. It looks as if sunlight never penetrates." *As do you, sometimes.* "How horrid to live there, especially if the area is full of criminals. Can't anything be done?"

"The St. Bride instinct to make all right," he said. "The only solution would be to pull it down, I suspect. Seven narrow roads meeting at one point has to be oppressive."

She cocked her head. "The very opposite of a square, you mean. How interesting. I've never thought about the way streets and towns come to be. After all, most just grow higgledy-piggledy. Perhaps that's the better way."

"I have to point out that some of the worst London warrens have grown higgledy-piggledy."

"And some squares and terraces are both designed and pleasant. Is it possible that some places are blessed whilst others are cursed?"

"As with Brideswell. Do you regret the fact that one day you must live elsewhere?" he asked.

"I'll not be far away."

"What if you fall in love with a man from far away?"

Mara assessed his question. Was he speaking of himself? "What of you?" she asked. "Do you regret not being the heir to Long Chart?"

"Not a bit."

"But you must love that part of the country," she probed. "Will you choose an estate nearby?"

"I may make do with rooms in Town."

"What of the children? They need the country."

He seemed surprised. "I suppose they will. They'll always have Long Chart, but you're right."

He made it sound like a burden, so Mara said, "It will be fun to pick the exact spot you want rather than being obliged to take on a place, like Simon and Marlowe."

He smiled at her. "You really dislike that place, don't you?"

"It's a cursed spot. All that money and effort, all that classical perfection, and for what? Whom did it ever make happy?"

"The workmen employed, the servants employed now to keep it up."

She grimaced but agreed. "They could have been used to create something more . . . joyous, however. Have you ever *been* to Marlowe?"

"Yes."

That startled her. Hurt followed, because Simon hadn't told her. "When?" she asked.

"A few weeks ago. My first foray beyond Long Chart."

"Not one I'd choose," she said.

"Simon was there."

It was a simple testimony to friendship, but that, too, hurt. *What of me? Will you ever be content in a place simply because I'm there?*

"I still shudder at the thought that our family might have had to move there," she said. "It's . . . it's soulless. It can shrivel a person. The old earl was a solitary invalid there for decades. His son spent as much time as possible elsewhere, and when there lived in one of the pavilions, but he still came to a grim end."

"Control your imagination, Mara. It's just a house."

The words came without thought. "I wish it would burn down."

"Unfortunately, so much stone and marble is hard to fire. It could always be demolished."

"No, it couldn't. That's the point. People visit from around the world to adore its perfection. You see how unfair that is? A blight ought to be ugly."

He leaned forward and took her hands.

Through gloves she felt a spark that almost made her gasp. "Don't care so much, Mara. For survival, don't waste your fire on impenetrable shadows."

She tightened her fingers on his. "Isn't that what fire is for — to chase away shadows?"

As I wish to do for you.

Perhaps he understood, for he let her go and leaned back. "A candle flame deprived of air dies." He turned to look at the outside world. "We're passing the Bank of England."

She took the deflection and made suitable comments on that, the Royal Exchange, and other places of business.

But then they saw the masts of ships on the river and Dare said, "There looms the shadowy edifice itself."

The external crenellated walls of the Tower of London rose around the famous square White Tower. Even in sunlight with flags and pennants flying the place looked grim and the darker moments of history no longer seemed romantic.

Perhaps she was picking that up from Dare, who was full of shadowy complexities. She could even understand his warning that his darkness could extinguish her light.

As they climbed down from the carriage, walked over a bridge, and through a looming arch, Mara felt as if she was entering a prison, as if terrible things might happen here, trapping her in the dark. The Tower was a prison, though rarely used now. It had been a terrible one once.

When they walked through another arch, however, they emerged into spacious daylight and her shivers seemed ridiculous.

"Houses and grass. Why didn't I expect that? This used to be a favored royal residence, after all."

A warder in his Tudor-style red uniform hurried to take their entrance fee and be their guide. She saw other visitors strolling around, each with their own guide.

"Sir, ma'am," said the yeoman, "permit me to show you all the places that formed our great nation's history. Here before you is the famous White Tower, built by William the Conqueror over seven hundred years ago."

Mara listened to the man's well-practiced patter as he showed them around the White Tower and the armory, which had once delighted Dare. Hardly surprising if weaponry no longer pleased.

Then their guide led them back the way they'd come to look at Traitor's Gate ". . . through which so many have arrived by boat never to leave alive."

Mara shivered in a more pleasurable way, for this was all far in the past. She went eagerly into the squat Bloody Tower, where the poor princes had been murdered four hundred years ago. But then their guide offered to shut them in a bleak chamber said to be the boys' last sleeping place so they could experience imprisonment.

"No, thank you." Dare spoke calmly, but Mara sensed sharp desperation.

"Oh, no, indeed!" she gasped and clutched his arm. "I could not bear it. Do let's go back into fresh air and sunshine."

She clung to Dare as if for support as they returned down narrow stairs, her mind whirling. Had he been imprisoned during his long absence by more than wounds and opium? By whom?

"The menagerie," she said, as soon as they emerged. That had been one of his favorite places. "I long to see the elephant!"

The guide, clearly worried about his tip, hurried them there. "Over the ages, many foreign princes have sent animals as gifts to our monarchs, and they have been housed here. Lions, tigers, elephants. Many have reproduced or been replaced. . . ."

Mara went in eagerly, despite a strong odor, but why hadn't she realized that the beasts would be caged? Some monkeys ran about freely, sometimes grabbing at passing hats, but a great maned lion lay in the lower half of a two-story cage, surely pining for open ground, and a tiger paced, eyeing them with malevolence.

Distress washed over her and she didn't know if it came from the beasts or from Dare. She set a rapid pace, saying as an excuse, "How terrifying if they were to escape!"

"I assure you, ma'am, they are completely safe," the yeoman said. "Tame, even. The tiger's cage was inadvertently left open not long ago, and he did not so much as seek to leave."

Mara paused to look back at the glowering animal. "How sad."

"Not for the public strolling around at the time," Dare pointed out, steering her on.

Even the enormous elephant, grasping hay with its trunk and feeding it into its mouth, could not delay her. She had to get out of this place and she was sure she was picking up the desperation from Dare.

"The jewels," the yeoman tried as they exited. "You will want to see the Crown Jewels, ma'am."

Mara wanted to escape the Tower completely, but Dare was saying nothing and it would seem peculiar. Jewels sounded safe enough. As they followed the yeoman, she babbled cheerful nonsense, but then they were ushered into another small cell-like room.

It was even barred down the middle, presumably to prevent anyone grabbing the jewels and running off with them. A sentry stood by as additional security, even though the only thing visible beyond the bars was a wooden cupboard.

At least the room was lit by ample candles, but Mara knew the Tower had been a terrible choice. The very stones seemed steeped in suffering. She was about to say that she'd lost interest when another party joined them — a middle-aged couple and two daughters in their teens. Guides chivied them all toward the viewing benches.

Dare didn't object, so Mara didn't either.

A young woman walked into the area beyond the bars.

She opened the cupboard and took the coronation orb out to display, reciting information at such speed and with so little interest that Mara had to bite her lips hard not to laugh. She glanced at Dare, and he might be having a similar reaction. The other party was ooohing and ahhing.

The orb was impressive for its history and the jewels flashed fire in the candlelight, but both she and he were no strangers to fine jewels.

The orb was followed by the scepter and a number of other pieces until, last of all, the crown, set with the most magnificent stones.

When they escaped blinking into daylight, Mara said, "The Crown Jewels are important for what they symbolize, but I'm never as impressed by huge gems as I feel I ought to be."

"Your husband will doubtless be grateful." Dare looked to their guide. "Where now, sir?"

Mara appreciated his willingness to carry on, but he looked distressed. He might even be sweating.

"I'm sorry," she said, "but can we leave now? I'm quite fatigued and we can always return."

She saw the flash of relief before he hid it. He tipped the warder and they walked briskly out of the Tower. As they passed through the last arch, Mara felt able to breathe properly again.

Their footman awaited. "The carriage is at the Yeoman's Arms, milord. I'll run and get it."

"Wait." Dare turned to Mara. "Perhaps you would like refreshments before we return. It's already gone noon."

The sense of oppression had lifted, but Dare still seemed strained, so Mara agreed. They strolled to the inn, the footman running ahead so by the time they arrived a private parlor was ready for them plus an adjoining room containing a washstand and a very welcome chamber pot.

Mara returned to the parlor to find pie, cakes, and tea laid out, but no Dare. She resisted an urge to run in search of him, but couldn't stop pacing the room.

She forced herself to sit and pour a cup of tea. She added more sugar than usual, drank it, and did feel better. But where *was* he? There was no clock in this room but she felt as if they'd been apart for an hour.

She tried to tell herself she'd imagined Dare's distress, but she knew she hadn't. It had felt as if their minds were joined, as if she experienced his fears.

Had he been imprisoned? By whom?

The French? But why, and they had lost the battle, so if he had briefly been imprisoned, he would soon have been freed.

The Belgian widow? She had nursed Dare back to health, but he'd said she was evil. Had she kept him prisoner? How?

And where was he now?

Of course he hadn't wandered off like a lackwit.

Of course he hadn't fallen ill somewhere.

Of course he hadn't been kidnapped!

All the same, it was as if she tasted his distress in the air.

Then he strolled in, so completely in order she wanted to hurl the plate of cream cakes at him. He didn't even apologize or explain, but simply sat and said, "I don't think the Tower lived up to your expectations."

He couldn't have been absent as long as she'd thought. She was an idiot deranged by love. She found a smile and poured him tea. "I'm not sure what my expectations were, but I'm glad we came."

Yes, she was. This was the longest time she'd ever spent alone with Dare, and here they were, taking tea in a cozy parlor. Like husband and wife.

She wanted to ask important questions — about opium and about imprisonment — but it would be better to keep things light. "The Tower was excellent research for Castle Cruel," she said.

He helped himself to pork pie. "How far have you progressed with that?"

Mara had hardly given it a thought, so she said, "I'm stuck on problems. Anne can't be a village maiden. The villagers would object to her ill treatment."

"In these egalitarian days, perhaps. In Caspar's time they'd be cowed in terror."

Mara finished her pie. "True, but Canute the duke would hardly be marrying a village maid. It makes no sense."

His eyes twinkled. "You expect this to make sense?"

"We have to try. I think Anne is Caspar's ward and was betrothed to Canute when they were children, but then he disappeared and was presumed dead."

"Perhaps, then, he should be the captive corpse."

"He can't be. He's the hero."

He raised a brow. "Mara, Mara, are you saying that only the male can have the active part?"

She paused, a forkful of cream cake halfway to her lips. "He's the captive, she's the rescuer? Oh, Dare! I do like that."

"I thought you might." He slid back and contemplated the beamed ceiling. "Poor Canute's a captive, trapped in a loathsome crypt/Brave Anne Whyte seeks him, although by scorpions nipped." He smiled at her. "I've been working on my iambic pentameters."

"So I see, but scorpions?"

"If we cannot be brilliant, we can be unique."

Mara finally put the cake in her mouth, savoring its light sweetness, but also the lightness of Dare. She tried to come up with more poetry. "Virginal Anne faces scorpion sting. . . ." She pulled a face. "Virginal Violet would have a better ring."

"No — even though you proposed it so poetically."

"I did, didn't I? But why not Violet?" He looked mischievously secretive, so she added, "Tell, Dare."

"There's a rather notorious lady called Violet Vane. She's not at all virginal, with or without a Y." He laughed. "That could become deeply philosophical, couldn't it? Do we know the *why* for poor Violet's fall from grace? *Why* is she not a blushing violet, but instead a blatant one? Can," he added pensively, "a violet blate?"

"Stop it!" Mara protested, in danger of choking.

"I was just getting into the flow of it," he complained. "But very well. Our heroine must remain Anne Whyte, Y not I, who is fighting off a scorpion."

"I or Y?" Mara asked.

"I," he said, frowning at her. "And a headless knight —"

"I or Y?"

"Perdition! There must be monsters who are I-less."

Mara grinned. "A mad, blind monk."

Dare applauded. "Which our heroine — don't say it — must fight — don't say it — while Canute, the poor laggard, cannot."

Mara laughed again, feeling sublimely happy. Dare was back.

"We've made him a corpse," she pointed out, "so his laggardliness is not entirely his fault. Do you think he'll mind being rescued by his lady?"

"If I needed rescuing, I'd feel churlish to quibble."

Mara winced. Dare *had* been rescued by a lady — a woman, at least. She ate the last morsel of her cake.

"Despite the delicious sound of the word 'corpse'," she said, "it makes no sense to hold a corpse captive. What can it do?"

"Rise to haunt. We need a new title. *The Ghastly Ghoul of Castle Cruel?* A rhyme, begad, to boot."

"He moans and groans and trails his drool/He is the dread Canute!"

"Bravo!" He applauded and smiled brilliantly at her, and for a moment, she felt faint.

"What if Anne were the ghoul," he asked,

"sneaking around disguised as a ghost in search of her beloved?"

"Terrifying the servants."

"Methinks," he said, "you base the lady on yourself."

She looked at him. "Simon told you?"

"That you walked the monastery ruins on Halloween one year, dressed as a white nun? I wish I'd been there."

"I, too," she said lightly, but meaning it deeply. She pushed the plate of cakes toward him. "You really should have one of these. They're delicious."

"Obviously. You've had two." He rose. "We should be on our way or Ella will send out a search party. I'll order the coach brought around."

Mara watched him leave, feeling pulled out of paradise. When she considered his plate, she noticed he'd eaten only one small piece of pie. Once, he'd loved cakes.

She pulled on her gloves and followed, unwilling to let the darkness creep back in. As she settled in the carriage, she said, "I think this novel should be a cooperative effort. We're far more inventive together than separately. *The Ghastly Ghoul of Castle Cruel,* a novel in verse by . . ."

"Dara Saint Mara," he suggested lightly. But there was definitely some dimming of his former brilliance.

"Perfect!" she declared. "We need to do more research as well. What about Westminster Abbey tomorrow? It must have crypts. In fact, I think it has effigies of famous monarchs."

She waited, breathless.

"Why not?"

"And torture chambers at the waxworks." Days stretched ahead, days just like this one, their fanciful novel their excuse. "Thank you for bringing me here, Dare. I particularly enjoyed seeing more of London. I like to be aware of the wider world."

"I could say *be*ware."

"We can't spend life being wary," Mara stated.

"Many do and the result is often blessed."

She had to ask. "Do you wish you'd not gone to Waterloo, Dare?"

He flinched.

"I'm sorry —"

"No. It's all right. I had no choice, especially with Con returning to the army."

"But he was a soldier from sixteen, wasn't he?"

"He sold out in 1814 and thought he was done with the bloody trade. He had the experience and the training, however, and was needed."

"Because the veterans had been sent to the Americas."

He nodded. "I lacked both experience and training, but when I knew how much he hated the thought of more fighting, I couldn't hold back. I was young, healthy, and expendable."

When she protested, he said, "A younger son with an older brother already father to a son. The only reasons to stay at home would have been indolence or cowardice."

"That's not fair. Few men who weren't trained officers went to fight at Waterloo."

"Those who tried weren't welcome. I probably wasn't, but I'm a duke's son with many strings to pull. I could go, so I did, but I wasn't being sacrificial, Mara. I remember a fierce desire to be in on the game."

"But do you *regret* it? Oh, I'm sorry. That's a stupid question."

"No, it's not. I don't. Any victory is a consequence of a million small acts. Perhaps one of mine made a difference. I remember being good at what I was doing."

Mara wasn't sure this discussion was wise, but she treasured his sharing such matters with her. "What were you doing?"

"Riding hell for leather here and there carrying messages."

"You were always a magnificent rider."

He returned her smile. "Mad, you said once, I remember."

"When you won that race to Louth. You jumped the tollgate!"

"It was in my way."

Mara couldn't help but ask. "What happened? In the battle."

He grimaced. "I wish I knew. I think I remember my horse going down, but beyond that, it's hard to be sure what's real and what's the result of wanting to remember. Of the early time after the battle, nothing, which is probably a blessing."

What do you remember from after? she wanted to ask. *Were you imprisoned?* But something about him choked off the question and an awkward silence settled.

"Was last night your first visit to Covent Garden?" he asked.

It was clumsy, but she grasped a safe subject. "My first to any London theater."

"Did you enjoy the play? And what," he asked with a lighter expression, "did you mean about barnacles?"

She laughed and described the Scilly brothers. They went on to discuss the play and some of the better ones they had seen.

Then Mara remembered some good news. "We're finally going to Almack's next week.

Will you attend?"

"Heaven forbid."

"But then who will dance with me?"

"Half the men in Town. If you've ever unwillingly sat out a dance, Imp, I'd be astonished."

She wrinkled her nose at him. "Oh, very well, but it's only because I'm a good dancer."

"It's because you're pretty and charming."

Something inside did a somersault. "Am I? Truly?"

She held her breath, but he merely gave her a look, just as one of her brothers would.

"A lady needs constant reassurance of her charms, you know."

"You lack a mirror?" he asked.

"At the moment, yes."

"I assure you, the visit to the morbid Tower has not dimmed the glow of your complexion or creased it with wrinkles. It has left your lips full and pink, your eyes clear and bright, and your figure, as best I can see" — his eyes traveled up and down her, leaving a sensation almost of fiery touch — "in charming perfection."

"Perfection!" she declared over a racing heart. "Alas that it must fade with my youth."

"No. Yours is a beauty for the ages, Mara,

because time cannot dull the spirit."

Clever repartee fled. Mara licked her lips, trying to read his features. "That didn't sound as if you think of yourself as my brother."

She saw wariness tighten his muscles. "A brother can appreciate the charms of a sister."

"I don't think I'd describe Simon in quite those terms."

"I should hope not."

Mara sucked in a breath. "You know what I mean. Dare, I think I love you."

His face turned blank. "You feel sorry for me, Imp, which is quite a different thing."

Imp. She recognized that name as an enemy now, a way of pinning her as child or sister.

"No, I don't. Or, at least, I do feel sorry for you. For being wounded. For . . . for having to fight free of opium. It's all unfair, but that's not it. It's the most peculiar feeling, like a fever, but I can't think what else it could be."

"The influenza?"

He was building a wall between them. She should have kept her stupid mouth shut. Tears threatened, but she knew tears would crown the disaster.

"I'm sorry," she said. "I've embarrassed

you. Now you'll probably never want to see me again."

"Of course not. I mean, of course, I will. Damn it, Mara —"

"Don't." She saw the way out and rushed for it. "You're probably right and it's a passing phase. I have a sad habit of falling into and out of mad passions," she lied. "I remember the time I haunted Louth because I'd tumbled into infatuation with a physician there. And I practically swooned at Sir Richard Jasper's feet."

She burbled along in this way, exaggerating youthful infatuations, making up more, and then carrying on desperately to relate all the embarrassing behavior of friends and neighbors. Somehow she talked her way back from the brink of disaster. From idiocy in love she moved on to idiocy in fashion and they entered Grosvenor Square engaged in a discussion of furnishings and Chinese ornaments.

When the carriage stopped, Ella's house looked like a haven. Even waiting for the footman to open the carriage door was a trial. Dare had climbed out and stood ready to escort her to the door and she wished he hadn't. She needed to escape and weep for her folly. At the open door, she managed a smile as she thanked him for the outing.

He took her hand, his expression somber. After a long moment, he said, "Don't, Mara."

If he intended more, he was interrupted.

"Mara, you're home at last. Don't rush off, Dare!"

Mara turned and there was her devil's hair brother, Simon, striding toward them, smiling.

CHAPTER 10

Because Dare still held Mara's hand, she felt it tighten before he released it. Yet when she looked at him, he was smiling, and when he spoke, she heard no tension. "Simon the tardy, arrived at last."

She realized for the first time just how skillful an actor Dare was. He must long to escape as much as she did, but they were trapped. He had no choice but to enter the house with her, and when the front door clicked shut, it felt like a cell door.

She gathered her resources and went to kiss her brother's cheek and chatter. "We've been to the Tower. *Very* dreadful and fascinating. When did you arrive? Is Jancy here? Ah, I see she is."

She went to hug her newest sister-in-law and friend, who was coming downstairs, bright with welcome.

Simon's wife was Jane for public usage, but preferred the name Jancy in the family and it suited her lively, generous nature. Simon adored her, and so did the whole family. Not surprising, as she was as lovely inside as out.

Jancy's Scottish father had given her red-gold hair and a delicate complexion dusted with freckles. Her mother had been of simple stock, however, so there was nothing delicate about the rest of her. She was a perfect, sensible St. Bride.

She'd never babble to a man that she loved him. Mara wanted to pound her head against the nearest wall over that.

"What's the matter?" Jancy asked.

Mara put on a smile. "Nothing but a need for tea."

"Come upstairs, then. Ella's pouring. We've only just arrived here."

They turned to go up and Mara said, "The baby's beginning to show. You're well?"

Jancy blushed, but said, "Completely."

"Your baby and Ella's will be about the same age. That's perfect."

Perfect. At the top of the stairs, Mara glanced back to check on Dare. He was close behind them, listening to Simon, seeming at ease. He and Simon were old and deep friends. She prayed she hadn't threatened that.

Then what her brother was saying caught her attention.

"Gas?" she asked. "At Marlowe House?"

"Yes. Come into the drawing room and I'll tell all."

Ruth hurried up and Mara took off her gloves, hat, and spencer so the maid could take them away. Then she went into the drawing room and sat beside Jancy on a sofa.

"An *explosion?*" she asked.

"No," Simon said. "How you do rush to dramatic assumptions. Austrey had gas piped into the library for lighting, though what possessed him, I can't imagine. He wasn't even bookish."

"It's fashionable," Ella said, passing cakes. "I don't care for it myself. Apart from the danger, it's too bright. Give me lamps and candles any day."

"But bright must be excellent for reading," Mara said.

"It *hisses,*" Ella said, "and always smells a little. It can't be healthy."

"This smell is more than a little," Simon said. "The housekeeper ordered the windows opened, but she didn't seem to realize the dangers."

"You must not live there until the whole system is removed," Ella said.

"Certainly not until it's been made safe. We took one sniff and ordered the house evacuated. The servants are taken care of and now I need to find a hotel."

"I wish I could invite you here," Ella said, "but we have no spare room."

"No matter —"

"Come to Yeovil House."

To Mara, Dare's words seemed strange, as if spoken reluctantly from another sphere. He looked quite normal, however, and before Simon could speak, he added, "You know there's no shortage of space, and with my parents away, I'm rattling around on my own. Do please come."

Simon hesitated, but then said, "Thank you. It won't be for long. Either the house will be in a fit state soon or we'll rent another."

Mara struggled with temptation and lost. She'd been expecting to move to Marlowe House with Simon and Jancy, and couldn't bear to be stuck here any longer, especially with such an exciting alternative — to live under the same roof as Dare.

She angled closer to Jancy. "Ask to have my company," she murmured.

Jancy flashed her a look, but she was quick-witted. "Simon, can Mara join us? I was depending on her advice about London."

"She doesn't know London any better than you," Simon said.

"But she has a book."

Dare was looking at Mara in an all-too-perceptive way. Lord, how could she have forgotten their recent, disastrous conversation? It must look as if she was pursuing him.

"A book?" Simon asked.

"*A Young Lady's Guide to the Educational Delights of London,*" Mara said. "A gift from my ecclesiastical godparents. Very informative, but I'm sure Jancy meant more general social knowledge. I might not have London polish, but I've lived in society all my life. I'd be willing to assist in any way I can."

"More than willing, you'd be delighted," Ella corrected.

Mara flashed her a look, alarmed that Ella had guessed her feelings for Dare.

"We're a little dull here," Ella continued with a smile. "I like dull, especially at the moment, but of course Mara would prefer more lively days."

"My soul shudders with dread," Simon said, but he turned to Dare. "Are you willing to take an extra guest if she promises to behave herself?"

"I will be *perfectly* behaved," Mara protested. She sent Dare a bright smile, hoping he'd understand that it was a promise not to embarrass him or herself ever again.

His eyes held hers for a moment, but then he said, "I don't believe even Mara can overstretch Debenham hospitality."

Even Mara?

Sick inside, she plunged into chatter. "Will this mean I'll meet more Rogues? I met Lord Middlethorpe and Sir Stephen Ball last night," she told Jancy. "And their wives. Oh, that reminds me. We're to go on an expedition in search of a silk warehouse. The wives, I mean. I mean, *I'm* not a wife." She pulled a face at her laughing family, hoping none of them guessed why she was babbling, and why her face was burning. "You're a Rogue's wife, Jancy. If there's room in the carriage, would you like to come?"

Jancy's eyes flickered. "If that's all right, Simon?"

"Of course. I have to deal with the gas. Buy lots of silk, my love."

He said it with a smile, but Mara felt a trace of strain in the air. That was the one blemish in this blissful marriage — money. Jancy had grown up poor and valued a penny where the St. Brides valued a pound.

Simon longed to pour out his wealth for her pleasure, but Jancy fretted over every extravagance.

That was an area where Mara could earn her keep. She wasn't careless with the pounds, but she had no difficulty with spending on reasonable things. In their circle the best quality was often reasonable. In fact, it could be essential.

Jancy was a new viscountess and would one day be a countess. She was also an outsider, a person known to be of lowly birth and with no ton connections. Many would be looking to find fault. Everything would go more smoothly if she, her home, and her entertainments were up to snuff.

Dare rose. Mara noticed he'd not touched his tea or cake. "Please excuse me. I, too, have matters to deal with, but I'll make sure all is in readiness. How many servants will you be bringing, Simon?"

As he and Simon discussed the details, Mara turned to Jancy. "Thank you," she said quietly. "As Ella said, it is a little quiet here and I'm a sad bother to her."

"It's a wonderful idea. I'd be terrified of London in my own home, never mind living in a duke's house. Simon laughs at me, but it's not easy."

"Don't worry. You'll soon find your feet,

especially with me to help."

Mara hurried upstairs to supervise the packing of her trunks, resolving to keep her silent promise to Dare. She wouldn't pester him. She would act the perfect young lady and wait for him to court her.

But please let it be soon!

Dare traveled back to Yeovil House in a coach that now seemed full of memories of Mara. Perhaps even her light perfume lingered.

They'd been face-to-face in here for so long and at times it had felt overwhelming, yet he'd had no desire to escape. Her bright eyes, her attention, her very presence had been light for his dark spirit.

She'd said she loved him.

He should be fleeing back to Somerset. For her sake. Instead, he'd invited her into his home. What insanity had possessed him? True, he'd invited Simon and Jancy, but all the same. To invite anyone . . .

He'd seen no choice. How could he not offer hospitality to his closest friend when he had eight empty bedrooms?

He closed his eyes and rested his head back, aware as always that a little opium would wipe all these cares away. He'd taken his noon dose at the Yeoman's Arms, congratulating himself that he'd carried it all morning without succumbing to temptation.

He'd never tried that before. He'd truly felt no temptation until the oppressiveness of the Tower had weighed on him — prison cells, cages, poor trapped animals with hate in their eyes. . . .

Mara hadn't seemed to notice his distress, thank heavens, but it had been a blessing that she'd tired. If she'd wanted to explore every nook and cranny he didn't know what he'd have done.

She'd said she loved him.

Despite her scrabbling attempts to escape, she'd meant it. At that moment, she'd meant it and hunger had roared in him, hunger worse than that for opium. To claim her, to possess her, to feed off her light and beauty.

To consume her.

That was what he feared above all. That the darkness inside him would swallow all the light — in his family, in his friends, but especially in Mara St. Bride.

The damnable, magical St. Brides.

As a tribe they were too tenderhearted for the real world. The hungry must be fed, the sick cared for, the injured healed, the oppressed defended. Those cursed with Black

Ademar's hair were the worst. They would plunge into an inferno in their cause.

That had almost killed Simon. Nothing must be allowed to harm Mara, most especially himself.

She'd said she loved him.

When he broke free of the beast.

If he broke free of the beast . . .

What if he stopped now? If his recent dose was his last? In a few weeks he could have victory.

If he could endure it this time.

Surely he could with such a prize at the end.

But as he reached the house, he realized he had put that option out of reach for now. Simon, Jancy, and Mara would arrive within hours, so he couldn't flee London to endure hell.

He descended from the coach and went into the house, where he summoned Mrs. Hunstable and gave her instructions.

"Two bedrooms. Viscount Austrey and his wife should have a parlor as well, I think. Which ones face the street?"

"The blue and the brown, sir. And the brown has a parlor adjoining. Both are noisier, however."

"They'll do." He saw her realize that they

would be farthest from the ballroom at the back.

"Provide all that might be needed. Wines, fruit, brandy. And the meals will need to be more varied, especially dinner. . . ."

What else?

"Don't you worry, my lord," the house-keeper said. "Just let me know if there's anything in particular the ladies and gentle-man would or wouldn't like, and I'll see to everything."

She might as well have patted him on the head. In his attempt to appear normal, he was acting as he never had before. In that other life that seemed a distant dream, he'd have carelessly told her the number of guests and left it all up to her.

He escaped to his room. Salter was there, assessing him for the ravages of the expedi-tion.

"I'm alive and in one piece, but there's a problem."

"Yes, sir?"

When Dare explained, Salter said, "A little early for this, sir, but these aren't strang-ers."

"No." Dare couldn't find words to speak of Mara. "I thought of giving it up entirely."

"Most unwise, sir."

"You're right, of course. Get Ruyuan. We

need to discuss strategy."

Dare waited for his mentor, inhaling and exhaling, as he'd learned could calm his desperate mind, aware of a new and unforeseen burden.

The thought of taking opium when under the same roof as Mara St. Bride revolted him.

CHAPTER 11

At half past three, Mara traveled to Yeovil House with Simon and Jancy, excited, but tense with awareness that she was returning to the house she'd so scandalously visited three nights ago. No one could possibly recognize her. No one but the kitchen boy and the groom had even seen her, and she'd been huddled in the blanket. Yet her nerves were wound tight.

She would be under the same roof as Dare. They would meet a dozen times a day. She must make absolutely sure not to embarrass them both again. But she seemed to lose control of her wits around him.

"Sit still," Simon said. "You're as fidgety as a five-year-old. Was Ella's as dull as all that?"

"I spent most of yesterday sewing clothes for orphans," Mara complained. "And nearly every night we had politicians for dinner."

"Tasty," Jancy said, causing laughter.

"Tough as old boots, I'd think," Simon said. "Poor Mara. No dissipation at all?"

Smile brightly. "Not a scrap. Speaking of which, I long to go to Astley's. Dare wouldn't take me."

Simon studied her. "How does it come that he's squiring you around at all?"

Mara's mind flashed to her misadventure with Berkstead so fiercely that she felt her brother would see everything. "I asked."

When Simon shook his head, Mara saw an opening. "Should I not have done that? He seems recovered. Not his old self, but healthy. He did seem a bit blue-deviled, however, so I thought it would be good for him as well as for me. I do cheer people up — you know I do."

"Or drive them demented. I assume he's able to tell you to go to the devil if he wishes."

"I doubt he'd be so rude."

"Which is the problem. Sometimes you require it."

Mara's "Don't be horrid!" clashed with Jancy's "Simon!"

Mara smiled at her sister-in-law. "You know we squabble all the time. Seriously, Simon, how is Dare? I assumed he was free of the opium, but now I wonder."

Simon grimaced, clearly unwilling to share confidences. "He's reduced his dose to a low level, but it seems that the final break is very difficult."

"Why?"

"None of your business. You have Jancy's company now and my escort. Leave Dare alone."

Mara wanted to snarl or cry but she tried calm reason. "I'm going to be under his roof, Simon. Might I not need to know a little about these things?"

"Oh, very well. The doctors can't agree on cures for the addiction. Many think there's no point in trying and that it's better for the opium user to simply take a little every day."

"I know that. I assume Dare won't accept that."

"No, but stopping suddenly is horrendous — it can kill — so he's chosen the slow reduction method. It's worked pretty well thus far, and it's given him time to recover physically, but it seems the end must be taken at a leap."

Mara frowned. "And he can't do that? I would have thought Dare up to anything." Simon's surprise made her aware of her words, which sent heat into her cheeks. "I've always thought him splendid. You know that."

"Yes." His look was speculative, however, and not pleasantly so. Mara almost asked what he'd think about her marrying Dare but she had some sense and control left.

She was saved by the carriage rocking to a stop in front of Yeovil House, but she descended feeling as if the woman's-head door knocker might cry out the scandal of her last visit here. All that happened, of course, was that the door was opened by an impassive footman and they walked in.

Last time, distressed and by the light of only one candle, Mara hadn't noticed the paneling, the ornaments, and the weighty portraits of men and women in robes of state, including the present king and queen.

Mara braced to behave perfectly toward Dare, but their only welcome came from the footman, a maid, and a cap-wearing woman in a brown-and-gold-striped dress and white lacy apron. She introduced herself as Mrs. Hunstable, the housekeeper, which surprised Mara, for housekeepers generally dressed more soberly.

They were taken up the grand oak staircase to front-facing rooms next to each other. Hers was only a bedroom, but Simon and Jancy also had a parlor.

As she waited for Ruth and her luggage to arrive, Mara took off her outer clothing and surveyed her new quarters. She decided she liked the room better than the one she'd had in Ella's house, perhaps because it reminded her of home.

She hadn't realized how much she liked a carpet that showed slight paths of wear and upholstery that was a little faded. She even liked the hint of time in the air that blended with the lavender sachets.

She sat on the small sofa by the fire, taking the first calm moment for hours. Simon was right. Now he and Jancy were here, she had no excuse to tease Dare into taking her out and about. At least she'd be with him in the little ways, the family ways.

Unless he avoided her.

He'd said he had business to attend to, but she thought that had been an excuse to flee. If she were fanciful she could say she sensed him somewhere in the house now. If he was avoiding her, she didn't blame him. How could she have been so foolish as to blurt out her love like that?

Because she'd never been in love before. She'd fancied herself in love, but it had never been like this.

She rose, unable to sit still. This feeling — influenza, he'd said, which made her laugh even though it had been thrown up as a shield — was all-consuming. She wanted to prowl the house in search of him. To stand in a corridor in case he should pass by. She remembered stories of Lady Caroline Lamb haunting Byron's doorstep, often in disguise. She was going to be a similar laughingstock!

More to the point, she was in danger of distressing Dare when he already lived on a perilous edge.

A knock brought distraction — the luggage and Ruth. It also provided an excuse to leave her room, but where should she go? Simon and Jancy seemed to pine for time alone together. She'd never understood that lovers' behavior before, but now, if she could share a private room with Dare, she'd never want to leave it.

She went out into the carpeted corridor, its walls hung with paintings, and set with occasional tables, chests, and chairs against the walls. The house was quiet enough to be deserted though she supposed the children were in their quarters.

She could go in search of them and thus, perhaps, find Dare.

Stop that. She went downstairs and asked a footman for directions to the drawing room.

"There's the large and small, milady, and also the library, where the family often likes to sit."

"The library then."

Books would distract her mind. She had her novels, but they were being unpacked upstairs. And besides, she needed no more tales of fancy or husband hunting. Some sensible sermons would be more the thing.

The Yeovil House library was more parlor than library, for the shelves held a small collection that turned out to be mostly gazetteers, almanacs, Hansard, and bound annuals of magazines.

She was browsing the *Gentleman's Magazine* for 1815, looking for reports of Waterloo, when the door opened. She knew who it was before she turned, her heart thumping.

Dare was clearly as startled to see her as she was to see him. And wary. Was he afraid of what she might do or say?

Thank heavens that bright cheeriness came so naturally. "I hope you don't mind my exploring here. Such an interesting collection. I mean, eclectic. A bit of this, a bit of that."

She turned to put the book back on the shelf, wincing. There was cheeriness and then there was inane babbling.

"I hope everything is as you wish," he said.

"Perfectly." She composed herself and turned back. "It's very kind of you to invite us here."

"That's as ridiculous as suggesting Ella is kind to invite you to her house."

"Because Simon's like a brother to you. You didn't precisely invite me, however."

And I am not your sister.

"All the same, you are welcome."

"Am I?" It popped out and he almost flinched. "I won't distress you, Dare, as I did in the carriage —"

"No —"

She raised her hand to stop him. "I did. Such silliness. But I do care for you. You've been part of my family for years. We all care for you, but we can be overwhelming and now here we are in your house. A Brideswell invasion. You know what that means. Intrusion and interference, fuss and hovering, all with the best intentions."

"I —"

"If we disturb you, tell us to go to the devil. If we can help, ask."

He closed his eyes for a moment and she thought she'd blundered again. But then he smiled. She could see the strain behind it, but it was a true smile.

"A Brideswell invasion," he said. "I should

welcome you with flowers and pealing bells. As I said to Simon once, please just put up with me. You're right. Having anyone here is a strain, but sometimes strain is good for us. Or at least necessary. I am too much alone."

"You were at the theater last night."

"The insistence of friends. And . . ."

He seemed to stop himself saying something else, but he came farther into the room. Mara turned to watch him, to study his expressions, seeking guidance. Should she leave? Had he moved merely to open the way to the door?

He stood by the fireplace with his back toward her. "I'm addicted to opium," he said. "I'm sure you know that. I'm fighting to be free. I will be free. I thought the process would be . . . not easier, but simpler. Steps to be followed. Steep steps, but not impossible. Now I wonder if it's possible." His hand on the mantelpiece tightened to a fist. "If even when I stop taking it, I'll hear its siren song all my life . . ."

Mara gently closed the door, her heart thundering at this intimate revelation. She longed to take him in her arms. Not as a lover, though she wanted to be his lover, but as she would a sister or brother in pain.

He turned to face her and it was as if his

features had previously been held in normal lines only by willpower — willpower that was now exhausted.

She stepped forward, but stopped herself. Fragile as cracked glass, she remembered.

"I'm taking as little as I can bear," he said, "three times a day. It's rather a long time since the noon allowance, so please excuse any present peculiarities."

He'd taken some at the Yeoman Inn? That explained so much. His distress in the Tower. His delay in joining her. His subsequent brightness. But had that precious wit and clarity all come from the drug?

"Is there anything I can do?" she asked. "In general, I mean."

"No." She saw his chest rise and fall. "I do hope to win."

"You will. Of course you will."

She needed to do something. Looking down, she saw the flower brooch set at the low neckline of her gown and fumbled it free. She went to him, watchful for distress.

"In the past, ladies gave knights favors to wear for victory in combat." She reached for the lapel of his jacket. When he didn't resist, she fixed the brooch into it, aware of his warmth and perhaps also of his frantic heart. "May all your enemies be vanquished, my lord."

Though his face remained drawn, a smile showed in his eyes at their old joke. "With your favor, my lady, how could it be otherwise?"

He took her hands and raised them to his lips, first one and then the other, pressing his lips to the knuckles of each. His own hands were too cold, so she curled her fingers around them, trying to share her warmth.

"Dare . . ." she said, seeking the right words.

"Mara?"

Mara and Dare jerked apart and turned to where Jancy stood in the doorway, turning pink. "Oh. I . . . I came to see if you wanted to go for a walk."

Mara desperately employed her bright smile. "An excellent idea. I'll get my outer clothing and be with you in a moment."

As Mara hurried away, Dare met the clear blue eyes of Simon's wife. Jancy was young, as young as Mara, but like Mara she was not at all naive or silly.

"I won't hurt her," he said.

"Of course you won't. Why even think it?"

Because she truly loves me and I may be as helpless to resist that as I am to resist the beast. Her touch steals my breath; her look makes me believe I'm a better man. But I'm not. I'm too painfully aware of having her beneath my roof and of her lovely ripeness for bed. Even though I'm not sure I'm capable of love anymore — of the sort of love a jewel like Mara deserves — I'm discovering that I'm very capable of lust.

He forcibly stopped his wildly running mind and sought Jancy's question. Ah, yes. Why did he think he might hurt Mara? He fought a laugh. He lived in fear of hurting everyone around him.

"I'm somewhat unpredictable. Even to myself."

"Simon thinks you're trying to reduce the opium too quickly. He tells me not to interfere, but I'm not always an obedient wife."

"An obedient wife would be a dead bore. However, would you tell a drowning man not to struggle for the shore?"

"But panic never serves. I think you should —"

"Don't!" It came out more viciously than he'd meant and he closed his eyes. "I'm sorry. But don't. Don't carp at me. Not now. After six o'clock, you can nag all you want. I probably won't care."

It took effort to open his eyes and look at her, and when he did, her cheeks were flushed with mortification. Simon would kill him.

But she spoke calmly. "I'm sorry, too. Silly of me."

They both heard footsteps.

"You're loved too much, you see," Jancy said, then left, closing the door. He listened to faint voices and then the closing of the front door.

Gone, gone, gone.

He roamed the room, unable to remember why he'd come here, feeling more alone, more abandoned, than he could remember. Two brutal desires tormented him — for Mara and for the beast. One he might never have. The other was in every druggist's shop, his for a penny if he only surrendered.

The ticking of the heavy marble clock on the mantelpiece beat in his head. Two hours still to go and the damned thing ticked so slowly. He grasped it as if he could force it to speed. Or could strangle its ponderous pace. He definitely tried crushing it. Pain sometimes helped.

He forced his hands to loosen.

Having others here, friends, damned friends, damned interfering friends, was going to be hell.

But then, what wasn't?

CHAPTER 12

A stroll around St. James's Park was just the thing, Mara decided, after that intense exchange with Dare. That didn't mean she wouldn't rather be in her room, picking with feverish intensity over every word spoken, but that way lay madness.

A footman in Simon's livery walked a few yards behind them. "Do we really need an escort?" she asked as they turned into Duke Street.

"Simon fusses."

"What harm could he imagine coming to you here?"

"I think he fears I'll get lost. He says there are some rough areas near here."

"That's true, but I think it's simply that he loves you so much."

Jancy smiled, but said, "I only wish we ladies were allowed to be as protective of our men."

Mara squeezed Jancy's arm, knowing how

terrified she had been for Simon when he'd been wounded. The thought of Dare being wounded again made her shudder. The thought of him dead . . .

It was impossible. Mara touched her bodice to be sure the brooch was not there. A talisman. If there was any magic about Brideswell, she prayed she'd given Dare some of it.

"Dare and I were talking about that," she said, and told Jancy about Anne searching for her imprisoned Canute.

"You're truly planning to publish a novel?" Jancy asked, looking alarmed.

"Oh, no. It's just for fun. Dare needs fun."

Jancy nodded. "Yes, you're right. Simon tells such tales of him, but now he treats him like a mental invalid, if that makes sense."

"Yes. Yes, it does, and I'm dragging him out of bed and into races. I might be doing harm, though."

Jancy touched Mara's arm. "I'm sure you're not. There's something about him that wasn't there a few weeks ago."

"Breathlessness?" Mara joked.

Jancy smiled but shook her head. "Perhaps more like an invalid who's finally been in the sun a little. Oh, look, there are Dare's little ones. Shall we join them?"

Mara turned and saw Pierre and Delphie playing with a ball under the care of their two maids.

"Of course," she said, turning to walk that way, but also savoring the idea that she had brought sunshine into Dare's life. "How do you come to know the children? Did he bring them when he visited Marlowe?"

"They go everywhere with him. But I've also met them at Long Chart. We visited there on our arrival. Unfortunately I was in mourning and they're wary of women in black."

"Why?"

"Their mother dressed in black."

"The woman who took care of Dare? Do you know anything about her?"

When Jancy said, "Not really," Mara knew she was lying.

"Not even her name?"

After a moment, Jancy said, "Thérèse Bellaire."

The children had seen them and were running toward them smiling.

Mara smiled back and used their full names. *"Bonjour, Mademoiselle Bellaire, Monsieur Bellaire."*

Both children froze. Delphie's face quivered and Pierre's jaw set. With impressive dignity, he said, "That is not our name, my lady."

Mara almost stammered. "I'm so sorry. I thought . . ."

"Our name is Martin." He pronounced it the French way: *Martan.*

"I will remember. Names can be so very confusing! Last year my father was Mr. St. Bride and now he's Earl of Marlowe. And my brother went from being plain Simon St. Bride to Viscount Austrey."

"I will always be Pierre Martin," the boy said, "for I am not an aristocrat, me. But I hope one day to be Admiral Martin."

"Well, do you know," Jancy said in a comfortable tone, "I think you should consider becoming Peter Martin." She pronounced it in the English way. "Only imagine if we fall into war with France again. An admiral with such a French name might have difficulties."

The boy was clearly struck by this and mouthed, "Peter Martin . . . Thank you for the advice, Aunt Jane."

Delphie dropped a curtsy, pretty skirts spread. "Bonjour, Aunt Jane."

Mara could have wept at the difference between their treatment of Jancy and of herself, especially when she hoped one day to be their mother. She was trying to think how to make peace when Delphie came close to touch the flower-sprigged fabric of her gown. Mara crouched down to give the little girl better access to the ribbon work and embroidered spring flowers on the spencer.

"C'est belle," the girl said, little fingers adoring.

"Thank you." As Jancy didn't speak French, Mara didn't. "Did you know that Lady Austrey and I are staying in Yeovil House for a few days?"

Pierre answered. "Yes, ma'am. We have been told not to bother you."

"I'm sure you could never be a bother," Jancy said. "May we visit the schoolroom later and see your toys and lessons?"

"But of course, Aunt Jane. You can see my sailing ship. It was Papa's when he was a boy. It needs repairing, so Papa and I are working on that. Perhaps Uncle Simon would like to help? I will let him help me sail it when it is ready."

The image of Dare and the boy working together to mend the boat caught at Mara's heart. From there, her mind slid to another picture — of a comfortable parlor in which Dare and the boy worked on the ship while she and Delphie worked on some pretty craft. Of a baby in a cradle, which she rocked with one foot as she'd often watched her mother do. At Brideswell, babies were not restricted to the nursery.

The image was so clear it felt like a foreseeing.

For that reason, she didn't ask the children to call her Aunt Mara. She rose from her cramped position and listened to chatter about lessons and toys — Delphie was particularly fond of a dolls' house — and then she and Jancy left, promising a visit.

"I wonder why Dare hasn't given the children his name," Mara said as they walked on. "Peter Debenham would be even better than Peter Martin, and Delphie Debenham, especially with a generous dowry, could one day marry very well."

"The issue of their real parents must be settled first."

Mara stopped. "Their *real* parents? Their mother was this Madame Bellaire and she was a widow. And now she's dead."

Jancy's ready color flared. "Oh, dear."

"Jancy, tell me the truth."

Jancy sighed. "They were not her children. They are probably orphans of the war."

"And Madame Bellaire took them in?" But that wasn't it, either. Mara suddenly recollected Dare's one-word description of the woman. *Evil.* "Jancy, I need to know."

"Perhaps you're right."

Mara went to a stone bench and sat. "I am."

Jancy sat beside her, but pulled at the tips of her cream leather gloves.

"Tell me everything."

Jancy sighed. "That Madame Bellaire was not a good woman, Mara. Don't ask me for details, for it's very complicated and involves a lot of secrets, but she was close to Napoleon and sometimes spied for him. So after Waterloo she was in a difficult situation. She had lost her access to power and wealth, but she thought she had money in England. She lived here in 1814." After a moment, she added, "Running a brothel."

"Oh. *That* sort of close to Napoleon."

Jancy blushed. "Probably. Anyway, she assumed the identity of the Belgian widow of a Lieutenant Rowland who'd died in the battle."

"Did he have a wife? Widow?"

"No, but she forged the record of a recent marriage and it wasn't questioned. It would have entitled her to assistance from the army in getting to England, you see, and even a pension if she could keep up the deception."

"But how did Dare come into this?"

"No one's quite sure. Either she found

him on the battlefield and then came up with a plan to keep him in her power, or she found him after she'd woven the Rowland web and adapted it."

"But why Dare at all? Adding a seriously injured man to her burden can't have helped."

"She probably would receive more help to get a wounded officer back to England than if she were traveling as a widow. But it was really an act of spite or revenge. She hated Nicholas Delaney."

"Why?"

"It's complicated," Jancy said again. "They were lovers once and he left her."

"That's it? She sounds mad."

"I'm sure she was, but in a vicious way. And then he dared to reject her a second time and love his wife."

Mara shook her head, but returned to the main issue. "And the children?"

"It's assumed she scooped them up to support the illusion of a family and garner even more sympathy and aid."

"She just *took* them? What a carrion crow."

"Especially as she probably stripped poor Rowland of any identification and left him to be buried in a mass grave. His family has been notified, of course, and what little remained of his possessions has been returned to them."

Mara considered what she'd learned. "But once she was in England, why didn't she claim her money and disappear?"

"Her money wasn't readily available — and that was definitely the Rogues' doing — but she'd probably always intended to use Dare to make Nicholas Delaney suffer. She even kidnapped his daughter, Arabel."

"What a monster. I suppose King Rogue killed her, and good for him."

"Actually it was someone else — a Major Hawkinville. But Nicholas was involved in stopping her, along with other Rogues."

Mara turned to look at the children playing in the distance, so safe and happy. "How horrible she must have been for them to fear even her name." Then Mara saw the full implications and turned back to Jancy. "They might have parents somewhere who are looking for them? Oh, no! Poor Dare."

"There are no reports of similar children missing in the Brussels area, but with the allied armies gathered to fight the French, they could have come from anywhere, so the search continues."

"They must be orphans," Mara stated, wishing stating it could make it so. "If someone was looking for them, they would have found them by now."

"Even if their parents are simple people? Peasants, even? Pierre remembers a little of a farm."

Mara raised her chin. "Then they're better off with Dare."

"Mara! Only imagine if they do have parents who love them and who are seeking them."

Mara knew Jancy was right, but she was fighting for Dare, perhaps for his sanity. "I'm sorry if I sound hardhearted, but Dare needs Delphie and Pierre. I suspect that at times they have been his reason to live."

Jancy studied her. "You love him."

Mara looked away, blushing. "He's been like a brother since I was seven."

Jancy said nothing.

"Oh, all right. I love him." She looked back at Jancy. "I didn't know. Then it hit me like . . . like walking into a tree! And now I can think of nothing else."

"Yes."

"It was like that with Simon?"

"It was more complicated, but yes."

"I don't know what to do," Mara said. "I have the hair, so I want to hunt him down like a panther. I might do it if he wasn't . . . Oh, it's silly to call him frail or ill, but it wouldn't be fair." When Jancy didn't respond, Mara said, "It wouldn't."

"No, probably not."

"But what if he never is truly well? What if he has to take opium for the rest of his life?"

"Would you mind?" Jancy asked.

Mara thought about it. "No. That's what he's doing now and I love him now. I want him free for his sake, but no, I wouldn't mind."

Jancy stood. "Then happy hunting."

"You think I should?" Mara asked as she, too, rose.

"Such love has to be a blessing and strength. But if it all comes to disaster, don't tell Simon I recommended it. Oh, there's Hal and Blanche."

Mara turned to see a couple strolling along the path, lost in smiling conversation. He was tall and dark, with his empty left sleeve pinned across his chest. The lady on his right arm was petite and lovely, with coils of startling white hair beneath an outrageously pretty straw hat crowned with yellow blossoms, which matched the sunny stripe in her cream-colored dress.

Mara went with Jancy toward them. She'd met Major Hal Beaumont and his new wife, Blanche, at Simon's wedding, and Hal had played a significant part in getting Simon home safe from Canada. Not surprising when he was a Rogue.

"Hal, Blanche, how lovely to see you." She chattered to them about London and gas and Yeovil House, and the dull play at Covent Garden. "I'm sure you'd never act in such a preachy piece," she said to Blanche.

"You're right there," Blanche said.

"You should have seen her in *The Daring Lady*," Major Beaumont said with a proud smile. "It was all the rage last year. Perhaps it'll be revived."

"Not by me." There was something brittle in Blanche's tone. "I'm concentrating on classic pieces. So Dare's in Town, you say?"

The deflection was extremely obvious.

"Yes," Jancy said, "and I'm sure he'd be pleased to see you both. Not that it's my place to offer invitations . . ."

"A fellow Rogue doesn't need one," Mara said, rescuing her. "Does he, Major?"

"Never. I'm glad he's here. It's a good sign."

Mara and Jancy took their leave and continued on out of the park.

"What's going on there?" Mara asked as soon as they were out of earshot. "I thought their wedding had made everything perfect, but they seemed on edge."

"Hal wants Blanche to continue with her career including breeches parts like that in *The Daring Lady,* but she's trying to transform into Mrs. Hal Beaumont and be accepted by society. He wants that, too, but he wants both."

"That's not impossible, is it? Wasn't the actress Harriet Mellon presented at court recently after her marriage?"

"But she gave up the stage. There are other differences as well." Jancy glanced at Mara. "I suspect no one told you her history."

"No. What of it?"

"Blanche was born a butcher's daughter." Jancy glanced behind at the footman, who was a discreet six paces behind them. Even so, she lowered her voice. "She was thrown out when she got with child at fifteen. She survived by . . . by selling her body."

Mara tried not to show her shock. Lovely Blanche, a whore?

"Hardly anyone knows about that," Jancy continued, "but it weighs on her. A more public problem is that she was Lord Arden's mistress for a number of years, and then became Hal's."

"Lord Arden the Rogue?" Mara gasped. "Oh, my. I was aware at Simon's wedding of something — a touch of scandal — but I thought it was merely the breeches parts and all that. Does Major Beaumont mind that she was Lord Arden's . . . companion?"

She'd never thought herself mealy-mouthed before.

"I don't think so. They're all friends, in fact — Lord and Lady Arden and Hal and Blanche. This is a secret, too, but Blanche and Lady Arden wrote *The Daring Lady.* I gather it's full of saucy comments about men, and in the end, the lady captures her hero at sword point."

"I do like the sound of that."

"It was a roaring success and a scandal at the same time. But you see, Blanche never made any secret of being Lord Arden's mistress, nor of being Hal's, which creates problems."

"It's a pity. Hal deserves happiness."

"He is happy, but Blanche won't visit places like Yeovil House. She'll visit the Rogues' houses, but not their parents'. Some point of honor she won't move on."

"What a tangle."

"It's why Blanche resisted marriage for years," Jancy said. "Hal traveled to Canada because he hoped absence would force Blanche to marry him. That worked, but marriage, even with love, doesn't solve everything."

Was Jancy thinking of herself?

"Surely it can, over time, with compromise," Mara said. "Blanche is wearing some touches of color now, when before she always dressed in pure white, I understand."

"She's using it to distinguish her two lives — pure white for Blanche Beaumont, actress, and colors for Mrs. Hal Beaumont, the military hero's wife."

"We have to do something," Mara said.

"Mara, even a St. Bride can't solve this."

"What about the Rogues, then?"

"Make the ton accept an actress with a shady reputation as one of their own?"

"Why not?" Mara asked as they entered Great Charles Street. "I'm surprised they haven't started already."

"Perhaps they're minding their own business."

"That would be very foolish."

Jancy groaned again.

When they returned to the house, Mara went up to her room considering Hal and Blanche's situation. Ruth had put Juliet's Tomb on a table. Mara moved it to pride of place on the mantelpiece, thinking about love. Cupid did sometimes shoot his arrows rashly, but once done, it was done.

Blanche and Hal were sealed forever. There had to be a way to make their path smooth. She went down to dinner prepared to raise the subject. Mainly, however, she was hungry for Dare. It seemed so long since she'd seen him last.

The news that he'd sent his apologies knocked everything from her head. Jancy and Simon didn't remark on his absence, and with servants in the room, Mara didn't feel able to, either, but her appetite fled. Was she such a bother to him that he'd avoid her throughout their stay here?

After dinner, when they took tea in the small drawing room, she asked, "Is Dare all right?"

"What's that supposed to mean?" Simon asked curtly. "Of course he isn't. We shouldn't have come here."

"He wouldn't have invited us if he hadn't wanted company," Jancy said.

But he didn't invite me, Mara thought. Should she ask to return to Ella's house? Everyone would speculate over that.

Perhaps Dare would benefit from time alone with Simon. Comfortable manly talk.

"It's a shame that he didn't dine with us," she said, "for then he'd be sipping brandy or port with you and you'd be spared tea and gossip with us. Why don't Jancy and I take the tea tray to her parlor to talk about babies and silk, leaving you in freedom?"

"I do have some interest in babies and silk, you know."

"But women need their secret discussions,

too," Jancy said, rising and picking up the tea tray.

He instantly took it from her and insisted on carrying it upstairs, even though Jancy was the sort of woman who'd hewn and hauled for herself. Mara followed behind, aware of all the little ways Jancy and Simon cared for each other, the ways they were one. They glanced into each other's eyes as they spoke. Their bodies leaned very slightly toward each other, as if yearning to be joined.

She longed for that with Dare. To be free to cherish and protect, to comfort and support. To know, even in the busiest, most separated day, that come night, they would be alone together and joined.

I am alone too much, he'd said, but clearly he didn't want her company. She hoped Simon would find him and be welcomed, but she doubted even Simon could touch the isolation in which Dare was imprisoned.

She'd planned to burst open that prison, but in her new uncertainty she wondered if, like the tiger in the menagerie, Dare might be unable to survive without the bars.

CHAPTER 13

Simon left the parlor uncertain what to do. Over the past six months Dare had spoken and written to him honestly about the beast, as he called opium. The reduction had gone well, if slowly, and Dare's spirits had generally been high.

Until two attempts to cut free entirely had failed.

After the second attempt in March, Dare's parents had feared suicide. The duchess placed great faith in Salter, who at the time had never left Dare's waking side — but now Dare had broken free of that. And he was spending time alone with Mara.

In a different situation Simon would have been delighted. Dare, even on opium, was a worthy brother-in-law. It was the battle he fought that made him unpredictable and dangerous.

Jancy had interrupted them in the library holding hands, looking at each other intently. "With other people," she'd said, "I'd have thought them lovers."

Dare and Mara.

Mara was pure sunshine. She had the St. Bride brightness and generosity, but Black Ademar's heritage made her passionate and reckless. Part of him wanted to offer her to Dare like medicine, but most of him wanted his sister to have the best, most unshadowed future imaginable.

He walked down the corridor toward Dare's room, trying to decide the best thing to do. If Mara was upsetting Dare, he'd find an excuse to send her back to Ella's, or even to Brideswell. If Mara wasn't upsetting him, if Dare was beginning to fall in love with her, he might have to warn him off, which would be hell.

Then he paused. Whispers. Childish whispers.

"Quelqu'un arrive," one whispered in French.

"Attendez un peu."

One had whispered that someone was there. The other had replied that they would wait.

"Bonsoir, mes enfants," Simon said.

Two heads peered around a corner. *"Bonsoir,* Uncle Simon," Pierre said, in the mixed French and English they often fell into. "We are looking for Papa. He has not come to see us at *l'heure du coucher.*"

"Perhaps he's unwell." The children knew the truth. How could they not, having shared hellish confinement with Dare for most of a year?

"But where is he?" Pierre demanded.

They were as protective of Dare as he was of them, but if Dare was in real difficulties, he wouldn't want the children around.

"Which is his bedchamber?" Simon asked.

"That one *là,*" the boy said, pointing. "But he is not there."

"Then perhaps he's out."

Pierre shook his head. "He would say if he was to be out."

Simon was very unsure what to do for the best. He didn't doubt the children's word, and he knew Dare put their comfort first. He probably did always warn them of any disruption to the pattern of their days.

"Return to the nursery. I'll find your papa and send word."

Two pairs of solemn eyes studied him, too knowingly. Awareness of what these children had seen and experienced could break his heart.

But then Pierre nodded. "*Merci,* Uncle Simon." He took Delphie's hand and led her away. Simon noticed the small black cat that followed. Their other guardian, Jetta.

The cat had been a stray that had attached itself first to Nicholas's daughter, Arabel, then to these children. There was little a cat could actually do about the dangers of the world, but it was always comforting to see the way it watched over the little ones.

Simon considered his quest and decided he needed more information. He went to his room and rang for his valet.

When Trafford arrived, Simon asked, "Do we know where Lord Darius is at this moment?"

"No, milord. Though I heard mention of his treatment room."

Feeling horribly like a nosy parker, Simon asked, "And where is that?"

"I don't know, milord. Mr. Salter may."

"Salter's not with him?"

"No, milord. He is presently in the upper servants' drawing room, playing cards with Alstock. The head footman," Trafford added as explanation.

"Please ask Salter to come here as soon as may be convenient."

When Trafford left, Simon shook his head at the formality of that request. Life at Brideswell and in Canada had not prepared him for the servants' world in a great house. Marlowe was particularly challenging, but he and the staff there had silently agreed to a form of coexistence. Within the central house, the most formal part, Simon tried to live up to their expectations. In his home in one of the attached villas, they did things his way.

Did the senior servants at Marlowe have a drawing room? Almost certainly, and with their own servants to wait on them.

A knock brought Salter. Simon invited the man in, unsure, as always, how to treat him. He was more than a valet, but not quite an equal. Simon didn't care, but Salter might.

"I encountered the children, Salter. They're worried because Lord Darius hasn't visited them."

Salter's eyes went to the clock. "I'll see to it, my lord."

He would have left, but Simon said, "Wait. Where is he?"

Salter turned. "He will be in the house, my lord. I'll find him."

"Is he in . . . difficulties?"

The man's eyes met his. "Perhaps, but of no great seriousness, I assure you, my lord."

"You mean he's not slitting his wrists. Forgive me, but from an outsider's perspective, everything looks serious."

The man weighed his words. "Lord Darius is impatient to be free and frustrated by not being so. Also, new excitements and stresses exert strain."

"And then what happens?"

"He cannot act as he wishes."

"We shouldn't be here?"

"Lord Darius invited you, my lord, and he always enjoys your company."

It was like fighting cobwebs, but Simon appreciated that Salter would not gossip.

"I would like to see him when that's possible. And some message should be sent to the children."

Salter bowed and left.

Simon paced his room, wishing the previous Lord Austrey hadn't taken it into his head to put gas lighting in Marlowe House. He'd thought Dare was in a better state than this. He'd seemed normal — whatever that meant.

Normal compared to the Dare he'd found when he'd arrived back in England last October. That Dare had been thin, pale, and living on a fragile edge.

He was much better now, but nothing like the old Dare. He hardly ever showed a hint of spark, of mischief. Unfair to want Dare to be a person from years ago, but how could anyone help it? Everyone wanted to see the quick wit, the pure lighthearted brilliance that had been Dare Debenham.

Another knock brought Salter again. "Lord Darius would like to speak with you, my lord."

Simon suppressed a stupid "He's all right, then?" and followed, beginning to feel that he'd made a fool of himself. Perhaps Dare, like the rest of humanity, sometimes got a headache or an upset stomach. But he'd forgotten the children. That had to be serious.

He was taken to Dare's bedchamber, where he found him fully dressed and apparently normal.

"Thank you for carrying the message from the children."

"Of course. Why did you forget?"

Dare's lips twitched. "Ambition. Desperation. Despair . . . I took it into my head to stop this nonsense once and for all so I didn't take my evening dose."

"And that makes you forgetful?"

"That makes everything other than the untaken opium unimportant."

"And now?"

Dare's smile twisted. "All is well with the world. I must go and see Pierre and Delphie, but I wished to speak to you." He hadn't exactly been looking at Simon as he spoke, but now he definitely looked away.

"To assure you that I am no danger to anyone."

"To Mara," Simon said bluntly.

Dare's face twitched, but it seemed more of a frown than a grimace. "I assure you, she's in no danger from me."

"But are you in danger from her?"

Dare looked at him then, surprise and a touch of humor making him heartbreakingly like the boyhood friend. "Of course not."

"Are you sure? She's a devil when on crusade."

"It's the hair."

"I'll send her back to Ella's —"

"*No!* No," Dare repeated more calmly. "What she needs is other interests. Provide entertainment and she'll forget me."

Simon wondered. He remembered his own falling in love, which had perhaps been a slow slide but had felt like a shocking tumble, and completely uncontrollable.

But he said, "A good idea. Will you join the revels?"

"Whenever I'm able." Dare glanced at the clock. "I must go."

"Yes, of course. We'll move out soon."

"Don't rush. It's good for me to have you here and I promise not to be impetuous again. Slow and steady wins the race, as they say." His tone was desert dry.

He walked to the door and Simon went with him. "Does the race ever end?"

"On my birthday, June twenty-fourth. I'm resolved on it. Do or die. But don't worry. I intend to return to Long Chart for Armageddon."

Simon watched Dare walk away, then turned toward his own room.

Armageddon — the mighty battle at the end of the world. From what he knew of the attempt to cut free of opium, the concept was appropriate. Dare had said once, "We take opium to smother pain, of mind, of body, or both, but I think we bottle it up. And one day we have to let the demon out."

He went to the parlor and found Jancy and Mara playing chess.

"Well?" Mara asked.

Tight as a wound spring, he thought. "He was feeling under the weather, that's all."

"Because of opium," Mara said.

Simon found he couldn't lie outright. "Yes, but he's fine now. He's with the children."

"And he wouldn't go to them if out of sorts. Simon, I've been wanting to talk to you. I need to know more —"

"No, you don't. Don't interfere, Mara."

"I'm not interfering! Well, perhaps I am, but I can't ignore the suffering of a friend, especially when under his roof."

"I told you. Dare is slowly reducing the amount of opium he takes, which allows his body to get used to less and less. He's on a low dose now and in time will be able to do without it entirely. That's it. But it's a difficult process, so he doesn't need extra aggravation."

"I hope I'm never aggravating, but I didn't mean that. Was he imprisoned? He seemed upset by the dungeon in the Tower."

Damn. Simon sat by the fire. "Yes."

"By the French?"

"No."

"Then by whom? Tell me, Simon!"

"By the kindly widow."

Her eyes went wide. "Madame Bellaire? No wonder he said she was evil."

"His wounds were his prison to begin with, and she probably had good reason to give him laudanum, but she gave him more than necessary for longer than necessary, and then continued to feed it to him when he no longer needed it at all. By the time he understood what was going on, the damage was done. His addiction became a prison of sorts, but the true one was the children. If Dare rebelled in any way, she would punish them for it."

Mara turned pale. "Dear God."

"And at the end, he and the children, including Arabel Delaney, were truly imprisoned — locked in a room, unsure of their fate."

Mara inhaled. "No more dungeons, then. And probably he will be better without my bothersome company. You and the Rogues will drag him out, though, won't you?"

"Perhaps we trust his judgment more than you seem to."

"I didn't force him to anything. I merely asked. You might have to ask. He probably went to the theater because someone took the trouble to ask."

Simon wondered if she was right. They'd all been carefully letting Dare set the pace, but perhaps he did need help. He'd find out how Dare had come to be at the theater the other night with Stephen and Francis. He'd talk to the other Rogues, even though it felt wrong to be discussing Dare behind his back.

"And speaking of Rogues helping Rogues," Mara said, "what about Hal and Blanche?"

"What about Hal and Blanche?" he asked.

"I gather they're not completely happy because Blanche doesn't feel comfortable among the ton. The Rogues can solve that, can't they?"

"How?" Simon looked at Jancy, suddenly desperate for the ease of her company.

She rose. "After such a day, I need to go early to bed. We can discuss that tomorrow."

"Oh, of course," Mara said, a slight blush showing both her innocence and her understanding. "Good night."

Mara stood in the corridor feeling decidedly sorry for herself without being entirely sure why. Because Simon and Jancy were going to be enjoying marital love? Her turn would come.

Because she'd been warned off interfering with Dare and had tacitly agreed? That certainly hurt, especially when it seemed she might never see him here.

She should go into her room, but it was early and she was restless. Instead she strolled down the corridor.

Dare was with the children, thus presumably on the next floor up, but he would come back down eventually. To his bedroom. She should know where that was from her illicit visit, but she'd not taken in details.

Was this the corridor she'd walked with Dare that night? Yes. She recognized a portrait of a very ugly child clutching a pug dog. Then this, she thought, walking toward the last door on her left, is his bedroom.

She paused to listen, but of course there was no sound. After a glance left and right to be sure no one was watching she laid her palm briefly against the polished oak, trying to sense . . . what? A memory of him?

What nonsense. She hurried away. She should go to her room and read, but she was too restless for even *Tales of Fancy.*

The big house lay silent around her. She crept downstairs, feeling like a sneak thief, but finding that rather exciting. She jumped guiltily when she encountered a maid leaving the dining room with a broom and cloth, but the woman merely curtsied and hurried on her way.

Mara continued down to the hall, then looked up the stairs, remembering Dare carrying her, but no ghostly representation of that time revealed itself.

She suddenly felt completely alone. The servants were doubtless enjoying a bit of time to themselves before bed. Dare was with the children. Simon and Jancy had each other.

She was not just alone but lonely — a most unusual condition. Loneliness was never a problem at Brideswell, and in Grosvenor Square she'd had Ella's company. And politicians for dinner, she thought with a smile, remembering Jancy's joke.

She went into a dark reception room to look out at the street. She'd crept down that street barefoot, huddled in a blanket. Anything could have happened.

Many things had. There's been such intimacy that night — she could still *feel* Dare bathing her feet. There'd been nothing like it since — until he'd taken her hands in the coach and, later, in the library here. And kissed them.

If Jancy hadn't come in, would he have kissed her lips?

Fingers to tingling lips, she left the room. She really should go to bed, but she wasn't at all tired.

Unlit candles stood ready on a table. She picked up one and lit it at the night candle, which was guarded by glass. Then she indulged in a tour of the ground floor rooms — another reception room, the dining room, and a small parlor that probably served as a morning room.

She considered a closed door, then gingerly opened it to see a pedestal desk and leather chairs near an empty fireplace. This was probably where the duke received visitors who didn't warrant entry to the family part of the house.

She was closing the door again when she

spotted a group of miniatures on a wall. She went closer, raising the candle to shed better light. As she'd hoped, they were of the family.

The two oval portraits in the middle must be the duke and duchess when quite young. To their right hung a picture of a stocky man with thinning hair. There was enough of a resemblance to say it was Lord Gravenham, Dare's brother, though he looked older than the twenty-nine she knew him to be. The round-faced woman alongside must be his wife and the two infants his sons.

On the other side of the parents hung a picture of a smiling young woman with loose brown curls. That must be Lady Thea but Mara scarcely gave her a glance because she'd seen the picture of Dare.

This was the Dare she remembered — hair longer, a twinkle in his eyes, a smile on his lips — a smile that promised mischief and adventure. She raised her hand to touch it.

Alerted by something, she whirled, sending her candle flame flaring.

He stood in the doorway, without coat or waistcoat, his shirt open at the neck. In his arms he carried a languid black cat.

"I'm sorry. I was just . . ."

"Wandering," he said.

"Prying," she admitted. "But I really didn't mean to."

He walked toward her, and to her shame, she took a step back.

He stilled. "Jetta only bites enemies."

Mara reclaimed her step, though it brought her too close to this half-dressed mystery of a man. "Then assure her I'm a friend, please."

He glanced down. "A good friend, Jetta." He looked back at Mara, his eyes strange in the panicked light of her guttering candle. "Is there anything you require?"

"No. I'm sorry."

"Poor Mara. From tedium to tedium." His long fingers pleasured the cat, which watched Mara from slitted eyes as if warning her away. "It will get better," he said. "You'll soon be out until the early hours, dancing and flirting."

"I hope so," Mara said, but it was a lie. She'd be fulfilled in this dull room alone with Dare. Silence pressed and she scrabbled for something to say. "Yeovil House is larger than it seems."

"You can see why I was eager to have guests."

"Even though you avoid them?"

His fingers paused for a moment, and then resumed their work. "My apologies."

"No, mine. You were unwell."

"Yes."

Mara felt as if she wandered a cliff edge in a fog, but couldn't make herself leave for safer ground. "Will she mind if I stroke her?"

"I doubt it."

She put her candle on a small table, moved closer, and reached out. Seeing no objection, she stroked the warm fur. "She's lovely."

"She's full of her own importance. Don't puff her up farther."

A faint, deep purr made Mara laugh and she thanked heaven for it. She was fiercely aware of being too close to Dare, of their fingers almost meeting as first he stroked, then she did. In harmony.

"She's the children's cat," he said, "but once they're asleep, she prowls to make sure all is well."

"As do you?"

"No, I just prowl. You should go to bed."

Her hand stilled on the warm, silky body. "Or?"

He stepped back, taking the cat out of reach, creating cold air between them. "Or you'll be too tired for adventures tomorrow. A silk hunt, I believe."

"Yes."

He glanced at the pictures and said, "He's dead, Mara." Then he walked away.

He'd reached the door before she found voice to call, "No, he's not!"

He continued on without hesitation.

Mara ran to the door to watch Dare mount the stairs by the low light of the one hall candle. She blew out her own candle and returned to her room through the same gloomy shadows.

The next morning that encounter with Dare had all the qualities of a dream, yet Mara knew it had happened. Jumbled nighttime thoughts had not interpreted it for her.

She ate breakfast in her room, but found herself finished and dressed for the visit to the silk warehouse far too early, so she wrote to her younger brother and sisters. She wrote letters to Benji at school and Jenny and Lucy at home, describing the cork exhibition. She even added drawings of a volcano.

She still hadn't seen Vesuvius erupt, but this didn't seem a good time to ask about that.

She sealed her letters and put them aside, still with time to spare. What to do? Then she had an idea. She could visit Pierre and Delphie and find out what they thought of the cork models Dare had bought them.

She rang for a footman to guide her to the children's area. If Dare happened to be there, that would be cream on the cake. She found the children alone, however, apart from a maid, but they seemed pleased to see her.

The schoolroom was bright and furnished with soft chairs as well as the wooden ones at desks. It felt like the nursery rooms at Brideswell, because most things had clearly been used by generations of Debenhams.

Had Dare played here?

Almost certainly.

Paintings hung on the walls of the sort most likely to appeal to children — a vivid Italian landscape, a naval battle full of smoke, a child playing with kittens, and a medieval picture of jousting knights. A miniature suit of armor stood in one corner.

The two cork models sat on a low table.

"Papa says we will go one day to see the volcano explode," Pierre said.

"I think that will be frightening," Delphie whispered.

Mara touched her hair. "I'm sure you won't have to attend."

"But I like to go with Papa."

So do I, thought Mara.

"Milady Mara, please to come see *mes*

soldats!" Pierre took her hand and tugged her toward the table, where miniature armies stood in ranks.

But Delphie clung to Mara's other hand. "No! You must see *ma maison de poupé.*"

Feeling like the baby contested between two mothers before Solomon, Mara said, "House, then soldiers."

Pierre gave in with good grace, but did not go with them to the dolls' house. It was a magnificent work. Sitting on a low table, it was as tall as Mara. Three sides had been removed to show the rooms, but the front was in place.

"Why, this is Yeovil House," Mara said, studying the details with delight.

"*Oui,* milady." The house was on a turntable, and Delphie rotated it to point to a room. "Here we are." It was the nursery, containing four dolls roughly representing a boy, a girl, and two maids.

"It's magical," Mara said. "I see bedchambers, the library, and the duke's reception room." In the basement the kitchen and scullery were occupied by little dolls representing servants. Plaster hams and other meats hung from the ceiling. "I feel as if I could step inside."

"*Moi aussi,*" Delphie said. "I like to think where Papa might be."

"In the kitchens?" Mara teased, and Delphie laughed.

"Papa is never in the kitchens."

"Then where is he now?" Mara certainly wanted to know.

Delphie began to turn the dolls' house. "He is not in the dining room. He is not in the grand drawing room. . . ."

As the child went through her inventory, Mara marveled. It was an astonishing work.

"He is not is his bedroom . . ." Delphie chanted.

Mara recognized Dare's room and felt her cheeks heat.

"That's my room," she said, pointing it out.

"*Alors,* then we will put you there." Delphie picked up a figure and placed it in the room. Mara didn't complain that it was a rather severe-looking older lady.

"My brother and his wife, Lord and Lady Austrey, have the rooms next door."

"*Oui?*" Delphie chose a male and female figure and placed them on the bed, which made Mara bite her lip.

"Papa is not in the ballroom," Delphie said, turning the house to show a room that took up most of the back. "One day there will be a grand ball there and Papa says we may watch a little. There is a gallery, you see? Musicians will be there, but they will not mind us being there a little."

Delphie continued, pointing out all the other places where Papa was not. Mara couldn't hold the question back. "Then where is Papa?"

"In Feng Ruyuan's room," Delphie said. "At this hour, he always is."

She pointed to a bedchamber where a figure that looked a lot like Dare stood beside an Oriental one. Feng Ruyuan, Mara assumed, whoever that was. He was shown with a completely bald head and wearing something like a monk's robe, but in red.

"Who is Feng Ruyuan?" Mara asked, feeling as if she'd been shown a portal to another world.

"Papa's friend. He comes to visit us, but we do not go to visit him, because there Papa fights the beast."

The little girl could as well have said because there he does his accounts or there he cleans his guns.

Mara could think of nothing to say, but Pierre expanded for her from across the room. "One day Feng Ruyuan will teach me the way of the dragon."

"Me, too," Delphie said.

"The dragon is not for girls."

Delphie turned on Pierre, hands on hips,

225

breaking into French. "I asked Uncle Nicholas, and he said it was for girls who wish it!"

"A lady would not wish it, and one day you must be a lady."

"I do not *want* to be a lady if it means I cannot be a dragon!"

"Delphie, Pierre!" The maid swooped down in a flurry of French, scolding and calming at the same time. Then she said in English, "Now you must apologize to Lady Mara for your bad behavior."

They did, but anger clearly simmered. Mara sympathized with Delphie, but sought a deflection. "Why don't you show me the soldiers now?" she said to Pierre.

Delphie grabbed at her skirt. "You will prefer my dolls."

Mara freed her skirt from clutching fingers and took the girl's hand. "Come with us to the soldiers, Delphie. Soldiers are little dolls, really."

"Now you've torn it."

Mara looked up to find Dare there, amused. She'd already seen the shock and horror on both children's faces at her careless comparison.

After greeting Dare, Pierre turned back to Mara in combative mode. "Milady Mara —"

"Pierre," Dare interrupted. "A gentleman never contradicts a lady."

"But, Papa, what if a lady is wrong?"

"A lady is never wrong. And Delphie, a young lady never argues with an older one."

Delphie wrinkled her brow and looked to Mara. "Truly?"

Mara burst out laughing. "It would be very tedious, wouldn't it? But arguing is hardly ever worth the trouble. Unless it is an issue of conscience, and then we must stand firm. I apologize for offending you both, and if your papa agrees, I will first inspect the army and then the dolls."

Delphie reluctantly agreed to this, but would not go to the toy soldiers with them.

The soldiers were detailed representations of French and British regiments drawn up, Mara was told, as if for the battle of Salamanca. "Papa was not in the army in Spain," Pierre informed Mara, "but Riggs was, and he tells me exactly how it was."

"Riggs is one of the grooms," Dare supplied.

Mara admired the detailed models and watched a little action, but she couldn't help think of lives lost. Pierre played the English side, forcing Dare to take the French, but he didn't seem to mind, or be experiencing any shadows from Waterloo.

When she let Delphie tow her away, neither male seemed to notice.

Delphie took her to a rocking chair, which held three dolls. Mara admired Lucille, a baby doll with a perfect porcelain head and a lacy layette, then Belle, a fashion doll with a wax head, elaborate hair, and a silk gown in the style of the past century.

The third was . . . well, to call it a rag doll would give it too much credit. It seemed to be made of twigs with scraps of cloth wound around it to form a crude body and suggest a skirt and bodice. The head was only a stuffed ball of rag with inked-on features.

Delphie picked it up. "This is Mariette, my special friend. Say *bonjour,* Mariette." Pretending to be the doll, she said in a squeaky voice, *"Bonjour, madame."*

Then she addressed the doll in French. "No, Mariette, this is not a madam. This is a milady. Milady Mara, a friend of Papa. Her brother is a Rogue, so you may trust her." Resuming the squeaky voice and turning the rag head toward Mara, she said, again in French, "Good day, Milady Mara. You may hold me if you wish."

Mara found herself holding the assembly of sticks and rags and fighting tears. These innocent children had shared Dare's terrible captivity. This doll must have shared it, too.

"I'm honored, Mariette," she said in

French. "You must be happy here in this lovely schoolroom."

A conversation followed that might have gone on forever if Dare hadn't interrupted. "I came to invite you on an expedition, children."

Attention fixed on him. "*Oui,* Papa?" Delphie grabbed Mariette without seeming to realize it. "Where do we go?"

"To the exhibition of things made of cork." When the children cast a dubious glance at their cork models, he added, "The real ones are much larger and better. You'll enjoy them."

"We will see the volcano explode?" Pierre asked, his eyes lighting. "You said it exploded, Papa!"

"Erupt," Dare corrected. "If you are quick."

Pierre ran into the next room. Delphie paused long enough to give Mariette to Dare, and then raced after. Dare stood looking wryly at the doll, a finger stroking the rag head.

"You made her, didn't you?"

He started. "There were no toys. I made some for Pierre, too — small swords and even boats if we could get away with it. But Pierre doesn't cling to any of those things. I don't know why Delphie treasures this."

"Because it's not 'this,' " Mara said, "but Mariette."

"I suppose so. Pierre would sometimes hold her, too. He'd pretend to be protecting her, but really, he was cuddling her. I don't think he does that anymore."

"He might. If no one is looking. Perhaps boys need dolls, too, and not just little soldiers."

He gave her a skeptical look and replaced Mariette with her pretty companions. "You'll be in accord with Nicholas. His daughter has a toy soldier and I'm sure his son will have a baby doll."

Mara touched Mariette's rag head. "What about your sons and daughters?"

"Other than Delphie and Pierre?"

They're not truly yours, Dare. What if their parents come to claim them?

"Yes."

"I may not marry."

"But if you do?"

"Then I hope to let my children be what they will be. As long as they be it with good manners. For there is no civilization without courtesy, and civilization is our greatest treasure."

She understood as clearly as if he'd said it that for him civilization could not include opium. He would not allow himself children

230

of his own until he'd defeated the beast.

"You promised not to visit the volcano without me," she complained, but made it clearly a tease.

"Do you want to come?"

"I wish I could, but I'm promised to the silk expedition. Will you take me another time?"

"Of course."

That eased all her anxieties about him avoiding her. The children returned and the three of them left. Damn silk, Mara thought, but perhaps she could find time later for them to work on Castle Cruel.

She hadn't noticed the cat, but now Jetta slid from behind the curtain to curl up on the chair with the dolls.

"So you like Mariette, too, do you?"

The cat, of course, didn't answer.

Mara left the room, thinking about Dare. She was used to untangling problems and healing wounds, but here she risked doing more harm than good.

He's dead, Mara.

Had the Dare of her golden memories truly been killed by this evil Thérèse Bellaire?

When she reached her room, Ruth said, "There you are, milady! The coach has arrived. Hurry up."

231

Mara rushed into her outer clothing, then down to the hall, where Jancy was waiting.

"Come on," Jancy said nervously. "They're waiting in the coach."

Mara went, but said, "They're friends, Jancy."

"I've never met them before!"

"They're friends anyway."

Indeed, within moments of setting off, Lady Ball and Lady Middlethorpe insisted on being Laura and Serena. "After all," Lady Middlethorpe said, "we're all Rogues together."

Mara didn't remind her that wasn't true. It would be, one day soon.

CHAPTER 14

An hour's drive took them to an older brick building with only a small sign to identify it as a place of business. Beneath Chinese characters were the English words: *Lee's Finest Silk Emporium.* When the footman knocked on the red door, Mara wondered if such an English group would be denied entry.

After a moment of surprise, however, the Oriental who had opened the door bowed his wealthy visitors in.

They all gasped at the treasure chest of silks. Colorful bolts stacked shelves from floor to ceiling and a dozen Chinese men climbed up and down ladders fetching bolts to tables, where others cut lengths. Sometimes whole bolts were carried through to the back, where presumably they went on their way to the purchaser.

There were other English people here, inspecting and purchasing, but their elegant party, footman in attendance, was clearly out of place.

A man came forward to greet them. He was dressed like the rest in a long robe, his hair in a pigtail, but his robe was of splendid embroidered silk and he wore a black hat.

"We are mostly a wholesale business, honored ladies," Mr. Lee said, bowing from the waist. His English was accented but excellent. "But you are most welcome."

They were offered tea, without milk or sugar in very small cups without handles, and also a room for their comfort. Jancy, being pregnant, appreciated that. Then they were taken on a tour of the establishment by Mr. Lee himself.

Mara had no intention of buying anything; she had all the clothes she needed and no home to decorate. She simply enjoyed the abundant beauty and subtle perfumes. Sandalwood. Perhaps incense. Others she couldn't identify.

When Jancy dithered over a length of pale blue figured silk she clearly wanted, Mara took up her duties. "Buy it. It's lovely."

"Look at the price! I'm increasing, so anything truly fashionable won't fit in a couple of months, and by next year you'll say it's all out of fashion again."

"You have weeks in society ahead," Mara

said, "and first impressions count. A good mantua-maker will allow for expansion. As for next year, fashion rarely changes dramatically."

"Oh, yes, it does. More trimming, less trimming. Fringe this year, flounce the next. And color. Remember, I'm a haberdasher's daughter."

"Celestial blue last year, azure blue this. Jonquil yellow last year, primrose this. The true differences are so slight as to be meaningless and retrimming is easy. She'll have a dress length of that," Mara told the clerk. "A generous dress length. Jancy, how much?"

"Ten yards, but that silk is almost identical and better value."

"You mean cheaper. This is a much better quality." She addressed the clerk. "Isn't it?"

He bowed. "Yes, honored lady."

"He'd be bound to say that," Jancy grumbled, but she agreed to the purchase and to another of a moss green embroidered in white and gold.

"It will make a spectacular ball gown," Mara encouraged. "Everyone will be talking about Lord Austrey's lovely wife."

Mara saw the result of her calculated words. Jancy would suffer the torments of hell for Simon; paying a little more for silk than she was comfortable with — well, a lot more — was bearable.

On the principle of striking while the iron is hot, Mara said, "And, we hope, Lord Austrey's lovely home."

"If you mean Marlowe House, it isn't Simon's. It's his father's."

"As Father hates London, it might as well be."

"Even so, I have no idea what might need to be refurbished. We were hardly inside before we rushed out again."

Mara had to grant that. "Take swatches of anything you like. Or that Simon might like."

"Tyrant!"

"Pinchpenny!"

They grinned at each other and Jancy set about commanding swatches of curtain and upholstery silks. Mara left her to it, thinking about the power of love. What would she do to please Dare?

Anything.

She paused to consider that.

She really would.

She'd even wander the world with him, for to be without him would be worse.

"That's pretty." Jancy had come over. "Buy some."

Mara focused on the silk in front of her

236

— a heavy white satin embroidered with garlands of pink roses. Lord, it reminded her of the dressing gown her sister-in-law had given her for her last birthday. She hated it, but wore it anyway. After all, no one but Ruth saw it.

"It's not quite in my style," she said.

"I didn't think so, but you were smiling at it in such a way. What about this? Or this?" She picked out a number of rolls of silk, all lovely. "You must buy something, Mara, after bullying me into spending a fortune."

Mara gave in and ordered a length of peach sarcenet. In a while she'd discover a distaste for it and give it to Jancy, whom it would suit wonderfully.

Everyone was satiated, so they took their departure, leaving an even more satisfied merchant behind. It was gone noon, however, and Mara had a very unsatisfied stomach. She saw no sign of an inn suitable for ladies, but when they entered the coach, the footman passed a wicker basket to Serena. She opened it and offered fruit, cakes and cider. Completely content, they relaxed into talk of fashion and society as the carriage set off back to St. James's.

Mara remembered the matter of Hal and Blanche and raised the subject.

"You're right," Serena said. "We must do

something."

Laura looked doubtful. "Any number of men must have met Blanche with first Lucien, then Hal."

"The Rogues launched me into society," Serena said, "even though my first husband had involved me in some less-than-proper matters. None of the men involved stirred the pot. There aren't many willing to offend the Rogues."

"But you, at least, were married," Laura pointed out. "Of course I want to help Blanche, but how horrible if it went wrong and the ton publicly snubbed her."

"It's not as if Blanche went from man to man," Serena protested.

Mara wondered if Serena really didn't know about Blanche's early career.

"We need a council of war," Serena decided. "Dinner on Monday at our house for all the Rogues who are in Town?"

"Parliament allowing," Laura said. "The sittings are running very late."

"Then dinner will run even later. I'll have Francis write to tell Nicholas in case he can come up. Do we invite Hal?"

"How can we not? But I think Blanche is performing that night, so he won't come."

Mara asked, "Is a Rogue's sister permitted?"

"Of course," Serena assured her. "This was your idea and we should recruit anyone who can help. St. Raven's in Town. A duke is always useful, and he's almost a Rogue, anyway."

The carriage had come to a halt outside Yeovil House, but Mara paused before leaving. "Why do you say that?"

Serena laughed. "He was born to be a Rogue, but for credentials he's foster brother to Lady Anne Peckworth. She was virtually jilted by two Rogues — first Francis, and that was my fault, then by Con, who met an old love. The Rogues felt guilty, especially with her having a limp, so took her under their wing."

The footman had the door open, and their packages were already being carried into the house, so Mara said her thanks and left.

"How unfair," she said as they walked in, "that St. Raven can become a Rogue merely by being the foster brother of someone who almost married one, but a sister is beyond the pale."

"I don't think he's truly considered a Rogue," Jancy soothed as they climbed the stairs. "Merely a close associate. As a sister, you are closer."

"Dare's sister isn't. In fact I can't think of any sister who is part of the group. Only wives, and I'm not making any progress there."

"You're too impatient."

"Perhaps I should kidnap and ravish Dare. Isn't that the way valuable spouses are captured?"

Jancy shook her head. "Wait until he's well."

"Before kidnapping and ravishing him?"

"No, of course not."

"I *shouldn't* wait?" Mara teased as they paused outside Jancy's door.

"Stop it!" Jancy said, laughing. "I mean that when he's well all might fall into place. I believe you are special to him. Simon said that no one had persuaded him into society before you."

"The park and the Tower are hardly society."

"But he invited himself to join the theater party. Simon wonders why. I think it's because he knew you'd be there. Did he know?"

Mara thought about it. "Yes."

"See."

Mara contented herself with an "Oh" before hurrying to her own room. She stood there, grateful Ruth was elsewhere. Could it be true? That he'd spent an evening with his friends because of her? She reveled in that idea like a cat rolling in catmint.

She dreamily removed her gloves and bonnet, but then the clock on her mantelpiece struck two and her stomach rumbled. The light food eaten in the carriage hadn't made a true meal.

If only she could take a late luncheon with Dare. It had been so long since she'd seen him, and they did need to work on Castle Cruel. She rang the bell. When Ruth arrived, she asked, "Is Lord Darius at home?"

"I think so, milady."

"Do you know where?"

"No, milady. Keeps a lot to himself, or so I hear."

Mara wanted to reprove Ruth for a touch of disapproval, but it wouldn't help and she'd remembered her resolve not to pester him. Even though he'd invited her to go to the cork exhibition with him and the children, she decided to be demure for once.

She ordered for herself, but couldn't resist asking, "What do they say in the servants' hall about Lord Darius?"

"Well, milady, you know I don't hold with gossip," Ruth began, then continued. "They're all old family servants so very fond of him, as I'm sure is right, for he was a right merry gentleman and very considerate of others. But . . ."

Mara had been waiting for the but.

Ruth lowered her voice. "They say as there's strange goings on in the ballroom."

"In the *ballroom?*"

"Yes, milady. I was warned directly never to go there, and especially at night."

"Dances?" Mara asked, imagining wild romps with disreputable guests. She rather liked the idea of Dare holding wicked parties. In fact, she'd like to join in.

"No, milady. Just he and Mr. Salter and some others *jumping around.*"

Mara was tempted to laugh, but it wasn't funny. It sounded mad.

"And," Ruth went on, her voice a whisper by now, "they hit one another with sticks."

"What?"

"It's true, as I live and die! Tom — he's the second footman — was up there on his proper business one afternoon and heard noises, so he went up into the musicians' gallery — you won't say anything, will you, milady?"

"No, of course not."

"He was concerned, it being the afternoon, and nothing funny usually happening in the afternoon, you see? And he saw Lord Darius and Mr. Salter fighting with sticks. Long ones. Mostly they hit stick against stick, but sometimes, he said, they hit each other. Hard, too."

Mara felt as if she'd popped out of a dizzy whirl back to firm ground.

"Quarterstaff," she said, realizing she could feed some information the other way. "It can be considered a sport. It was a popular weapon in medieval times. It's no more peculiar than boxing."

"Oh." Ruth seemed rather disappointed.

"Simon and his friends used to play at quarterstaff. Don't you remember? They'd be out in the paddock whacking, blocking, and hitting. Sometimes they'd hit each other then, too, though they never meant to. I remember the time they did it on a tree fallen across the stream, acting out the story of Robin Hood and Little John."

Abruptly Mara remembered that that game had been Dare's idea. It formed in her mind as a brilliant summer scene with laughing youths toppling off the fallen tree into water and excited girls cheering them on from the banks. She'd been about eight and Dare a lordly, magnificent sixteen.

Mara came out of the past. "Thank you, Ruth. I'll have my refreshments now, please."

When Ruth had left, Mara frowned over Ruth's stories.

Quarterstaff wasn't so very peculiar, so

perhaps the leaping around at night wasn't either. It felt it, however, and he was such a good actor. Was he really on the brink of some insanity?

No, of course not. But she knew that later she would investigate what went on in the ballroom at night. Delphie had pointed out the musicians' gallery.

There were many hours before then, however, so she tried to work on *The Ghastly Ghoul of Castle Cruel.* That seemed ground for healthy amusement.

She wrote down as much as she could remember of their inventions at the Yeoman's Arms, then remembered saying the Tower could be a model for their castle. She drew a plan along those lines and ended up quite pleased with it.

She marked dungeons, torture chambers, and secret passages through which Anne Whyte could wander in her ghostly disguise, and in which she could encounter the scorpion — without a Y, the headless knight — without a Y, and the eyeless, mad monk.

She was smiling, but aching with sadness, too. She knew now that much of that creativity had been fueled by opium. At other times Dare seemed somber, and he was often tense.

Which was the real Dare Debenham?

Whichever, she now had reason to spend time with him. She glanced at the clock and began to add to their cast of characters.

Anne Whyte — smiling, she added, *Virgyn.*

Canute Ornottocanute, Lost Duke of Dawlish. Temporarily deceased.

Ethel the Ready, gallant serving maid.

With a chuckle, she added: *Ethel the Unready, her lazy cousin,* and *Halfacanute, the duke's midget twin brother.*

Halfacanute had actually been a king of England, though she was sure the name had meant something noble back then. She couldn't wait to share this idiocy with Dare.

Jancy knocked and came in. "What has you amused?"

Mara shared her embellishments and Jancy laughed. "What madcaps you both are."

"Oh, I do hope so." Mara impulsively asked, "Would you read the cards for me?"

Probably only Mara and Simon knew that Jancy could tell fortunes with cards. It was part of her secret heritage, from her early life among a gypsy family.

"Oh, I don't know. . . ."

"Please. I need some guidance."

"The cards are cryptic, Mara. They're easily misunderstood."

"They told you Simon wouldn't die in the duel."

"And predicted his injury, though I didn't want to believe that."

"So they tell the truth. I want to know."

Jancy bit her lip.

"Please!"

Jancy sighed. "Very well."

She left and returned with a lovely silk bag. When she opened it, however, she took out a dirty, greasy, rag-edged pack. Mara couldn't help but wrinkle her nose.

"A present from the woman who taught me," Jancy said, sorting through them. She showed Mara the queen of clubs. "This is you. Clubs are outgoing, determined, and focused on their goals."

"She looks like a shifty-eyed piece to me."

Jancy smiled. "These are homemade, but perhaps you are a bit shifty at times."

"I prefer to think of it as cunning. What are you?"

"A diamond. Fair in color, hasty in nature."

"Why did you hesitate before saying that?" Mara asked.

"I had this exact conversation with Simon. The night before the duel."

Mara touched her friend's hand. "I'm sorry."

"No, it's all right. Just peculiar. I'm not sure we should do this."

"Do you think the cards *cause* things to happen?"

Jancy shook herself. "No, of course not. Very well. Cut the pack a few times."

Mara wasn't keen on even touching the cards, but she did so. "It's a small deck."

"We only use the top thirty-two." She spread the cards roughly on the table. "Pick eight."

Mara did so, then three more times, building eight piles of four. Jancy then set each pile out and turned over the top card of the first pile.

"The king of clubs." Jancy smiled up at Mara. "A good loyal man in your life, and that's true. That's Simon's card." She turned the next one. "The queen of diamonds. That's me. This feels like an excellent spread. Next, the queen of clubs. Everyone in place."

"Except Dare," Mara pointed out. "What card would he be?"

"From the way Simon talks of him in the past, the king of hearts. A joyous, generous man."

Mara nodded, delighted by that image, but wishing Berkstead hadn't chosen the queen of hearts for his message. It soiled this, but at least she'd heard nothing from him since.

Jancy turned the next card, the nine of diamonds, and frowned.

"What?" Mara demanded.

"This turned up for Simon, too. It says to beware of sharp objects and firearms, and to be prepared for shocks."

Unease ran down Mara's spine, but she said, "Neither Dare nor I am likely to be involved with blades or firearms, and it doesn't predict death, does it?"

"No." Jancy turned the next card and smiled at Mara. "The eight of hearts — love from a light-haired man."

"Excellent."

The next card was the eight of diamonds and Jancy pondered. "This suggests brevity of some sort. A short journey, perhaps."

Mara made herself say it. "Or a short-lived love?"

Jancy met her eyes. "That, too." She turned over the nine of spades. "I'm sorry. Loss and thwarted plans."

Mara was tempted to sweep the cards from the table. "You're right. We shouldn't have done this. What's the last card?"

It was the ten of diamonds. "That's not much help," Jancy said. "It foretells change, perhaps a change of home."

"That would be when I marry. There's no other reason I'd leave Brideswell."

"True."

The question of who Mara would marry remained unanswered. When Jancy moved to gather the cards, Mara said, "There's no more? Ever the optimist, I hope for better."

Jancy's hands hovered. "The bottom cards are supposed to predict the more distant future."

"Let's see, then."

"Are you sure?"

"Yes."

Jancy flipped the piles over. The very first one was topped by the king of hearts.

Mara looked at Jancy. "That has to be good, yes?"

Jancy was smiling. "It's wonderful. It seems to say that there will be problems but Dare will be yours in the end."

Mara let out a breath she'd been unaware of holding. "What of the rest?"

"The ten of hearts. Lucky in love. The nine of clubs. More good fortune, especially in business or legal matters. The ace of diamonds — good news. The queen of spades — a widow."

"Not me, I assume," Mara said.

"No, but it is a warning card. The next card might add something." She turned it.

"The seven of spades. Difficult decisions. All I can say is beware of widows." She turned the next card, the eight of spades. "Disappointments." Quickly she turned up the last and smiled. "The seven of hearts — wishes fulfilled."

"So in the end all is well?" Mara asked.

Jancy gathered the cards. "If you believe in it."

"Don't you?"

Jancy slid them carefully back into their pouch. "Yes, I do."

"I don't suppose you could do a reading for Dare, could you?"

"No."

"Can't, or won't?"

"Won't. It's not right to pry into other people's lives, Mara. Be content with what you have. It seems your destiny is with Dare and it will be a happy one."

"With problems along the way."

"That can't surprise you."

"No," Mara said. "And at least sharp objects and guns are unlikely here in the heart of London."

"It can mean any kind of serious problem if it's unexpected."

"Not opium then, and I can't see how anything could be more serious than that."

Mara was whistling into the wind and knew it.

"Truly, Mara, this was an excellent spread," Jancy said. "All will be well."

Mara hugged her. "Thank you. Did you want something?"

"Help with fashion. Laura's sent magazines so that I'll have some ideas before we go to the mantua-maker."

"Lovely," Mara said, grateful for a diversion.

Assessing the latest designs — and laughing over some of the more absurd — passed the time until dinner. Mara changed her gown and went down, praying that Dare join them. It seemed to her that it would be proof that all would be well.

He did, and even gave an amusing account of the children's reactions to the volcanic eruption. Pierre had been thrilled. Delphie had clung to Dare, but seemed to have enjoyed it, too. "Not a delicate female, all in all," he said.

"What of you?" Mara asked. "Were you thrilled?"

"Tolerably. It's well done. Simon, we need to take Mara there before she erupts herself." His smiling eyes took any sting out of it.

"Tomorrow?" Mara said. "No, it's Sunday. And Monday we go to the mantua-maker's. That could take all day."

Jancy groaned.

"Tuesday, then."

"I don't see why not," Simon said. "And I confess, I want to see this wonder myself. By then, we should be at Marlowe House, however."

Mara almost gasped. She was frantically seeking an objection when Jancy said, "Are the pipes still there?"

"Yes, but the gas is turned off."

"All the same, Simon, I don't like it. Can't they be removed?"

"It'll make the devil of a mess." But then he said, "Of course, if you wish."

Mara could breathe again, but she was aware now of how short her stay in this house might be, and here she felt so close to Dare.

After dinner Simon proposed whist. Naturally, Mara and Dare became partners, which thrilled her out of all proportion to the situation. Whist was an excellent choice, however, being interesting and free of dangers. Sitting as Dare's partner also made it easy for Mara to keep an eye on him. She was ready to complain of tiredness if he showed strain.

She was bracing to do that when a rubber ended and Jancy rang for tea. Dare immediately rose as if restless, but he didn't leave. He turned to Mara. "Don't you play the harp?"

"It's her only accomplishment," Simon commented.

Dare's eyes stayed on her. "No. Will you play for us if I have it brought in?"

Mara was smitten with sudden shyness, but she agreed and sent for her finger pads. Being shy made no sense. She'd played in company for years and here her audience would be friends and family.

Dare had requested this, however, so she must be perfect.

And what other accomplishments did he see in her? She could not sing or draw well. Her handwriting was higgledy-piggledy. She was a good dancer; had he noticed that at the wedding?

When the harp was wheeled in, she tested it and then sat to play, fearing her hands would be too unsteady, too weak, even. She looked away from her audience and soon the music flowed.

Eventually she glanced at Dare. His eyes were closed, but it might be with pleasure, so she played for him alone, trying to send the rippling music into his distressed mind.

When she looked to the side she saw Jancy and Simon leaning together on the sofa, so naturally drawn to each other by familiar love. Oh, to be like that with Dare, she thought as she returned her gaze to the strings. The longing grew in her until it stole all power from her fingers.

The others stirred to look at her.

"I'm sorry. Lack of practice. My fingers cramped."

Dare rose and came to her. "Angel music. Thank you."

Mara prayed her blush could be taken for modesty. "As Simon said, my only true accomplishment."

"And as I said, no."

"Then what are the others?" she asked with a smile.

"Begging for compliments again?"

"As I said before, a lady can never receive too many."

"What about we poor fellows?" Simon asked from where he lounged on the sofa. "Unappreciated to a man."

Mara had forgotten anyone else was in the room. Gathering her wits, she surveyed both men boldly. "On the contrary. I see two fine specimens, in full vigor of manhood and beauty. Noble souls . . ."

"Warriors for truth and justice," Jancy

contributed.

"Tested by fire."

"Wounded in the cause!"

"Destined for greatness. Need we go on?" Mara asked.

Simon was laughing. "Spare our blushes."

"When a lady says that," Mara pointed out, "she *is* begging for more."

She looked up at Dare, hoping for laughter, but saw strain. He moved away, but aimlessly, or as if seeking escape.

Mara rose, pretending a yawn. "After my performance, and the effort of coming up with praise for two such unlikely specimens, I'm ready for my bed. Please excuse me."

No one objected, but Dare escorted her upstairs. Simon and Jancy were close behind and Mara wished they weren't. She ached to be alone with him, just for a moment. At her door, she hesitated, wondering if she could invite him in to see her plan of the castle, only for a moment.

Simon would have an apoplexy.

Dare wished her good night and walked rapidly away.

Mara had to go in and close the door, remembering her plan to investigate the ballroom. Ruth arrived with washing water, however, and there was nothing for it but to prepare for bed.

Once the maid left, Mara thought about dressing again, but that would be difficult and she didn't intend to be seen. She had to wait a little for the house to settle.

She went to the window to look out at Great Charles Street. Lit windows showed here and there. One house had so many lit that it might be hosting a party. A hackney coach rattled up and let down two laughing couples, who hurried inside. The coach passed beneath her; then two gentlemen strolled by in greatcoats and tall hats, talking.

Beyond these walls, life went on, the sort of full, merry life she was used to. Inside? Despite superficial normality, gloom slid around like an odorless gas. Prosaic Yeovil House was taking on the gothic aspects of Castle Cruel.

She didn't know how long she could endure this oppressive atmosphere, yet she had no desire to escape. To leave here was to leave Dare. Against logic, she saw it as abandoning him to fight alone. She'd given him her favor yesterday because he'd spoken to her about the opium and his struggles in a way she was sure he spoke to few others.

She wanted to believe that he needed her. She needed to understand. Was this leaping around in the ballroom simply quarterstaff work, or was it something more sinister?

It was time. Mara grasped the candlestick and left her room. Weighty floors and walls blocked nearly every noise. She heard faint voices as she passed Simon and Jancy's door, and then was alone with only the distant ticking of the downstairs hall clock. She set off in search of the ballroom.

She found the double doors, listened and heard nothing. That was no guarantee that no one was inside, but she sensed it was true. Instead of hunting for the back stairs to a musicians' gallery, she gingerly opened one door.

As she'd thought, the large room was deserted. No strange leaping tonight.

The room looked exactly as it did in the dolls' house with upholstered chairs lining the walls and three long windows breaking the facing wall. They let in moonlight and the panes cast silver tiles upon the floor. It looked like a setting for a faery ball.

Mara blew out her candle and put it down, and then she moved into the room to dance from square to square, weaving among imaginary dancers, humming music to herself.

CHAPTER 15

Dressed for his nightly battle in loose white trousers and shirt, Dare stood in the dark corridor watching Mara. She seemed a creature from another world, and she was. She was of the magical land of Brideswell, a place that in his mind held constant sunlight and laughter.

And he was an inhabitant of darkest hell.

This magic was different, however. She danced in moon magic in a loose robe patterned with flowers, her hair down around her shoulders. She was entrancing and threatening at the same time. But irresistible. He moved forward on bare feet and caught her outstretched hand.

She literally jumped and let out a cry, eyes wide with fright. But almost immediately she relaxed, smiled, and resumed the dance, her hand in his.

"What are we dancing?" he asked softly.

She changed the tune. "A waltz."

In waltz rhythm they passed down the room and he could almost see the others, the visitors from another realm. This felt like opium madness when he was already too far from his last dose for pleasant visitations.

Perhaps he was far enough away for two hungers to collide — the lure of the beast and the lure of a woman. The lure of this woman. Mara. She'd entered his mind like a melody only days ago, but the melody sang on through restless day and sleepless night. Now, her graceful movements, her eyes on his, her curves, her touch, her very smell, swept over and through him beyond all hope of sanity.

He should flee, but was as powerless to do so as if he had in truth been captured in a faery spell. The sweetest possible spell, one he wanted only to surrender to forever and ever.

They moved into the waltz steps, which meant he must put his hand over silk on her waist, feel the swell of her hip, fight the thought of her breasts.

Meager. That had been her word.

Perfect, he was sure.

Like all of her.

Her hand rested on his shoulder like a brush of impossible fire. They turned eyes locked, until the dance pattern swept them apart again. Oh, wicked dance.

Time ceased to have meaning, but each waltz step brought them closer until they turned at last, body against body. When the faery dancers moved on, they stayed together, hot, close, and in his case, aching with desire in a way he'd not experienced for so long.

"Almack's would definitely not approve," she said, her eyes bright with laughter, but with something else. Something he wasn't worthy of. Lost in the loveliness of Mara in his arms, however, with her lissome body pressed to his, her sweet perfume filling his disordered senses, he could not be noble.

He lowered her head to kiss her beautiful hair. "Not at all," he murmured. She moved so his lips slid to her cheek, then again so lips met lips.

He pulled back. "We mustn't."

She held on to his shirt. "Dance."

So they danced, twirling slowly until they swirled to a stop again, and this time the kiss had to be complete.

You mustn't do this! clamored in Dare's mind but the compulsion outreached anything he had ever felt for opium. To kiss Mara. At last. Fully. To run his hands down her back and explore the hot sweetness of her willing mouth, inhaling everything perfect that she was.

It was like consuming sunshine, peace, and home.

The heat of Dare's mouth sent a jolt through Mara, raising her to her toes to press closer to him. His lips claimed hers with a hunger that matched her own as perfectly as they'd matched in dancing. She arched against his strong arm, swept into delight and triumph.

He truly was hers!

They were turning still, slowly, slowly, as they shifted and explored, kissing, kissing, kissing. Their legs brushed with every movement, sending shivers through her, shivers of longing for more, ever more. She'd never imagined a kiss could be like this — so hot, so wild, so complete and everlasting.

She pressed her hands into his long, strong back, exploring the body of a man for the first time. He was wearing only loose pantaloons and shirt, and she could feel every inch of him with hands and trembling body. She felt his hands on her and he pulled her hips closer, closer to where she wanted to be.

Her breasts tingled and ached, and she rubbed against him, breaking free for a moment to breathe, to smile, to speak. To tell him how wondrously perfect this was.

He wrenched free of her.

"Dare?"

Eyes dark and wide he stepped back, back, back toward the door.

"Dare?"

He turned and ran.

Mara ran after him, but by the time she reached the door, the corridor lay empty in both directions. Silence ruled as if that kiss had never happened. She tried to calm her gasping breaths for they and her hammering heart deafened her, but it was hopeless.

For a magical moment all had been perfect, but she'd lost him as if he truly were a faery prince who'd now been dragged back into hell. No. She wouldn't let that be!

She ran to his bedroom and burst in.

It was empty.

She summoned the image of the dolls' house and ran to what she thought was the special room but paused outside the door, sanity creeping back. She heard no sound from inside. This time, when she reached for the knob and turned it, her hand shook.

She opened the door — into darkness. Then the weak light from the corridor lamps showed her not a room but a staircase. One of the plain service staircases.

She'd picked the wrong door!

She closed it. The correct door had to be nearby, but her courage had seeped away. Dare had fled from her as if she were a demon. How could she chase him down?

She stood hugging herself, rubbing her arms, searching desperately for a hint of sound that would prove he was still here, beneath this roof — in this world.

She knew now that image was true. He lived in two worlds. One was the ordinary world of sunlight, silk, and society, but he only visited that from a dungeon, where he was trapped by the beast of opium.

Well, then, she thought, straightening and walking back to her room, that had always been her quest — to rescue Dare. Nothing had changed except that she better understood the brilliance of the light and the intensity of the darkness.

And after that kiss, he was hers to care for, no matter how he fought that fact.

CHAPTER 16

Mara slept badly, but in the morning she tried to be lively for Ruth. Heaven help her if the maid learned of her nighttime adventure.

If only she had someone to talk to about it, but she couldn't imagine trusting even Jancy on such a subject. Jancy would be bound to tell Simon and Mara would be on a coach back to Brideswell within the hour.

Simon would fear kisses leading to more, to her losing her maidenhead before she married. And he could be right. If they'd kept on kissing, if Dare had slid his hands inside her clothes, if he'd whispered temptation . . .

Ruth returned with breakfast. "Come on, milady. You need to be up."

She was carrying the tray balanced on what looked like a bolt of black cloth. She put down the tray and passed over the package. "This just arrived, milady. You must have forgotten it."

The black cloth was wrapping stamped with white Chinese characters. Mara's purchase from Mr. Lee had been wrapped that way.

"It arrived on *Sunday?*" she asked.

Ruth sniffed. "I don't suppose such heathens mind about the Lord's day, milady."

Mara put it aside. "It's not mine, anyway. It must be Lady Austrey's. Give it to her maid, please."

Mara sat to her breakfast and to the ever-present thoughts of Dare. She'd spent half the night trying to come up with a magical remedy. Now she tussled with a more mundane problem. How would he treat her after what had happened?

He might hide from her again, but when she went down to go to church, he was waiting with Simon and Jancy. Their eyes met for one intent moment, but then they both acted as expected. Or in Mara's case, particularly brightly because of relief.

Jancy stepped close and softly said, "Did you want to keep the silk secret, Mara? I'll hold on to it for you."

"What silk?"

"The satin with roses."

"I didn't buy that."

"It was in that package," Jancy said.

"Perhaps Mr. Lee sent it as a gift."

"How strange. Was there a message?"

"There's a paper enclosed with Chinese letters on it. I'll give it all to you later."

Dare came over to offer his arm, and they all left the house.

"Is something the matter?" he asked Mara.

Again their eyes met, speaking of the past night.

"Nothing except that you fled," she said quietly.

"It shouldn't have happened. You shouldn't have been there."

"I don't regret it, Dare. I love you." She let her eyes challenge him to evade that.

But Simon and Jancy came abreast with them before he could react.

"I forgot to say that I had a message from Hal," Simon said. "He and Blanche will be at the Abbey today, too, along with Stephen and Laura. Testing the waters."

"No one is going to snub anyone in church, are they?" Mara asked.

"There are always subtle ways," Dare said, "but it's a good testing ground. Many of the old-fashioned sort attend service there and they're the ones most likely to be difficult."

They entered the ancient church to find it filled with the angelic voices of a boys' choir. Mara remembered she'd proposed a visit here to research moldering crypts, but this was more heavenly.

Especially to be attending Sunday service on Dare's arm. Almost like a married couple.

They joined the Beaumonts and Balls and during the service Mara prayed as never before — that Dare would be victorious over opium, and that they would be happily together for the rest of their lives. She remembered to also pray that the Rogues find a way to have Blanche fully accepted by society.

They emerged into sunshine and their party became a hub for friends and acquaintances. No one seemed to treat Blanche coldly, but Mara noticed that some people kept their distance. That was probably telling, for few members of the ton would lightly ignore the son of a duke, the heir to an earldom, and a prominent politician.

There was a preponderance of fashionable younger gentlemen in the group around them, many clearly delighted to see Dare back in the social whirl. She shouldn't be surprised. He'd doubtless been the heart and soul of every bachelor party before Waterloo. Mara reveled in his popularity, especially as many of the gentlemen discreetly flirted with her.

She flirted back with ease, delighted by the shower of invitations Dare was receiving. Until she realized he was hating all this.

He needed to be rescued. She caught Jancy's eye. Jancy said something to Simon. In moments the men melted away and their party was walking back to Great Charles Street.

"Being with child is such a convenience," Mara said to Jancy.

"And Simon hinted it so delicately," Jancy replied.

"Which promptly terrified them. Anyone would think you were about to give birth on the spot."

"Probably a very natural bachelor terror of anything to do with nurseries," Dare said.

"Oh, what fools these men do be," Mara misquoted, linking arms with him. He was still tense, she noted, but he'd be better now.

Simon and Jancy walked ahead, which left Mara exactly where she wanted to be — almost alone with Dare. "That went well," she said, "but I noticed how few of the older people came over. It's so unfair to Blanche."

"It was doubtless because of me, not her," he said. "I don't think association with me can help Blanche at all."

"Because of opium. That's nonsense. Any

number of people take it."

"And some are even addicted," he said, making nonsense of her evasion. "None, however, quite so infamously."

"There's nothing shameful about your situation, Dare, and only see how many well-wishers you had. Have you been treated coolly elsewhere?"

"I've not been mixing with society elsewhere."

She shouldn't have begun such a stressful subject. "I'll find a way to sort this out."

"The hair, the hair," he lamented. "Mara, don't."

Like a lightning strike, memories hit — of that moment as they'd returned home from the visit to the Tower, after she'd revealed her love. She saw in his eyes that he remembered, too.

"How can I help it?" she asked softly. "I do love you, Dare. There's nothing you or I can do about that."

"Even though it's a dread affliction?"

"You know that's not what I meant. And if you say you're not worthy of my love, I'll hit you."

His lips twitched. "You would, too. I do hope to prove worthy." He came to a stop, looking beyond her, frowning.

"What?" Mara asked, turning to see what

concerned him.

But then he spoke. "I shouldn't say this, but . . . Mara, will you wait for me?"

She turned back, hope uncurling, then blossoming at the look in his eyes. "Of course! But why wait? I'll marry you now. Soon, at least. As soon as you wish."

He laughed rather wildly. "No. When I'm free of opium."

"The lady sets the date, sir."

"In a normal world, the gentleman proposes."

She gripped his arm. "But I want to help you in the fight and how can I do that if we're apart? Soon Simon will take me to Marlowe House."

"Mara —"

"I always get my way — you know I do. Three weeks. Time for banns. We'll marry at home — Brideswell, I mean."

"If we marry, then yes, it must be at your magical home."

"It is magical, isn't it? And once you're married to me, we can spend as much time there as you want. It will heal you."

"Or I will pollute it."

She stilled. "Never say anything like that again."

"But —"

"Never."

The resistance in his eyes, the self-doubt there, terrified her into pushing harder. "So in three weeks?"

"I will not marry you while in this state," he said.

"I would marry you in a far worse state."

"But I won't let you sacrifice yourself for me."

Mara rolled her eyes. "It wouldn't *be* a sacrifice, you dolt. Do you love me?"

He hesitated, his eyes anguished, but then said, "Yes."

Mara paused to savor that precious gift.

"Would you reject me if I became sick?" she asked, as calmly as she could.

"No. But —"

"But this is *exactly* the same." She wanted to insist on a hasty wedding — she wanted him entirely in her protection and care — but she managed a light "At least we're betrothed."

"No, we're not."

"My lord, are you *jilting* me?"

"Mara —"

"What are you two arguing about now?" Simon asked.

He and Jancy had walked back to see what was delaying them.

Mara looked at Dare and took the most dangerous plunge of her life. "Dare just

271

asked me to marry him," she told her brother. "And I said yes."

She saw Dare's lips go tight and Simon's do the same thing.

"He should have spoken to Father first," Simon said.

"And will. Yes?" Mara asked Dare, who looked as if he had a blinding headache. Oh, Lord.

"If you wish," he said, sounding as if he'd make the same response to the question "Will you shoot yourself?"

"Let's get home," said sensible Jancy. "We can talk about the details there, but you have my congratulations, Dare."

"Mara is a ruby beyond price," he said flatly, "and I am truly unworthy of the honor."

The rest of the journey passed in a silence that even Mara was afraid to break. She became more and more afraid of the situation she had created. As they approached the door, she whispered to Dare, "There's no need to make our betrothal public yet."

"It will be as you wish."

"Stop that," she hissed. "Stop agreeing to everything. Stop being cold and distant. If you don't want to marry me, say so."

"I am not in the habit of lying."

She stopped. "Well, then . . ."

"I also want to throttle you," he said with shocking sharpness and walked ahead of her into the house.

Simon handed his hat and gloves to the footman. "Dare, we need to talk."

"Of course."

Mara wanted to insist on being part of the discussion, but Jancy took her arm and drew her upstairs to her parlor.

"Did he really ask you?" Jancy demanded as soon as they were in the room.

"He asked me to wait. Isn't that the same thing?"

"Not precisely."

"A fig for precision. He admitted he loves me." Sudden joy burned through everything else. "He *loves* me!" Mara flung herself into Jancy's arms and danced her around the room. "He loves me! He loves me! He loves me!"

Jancy extricated herself laughing, bonnet askew. "Stop it, you madwoman. Simon's furious, you know."

"Of course I know. He's my brother. But I don't know how he can be. Dare's his closest friend."

"And you're his sister. He wants only the best for you."

"The best is Dare." Mara whirled around

the room alone. "It has always, always, always been Dare!"

CHAPTER 17

In the library, Dare eyed his friend, considering how to stave off a physical attack without doing too much damage. His training with Ruyuan had made him dangerous.

Simon, however, ran a hand through his hair. "Did you ask her to marry you?"

"How can I say no and still be a gentleman?"

"So you didn't. She needs whipping."

Simon wasn't serious, but even so, rage stirred. "No. And don't berate her, either."

"She's my sister."

"And my betrothed."

"You're going to let her do that to you?"

Dare laughed. "Accept imposed heaven?"

Simon stared. "You love Mara?"

"Is it such an impossible notion? I'm sure men have been falling in love with her since she left the schoolroom. I'm the fortunate one she claims to love in return."

Simon's eyes narrowed. "Are you being

honorable?"

"I hope always to be honorable, but in this case, no. I had no intention of coming this far this soon, but I precipitated this. Seeing her the center of attention" — he paused, trying to make sense — "I was suddenly very afraid that some other man might snap her up before I had the chance. So I asked her to wait."

"Wait for what?"

"Wait for me to be free of the beast."

"And if you don't break free, you'd let her go?"

Dare turned away. "I would have to. If I can't free myself soon, I doubt I ever will."

"That's no reason —"

Dare turned back. "Yes, it is. It would be a crime against heaven."

Simon sighed. "I'm not having Mara labeled a jilt, so the betrothal must remain private."

"Of course."

"Dare, you know there's no one I'd rather welcome into the family." Simon made himself say the words. "Even opium addicted."

"I think I'd rather slit my throat than take opium at Brideswell."

"That's nonsense. It's in Mother's medical chest."

"You know what I mean. It's a daily defilement."

It was too close to noon for this. Body and mind were turning restless, making it hard to think. Or to think of anything but the ease the beast could bring. He poured brandy for himself and Simon. Sometimes it acted as a substitute, for a while.

"I am going to return to Long Chart as soon as Marlowe House is ready for you," he said. "This visit to Town isn't serving as I'd hoped."

Simon drank some brandy, watching him with burdensome concern. "What did you hope for?"

"I'm not sure anymore." Brandy burned down, a distraction for mind and gut. "To escape a place where everyone was so damnably considerate of me. To test my ability to be with strangers. To test my control where opium is available everywhere."

"All those have worked."

Dare drained the glass and refilled it. "There's another problem."

"What?" Simon asked.

"Didn't you notice how some people avoided us after church?"

"Because of Blanche, I assume. Not a good sign."

"Because of me."

"Because of opium? That makes no sense."

The glass was empty again, but more wouldn't achieve anything except embarrassment. "That and my mysterious absence. My association with a dubious woman."

"What dubious woman? As far as the ton is concerned, you were cared for by a respectable Belgian widow."

"Who is not here to bolster the story. Many wonder why it took so long for me to contact my family. We've claimed I was unaware of my identity all that time, but it's hard to swallow. Now I'm wondering if it's leaked out that my rescuer was Thérèse Bellaire. There are plenty of men who remember her brief but brilliant sojourn in London."

"Ran the best brothel the town's ever known. I'm sorry to have missed that."

"Don't be."

Simon winced. "Sorry. Scene of Nicholas's journey to hell, I know. But I don't see how that can be known."

"Which leaves us with a general belief that I didn't return because I was happily addled with opium. Which, leaving aside the happily, is mostly true."

Simon looked at his glass and put it aside.

"Don't you want to stay in Town until we decide what to do about Blanche? It's clear there's a bit of a challenge."

"What good can I be?" But Dare shrugged. "Very well. I'll do what I can while I'm here. God knows, the Rogues have done much for me. But I must go. This is another reason, Simon. My times of true sanity and civility are very limited."

Mara had no taste for dealing with her brother just yet, so once she'd shed her outer clothing, she picked up the piece of paper with Chinese writing on it and went in search of Dare's Chinese friend. In daylight it seemed easier to find the right door.

The man who opened the door was dressed in the red monk's robe, and like the figurine was completely bald. He wasn't old, however, and his height and broad shoulders suggested strength. He had steady, slanted eyes in a rugged, wide face.

Mara stepped back, suddenly nervous.

"I may help you?" he said.

"I'm Lady Mara St. Bride. I'm staying here."

"I am aware, my lady. May I help you?"

He wasn't inviting her into his room, which was hardly surprising, and Mara wasn't sure she'd want to go in, but she felt awkward hovering in the corridor. She offered the paper. "I received this. I wondered if you could translate it. I think it's Chinese. Are you Chinese?"

He took the paper. "I am, my lady."

He was addressing her correctly and Mara hadn't been as polite. "I'm sorry, sir, but I don't know the correct way to address you. Mr. Yan?"

"My name is Feng Ruyuan," he said, showing no upset at her mistake. "In my country the first name is the last. Thus in your usage I am Mr. Feng."

Mara dipped a curtsy. "Then thank you, Mr. Feng."

He smiled and looked at the writing. "Who wrote this note to you, my lady?"

"A merchant."

"Are you promised in marriage to him?"

"No, of course not."

"Then be wary. This message says, 'Have this made into a robe, my love, in preparation for our wedding night.' "

Heat swept up Mara's body into her face and she snatched the note back. "Thank you! Please, you won't speak of this?"

"This moment never occurred, my lady. But that is not a suitable message from any man except your promised husband."

He was right, but she *was* promised in marriage to the sender. It had to have come from Dare!

Mara hurried back to her room, even doing a little dance in the corridor. Dare must have asked Laura or Serena about something she'd seemed to want and not bought. The wondrous thing was that he'd been thinking of marriage before they'd left for church. She hadn't forced or tricked him into anything!

Then she remembered Simon. She still couldn't deal with him right now, so she rolled the paper into a tube and slid it between her breasts and slipped upstairs to the nursery.

She enjoyed her time with Delphie and Pierre — soon to be her stepchildren — but couldn't hide forever. She went down to lunch braced for battle, but the meal passed peacefully enough. Jancy talked calmly of commonplace things, Simon didn't refer to the betrothal, and Dare didn't appear.

That daunted her spirits, but she was sure he'd recover.

Afterward, they left to visit Ella and George. Mara enjoyed her sister's company and playing with little Amy, though it reminded her of Ella's objections to Dare's children.

That would end when they were Mara's stepchildren. No one in the family would tolerate exclusion. The marriage would be so good for Pierre and Delphie. Everyone would adore Delphie, and Pierre would revel in the flock of noisy male St. Brides.

Her relaxation shattered when Major Berkstead entered the room. She had been vaguely aware of the footman coming to say that someone had called, but had been absorbed in dressing a doll with Amy.

Caught sitting on the floor, she flashed a look at Ella, who winced back. George must have invited him up. Mara decided to stay where she was so Berkstead couldn't sit by her.

She did her best to ignore him, but he persistently addressed questions to her. When talking about international affairs, he said, "The blessings of peace. Wouldn't you agree, Lady Mara?"

Attention focused on a tiny bonnet, Mara replied, "Peace must always be a blessing, Major."

Conversation moved on to fish. "Like a piece of Scotch haddock myself. What's your favorite fish, Lady Mara?"

Mara looked at him and lied. "Eel."

He beamed. "Very tasty, eel. Did you enjoy the play the other night, Lady Mara?"

The wretch was daring to remind her of that message.

"I thought it ridiculous," she said pointedly.

His expression flickered. "Perhaps you prefer tragedy. Star-crossed lovers."

"I think *Romeo and Juliet* a sad waste of two young lives."

"Indeed," Ella interrupted. "Thank heavens such things no longer happen. More tea, Major?"

Berkstead allowed her to refill his cup, but his attention remained on Mara. "Do you agree, Lady Mara, that true lovers cannot be kept apart in our modern age?"

He was speaking of them. She tried to form a message that would penetrate his thick skull. "I do, Major. Those who love deeply enough have only to wait until they come of age."

"And before that," he said, "there is Gretna."

"Don't speak of such scandalous goings-on!" Ella commanded and directed conversation firmly onto the new exhibition of sculptures in artificial stone.

Mara returned her attention to little Amy, but winced at having let Berkstead trap her into conversation. She simply wasn't good at being rude. But did he really imagine she would climb down a ladder in the night to run off to Scotland with him?

She sent an urgent appeal to Jancy, and soon they were taking their leave. In the carriage, Simon chuckled. "Another suitor, Mara?"

"He was one reason I was eager to leave Ella's house. The man believes himself in love with me."

"That's not uncommon."

"But he believes me in love with him! He chooses to see us as Romeo and Juliet, thwarted by my cruel parents, who forbid me to marry far from home."

"What gave him that idea?"

Mara hoped any blushes were taken as agitation. "He proposed and wouldn't take no. So I offered that as explanation — you know it's more or less true. So now we're star-crossed lovers."

"Poor Mara," Jancy said, but she was fighting laughter.

"It is funny. I see that, but it's a tiresome trial."

Simon said, "I'm surprised he hasn't called at Yeovil House if he's so besotted."

Mara put on a bland expression. "He doesn't know Dare."

"Berkstead said something about encountering Dare in the run-up to Waterloo. But if not, knowing you would be excuse enough."

Did Simon suspect anything? He'd never suspect the truth.

"I hoped he'd realized his cause was hopeless," Mara said.

"A man in love is rarely sane."

Mara hoped that was the end of it, and in a way it was, but Simon added, "Dare's home is in Somerset. Almost as far away as Northumberland."

She'd stumbled into the discussion with Simon she'd been avoiding, but he seemed calm about it. "He intends to buy an estate near Brideswell."

Then she realized they'd never discussed such a thing.

"Fair enough," Simon said, "but he could inherit the dukedom."

"Gravenham has two boys already."

"Stranger things have happened. Look at the way Father became Earl of Marlowe. Besides, if anything should happen to Gravenham, Dare might feel obliged to move back to Long Chart to help raise his nephews, especially if the duke dies."

"Stop predicting disasters!" Mara exclaimed.

"It's not impossible," Simon said. "How would you feel in that situation?"

It took only a moment's thought. "Dare would need me even more."

Simon nodded and the debate seemed over.

"Did I do wrong, Simon? He did ask me to wait for him. Isn't that the same as asking me to marry him?"

"Not quite, but he wants you as much as you want him. Tread carefully, however. Stress and strain seem to make everything harder for him right now. The sooner we move to Marlowe House, the better. We'll stop by and see how things are."

Mara wanted to protest — she could easily have burst into tears — but neither would do any good.

All Mara had seen of Marlowe House before had been the high stone walls that surrounded it and a glimpse of the Grecian house through the gates. It didn't improve on closer inspection.

Though not as monstrously chilly as Marlowe in Nottinghamshire, the London mansion had mostly been decorated by the same taste. It was classically beautiful and completely soulless. Its chief sin for Mara, however, was that as soon as it could be lived in, she'd be forced to leave Dare's home.

They went into the problem room, the

library. It was more formally furnished than the one at Yeovil House, with impressive ranks of volumes in matching dark blue leather bindings.

"No smell of gas," Jancy said.

"The flow of gas was stopped days ago," Simon pointed out. "I'm not sure we should remove the system, you know. Gas gives an excellent light for reading and in time it will be safer."

Mara saw Jancy being swayed. "It might leak again," she said.

Simon frowned at her. "It can't."

But Jancy said, "The thought does make me nervous."

That settled it. "Then we'll have it all out," Simon said, mostly suppressing a sigh. "Come on. We might as well do a quick tour of the house while we're here. You can decide where to use all those silks, Jancy. The place does need cheering up a bit."

After the tour, Simon went to give orders about the gas, leaving Mara and Jancy in a chilly gray-and-white reception room.

"The rooms are a good size for entertaining," Mara said.

"Don't remind me." Jancy was only half joking.

"Don't worry. I'll be by your side, and you'll have the Rogues as support, too."

"I know. But Simon's talking of hosting a ball for Hal and Blanche."

Mara wanted to bash her brother over the head with a brick. A challenge like that was no initiation for a novice.

"That would certainly be a fiery introduction for a hostess," she said, "but it won't be so very terrible. I'm sure the servants here are competent, and you're sure to have a squeeze because the inheritance was so dramatic. The worst calamity is empty rooms. The Rogues will recruit all the influential people they can to help Blanche. It will be the event of the season!"

Jancy shuddered again.

Chapter 18

Mara had expected Dare to behave differently now they were secretly betrothed, but she was disappointed. He took dinner with them, but behaved in exactly the same manner as the night before. They played cards again. She played the harp again. When she saw Dare becoming strained, she claimed tiredness. He escorted her to her room.

She wondered whether she should raise the subject of the rose silk on the way, but it was no time to deal with any tricky subject. She said good night and went into her room as miserable as a woman could be who was promised in marriage to the man she loved.

A door shut next door. Simon and Jancy had come up. Dare's room was too far for her to hear the door, but he was probably in there preparing for his nightly battle.

Last night he had probably been coming to the ballroom for his jumping around.

He'd been dressed strangely. The pantaloons had been loose to the ankles and the shirt very plain. Something definitely did go on.

Ruth left. Mara waited longer than she had the night before and then left the room. The corridors were dimly lit, but she had no trouble in finding the set of service stairs that should lead up to the musicians' gallery. They were dark, however, and she wished she'd brought a candle as she felt her way up them, feeling for doors. She found one.

Dry mouthed, she turned the knob. As soon as she opened the door a crack, she heard thumpings and grunts. She slipped in, but couldn't see anything but a thread of light. There must be a heavy curtain at the front of the shallow gallery.

She stepped cautiously forward, groping for chairs or other objects, then closed the door behind herself. The thumps and grunts continued, making her wonder if she truly wished to see what was going on. She couldn't turn back now.

She shuffled her way forward, then froze when Dare gasped, "Damn you!"

Oh, God, what was happening?

She groped forward as quickly as she could, aiming for that thin crack of light. Dare cried out in pain. She almost ripped the curtains apart, but managed to restrict herself to making the tiny gap a few inches wide.

After the darkness the ballroom beneath her seemed brilliantly lit, though in fact only two stands of candles shed light. In that circle of unsteady light, she saw Dare, wearing the strangely loose pantaloons he'd worn the last time but no shirt at all. He was fighting Mr. Feng, who was dressed in similar pantaloons, but of red.

Mara simply gaped as the two kicked, struck out, whirled, leapt, even. She'd never seen anything like it, but at least no one was being tortured.

Her stunned brain began to sort out some of what was happening. They were fighting but not fighting. There was no intent to hurt or defeat.

Though Dare looked strong and skilled, Feng Ruyuan was his master. He seemed almost fluid, and when Dare's hands or feet connected with him, it was by Mr. Feng's will. She saw the way Mr. Feng sometimes halted a blow of his own that could have been ferocious if it had landed. Dare cursed him then.

Mara sank to her knees so she could just see over the balcony rail and watched, not knowing whether to smile or weep. Dare's chest heaved and sweat glistened, but he never paused. It was as if he were fighting something other than his opponent, something that must never be allowed to win.

Opium.

She swallowed. That chest was magnificent in ways not obvious when hidden by clothing. Dressed he seemed simply lean, but now she saw the defined muscles that slid and rippled with the complex movements. She also saw a jagged white scar down his side.

His leaps and turns meant that his legs were as strong. Of course he'd always been a rider, but she felt sure he hadn't been built quite like this a few years ago.

Twice Mr. Feng landed a blow and Dare cried out in pain. Mara had to fight not to leap up and protest.

Once, only once, Dare landed a true blow on his teacher's flank. He yelled, "Ha!" in triumph. Mr. Feng bowed, smiling.

Time ceased to have meaning, but Mara wondered at the stamina of both men. They had to cry halt soon. They did, but not as she'd expected.

A sharp command from the Chinese man brought Dare to a stand, feet slightly apart, hands joined as if in prayer. Only his chest moved, heaving in and out. The teacher faced him in the same pose, breathing hard, but able to speak. Mara thought it was English, but his voice was so soft she couldn't understand the words.

He spoke at length, in a calm flow that was almost a chant. When both men's breathing had calmed, he took something out of a pocket. A box? Yes, like a snuffbox. He opened the lid and offered it to Dare, who closed his eyes.

Then Mr. Feng walked closer, still talking, in a glide like a cat, the box held out so it ended up close to Dare's face, right beneath his nose.

And Dare began to gasp for breath again, shaking all over.

No. Mara only mouthed it, probably because she felt breathless herself. No!

The man was offering him opium. Tempting him with it, now, long after his last dose of the day. He was crooning temptation as he waved it slowly before Dare's face. Dare's hands were still pressed together, but Mara thought she could see the desperation in every line of his vibrating body.

She wanted to leap off the balcony and run to his aid. This was cruel torture. She only gripped the top rail harder and harder, struggling with Dare, trying to lend him her strength.

This must be a torture he had chosen. It was part of his battle — the one for which she had so lightly offered him a lady's favor.

Sweat poured off him now and muscles jumped in his arms and face.

Eventually, eventually, the master glided back, closing the box and sliding it into his red pantaloons. Then he flowed behind Dare and put his hands on his shoulders. Mara thought he could probably push him over with little effort, but instead he massaged, speaking again, this time soothingly. Dare shuddered, but in a different way, his head bending, his hands dropping to his side.

Mara drew slowly back, letting the curtains fall closed, and crept back to her room. What a child she had been.

Dare lay on the narrow bed as Ruyuan pummeled the beast out of his flesh. Overwhelm it. Overwhelm it in body and mind.

Under Ruyuan's tutelage, as his body had regained its strength, so had his mind, and that was his only true hope. He'd studied addiction and he knew that many won the bitter physical fight but fell back into the pit because they'd neglected their mind and will.

In many ways that had been the harder

struggle, because he'd once been physically strong, but he'd never paid attention to the deeper mental strengths.

He appreciated them now, just as he appreciated muscles and sinews that worked well, but he was going to be a strange sort of Englishman at the end of this. Rather like Nicholas, for he suspected he was deeper into these philosophies of mind and body than was obvious.

Each night, Ruyuan tested his will, and for twenty-two nights now he'd had the strength to resist. It had been a close fight tonight.

It had been a bad day in many ways, but heaven and hell combined. Mara had promised herself to him, but she didn't know what he was. How could she? Her image came from the past, from what he'd been before, like that miniature portrait she'd been admiring on her first night here.

She didn't know the addict who acted out his days and dragged himself through the night in a war it seemed he could only ever survive, never win. She didn't see him shake and sweat not to grab the relief Ruyuan offered. Or the times he'd broken and taken it.

He carried Mara's brooch, her favor, in his pocket at all times, and it gave him strength. He would become worthy of her. He must, for she was a devil-haired St. Bride and she'd persist in loving him.

Please God let that be so, but he must be worthy. He must never defile that trust.

The massage gentled and the music started, the Oriental flute that swooped and flew in ways so different to Western music. He wasn't sure he liked it as music, for it often seemed infinitely sorrowful, but it soothed his tormented mind.

Tonight, it made him weep.

"What have you been doing to yourself?" Ruth demanded the next morning.

"Not sleeping," Mara replied, feeling as if she'd been rolled down a hill in a barrel of dust.

"What's the matter, then? Toothache?"

"I just couldn't sleep."

"You always sleep." Ruth poured the washing water, but looked Mara over. She had eyes like a hawk for symptoms and problems.

What did a woman look like who was desperately in love with a man in desperate torment? Who wasn't sure who that man was anymore, but loved him anyway? Who wasn't sure how to help him, but had to try.

Mara yelped when a wet cloth was wiped

around her face. She grabbed it, and rubbed around her neck as well. "All right, all right. I'm up." She scrambled out of bed. "Why am I up?"

"You're going to the mantua-maker's with Lady Austrey."

"Oh, yes." Mara's eyes tried to close again.

"Do you want to go back to sleep, milady?" Ruth was looking truly concerned now.

"No." Mara stripped and began to wash.

"Very well, but what kept you awake, that's what I'd like to know. You been up to something else in the night you shouldn't?"

"Absolutely not!"

But Mara had been kept awake in the night by guilt. Even though it had been obvious that Dare's struggle was hard, she'd chosen to see it as a simple matter. That was because he'd carefully shown her his calmer faces — most of the time — but she should have known better even so.

She dressed and sat to her breakfast, wondering where he was now. How did he spend the rest of his nights? Did he return to fighting? Did he sleep at all?

Opium was supposed to make people sleepy, but in that case, why the jumping around in the ballroom? She wished she knew more. She stilled in pouring chocolate.

That was what she must do — learn all about opium.

From whom?

The calm features of the Chinese man came into her mind. She would talk to Mr. Feng Ruyuan. No, Mr. Ruyuan Feng, apparently. Why was everything so complicated?

She filled her cup and drank, comforted by a plan. But when Mara set out with Jancy, she would much rather have been staying behind, under the same roof as Dare.

From a reception room, Dare watched Mara leave, feeling both abandoned and relieved. Her presence in the house had become like an omnipresent melody — sweet, but playing so constantly in his mind as to create dementia.

Mara. Ademara. Ademara Saint Bride.

He'd written down what he could remember of their crazy plotting of *The Ghastly Ghoul of Castle Cruel* as a way of revisiting that magical time in the Yeoman's Arms. He'd added a few twists to share with her. A suit of armor that came to life and attacked. A faceless woman in a black dress. A ghostly child who wept in the night.

He'd tossed the papers in the fire because

they'd sucked him into his own hell — Thérèse, opium-dulled pain, and crying children wailing miserably as a child will when beyond hope. In time, they'd learned to weep in silence, and that had been even worse.

The children would be all right. He'd vowed that. They rarely shrank from strangers anymore, except women in black. They could be happy away from him for hours on end. They laughed and, more significantly, risked defiance. That, at least, he might be doing well.

Mara — that he was not doing well.

He should never have asked her to wait. It had plunged them deep into a thicket of thorns. Nor should he have danced with her in the moonlight. He certainly should not have kissed her.

He should have known how fiercely the fire would burn at a touch, at a taste, when distance from the drug stirred wild lust. If he'd not found strength to resist, God knows what he'd have done.

"Dare?"

Dare turned to face Simon, trying to conceal any trace of his thoughts.

He'd never been short of friends — sometimes these days he felt overwhelmed by them — but Simon was different. Despite their long separation, he was the closest, the best, the one to be trusted above all. He mustn't be hurt, mustn't be betrayed.

"A bad day?" Simon asked, too wise to ask if he was all right.

"A bad night, perhaps." Dare found some sort of smile as he crossed the room. He made a sudden decision. "So the women are away and we men may play?"

Simon's eyes showed a flicker of surprise and then instant delight. "An excellent idea. What do you fancy?"

Dare felt as if he'd already outstretched himself, but he didn't draw back. He grabbed the first idea to cross his mind. "Tatt's."

"Splendid idea. Let's be off."

They were both already dressed in breeches and boots, so they needed only hats and gloves before walking to the famous Tattersall's Repository on the edge of Hyde Park, lodestone for horse-loving gentlemen.

How many times had he gone there without a thought? Today it felt like a mighty enterprise. Dare realized it represented his Holy Grail, ordinary life. His key to deserving Mara.

Morning was his best time of day. When the sun rose, he'd survived another night. After the long struggle, the opium was particularly sweet. That was a danger in itself, but it gave him bliss, it gave him rest, and it left him feeling up to anything.

Opium could lessen restraint as well. He felt, like an itch, an alarming temptation to tell Mara's brother about the kiss in the ballroom. Thank God that Simon, wise Simon, was happy to talk about gas lighting and horses, specifically his need for a team for his curricle.

"Do you have a curricle in Town?" Simon asked as they approached Tatt's.

"I've not driven since before. Except for when I took Mara to the park."

"What did you use then?"

He'd stepped into a swamp. "Borrowed a rig from St. Raven."

"What sort?"

They'd walked through the building to the open ring where horses showed their paces. Dare seized distraction. "That's a fine-looking gray."

It worked, but Dare didn't fool himself that he'd entirely escaped. Especially as, damn it all, dark-haired St. Raven was present. Despite his marriage and reformed ways, the duke looked every inch the rich, fashionable rake. No one would think he'd own a tame vehicle.

Even worse, his companion, relaxed and

with the brown skin of a countryman that almost matched dusky blond hair, was Nicholas Delaney. Nicholas had been a regular and welcome visitor to Long Chart over the past nine months, often key to Dare's recovery, but Dare didn't relish facing him now.

As usual, he had damn all choice.

CHAPTER 19

As he and Simon strolled over to join their friends, Dare knew his brain must be thoroughly scrambled to have suggested coming here, to one of the most popular venues for London gentlemen outside of the clubs.

St. Raven, bless him, greeted them both without undertones and continued talking about a racehorse he'd recently purchased. Dare only wished he could whisper to him not to volunteer anything about a high-perch phaeton. He realized that even then he'd been trying to impress Mara like a preening youth.

An observer might think Nicholas Delaney's greeting equally casual, but Dare was aware of having being assessed in a glance. Apparently he passed muster — which meant Nick was losing his touch.

Then it got worse.

"Ah, that's what I like to see. Good horsemen with deep pockets!"

The grinning, sandy-haired man strolling across the ring toward them was Miles Cavanagh, another Rogue, an Irishman whose passion was breeding horses.

"That's one of mine," he said, indicating the gray. "What more need be said, my friends? Let the bidding begin."

Surrounded by loud conversation and cheerful teasing, Dare felt his brain scattering into pieces. He couldn't risk speech. God knows what he would say. When Simon drew him away, he went, feeling like a child.

"You'll want a closer look," Simon said, taking him over to the gray.

"Yes." Then Dare added, "Thank you."

He patted the hunter, which truly was magnificent, all sleek, rippling muscle with a proud, arched neck. The horse turned to look at him with an intelligent eye.

"Wondering whose hands you'll end up in?" Dare asked, moving to face the horse and inspect its teeth. Going through the motions. "Rather like a slave auction, isn't it? But Miles won't let you go to a bad owner."

Miles Cavanagh was a wealthy man and handled the sales of all his horses himself. He sold most of them in Melton during the hunting season, and only to men he knew to be good riders who took care of their animals. In London he had a private arrangement with Tattersall's. He showed some horses here, probably simply for amusement, but still handled the sale himself, giving Tatt's their cut.

The panic or whatever it had been was fading, but Lord, was that going to happen whenever he tried to lead a normal life? It hadn't happened at the theater, but that had been a sedate affair. He'd begun to fray after the church service.

He'd been at the theater in the evening. Did that make a difference? Or was his current state some residue of the situation with Mara, which had left him as raw as if he'd lost a layer of skin? He'd gone early to the ballroom last night, hoping for another encounter, but of course she hadn't come.

"What do you think?" Simon asked. "I could do with a hunter."

Dare pulled his mind to everyday matters. "You plan to hunt? Even now, married?"

"Luce hasn't given it up, and can you imagine Miles doing so? I missed four years of splendid runs and mean to make it up."

"What about Jancy?"

"Luce has that bloody great place near Melton that has the cheek to call itself a hunting box. He's been holding open house

305

for Rogues there in hunting season, wives, children, cats, and dogs included. But of course you know that."

Of course, Dare did.

"I was there in early 1815," Dare said. "It was a different world. Luce wasn't married then. None of us were other than Nicholas. Miles, Francis, and Con were there. Con had no idea he'd have to fight again. It was a good time."

Someone, probably Luce, had sent him an invitation this year. Riding to hounds, riding hell for leather as he used to, riding at all, had been beyond him in the winter, but he also couldn't have handled a noisy gathering, even of friends.

He hadn't done too well now, but he needed to be able to do this. Forcing Mara to live in quiet seclusion would be like keeping a precious plant in a dark cupboard.

He rested a hand on the horse, concentrating on the beast's character and steadiness as other men came to poke and pry. He had no doubt that his hunters had been kept, but a prime young addition wouldn't come amiss. And he realized he no longer had a Conqueror.

He spoke to the groom and leapt onto the horse's bare back to walk it around the ring, feeling its paces, its fluidity of movement.

"You'll not find fault with him," Miles called out with a strong Irish lilt. He always developed an Irish accent when into horse trading. "The finest bit of blood to come out of Ireland, to be sure."

"Stop sounding like a bloody huckster at a fair."

A burst of laughter didn't threaten Dare or the horse, and the horse was everything Miles claimed. Dare moved it into a canter, approving its response, its intelligence, and perhaps its liking. The animal had no reason not to like him. He was a good rider, though he hadn't ridden seriously in far too long.

He'd ridden with Mara that night, but at a walk.

He suddenly wanted to kick the horse to speed and burst through the circling men, out into the park to ride, ride, ride. . . .

Into another world.

Into the past.

Back to before.

That wasn't the way to reach freedom, but the desire, the slight taste of joy, the faltering belief that it was within reach, was a beginning. He halted the horse close to Miles and slid off. "Let's talk."

St. Raven protested that Dare had stolen the gray and Miles called for another of his horses to be brought out. "Sure and you'll like this one, your worshipful grace, even better. The sweetest goer, and stamina. You've never seen the like!"

St. Raven laughed and turned to consider a prancing chestnut.

"Five hundred guineas," Miles said.

"Very well."

Miles stared. "Dare, Dare! You're supposed to *haggle.*"

Dare's original acceptance of the price had been from indifference — another effect of the drug. But now something else stirred, the old mischief.

"But you wouldn't ask such an amount if you weren't in need, my friend."

Miles reddened. "What? What sort of unchristian idea is that? The beast's worth no more than four."

"But I don't mind paying five hundred if you need it."

They were getting an audience.

"Are you after insulting me?" Miles asked, pretending outrage. "Need? Need! Am I not the finest horse breeder in Ireland and owner of Clonagh as well? I'll not take more than four hundred, and that's an end of it."

"Heavens above, I'd never want to insult a friend. My apologies. We'd better make it three fifty to be sure of it."

Miles's eyes flashed, but then he burst out

laughing. "Ah, boyo, that's my old Dare! Done!"

He extended his hand and Dare slapped it in the old horse-trading way, painfully aware of everyone grinning, as if a child had performed a clever trick.

St. Raven tried to get the chestnut for three fifty, but Miles ruthlessly haggled him up to four hundred. "You're a bloody duke and can afford it."

St. Raven agreed to the deal but said, "And you're a bloody huckster and can buy us all a drink."

A new horse was led in, not one of Miles's, and a handler began to shout its praises. Voices seemed to swell all around and Dare wished he could escape. He went with the others toward the subscription room, praying he could hold himself together.

Nicholas said, "I have to excuse myself. Dare, I need to talk to you about something when you have time."

Dare saw the extended hand and grasped it. "Why not now?"

He was sure Simon, at least, understood what was going on, but farewells were taken in good cheer, with mention that tonight everyone was to dine at Francis's.

Hell.

They walked into the park in silence.

Eventually Nicholas said, "Don't talk if you don't want to."

"I don't know," Dare said, then laughed. "There's an idiocy."

"Talk is more than words."

"Yes. It's a fine horse."

"Yes."

"I assume Eleanor and the children are with you."

"Of course. Arabel's anxious to visit Delphie and Pierre."

Nicholas's daughter had been kidnapped by Thérèse Bellaire to intensify her pressure on the Rogues.

He'd been chronically weak from poorly healed wounds and lack of food and unable to do anything to protect the children as Thérèse worked out her devious plots. They'd been moved from the familiar cottage to Brighton and imprisoned. Then Thérèse had brought a new, terrified innocent, gloating as she told him it was Nicholas's child.

Thérèse had given him opium and left one more dose — an act of torture, not kindness. With no idea how long it would be before she returned, he'd fought the need to take it as long as he could, praying to spare the children the horrors that came when he was completely without the stuff for a day or two.

For some unfathomable reason, little Arabel had decided he was a trusted protector. Could she have remembered him? She'd been a mere baby when he'd last seen her and he'd never held her.

For whatever reason, she'd snuggled in his arms and the other two — his brave innocents who had been too accustomed to dark terrors — had comforted her. Delphie had even lent her Mariette and now Arabel had an ugly rag doll of her own.

Dare realized he'd drifted away and that Nicholas was patiently waiting. He'd asked if Arabel could visit.

"Of course," Dare said, walking on. "You know Simon, Jancy, and Mara are living at Yeovil House at the moment?"

"No. We only arrived last evening."

"He has a gas leak at Marlowe House."

Nicholas's eyes lit. "Really? What's he doing about it?"

"If you want to explore the mechanics of gas lighting, talk to him quickly. He's planning to have it all ripped out."

"Makes me wonder why I'm wasting time with you," Nicholas said amiably. "Is it presenting difficulties?"

He wasn't talking about gas.

"Not too many. They understand. It's a

big house." But then Dare said, "Mara . . ."

It had slipped past all his guards like a snake.

"Simon's sister," Nicholas said, but there had been a betraying pause. "I've never met her, but I gather she has the hair."

"Yes. Doesn't seem to want to wander as Simon did, but she's adventurous with a crusading inclination."

"Interesting."

Typical of Nicholas. He wasn't going to probe.

Dare didn't know if he wanted to talk about it or not. He wanted Mara St. Bride with a raw intensity that he couldn't talk to Simon about. Nicholas was undoubtedly the next best thing.

"I'm in love with her."

It seemed a tame hearts-and-flowers description, but it would do.

"And she?" Nicholas asked.

"She thinks she is. It could be pity."

"If you were pitiable."

"Don't be an idiot."

"Back at you," Nicholas said. "She might, I grant, want to be your handmaiden in the fight. She's what — eighteen?"

"Too young."

"The same age as Jancy. Is she too young?"

"Who?"

"Either of them."

Dare thought of Mara and Berkstead. That sort of escapade should emphasize her youth, but the way she'd dealt with it proved otherwise. As did his many experiences with her.

"No, but I can't have her until I cut free of the opium."

"How's that going?" Nicholas asked.

"Well up to a point. It's clear the last bit simply has to be done. Do or die." He meant that literally and saw that Nicholas understood. Dare asked the question he'd wondered about. "Have you been addicted?"

Nicholas nodded. "But not like you. I explored it. When I was with Thérèse, actually. Like many, I was seduced by the fancy of it expanding my mind, granting me great insights. But I saw in time that was delusion, or if not, that the price was too high. Breaking free of it was unpleasant but no more than that. But I hadn't been using it as long as you, or in such high doses. What does Ruyuan say?"

"I haven't put it to him directly, but I think he agrees that reduction has lost its purpose. I take so damn little. Why can't I simply stop?"

"It's not the way it works. Mara St. Bride might be an excellent handmaiden in the fight."

"Not if I lose," Dare said. "I'm terrified of destroying her."

"I'm sure she's stronger than that."

"I could die or go mad."

"You could be struck by lightning."

"You think it trivial?"

Nicholas touched his arm. "No, I don't, but —"

"You have to remember how it is! The pain, the screaming mind, the formless demons. The knowledge that relief is so easy and so close. The desperation for it that might lead a man to strangle his mother if she stood in his way."

Dare realized he was shivering.

Hell!

Nicholas gripped his arm tightly. "I don't forget. You can have all the help you need. You know that."

"What? Lock me up? Tie me up? I've heard of people who've done that and thought they'd won, but soon they're sneaking off for a little taste. Like a tiger unable to stay outside the cage."

Where had that nonsense come from?

Oh, the Tower.

Mara . . .

They'd halted again, within sound of the vehicles on Park Lane.

"So let's see," Nicholas said evenly, "you're afraid of leaving your cage for fear of wanting to return to it?"

"I'm afraid, damn it, of going to hell and back all for nothing. Perhaps everyone is right and I should learn to live with the dose I have. Is that temptation or sanity?"

"Only you can decide that."

"Whichever it is, I can't do it. I loathe the stuff and all it stands for."

After a moment, Nicholas said, "This is all my fault."

"Don't be stupid."

"If I'd not been a foolish youth and fallen under Thérèse Bellaire's spell a great many terrible things would not have happened. To Eleanor, to Luce and Beth, to Clarissa, to Arabel, to you."

Dare couldn't entirely deny it. Three years ago, Nicholas had been recruited by the government to seduce secrets out of his ex-lover, Thérèse Bellaire. It had been believed that she'd been part of a plot to bring the abdicated emperor back to power.

Nicholas had accepted the task. Dare could understand that. It was no more insane than his own need to take part in the last great battle against the Corsican Monster. For their generation Napoleon was the devil incarnate who must be stopped at any cost. The war had also been responsible for the death of two Rogues — Allan Ingram and Roger Merrihew.

It had been Nicholas's misfortune that he'd had to marry at about the same time, throwing him into the hell of being the sexual plaything of the woman he hated and hurting the one he loved. He'd almost destroyed his marriage and nearly lost his life, and there had been lingering consequences.

One tentacle had threatened Luce's marriage; another had tossed Dare into Thérèse Bellaire's claws; a third had almost ruined an innocent girl called Clarissa Greystoke; and a fourth had wrenched Arabel Delaney from her loving home and turned a blessed child into a fearful one.

Thérèse was dead. Luce and Beth were happy. Clarissa had been rescued from disaster by inheriting Thérèse's soiled money and both were now in the capable hands of a Major Hawkinville. Arabel and the children had almost entirely recovered.

The only victim remaining was himself. For the first time, he realized what his recovery meant for Nicholas and the Rogues. They wanted it for his sake, but it would signal the absolute end of Thérèse Bellaire and all her darkness.

"You did what seemed best at the time," he said to Nicholas, "but I can't accept any lingering trace of the woman. Taking opium daily for the rest of my life would drive me mad. The smell of it, even as I crave it, makes me want to vomit. Every dose is a surrender to something foul. It's like lying with a diseased whore, but one who has skills to drive a man to ecstasy. To be worth anything, I have to win free myself. Not under compulsion."

"I agree," Nicholas said. "That's why I asked Ruyuan to help you."

"And I thank you." As they walked on into the street Dare asked, "Do you practice his religion?"

"It's not precisely a religion, but a path."

Tao-jia," Dare said.

"To take life as it comes."

"It sometimes comes damn unpleasantly."

"But sometimes we invite the pain. Why did you come to London?"

"You think I shouldn't have?"

"I think," said Nicholas, "that you were placing rocks in the stream and thus creating turbulence. I don't see that as a bad idea. But then, I am too much a part of my world to be a dedicated Taoist."

Dare thought about his motives as they walked. He'd like to think he flowed like water, but he felt more as if he drifted like a ghost. A ghoul, trapped in Castle Cruel.

"I was stuck," he said at last. "I couldn't make progress and I couldn't make the final break. I hoped that different places and experiences would move me to a new point."

"It seems to be working then."

That startled Dare into laughter. "I suppose I hoped the point would be a little less sharp."

"They rarely are. Now I really do have business. I'll see you at Francis's tonight?"

The gathering of Rogues held too many possibilities of disaster, but Dare knew he had to attend. "Yes, of course."

"I assume I'll meet Lady Mara. I can't wait."

Dare walked back to Yeovil House thinking he should find a way to warn Mara. But about what?

CHAPTER 20

A lighthearted visit to a dressmaker with three friends should have been a perfect distraction, but it wasn't working.

Mara was trapped in a whirl far madder than she'd ever known and could finally understand why lovers behaved so insanely. She would haunt Dare, pursue him, sing serenades beneath his window. She understood poor Berkstead better now.

"Mara, are you all right?" Jancy asked.

She'd been sitting in silence for far too long. "Yes, of course. I'm sorry. I . . . I didn't sleep well last night."

Jancy smiled understanding, but all she understood was the strain of the secret betrothal.

Mara made herself take part in the discussions, though fashion seemed irrelevant. Who cared about the fullness of a sleeve or the cut of a bodice? Who cared about Circassian cloth as opposed to Manchurian?

But she had a job to do today — to chivvy Jancy into ordering the finest gowns.

She wasn't needed. Having purchased the silk, Jancy didn't balk at the cost of having it made up and settled to an earnest and knowledgeable discussion with the mantua-maker. Mara twiddled her thumbs, wishing she'd not come.

She and Dare might have been alone in Yeovil House.

Anything could have happened.

Also, she would have had opportunity to visit Mr. Feng to ask him about opium. Instead, she was stuck here amid fussing about flounces and fringing, satin and sarcenet and was soon going to embarrass herself by screaming.

At last all the decisions were made and they could leave, but now the other ladies wanted to stroll to nearby Bond Street and investigate more shops. At least talk turned from clothes to the dinner tonight.

"Nicholas has arrived," Serena said. "So we'll be sixteen."

That caught Mara's attention. "Who else besides Nicholas and Eleanor, you and Francis, Laura and Stephen and Jancy and Simon?"

"You and Dare," Serena said.

Of course she'd not meant that as a

couple, but Mara looked down to fuss with her spencer to hide a blush of delight. "That's only ten," she said.

"Miles and Felicity Cavanagh have arrived," Serena said, "and Lord and Lady Charrington are in Town. I've invited St. Raven and his wife as well."

Not long ago that would have stabbed Mara with envy, but now it didn't ruffle her at all. *You and Dare.* And it was truer than Serena knew.

"So who won't be there?" she asked. "Lord Arden, Lord Amleigh . . ."

"And Hal," Serena said. "Blanche is performing, and he never misses one."

They paused by a jeweler's window to inspect and discuss the items on display. Mara had an idea. She went inside, the others following. A young man hurried forward, eyes bright at the sight of obviously rich customers.

"I only want beads today," Mara warned him. "Do you have beads of stones, like jasper, jade, and quartz?"

Clearly he'd hoped for purchases of rubies, but he asked about size and cheerfully produced trays with containers of different colored beads.

"You wish to have a necklace strung, ma'am?"

"Something like that." Mara studied the many colors and textures. Some she recognized, some she didn't. She asked for names, pointing.

"White jade," the clerk said. "Malachite, obsidian, rose quartz, clear quartz, amber, garnet, blue agate, amethyst, lapis lazuli, red jasper, coral, bloodstone . . ."

Mara began to pick one each out of different sections, simply choosing colors and textures that appealed to her.

"What are you doing?" Jancy asked. "That will make a peculiar necklace."

"I'm going to collect a string of Rogues. Yes," she told the clerk, "I will need a string."

He summoned an assistant to bring it.

"I'll put on beads in the order I met the Rogues," Mara said, but realized that would put Simon and Dare at one end. "From each end," she added.

When the string arrived, she picked a dark red bead first. "For Simon. This is garnet, I assume."

The clerk agreed.

Mara wished she had more time to think about Dare, but let instinct be her guide. She chose a creamy gold bead.

"Topaz, ma'am."

Mara slid it onto the string. "Now Hal,

Francis, and Stephen." She chose the greenish-red bloodstone for the soldier, then turned to her companions. "You should choose for your husbands."

"Oh, no," Serena said. "It's your image of them that counts. I wouldn't have chosen topaz for Dare. But then I didn't know him before Waterloo."

Mara turned back to the tray, thinking how strange that was — that people might think the present Dare was the real one. But then what was reality? They'd talked about that in the coach.

She picked a green-flecked brown.

"Jasper, ma'am."

"That's for Francis," Mara said, "and this blue for Stephen."

"Blue agate, ma'am."

She put them on either side of the three beads. "How do I choose for the rest, though? I haven't met them yet."

"Then you wait," Laura said.

Mara grimaced. "I'm not good at waiting, but I suppose I must." She chose an assortment of about twenty stones. "There have to be six there that suit." But then she said, "There were twelve Rogues originally."

"Two are beyond earthly contact, alas," Serena said.

"Roger Merrihew and Allan Ingram,"

Mara said. "They should be represented." Mara looked automatically at the jet beads, so suitable for mourning, but then shook her head. "Pearls," she told the clerk. "I want two pearls of the same size. And I'll put them in the very middle."

"Mara," Jancy murmured. "The cost."

"It's the right thing."

"I never knew them," Laura said, "but Stephen speaks of them. It's terrible that so many men died so young because of Napoleon."

Laura said, "When the Rogues heard of the casualties at Waterloo, and of course they thought Dare one of them, Nicholas proposed a toast. Francis wrote it down and had it carved on a plaque in our church at Middlethorpe in memory of all the victims of the war. 'To all the fallen, may they be young forever in heaven. To all the wounded, may they have strength and heal. To all the bereaved, may they feel joy again. And we pray God, may there one day be an end to war.'"

Mara watched the clerk put her purchases into silk pouches.

Amen, she thought. *But the true end of the war for us all will be when Dare is fully healed.*

On returning to the house, Mara sent a

footman to ask if she could speak with Mr. Feng, but the man returned to say the Chinese man was not available. Instead, Mara took a nap — a strange enough event to put Ruth in a fret again.

It meant that she arrived at Lord Middlethorpe's Hertford Street house that evening with her wits sharp, but her emotions were a mess. Once she would have been innocently thrilled at the prospect of a gathering of Rogues, but that seemed of no importance now.

She'd promised Simon she wouldn't make the commitment public until she and Dare had spoken to her father. Dare didn't want it known until he was free of opium. She wasn't sure she could conceal her feelings for a moment.

As they entered the house, Dare seemed at ease, but she knew he wasn't. It was frightening how strongly she felt his shielded emotions. She wanted to take his hand, but had to content herself with being his acknowledged partner at this gathering of couples.

She was introduced to Miles and Felicity Cavanagh, an Irish couple, and to Lord and Lady Charrington.

Miles and Felicity were jolly and Mara took to them immediately. He was the sandy-haired sort of Irish and she the type called Black Irish because of their dark hair. It was said to be an inheritance of the crews of the Armada wrecked on Ireland's shores.

The Charringtons were another matter. The sleek dark-haired man was Leander, but Mara wasn't sure she would ever be able to use his Christian name. She remembered Simon talking of him as the perpetual diplomat and "foreign" — neither of which were admired traits in a schoolboy. He still was both smooth and foreign in ways she couldn't pin down. She felt an alarming temptation to dip a curtsy.

His plump wife didn't have that effect, but she was a surprise as well. Lady Charrington had been the widow of the famous poet Sebastian Rossiter, and thus his "angel bride." "How sweet the sight of dainty wife,/ Light-footing through the gloaming./A fairy trembling on the air,/My Judith gone aroaming."

Dainty? Fairy? Rosy-cheeked Judith reminded Mara of practical country ladies like her mother. Ah, well, she never had understood poetic metaphor.

The rakish Duke of St. Raven's wife was another surprise. Cressida St. Raven was a composed young woman with steady gray eyes who looked like a reforming influence, but St. Raven didn't strike Mara as tamed.

Then she met King Rogue. Despite appropriate evening clothes, Nicholas Delaney managed to look casually dressed, but there was nothing casual about his sherry brown eyes.

"The famous Lady Mara," he said.

"Famous?" Mara asked, prickling.

"You have the hair."

She touched it nervously and then wished she hadn't. "A blessing and a curse." Seeking deflection, she asked, "Your wife isn't with you, Mr. Delaney?"

"That depends on how precisely you mean 'with.' She's upstairs feeding the baby."

Babies made a safe subject. "How old, and boy or girl?"

"Two months, a boy — Francis — and he should be at home. London is dirty, both physically and psychically, but Hal and Blanche need help."

And Dare? Before Mara could decide whether she wanted to talk about Dare with this man, Lord Middlethorpe interrupted. "Mara, I have a complaint to make."

She turned to him, increasingly nervous. "What have I done?"

"I gather you're choosing beads for us all, and I am boring jasper."

Despite the humor in his eyes, she

squirmed. She'd picked it because he seemed so steady. "I could choose something else. . . ."

"Don't indulge him," Nicholas said. "But now you have to tell me what stone I am."

"I haven't had time to decide." Wishing she'd never started this fancy, Mara turned to Stephen. "I chose a blue agate for you, sir. I hope that doesn't disappoint."

"I think it's perfect," Laura said.

Her husband smiled at her. "Then I'll commission a necklace of it for you."

"How fortunate Mara didn't choose a sapphire," Nicholas remarked. "Have you decided on any more?" he asked her.

"Simon is a garnet, and Dare a topaz." She avoided looking at Dare by turning to the easygoing Irishman. "Would it be too trite to designate green jade for you, Miles?"

"Trite or not, I'm ever proud to be Irish!"

"And me?" asked Lord Charrington.

Mara thought quickly, surprised by how much she was disliking being the center of attention. "Malachite."

He laughed. "An excellent choice. The Tsar gave my father a table made out of a slab of the stuff. It's a great honor. Russian nobles value the status of such gifts more than gold."

"What bead for a duke?" St. Raven asked.

But Nicholas said, "Rogues only. Twelve we are, and twelve we shall remain."

"Except by marriage. Wives are full Rogues, remember." The speaker was an auburn-haired woman, who came over to take Nicholas's arm.

He smiled a ready welcome at her. "I grant you that."

The connection between the two was palpable and somehow both powerful and gentle. Mara felt more kindly toward Nicholas.

"Entry only by marriage?" St. Raven looked sorrowfully at his wife. "It'll have to be divorce, my dear."

Cressida St. Raven smiled. "I am not a-tremble, sir. Whom could you marry to gain entrée?"

The duke flashed a grin. "Dare." He fluttered his dark lashes. "Could I pass as a woman, do you think?" He strolled up to Dare and laid fingers on his arm. "Be mine, my lord, be mine. You bring such a precious dowry."

Dare slapped his fingers away playfully. "Too precious for the likes of you, you strumpet. I'm open to legal offers, however," he said to the room. "Let the auction begin."

Everyone laughed, but Nicholas pointed out, "Only Mara's in a true position to bid."

Everyone looked at her. Mara knew she was blushing fiercely, but the only thing to do was act along. She looked Dare up and down as if assessing his value, then circled him thoughtfully. "Entry to this select association is, I grant, of value. I bid" — she let the silence hang — "a farthing. Going, going, gone!"

Everyone laughed again.

"Alas to be valued so low," Dare complained, but his eyes said something else, something connected to love and kisses that deprived Mara of wits and speech.

Thank heavens Miles Cavanagh broke the moment. "That's the trouble with going to auction at the wrong market, Dare. Always make sure there'll be competing bidders, even if you have to provide them yourself."

"Then bring in some maids," Dare commanded.

"Or hold the auction again at Almack's," Francis suggested.

Mara took Dare's arm in a possessive way. "A deal is a deal. Isn't it, Mr. Cavanagh?"

The ladies applauded, and a grinning Miles said, "It is, indeed. You're bought and done for, Dare."

"For now, at least," Mara said, finally enjoying herself. "After all, a lady can always change her mind."

Dare sighed. "I'm devastated. Even at a *farthing* you think I might be overpriced?"

"There are certainly horses like that," Mara said. "Aren't there, Mr. Cavanagh?"

"No more of this Mr. Cavanagh, Mara, but you're right. Ask Francis about Banshee."

Lord Middlethorpe gave a smiling grimace and told a story of an ill-formed but speedy horse he'd purchased from Miles in order to trick Serena's brothers and get her jewelry back. Dinner was announced and he finished the story as they sat.

"Couldn't walk for a week," he said, but smiled at Serena by his side. "Worth every ache and pain."

Talk became general, and Dare said, "Couldn't you at least have set my value at sixpence?"

"But it is above rubies."

Their eyes locked and Mara wondered if they might kiss, but then they had to concentrate on soup. Mara listened to lively conversation, appreciating the relaxed friendship around her. The Rogues were not alike, but they behaved like the best sort of family — loving and accepting. Stephen and Leander even got into a political argument about Austrian policies without disrupting harmony.

At the same time Mara noticed how little Dare spoke, and how lightly he ate. A stranger would detect nothing amiss, but she did, and she was sure the Rogues were as aware and as protectively concerned. She also recognized what a burden this put upon him.

They all needed him to be healed, which meant to be the person he'd been before Waterloo, but it was like expecting him to be a performing monkey. Or expecting a corpse to revive.

She realized she'd hardly touched her food and ate before her plate was taken away and the next course put on the table.

Discussion of Hal and Blanche's situation held off until the meal was finished and the servants dismissed. Port and Madeira circulated along with nuts and small cakes, and Nicholas said, "I give over rule of this meeting to Labellelle."

Laura smiled at him. "Matters of acceptance in society are women's work, yes, and I'm the one with the most experience. The first foray will take place at Almack's on Wednesday."

"They'll never let Blanche in," St. Raven objected. "Not even under an armed escort of Rogues."

"Of course not," Laura said, "and she has

no interest in attending. But it will be the perfect place to introduce the subject."

"In what way?" St. Raven was clearly skeptical.

Nicholas answered. "Those present can make it an assumption that Mrs. Hal Beaumont is part of the ton, and that many people of significance would be offended if she were offered any insult."

St. Raven shook his head. "You Rogues have influence, but you don't have that kind of weight among the bastions of the *haut volée.*"

"But we can recruit," Nicholas said. "Various dukes, for example. Why else are you here? But also Arran, Yeovil, and Belcraven. Above all, however," he added, with the air of a silent drum roll, "we have the Dowager Countess of Cawle."

St. Raven whistled. "She'll do it?"

"She's Hal's godmother."

St. Raven laughed and raised his glass in a toast. "You Rogues. Do you have the Regent in your pocket?"

"Too fat and too much trouble."

"You really are impossible."

"Who is the Dowager Countess of Cawle?" Mara asked Dare.

"One of the quieter rulers of society. Whom she approves is approved. Whom she disdains is cast into the dark."

"Why does she have such power?"

"Probably because she can get away with it."

The others were running through names of people they could bring to support the cause. The Grevilles, the Burleighs, the Dunpott-Ffyfes, the Lennoxes.

"After Almack's," Laura said, "Blanche and Hal will appear at some friendly ton events, well escorted by Rogues, and we'll persuade Blanche to go around with some of us ladies now and then. The grand assault will be a ball at Marlowe House as soon as Simon and Jancy are ready to host it."

"How's the gas situation, Simon?" Nicholas asked.

"We'll have it sorted out in a couple of weeks."

Jancy, who'd been quiet throughout the meal, looked guilty.

"We're not short of ballrooms," St. Raven said. "I have one. So does Yeovil House."

"I want to do it," Simon stated. "Hal was my friend in need in Canada and helped get us all home safe. And besides, Marlowe — both houses and the title — carries such an aura of classic propriety it could bleach out the blackest scandal."

Simon wasn't taking Jancy's fears into account, but there was no point in arguing. Jancy would walk over hot coals if Simon wanted it.

Everything settled, the ladies moved to the drawing room for tea, still talking social strategy like generals before a battle. Felicity had no patience with the subject and sat to play the piano, surprisingly well, for she seemed a tomboy.

Mara decided to make some suggestions. After all, as she'd said, the finer nuances of society were no different in Lincolnshire than in London. Her ideas were taken well.

Conversation changed when Eleanor's infant was brought to her for feeding. Mara was startled, even though Eleanor managed it neatly beneath a large Norwich shawl. Babies were sometimes fed in public at Brideswell, but only before family.

But then, as she'd thought, the Rogues were a family, one to which she would soon belong. The simple bliss of that cast her into silence until the men came to join them.

CHAPTER 21

Mara studied Dare. It was getting late, but he seemed all right. She was about to join him when Nicholas said, "So, Mara, have you decided what bead suits me?"

She balked. "And if I choose not to?"

"Why would you do that?"

Why indeed? "Because Francis objected to my choice."

"I was only teasing," Francis said, surprised. "I'm sorry, Mara."

"I know that." This was getting worse and worse, but something about Nicholas Delaney set her on edge.

"So," he demanded.

Flint, Mara thought, close to tears.

"Nick."

Dare spoke only the one word, but it shot through the room like lightning.

Nicholas's brows rose a little. "Didn't mean to tease." He turned to his wife. "Eleanor, of course, is a pink pearl."

"Wretch!" his wife protested, and told Mara about a string of pink pearls that Nicholas had given her and that she'd given to her brother. Mara wasn't sure she followed the reasoning, but the story smoothed over the moment and conversation moved on.

Mara went to Dare's side feeling quivery. Perhaps his intervention hadn't been significant, but it had felt like a champion waving a sword, declaring that he would protect his lady.

His lady.

"Thank you," she said.

"Nick's playing some sort of game."

"Why?"

"He can't help it. Don't let him irritate you."

An edge of irritation in Dare told Mara that his calm was a thin veneer. He'd rescued her and it was for her to rescue him. She flashed a look at Jancy, who announced that she was tired and they all took their leave.

Dare spoke little in the coach back to Yeovil House and, after brief good nights, disappeared. Mara was grateful that Jancy and Simon were keen to retire to their own room because she couldn't have born idle conversation.

As Ruth helped her prepare for bed, Mara chattered about Rogues because that was what Ruth would expect. When she was finally alone, however, she sighed with blessed relief.

Lord! Only imagine liking being alone.

Of course she wanted not to be alone. She wanted to be with Dare. She pushed that out of her mind and took her beads out of a drawer. She laid them all out on the desk and studied them as if they, like Jancy's cards, could give insight.

She rolled the green jade. A simple stone for a simple man, Miles. She'd liked him for his uncomplicated good nature.

Leander, the sophisticated malachite, she wasn't so sure of. He had exquisite manners, but there was something distant about him. Reserved, perhaps. She liked his wife, and perhaps a man could be judged by the woman who loved him.

Stephen, the blue agate, made her nervous, but that could simply be his reputation. Laura Ball, a perfect jewel herself, had made him seem a little less awe-inspiring when she'd complained that he often became so wrapped up in parliamentary matters that he forgot to eat and which day of the week it was.

Francis, despite his poetic looks, was

sturdy jasper.

Nicholas? She studied her beads — amber, tiger eye. She was looking at those because of his eyes. She ended up rolling the topaz one between her fingers. Dare, glowing, golden, as he once had been, as he had been at times this evening, and at others. So briefly, like a fire struggling to stay alight but occasionally sending up flames.

She picked up her netted purse and shook out the coins. There. A farthing, a small brown coin, a mere quarter of a penny that did not reflect in any way the value of Dare in her eyes. But then, what could? She owned no rubies, and a full necklace of them wouldn't be enough.

She wanted to take it to him now, but looked at the clock and saw how late it was.

No. Better keep it until the safe sanity of daylight.

"If you carry on this way, Miss Mara, I'm sending for your mother!" Ruth protested.

Mara lay in bed, dull with lack of sleep. Being good and not hunting down Dare hadn't helped. Instead, her mind had run over and over the night before like . . . yes, like geese stampeding across a graveyard.

The look in Dare's eyes when she purchased him.

Farthings and rubies.

The way he'd stopped Nicholas Delaney's teasing, like a sword raised.

The rights and wrongs of wanting him to be the man he'd been before.

That gift of silk, which she didn't understand.

She opened her eyes to find Ruth studying her anxiously. "I think I drank too much wine. I have a headache."

"Well, really, what a foolish thing to do." But Ruth had returned to ordinary fretfulness. "I'll be off then to make my tonic."

Mara closed her eyes again and groaned. Ruth's tonics were foul, but they did no harm. Unlike opium. She hadn't learned more about it. Today she must speak to Mr. Feng.

She sat up just as Ruth returned. "Oh. You're up, then."

"Yes, and feeling much better."

Ruth brought over the glass. "Best to drink this anyway, milady. Especially when I've gone to the trouble of making it."

Mara downed the tisane with only a slight shudder. Not as awful as some. "Thank you, Ruth. I'll have breakfast now."

Mara glanced at the clock as she climbed out of bed. It was nearly nine o'clock! No wonder Ruth had been worried. She never slept in except after a late event like a ball.

What was planned for today? Whatever it was, it would only be a nuisance, a distraction from Dare. What a bother it was that she could no longer pester him into taking her on long carriage journeys. She desperately needed to be alone with him. At least they wouldn't be moving to Marlowe House yet, thanks be to gas.

She checked her appointment book and saw that she'd noted Dare's promise to take her to see the volcano. Perhaps she'd remind him. Almack's tomorrow.

Once, her first visit to that holy of holies would have been the moon and stars to her, but now it shone only as the place where she might first dance with Dare. Dance properly, in public, to music.

The various meanings of "proper" drifted her into memories both sweet and sharp until eagle-eyed Ruth returned with breakfast. To distract her, Mara said, "We need to decide what I should wear to Almack's."

"Something pale, milady."

"Virtuous and maidenly?"

"Which you are, milady."

"Alas and alack."

"Miss Mara!"

Mara gathered her wits. "Sorry. I was only teasing, Ruth." She sat to pour chocolate.

"So I'd think," Ruth scolded, and went

into one of her rants on the wickedness of men but Mara was trying to remember who'd said that, about only teasing.

Nicholas Delaney. After Dare had stepped in to defend her.

When people said they were only teasing it was rarely true. Had King Rogue deliberately needled her to stir that response from Dare?

"Eat something, milady."

Mara started and realized she'd only sipped at the chocolate. She buttered a piece of toast and took a bite. Was Nicholas on her side? Could he offer her good advice about Dare?

"So which one, milady?"

Ruth had draped three pale ball gowns over the bed. Mara glanced at them. "The pink."

"Very well, milady. With your pearls you'll look a proper young lady. Would that you lived up to it."

"Ruth, stop it!"

The maid turned red. "Stop what, milady?"

"Stop . . . stop *poking* at me. Anyone would think I'm the sort of hoyden who chased officers in the street and showed her garters."

"I'm sure I never would . . ." But then

Ruth burst out, "You're just not yourself, milady! And it all started when I helped you with that mad start of slipping out at night. I don't know how you ever got me to agree. You've been peculiar ever since. And here! Since we came here, it's been worse. You didn't . . . you didn't do something foolish, did you?"

"Of course I did." But then Mara realized what Ruth was asking. "What? No! Heavens, no. The truth is, I'm in love. I'm in love with Lord Darius." She smiled, but Ruth clasped her hands.

"Oh, I was afeared of that. What your poor parents will say!"

"They'll be delighted."

"To have you mooning over an opium addict from *Somerset?*"

The emphasis made Mara laugh, if a bit wildly. "We'll live near Brideswell, I promise." She still hadn't talked to Dare about that.

"That's something, I suppose, but —"

"And he will soon be free of the drug. You're not to say anything to anyone about the engagement, though. Not until we've had a chance to speak to Father."

"At least you're doing something as you should there, milady," Ruth said, still looking as if there'd been a death in the family.

"I will say as Lord Darius is very well thought of in this house."

"Of course he is. He's wonderful. Perfect, in fact."

Ruth rolled her eyes. "Ah well, I always knew you'd make a strange choice, with the hair an' all. And if he's free to live near home, that's something. We'll all be able to keep an eye on him."

Mara bit back a protest. It was true. Even if she married the most innocuous man in England, everyone in the area around Brideswell would keep an eye on her husband's behavior.

Ruth began to put the gowns away and Mara considered what to do with her day. Should she find Dare and discuss the matter of where they would live?

For some reason that made her nervous. She wasn't ready to raise that subject. In fact, she'd like some fresh air. "Go and see if Lady Austrey would like to go for a walk," she told Ruth.

"They're out, milady."

"So early?"

"Something to do with Marlowe House."

"Oh." Did that mean a hastening of the move? Mara hated that, but could do nothing about it. "Then you will accompany me, Ruth."

"Very well, milady."

Mara found immediate relief in fresh air. Yeovil House had become oppressive, but it wasn't the air, it was her knowledge. The house felt permeated with dark and heavy drama.

She walked briskly toward St. James's Park, grateful now that Jancy hadn't been available. With Ruth, she didn't need to talk and could plan her strategy. When she returned, she would request an appointment with Mr. Feng. He might be able to suggest ways in which she could help Dare and warn her away from doing harm.

Was it useful to persuade Dare into activities, for example, or was he better left alone? Was Castle Cruel an amusement, or might it stir foul memories? Was her cheerfulness a blessing or a burden?

She knew how to navigate society, but not how to work her way through these shadows. Her life had not been entirely free of sorrows, but they had all been the common ones of life, such as the death of her beloved Grandfather Baddersley when she was six, and of her baby sister, Alice, eight years ago.

They'd all worried about Simon, away so long and involved in war, but he'd returned home safely. They'd not known, thank heavens, about the duel and the wound that had almost killed him until it was all history.

Ignorance could be bliss, but it wouldn't help her now.

"Lady Mara!"

She'd been so deep in thought that it took her a moment to realize that they'd encountered Major Berkstead and he had spoken to her. Now he blocked her way, eyes intent. *Oh, please no.*

She probably should cut him dead, but couldn't bring herself to be so cruel. "Major," she said coolly, and walked on.

He fell into step beside her. "Dearest lady."

Ruth had fallen behind, but Mara only had to send her a look to have her interfere. What a scene that might be, however. It wasn't as if she was in danger in St. James's Park. It was dotted with people and in moments they would be walking by the spot where milkmaids sold milk fresh from the cows. A half dozen people were gathered there.

"May I buy you a syllabub?" Berkstead asked, in a tone more suited to an offer of death in the cause.

"No, thank you, Major. In fact, I must return home. I am expected."

Mara walked faster, hating feeling nervous. He matched her speed without effort. "I will escort you, dear lady." He lowered his voice. "This is the first time in too long that we've had an opportunity to speak privately."

Mara looked straight ahead. "We have no need to speak privately, Major."

His voice became softer still. "Ah, your maid — she is your guard? You will be punished? Then slip out of the house, my beloved. I am always on watch."

Mara stopped to stare at him. "Always on watch? Whatever do you mean?"

Ruth was alert now, looking ready to act.

"Can you think I would abandon you to oppression? Slip out of the house at the back, my beloved. I will set you free." He strode away, leaving Mara gaping.

Ruth came to her side. "What was he on about, milady?"

"Nothing, but . . ." Mara wasn't going to relate such madness to Ruth. But she hurried back to Yeovil House, eager now to be inside its strong walls.

Always on watch? It made her skin crawl. Then she thought of the mysterious gift of silk. Had that been from *him?* He could have followed her to the warehouse and asked Mr. Lee about something she'd admired. In that note, the giver had said she should make a night robe of it.

She'd burn it. She should have known Dare would never think that blowsy design to her taste.

She hurried into Yeovil House, knowing she must tell Simon about Berkstead, but she winced at the thought. She'd almost rather tell Father, even if it meant telling him all.

"Mara, what is it?"

She was so far away, she almost fainted at coming face-to-face with Dare.

"Nothing." She laughed shakily. "Just seeing you."

His brows rose, but he said, "You have a similar oversetting effect on me."

She laughed again, for happiness.

He looked so much the ordinary English gentleman. Well, never ordinary, but his expression was relaxed, his complexion healthy, and his clothes were the gentleman's casual uniform of dark blue jacket, buckskin breeches, fawn waistcoat, and top boots. He was carrying hat, crop, and whip.

"You've been riding," she said, delighted.

He passed the things to a footman. "I purchased a new Conqueror yesterday. Would you like to see him?"

"Yes, of course."

She let Ruth go and walked with Dare

toward the back of the house. "How many Conquerors have there been?"

"Four. The last came to grief at Waterloo. Poor horses. Our strife is nothing to do with them. We should fight our wars on foot."

"And rulers who start a war should lead their armies to battle," Mara said.

"Napoleon did," he said.

"Are you admiring the monster?"

"Merely stating a fact," Dare said as they went through a door into the servants' area. "But he abandoned his army in Russia. Probably necessary, but still vile."

Mara glanced around. "I think I remember this corridor."

"Shush."

She pressed against him in a deliberately flirtatious way.

"Do you want to be ravished in a store cupboard, wench?"

She pressed even closer. "Yes, please."

He laughed and steered her toward a back door she also remembered. The sleeping alcove was now empty.

"Perhaps when we're married?" she murmured as they went outside.

"Then your wicked wish will always be my command."

Wicked wishes rippled over her so fiercely that she could imagine her hair standing on end. "I can hardly wait."

He touched her back to move her through the small area of herbs and vegetables toward a gate into the ornamental garden. More wickedness shot out from that fleeting contact. If they stopped beneath a tree for a kiss, could anyone see them?

Mara glanced up at windows. Probably. But she kissed him anyway, a brief touch of lips to lips, a look from eye to eye that transformed the London garden to Eden.

Smiling, they linked arms and strolled on. This is what our life will be, Mara thought. Walking through gardens. Visiting a new horse in the stables. One day there would be children by their side. Very soon, in fact. They would have Pierre and Delphie.

"Are the children riding yet?"

"A little. For a long time they wouldn't go far from my bedside, but Thea was very good with them. She coaxed them outside, and then to the stables to get used to horses. Once I could go there with them, they began lessons."

They entered the mews where a magnificent gray was being rubbed down.

"He's splendid," Mara said.

"One of Miles Cavanagh's."

"Oh, that reminds me." With a smile she found the farthing in her pocket and presented it to him. "To fix my purchase, my lord."

He considered it, then slipped it into a fob pocket, but he held out his hand, palm up. "We should slap hands."

"Slap hands?"

"To seal the deal."

Mara took off her glove and slapped his palm. "Does that mean you're completely mine now, bought and sealed?"

He'd captured her hand and raised it for a kiss, his eyes warm on hers. "So it would seem. I am your slave for life."

She tightened her fingers around his. "I mean to hold you to that."

The horse's shifting hooves reminded them where they were. They moved apart, fighting smiles.

"He's a hunter," Dare said. "Will you object to spending time in the Shires next winter?"

She smiled at him again. "Not at all, even though ladies aren't allowed to hunt."

"Are you saying you'd want to?"

"Are you saying you'd let me?" she parried.

"You own me, not the other way around, but you've always been squeamish. You didn't even like to fish."

She pulled a face at the memory. "You all

teased me about it."

"Boys will be boys."

Mara slapped at a fly that buzzed around her face.

"Aha," he said. "A bloodthirsty creature after all."

She searched for any hint of battle horrors, but he seemed topaz bright. "I'll kill a fly and even a wasp if I have to. And ruthlessly attack unborn moths."

They moved closer to admire Conqueror, which preened at the attention. Mara could see the horse was already devoted to Dare. "I brought Godiva to Town, but haven't had a ride yet."

"Then we must," he said as they strolled out of the stable. "Tell me, fair lady, do you ride her naked?"

Mara swatted at him. "Godiva, sir, is the horse, and thus always naked."

His brows rose. "You ride her bareback?"

"No, but a saddle doesn't cover — Oh —" She broke off, red-faced. "This is a ridiculous conversation!"

He laughed, and she laughed, too, for pure pleasure at his wicked teasing.

"We could ride tomorrow," he said.

"Lovely. When?"

"Ten?"

"Nine," she countered. "Rides should be early."

"Eight, then."

"Seven?"

His eyes danced. "Mara, Mara, you'll never win that sort of challenge. Eight will be early enough."

She laughed again, not caring if the world heard her love in it. "Eight it is."

By silent accord they didn't return directly to the house but walked down the lane to the street. He took her hand, skin to skin, and the simple contact carried astonishing power. Didn't they speak of handfasting? Now, weaving her fingers with his, she understood why. Flesh to flesh entwined like the honeysuckle that tumbled over a wall here.

"This could almost be in the country," she said, looking at the plants that flourished where hooves and wheels never reached. She paused to inhale the sweet scent of all flowers. She looked at him. "We should go to Brideswell to talk to Father."

His jaw tightened and he looked away. "I won't marry you while addicted, Mara."

"When will you be absolutely free? How long before you can be sure? How long before we can be open about our love?"

"Months, at least."

She opened her mouth to argue, but switched her ground. "I at least want my father's consent. As soon as possible. I mean it, Dare."

He looked at her with love, but a touch of despair. "What if your parents don't agree?"

She took his hand. "They will. When?"

After a moment, he said, "We're committed to Almack's and then the ball at Marlowe House. After that, whenever you wish."

Mara realized she could raise the subject of where they'd live. Still holding his hand, she said, "Dare, I've been assuming that we will have a house close to Brideswell. A place in Town as well, but . . . Is that what you want?"

What was she going to do if he said no?

"Move a St. Bride away from their hive?" he said. "A crime against nature."

"Oh. I thought you might think . . . because Simon . . ."

"Simon doesn't have the same bond, but if he could, his country home would be there rather than at Marlowe. Brideswell is a special place, Mara. Perhaps I'm only marrying you for that."

"Perhaps I'm only marrying you to become a Rogue."

He laughed, and they came together for a kiss.

Suddenly, he pulled her hard against him in a fierce, famished kiss. She wanted to return it wildly, but they were in a public place. She broke free to gasp, "Dare, stop!"

He wrenched back from her, looking shocked.

But then she realized someone had dragged him away from her. Dare whirled — to face Major Berkstead.

"You cur!" Berkstead roared and swung a fist.

Though off-balance, Dare slid by it. "Stop it, you madman —" He blocked the next fist with his arm and again turned so that Berkstead stumbled, but the man threw himself back into attack, red-faced and mad-eyed.

Dare punched Berkstead in the chest. The man staggered back, wheezing, but managed to grab Dare's jacket. They both tumbled to the ground.

"Stop it!" Mara screamed, but then realized Berkstead wouldn't and Dare couldn't. She looked around frantically, but no one seemed to be coming to help.

Berkstead grabbed a stick, a bit of tree limb as thick as Mara's arm and swung it at Dare's head. Dare rolled away and to his feet with the fluidity Mara had seen in the ballroom. He was focused now in the same way, but he let Berkstead struggle to his feet.

Berkstead showed his teeth and swung the stick, then attacked again. Mara wasn't at all surprised when Dare kicked it out of Berkstead's hand and, almost in the same movement, punched him in the belly. When Berkstead staggered back, however, Dare kept going, landing another ferocious blow on the man's body. And another.

"Dare, stop!"

People were running toward the fight now — grooms from the stables, someone behind from the street, but they were too far away. Berkstead was glassy-eyed, but Dare still attacked.

Mara picked up the stick and whacked Dare hard across his back.

He whirled, smashing the stick from her hands with one fist, the other moving toward her, hard-edged as a blade.

He stopped dead, ashen with horror. "Mara?"

She'd flinched, but she said, "It's all right. I'm all right. I couldn't let you kill him."

She reached for him, but he turned away, slowly, clumsily to where Berkstead leaned heavily against a wall, clutching his body, blood pouring from his nose. Three grooms ran to him, shooting astonished and nervous glances at Dare. On the street side, two older gentlemen had paused, seeing that the action was over, but they were staring, too.

It could only have been minutes. Less than a minute, even.

Mara took Dare's arm. "Thank you. For protecting me." He was still pale and she could feel tremors running through him. "Come along. Come back to the house."

He shrugged her off. "Is he badly hurt?" he asked the grooms.

"Maybe cracked ribs, milord —"

Berkstead wheezed. "You're a madman. You should be locked away. First you attacked a lady, then me."

"He did not attack me!" Mara spat. "It's you who is mad."

"Kiss him in the street of your own free will, did you?"

"Yes. We're to marry."

Berkstead's angry color bleached. "No."

She'd spilled the secret before witnesses, but what else could she have done? "Yes," she said, loudly and firmly.

"Assist him back to his rooms and do whatever's needed," Dare told the grooms. "Come."

He put an arm around Mara and drew her back toward the mews and the house. Faint tremors still ran through his body, and she probably trembled, too. At her words, Berkstead's expression had turned to one of deadly hate.

Mara couldn't have chattered to save her life. Her heart still raced and her breath came shortly, but it was something about Dare that silenced her.

He stopped in the garden behind the house. "Why was Berkstead there?"

"What?"

"Why was Berkstead in the lane? Why did he think he had the right to protect you?"

"*What?*" Mara repeated. "The man's an idiot! He believes he's in love with me. He believes I'm in love with him."

"Not surprising when you gallivant in the night with him."

"A mistake. I admit it. I've told him clearly —"

"You've been meeting him?"

Mara's rare anger burst into flame. She shoved him. "Don't make this my fault. It would have been nothing if you'd not turned into a killer." At the look on his face, she said, "No. No, Dare, I didn't mean that. . . ."

But he'd already turned and was striding toward the house.

She ran after. "Don't. Don't walk away from me like this." She grabbed for his arm. "Stop!"

He whirled, wrenching free. "Leave me alone."

The cold force of his words froze her and she could only watch as he disappeared into the house.

She realized she was crying when a scullery maid came out with a bucket of slops and stopped to stare. Mara pulled herself together as best she could and turned into the house and up to her bedroom, where she sat, shivering and hugging herself.

When someone knocked on the door, she didn't know how much time had passed. She went to open it, unsure whether she wanted it to be Dare or not.

It was Jancy, looking worried. "Are you all right?"

Mara tried for her normal manner. "Yes, of course. Why?"

Jancy came in and shut the door. "Because Dare told Simon he can't marry you and then refused to say anything else."

"What?" Mara rose, but the room whirled around her and she had to grab on to a chair for support. "I have to speak to him!"

"Not yet," Jancy said, putting an arm around her. "Sit back down. I'm sure he didn't mean it."

Mara let Jancy settle her on the sofa near the fire, wishing she were sure of that. He'd spoken so roughly, so coldly. Her misery was too deep for tears.

"What happened?" Jancy asked. "We heard about a fight in the mews lane and Dare almost killing someone."

"It was horrible. Berkstead attacked Dare."

"Why?"

"Because the man's mad. We were kissing. . . . Dare tried to reason with him. . . . Do you know he uses a kind of fighting to combat the opium?"

"No. What do you mean?"

Mara explained what she'd seen, though not the whole of her nighttime adventures. "He's so strong and fast. I thought he'd kill Berkstead, so I walloped him with a stick. And he turned on me."

For the first time, Mara realized that her hands stung, that she had some scrapes from when the stick had flown from her grip.

Jancy looked at the marks. "Did he hurt you in any other way?"

"No, of course not." But then Mara said, "Almost . . ."

"Are you afraid of him?"

"Of course not. I'm a little afraid of what he can do. And of his anger. I don't remember him ever getting angry with anyone. Before."

"You probably never saw him when he was attacked."

"No one would have had reason to attack him back then."

"So why did Berkstead attack him today?"

Mara blushed. "Probably because we were kissing." She sighed and told Jancy about the theater and the silk, and the content of the message in Chinese.

"Mara, you should have told Simon days ago!"

"I only just realized the truth of the silk, and I will never risk another duel."

Jancy covered her mouth with her hand.

"See? I didn't tell Dare for the same reason, and because he has enough to worry about. I thought it would blow over. I never imagined that Berkstead would cling to this obsession when I steadfastly discouraged him. Now everything's ruined!"

"No, it isn't. It will sort out."

Mara shook her head. "I ripped up at Dare and now he hates me."

"Hates you? That's impossible."

"I told him he'd turned into a killer."

"Lord above, why?"

"Because I was so furious at him. For accusing me of sneaking out to meet Berkstead. And because he did. Turn into a killer. But I wouldn't have said it if I hadn't lost my temper."

"I didn't know you had a temper," Jancy said.

"I have the hair." Mara sighed. "Hardly anything ever happens to make me angry, but yes, I have a temper, and now I've ruined everything."

Jancy stood. "I'm going to order hot, sweet tea, and talk to Simon. Stay here and don't do anything else stupid."

Mara decided that taking off her hat and pelisse wasn't stupid and did so. She washed her hand in cold water, dabbing at the scrapes. She wasn't afraid of Dare, not really, but she didn't like the trapped violence in him. It wasn't part of the real Dare.

And she was still furious that he'd leapt to such vile conclusions. She saw her plan of the layout of Castle Cruel and tore it up, tossing the bits on the fire.

Then she burst into tears. She was still sniffling when Jancy returned, accompanied by Simon, carrying the tea tray. Simon did not look pleased.

Jancy poured tea and Simon waited until Mara had drunk some before speaking. "Jancy's told me about this Berkstead. You doubtless went beyond the line to encourage him to such folly."

Mara blushed and prayed he never knew how far beyond the line.

"I'll make it very clear to him that he'd better stay away from you."

"You won't call him out," Mara said.

Simon glanced at Jancy. "It would take a lot to get me to another duel. If he won't bend to pressure from me, I'll pile on Rogues until he buckles."

Mara accepted another cup of tea. "What about Dare?"

Simon grimaced. "He's not available and I can hardly force my way into his bedroom."

"I wish you could. I worry."

"So do I, but he has Salter and Feng Ruyuan."

"When you do see him," Mara said, "tell him I will not be jilted."

"Are you sure?" he asked. "That you want to marry him?"

"You don't trust him, Simon?"

"Yes, but it won't be easy."

"I don't want easy." Mara sighed. "Yes, I do, for Dare, for both of us, and we will have that one day, but if I must struggle to get there, so be it. But I do hope we can leave London soon. I want to get him to Brideswell. When will this ball for Hal and

Blanche be held?"

"It will take a week or so to extract the pipes and clean up the mess."

"I was being silly," Jancy said. "You said there's no gas flowing through those pipes anymore, so there's no need to rip them all out. We could move there today."

"No!" Mara protested. Quickly, she found a reason. "There's Almack's tomorrow."

"What has Almack's to do with it?" Simon demanded. "You can attend from Marlowe House as well as from here."

"There are preparations. Jancy and I need to rest. A hairdresser is to come." Then Mara found a reason that made sense. "We can't leave now. It will look as if we've fled Dare."

He pushed a hand through his hair. "I suppose you're right. On Thursday, then. But we can send out invitations for next week, and begin preparations."

"Less than a week for a ball?" Mara said.

"Musicians, food, wine. What else is needed?"

She rolled her eyes. "This is a London ball, Simon, not a hop with the neighbors."

"Do you want to get Dare to Brideswell or not?"

Mara gathered herself. "Yes, yes, of course. It can be done."

"It can?" Jancy asked weakly. "We'll have a poor attendance, however."

"For the first ball at Marlowe House in years, with hints of a scandal attached? It will be a crush."

Mara ignored Jancy's moan. "I'll do most of it, and the Rogues will help. The house is in perfect condition. You'll need more staff, but probably the Rogues can lend some. Better than bringing in strangers. For enough money the food and wine can be produced overnight. The same applies to decorations. Fresh flowers. Masses of them. For enough money, almost anything can be achieved overnight."

Jancy gave a pained squeak.

"Cost is irrelevant in this case," Simon said. "Sorry, Jancy, but it is."

Jancy pulled a face, but said, "Yes, of course. I'll probably wince all the time, but I agree."

"You don't need to see a single bill." Mara put down her teacup. "We'll start planning immediately and order invitations engraved. That, too, will need special speed. Simon, you can leave this with us for now." When he reached the door, however, she couldn't stop herself from adding, "If . . . when you see Dare, please tell him that I must speak to him."

CHAPTER 22

Dare, however, might as well not be living in the house at all. After lunch, Mara visited the schoolroom and found the children unhappy because he'd sent a message to say he wouldn't be able to visit them again that day.

Where had he gone?

A busy day was a mercy, but through it all — a visit to Marlowe House to confer with senior staff, to Fortnum and Mason, to the printers and vintners, then to a florist — Mara was never free of worry about Dare. She needed to see him so badly it was a deep ache.

That night she crept through the house but caught no trace of him, and in the morning, she asked Ruth if he'd left.

"Not as far as I know, milady."

"But are you sure?" Mara was suddenly certain that Dare had fled. She'd never imagined that people could sense the presence of others in this way, but she was convinced. "Go and ask."

Ruth made a prune face but she went away and returned in a while with the news that yes, Lord Darius had spent the night elsewhere, but had recently returned. "Now can we decide what you'll wear today, milady?"

"I don't care."

With a scowl, Ruth produced a plain blue dress that was years old. Mara had only brought it to London in case she should end up helping Ella in some menial task. She didn't complain, however. It suited her mood. If Dare was determined to avoid her, how could she mend their shattered situation? She didn't even bother with the corset she didn't need. In this gown, no one would know.

When she went to Jancy's parlor to ask Simon for help, he told her to leave Dare alone, even adding, "You've done enough damage."

She burst into tears and he fled with the excuse that Marlowe House must be ready for them the next day. That made Mara cry even more. Jancy tried to comfort and reassure her, but then even she lost patience and deserted her. Mara didn't blame her. She'd hardly ever cried since being a child, but now, sprawled against the arm of the sofa, she couldn't stop.

"Mara?"

She looked up. Dare stood there, somber. No, anguished.

She gulped, sniffed, straightened, and tried for a smile. "Don't worry. I'm all right." Tears kept leaking, however, and she brushed them away.

He sat on the sofa and took her in his arms. "No, you're not, and it's all my fault."

She pushed back to look him in the eye. "If you say things like that, I'll cry again."

"You're still crying now," he pointed out, wiping tears with his thumbs. "My dearest Mara, what am I to do?"

"Say that again."

"What am I to do?"

He was teasing, which stopped her tears like a plug.

"My dearest Mara," he repeated, but he rested his forehead against hers. "Don't you see that I'm like a bad horse? You are fond of me and I of you, but I could still hurt you."

She drew him closer, held him tight. "You are not, could never be, a bad anything. As for hurt, you hurt me by disappearing, by trying to end our betrothal. No pain could ever equal that, Dare. Except your death."

"I almost hit you."

"But you didn't. And you thought I was another assailant."

His eyes didn't waver. "I could have killed you. I've trained in these things. It helps me to fight the opium, but —"

She touched his lips. "I know. I sneaked into the musicians' gallery three nights ago. You're dangerous, but Feng Ruyuan could kill you in a moment."

He laughed slightly. "True enough."

She stroked his hair. "Do you mind? That I spied on you? I meant no harm. I simply care too much not to."

"If we are to do this, I want you to know all about me."

She cradled his face, cherishing his cheeks with her thumbs. "I know all I need to know."

She pressed her lips to his, but then he took over, kissing her slowly, then deeply, then as hotly as he'd kissed her in the lane. They were alone now, private now, and she had no reservations. When his hand brushed her breast, she captured it and pressed it there.

She saw his reaction when he realized she wasn't wearing a corset. She felt her nipple harden against his palm.

"Jancy's not going to come back," she

whispered. "Show me more of this. Please. If you love me, please . . ."

With a sigh and a groan, he began to rub his hand gently over her breast, sending ripples of pleasure through her. She pressed her hips closer. "That's wonderful."

He pushed her sleeves off her shoulders, freeing her breasts to cool air, then to his hot mouth.

Mara melted against the sofa, liquid, languid, and yet fiercely burning, hands clutching at him, stroking him, loving him. She slid hands inside his jacket, kneading his flesh, and met his hungry mouth in another famished kiss.

When he moved over her, she felt the hard ridge of him and arched against it, driven mad by his clever mouth, by his weight, his scent, his heat. She spread her legs, urging him between her thighs. "I need you. I need you now, Dare. Now."

But he drew back. "Mara, this is wrong."

She grabbed his shirt. When had his jacket and waistcoat gone? When had she untied his cravat and tossed it on the carpet?

"We're as good as married. Don't stop now. I can't bear it if you stop now!"

He gathered her into his arms — "hush, hush" — and slid his hand up under her skirt and between her thighs. She opened wider, and when he pressed there, she laughed into his shoulder for the sweetness of it.

In moments she was lost, feverishly swimming in ecstasy, clutching, nibbling, kissing. He caught her cries in a kiss, as the sharpest pleasure she'd ever known shot through her again and again and again.

She might have passed out. Certainly when she became aware of hot sweat and thudding heart, time seemed to have passed. She opened her eyes to look up at him.

Various words came to mind but all seemed inadequate, so she spoke to him with kisses and with touch, trying to tell him that way how much she loved him and what pleasure she'd felt.

She longed for more, to belong to him more deeply still, but she saw he couldn't allow himself that yet. She could wait until her wedding night. For now, she would cherish him in every other way she could, pressing close, stroking his hair, murmuring her love, sensing his pleasure in these simple things.

Eventually, he stirred. "I don't know how Jancy is keeping the world at bay, but we should relieve her of duty." He pulled up her bodice and straightened it.

"Oh, good Lord!" Mara was suddenly

plunged back into the real world. She fussed at herself, then at him. "I ripped your shirt!" But then she was distracted by his beautiful, muscular chest, kissing it, licking it, tasting his sweat. . . .

A shudder ran through him, but he pushed her away. "You enchant me. Literally. I shouldn't have done this. We shouldn't have done this."

"Yes, we should, and if you're powerless before my magic, we'll do it again. Soon." She reached for him, half in jest. Laughing, he escaped to stand, to fasten his torn shirt and look for his other clothes.

Mara stood to restore her own clothing, but mostly she watched Dare, loving the intimacy of the moment. He put on his waistcoat and found his cravat, then peered into the small mirror on one wall as he did skillful things to it.

"Why don't men just knot a cloth around their necks as they used to?" she asked.

"I don't know why we wear such things at all." He finished, pulled on his jacket, and turned to her. "Do I pass muster?"

She went to fiddle with his clothing, mostly because she wanted to. Then she turned for inspection. "What about me?"

"Remarkably in order. And," he added, stroking her bodice, "there is nothing at all lacking about your breasts."

Heat rushed into her cheeks, but it was a flush of pleasure. "You don't mind? That they're small?"

"My dear idiot." He offered an arm. "If we're to retain a scrap of sanity, we must leave this room."

Mara took it, but she asked, "Are you all right now? You know you could never hurt me?"

"On the contrary," he said, "I'm sure I will. But as little as possible. That I vow."

Mara had hoped all the shadows were gone, but she tried not to show disappointment as they stepped out into the corridor. There was no sign of Jancy. No sign of anyone, in fact.

"The world has come to an end?" he asked.

"It's certainly changed, but this house is often like this. It's why I've been tempted to wander in the night."

"Wander as you will, my love, but by the time we return home tonight, you'll be too tired."

"Almack's," she said, astonished that she could have forgotten. She smiled up at him. "Tonight, we dance."

If not for Almack's, Mara might have dreamed the day away, but she wanted everything to be perfect for her first appearance at a significant London event. She also had to keep an eye on Jancy, who was suffering an extreme attack of nerves. Jancy could never quite rid herself of the fear that she'd meet someone from her home area of Carlisle who could reveal her lowly origins.

Mara kept Jancy company during her first experience of a fashionable London coiffeur. Her thick red-gold hair was arranged into a complex confection that included an amber, pearl, and diamond tiara to match the other jewelry Jancy would wear.

Mara had to leave then to have her own hair arranged, but her curls required less work and they were soon in order and scattered with pink rosebuds and tiny brilliants. Her gown of white gossamer silk over pale pink satin was a favorite and she knew it suited her.

She rejoined Jancy to help with the final touches, and to genuinely admire the gown made from the green sprigged with gold. Jancy looked wonderful and could see it for herself in the mirror. She smiled at Mara. "I think I'm ready."

When they went down, Simon came forward, his eyes bright with appreciation. Mara looked to Dare, whose eyes, she thought, were much the same.

"What shade is that?" he asked.

"Maiden's blush. Truly. They give colors the most ridiculous names. Do you know the old French court used to have a color called *caca de dauphin?*"

When Dare and Simon laughed, Jancy demanded, "What does that mean?"

"Excrement of the baby prince," Mara told her.

"You made that up."

"I did not. It's a greenish yellow. There was *langue de reine* as well. Tongue of the queen. A deep pink."

Dare kissed her hand. "And," he murmured so only she could hear, *"cuisse de nymphe émue."*

Mara blushed, for the translation was "thighs of an aroused nymph." *"Langue de coquin,"* she chided.

"How can I help but have the tongue of a Rogue?" He draped her white velvet cloak around her shoulders — and stole a kiss at the nape of her neck.

"Stop it," she said, not meaning it at all. "I am determined to be the perfect young lady tonight."

"Then perhaps the bodice is a little low?"

Mara followed his look down to where rosebuds nestled between her breasts. The neckline only just covered her nipples. "It's the fashion. And the bounty is the deceptive work of an excellent corset. As you know?" she added, with a look.

"You were going to be a perfect young lady," he reminded her.

She laughed as they went out to the carriage, but suddenly realized that he must already be hours past his last dose. Her look must have been eloquent, for he said, "I took my dose later than usual. I can survive."

"I'm glad we can speak about it."

"I wish there were no necessity."

She sought the right response to that, but they were at the carriage door and Simon was urging them inside.

Almack's was everything Mara had hoped, being packed with the noisy, glittering elite, but as they threaded their way into the crowded rooms, she was more concerned with her charges — Jancy and Dare.

Jancy was clinging to Simon too much, but at least he was at ease. He'd probably never attended an Almack's assembly before, but he and she shared an ease with new people and new situations. It was a bold confidence that could sometimes lead them too far. Simon had almost died in

Canada, and she had almost ruined herself that night with Berkstead.

She resolved to be very careful tonight.

Dare didn't need her care. He was being greeted by friends left and right, and if anyone was concerned about opium, they were hiding it. Lady Downshire, one of the patronesses, paused to ask after his health and fondly admonish him to behave. "I don't forget the feathers," she said.

When she'd moved on, Mara asked, "Feathers?"

He smiled. "I have to have some secrets."

Then the other side intruded — the remnants of war. A grizzled-haired military man came over and was introduced to Mara as Captain Morse, whom Dare had met in Brussels. A Lord Vandeimen joined them — a dashing blond with a scar on his cheek that rather enhanced his looks. His wife was a fashionable lady who must be some years older.

What a variety of couples in the world, to be sure.

Mara prayed military talk wasn't upsetting Dare.

"There's no stopping them," Lady Vandeimen said with a smile, then added softly, "Don't worry. Dare is a beloved cousin of mine, and Vandeimen is a close friend of

Lord Amleigh."

Part of the Roguish contingent. Mara wondered just how many of the glittering throng were.

"Is this your first visit to Almack's, Lady Mara?" Lady Vandeimen asked in a normal voice.

Mara took the hint and chatted of the crush, the fashions, the famous and infamous. She saw the Charringtons and another couple talking to Simon and Jancy. St. Raven and his wife joined that party.

A flurry drew her eye to the entrance.

Stephen and Laura had just entered and were attracting people like magnets. Or at least, Laura was.

"Labellelle," Lady Vandeimen said. "I'm so glad to see her happy."

All was well. The Rogues and their friends would be dropping mention of Mrs. Beaumont into every ear, and the dancing would soon begin. She'd dance with Dare.

Then a woman cried, "Mara!"

Mara turned to see two friends struggling toward her. "Sophie, Giles! When did you arrive?"

"Last Friday," said Sophie Gilliatt, gasping slightly, her guinea gold hair already trying to riot. "I would have sought you out earlier, but it's been rush here, race there, and such a panic over vouchers to come here." They chattered about London and Lincolnshire, but then Sophie said, "He's very handsome."

Mara blushed, realizing she'd been stealing glances at Dare. "Lord Darius Debenham, Simon's friend."

"Oh, I remember him. He's matured very well."

Sophie's appreciation made Mara smile, but Giles said, "Make him sound like a cask of port. Anyway, he's not a Lincolnshire man."

"He's a younger son," Mara said, "so that doesn't matter."

Sophie said, "Oh-ho!" but Giles glowered. Mara remembered that he was one of her suitors.

"Wasn't he the one who organized hedgehog races at the summer fair one year?" Sophie asked.

Mara laughed. "Yes, that was Dare."

"And a jousting tournament on the river in boats." Sophie slid another look. "He's very changed." This time it wasn't a compliment.

"He was at Waterloo and seriously injured."

"I remember now."

Giles said, "Thought dead, then mysteriously appeared. A bit fishy if you ask me."

"Which no one did," Mara said hotly. "It wasn't at all fishy. His wounds were serious, and for a time, he didn't remember his name. Then he was too weak to get home."

"Fishy," Giles insisted. "Do you really believe that he couldn't get word to his powerful family?"

"You're being horrid, Giles," Sophie said. "Stop it."

"That's because Mara's broken my heart."

He was trying to make it a joke, but Mara feared it was a little bit true. She laid a hand on his arm. "If I thought so, dearest Giles, I'd die of shame."

He pulled a face, but covered her hand. "And that'd be a sorry waste. I hope he's good enough for you, though."

"Thank you."

The music changed. Mara had hoped to dance first with Dare, but with her hand in Giles's, she had no choice but to walk out with him. Dare asked Sophie to dance. At least Sophie would soon realize what a gem he was.

Mara loved to dance, so any tendency to pine was swept away by music and the lively patterns. As she moved up and down the line, she caught a glimpse of another entrance.

The magnificently bosomed woman in a gown in the style of the previous century had to be the Dowager Countess of Cawle. The many going to pay their respects were mostly older, which was excellent. They were the ones who might be hardest to convince to accept Blanche.

The woman's style of dress was a good choice, for she was the sort made to be well-rounded. The modern high waist and simple fabrics did tend to make a large women look like a bulging sack. Mara liked the spirit of the woman who refused to bow to fashion.

When the dance ended, Mara made sure to join Dare and Sophie for the promenade so that the next dance would be with him.

As he took her hand to lead her into a set of eight, Mara felt as if she floated, and she smiled into his eyes in memory of their moonlit dance. Alas, this wasn't a waltz, so she and Dare would spend little time with each other. It was still a unique joy, and she wove the patterns smiling.

But then she became aware of something amiss. Had somebody shocking managed to gain entrée? Was someone drunk? The drinks at these assemblies were deliberately mild to avoid that.

But then she realized it was closer to hand — literally. As she joined hands with a uniformed officer of about forty, she saw anger on his chunky face. His cheeks were flushed, and she didn't think it was with exertion.

As they stepped one way, then the other, she said, "I admire our soldiers very much, sir, and thank you for your service."

"I thank you, ma'am," he said, but gruffly.

"Were you at Waterloo, sir?" Mara persisted, bright and smiling.

"Unfortunately no, ma'am. I was in Canada."

The dance separated them. Simon had made enemies in Canada. Was his anger directed at her as Simon's sister?

When she reached Dare again, he asked, "What's the matter?"

She smiled. "Nothing when I'm with you." It was no effort to look into his eyes as the dance required.

When she joined the officer again, she probed. "My brother, Lord Austrey, was in Canada until recently. In York. Perhaps you knew him? He was Simon St. Bride then."

"Alas, no, ma'am. I was in Lower Canada, in New Brunswick."

The "alas" was merely polite, but she could detect no animosity. She tried another tack. "We are exiles from our London home, which suffered a leak of coal gas. Fortunately Lord Darius has given us refuge at Yeovil House."

The man's face pinched as if he smelled gas here. His ill feeling was directed at Dare?

Mara danced on wondering, Why, why, why? Merely because of opium? That would be horribly unfair. Perhaps the ill will was some lingering resentment over a prank. Dare's pranks were always gentle, but one could have annoyed the man. Still, the officer had not been at Waterloo.

The dance ended with her no wiser. Mara danced next with St. Raven, who flirted in a satisfyingly rakish way. But then she shivered. It was as if a chilly fog was creeping through Almack's Assembly Rooms. Mara tried to deny it, but then she caught Sophie looking at her as if someone had died.

St. Raven was still smiling, but he sensed it, too. Mara couldn't see Dare.

As soon as the dance ended, they wove through the crowds to Simon's side. "What's happening?" she asked, wafting her fan and looking, she hoped, as if she hadn't a care in the world.

He, too, was politely smiling, but she could see tension in his jaw. "Never mind for now, but may I let it slip that you're engaged to marry Dare?"

So it was about Dare, and it was bad. Her

gaze had found him. He was talking to the Charringtons and another couple, but people were shooting glances at him.

"If he's allowed to marry me he must be a sound 'un?" Mara asked. "What is it, Simon?"

"Nonsense, but nasty. Let's join him."

Simon took her over to Dare, handing her off in a manner reminiscent of a wedding. It was easy for Mara to smile at Dare, and he returned it. When Simon stepped away, Mara asked, "What's happening?"

"I don't know."

Of course if anything was being whispered, he'd be the last to be told. The next dance struck up, and it was a waltz.

"At last," Mara said and they stepped onto the dance floor.

For the next little while, Mara pushed aside all cares. Whatever the problem, Simon would be telling people about their betrothal and that should do the trick. If the St. Brides of Brideswell were happy to let a daughter marry Lord Darius Debenham, nothing could be seriously amiss with him.

When the dance ended, the Charringtons and Balls moved around them, almost like a guard, though a smiling, lighthearted one. Mara felt able to go to the ladies' retiring room, which she needed, but when she entered, conversation stopped. Soon the three ladies who'd been there left and she was alone with the maid.

She eyed the elderly woman. "If I asked, would you tell me what they were saying?"

The woman cocked her head. "Would you be Lady Mara St. Bride, ma'am?"

"I would."

"Well, then, they were gossiping about your husband-to-be, a Lord Darius. Saying as he turned coward at Waterloo and hid to avoid the battle."

Mara gasped. "That's a horrible lie. He was serious wounded!"

"But as they have it —"

Two women walked in and the maid fell silent. The women looked at Mara and pasted bright smiles on their faces before going behind curtains to use the chamber pots.

Mara did the same, then left, burning with fury. Dare, a coward. This was wicked! And heavens! Word of the betrothal would be all over England before they'd spoken to her father. She remembered with difficulty to look as if she hadn't a care in the world as she entered the ballroom.

Probably many of the people here were unaware of undercurrents. She could see enough who weren't, however, people who were talking in a secretive way, casting sideways glances at Dare. She saw two of the patronesses with their heads together. They couldn't go so far as to ask Dare to leave, could they?

He was still surrounded by friends, friends of respectability and high rank. A distinguished older couple joined the group as Mara hurried over.

She was introduced to the Duke and Duchess of Belcraven — a charming lady with a hint of French still in her voice, and an austere gentleman, but with kind eyes. Lord Arden's parents. They were clearly willing to lend their support, but she heard the duke say something about unfortunate.

Dare looked pale and strained, and she longed to whisk him away to safety, but of course to leave now would be the worst possible thing. What time was it? How long before the opium wore off entirely, and what would happen then?

She slipped in next to Simon. "Someone has to deny the rumors."

"You heard, then?"

"It's wicked."

"Yes, but no denial will count unless it comes from someone who would know. I wish Con were here. He fought at Waterloo."

"What of Lord Vandeimen? He seemed to know Dare from Waterloo. And a Captain Morse."

"I'll ask them."

Simon moved away, but soon returned. "Couldn't find Morse, but Vandeimen says he never saw Dare at all during the battle. There'd be no point in a lie. He's finding a Major Hawkinville. Says he might do the trick."

"Dare needs to get away."

"I know," Simon said, not bothering to point out why it was impossible.

Mara returned to Dare's side, trying to radiate unshadowed delight. Then a tall man strolled over, a red-haired woman by his side. "Dashing Deb, as I live and breathe." He spoke a little louder than necessary.

Dare started, but managed a grin. "Hawk Hawkinville. Surviving without armies to shuffle around?"

"Shuffling cattle and drainage ditches instead. Not much difference in the end." He introduced his wife, then said, "Glad to see you looking well, Debenham. The Duke often says how well you served."

Mara slowly exhaled. People nearby had to hear, and "the Duke" was, of course, Wellington. Mara had no idea why Major Hawkinville could invoke his name this way, but it was a blessing.

Then Hawkinville turned to her. "Will you grant me the next dance, Lady Mara?"

She dipped a curtsy. "Of course, Major."

Dare partnered the Duchess of Belcraven, and the Duke took out Mrs. Hawkinville. The atmosphere was changing, but only to one of confusion. How could this be completely wiped away without facts?

At the end of that dance, they decided they could leave. Jancy had made a modest comment to Lady Downshire about her delicate condition, and that was their excuse.

Dare appeared calm in a frozen kind of way, but once in the carriage, he asked, "Very well. What is it now?"

He sounded so weary that Mara wished she could take him in her arms.

Simon spoke bluntly. "Someone's spread the story that you ran from the battle. That you hid in some bushes. That your wounds came about when those bushes were overrun by our own cavalry in pursuit of fleeing French."

"Dear God. I've always been afraid of that."

"It's not *true!*" Mara exploded.

He looked at her. "How can I tell?"

"Because you are who you are."

Dare's lips twisted. "I wish I were sure of that."

CHAPTER 23

When they arrived back at the house, Simon proposed a council of war, but Dare said, "I'm sorry, Simon. Not now," and went upstairs.

"Damn, I forgot."

Jancy took his arm. "There's nothing to do tonight that can't be done tomorrow, love. Come to bed."

Mara went upstairs with them and entered her room feeling selfishly deserted. She needed to talk over events, and she needed to be with Dare. She had some idea now of his nightly battles and tonight could be dire.

Ruth arrived with hot water and began helping Mara out of her clothes. "And how was it, milady?"

"It?"

"Almack's, milady!"

"Oh, as expected." But if she didn't want Ruth in a fret, she had better show some enthusiasm. "Sophie and Giles Gilliatt were there."

"That must have been nice, milady."

"And I met the Duke and Duchess of Belcraven. They're the parents of one of Simon's friends." She dredged up names of other people who might satisfy Ruth's interest, but was profoundly grateful when she was finally in her bed.

But Ruth hovered. "Are you all right, milady?"

"Yes, of course. Just a little tired."

"From a bit of dancing? That's not like you." Ruth put her hand to Mara's forehead.

Mara brushed it away. "I don't have a temperature, Ruth."

"Just checking. It's a nasty place, London is. All sorts of dirt and disease."

Including, Mara thought when she was finally alone, gossip. Who could have invented such a horrible story?

Or is it true?

Definitely not.

But Dare feared it.

It isn't true. It isn't!

He must be so anguished, but he had people to care for him. Salter, Feng Ruyuan.

She couldn't bear it. She climbed out of bed, put on her wrap, and left her room. As usual at such an hour, the house was silent, so she hurried along without fear of being caught. She wasn't sure she cared anyway.

She reached the door to the musicians' gallery and opened it — to be met by silence. She stepped carefully up to the curtains and made a chink to look through. The ballroom was empty. Something was definitely wrong.

Mara left the gallery and went carefully down the dark stairs to the corridor with its occasional night lamps. She needed to see Dare, to know how he was, to help him if possible. She had the right by love, both hers and his.

She went to Mr. Feng's room and listened at the door, but heard no sound. She moved on to the door to Dare's bedroom and tapped, surprised by how little hesitation she felt. The door opened and she faced Dare's stone-faced man, Salter.

"Is Lord Darius here?"

"No, my lady."

"He's with Mr. Feng?"

"No, my lady."

"Then where is he?"

After a moment, he said, "I don't know, ma'am. He came up and changed. Then he disappeared."

"This isn't good, is it?" She'd never spoken to Salter before, but she knew him to be a kindred spirit at this moment, a comrade-in-arms.

"No, ma'am. What happened?"

Mara stepped into the room and closed the door, then gave him a quick account of Almack's. "Could it be true?"

"No."

"You're sure?"

His eyes narrowed. "You're not?"

"I'm in love. I know what that does to a person's judgment."

His grim face relaxed a bit. "It isn't true, ma'am. I've lived so close with Lord Darius this past eight months that I know him better than he knows himself. The mind's a funny thing and can invent a lot, especially under the influence of opium, but the truth is always there. There's none of that sort of cowardice in him. The mind can lie to itself, especially to try to bury shame, but only to a point. He has no memory of anything like that."

"Have you told him that?"

"Haven't had the chance, have I?" Salter said.

"Where will he have gone?"

"I don't know, ma'am. We haven't had anything like this since we've been here."

"We must search."

"It's late, milady —"

"I can hardly sleep in this situation!"

Salter shook his head. "I mean, he's a long way from his last dose. There might be difficulties."

"All the more urgency in finding him, then. Get Mr. Feng to look, too."

She left the room and prowled the corridors, trying to sense Dare. Something turned her attention toward the upper floor. Dare wouldn't go to the children's quarters in distress, but she was pulled that way. She had to check.

As she'd suspected, the schoolroom was dark and deserted. She blew out her candle before carefully opening the door into the children's bedroom. By moonlight, she saw two beds, two sleeping children, and no one else.

The next door was closed and she realized there were sounds from within. Creaking floorboards, thumpings. Was Dare fighting Mr. Feng in there?

She eased open the door into an empty white room lit faintly by moonlight. Dare was in the room alone, like a ghost in his loose white clothing, bouncing from wall to wall, thumping the walls with his fists, not hard, but desperately.

Wary of startling him into hitting her, Mara said, "Dare?"

He froze, his back pressed to a wall, hands spread as if seeking something to clutch on to.

Cracked glass.

Fear made Mara tremble — fear of doing harm, a worse fear of being rejected — but she didn't feel she could leave him to go for help.

"Salter says it can't be true."

"How can he know?" Perhaps she heard shivering in his faint voice.

"He seems to think he knows you very well. He's worried about you."

"He's always worried about me. Everyone's worried about me. Apart from the people who are disgusted with me."

She walked up to him. When he turned his head away, she gripped it between her hands and turned it back to face her.

"Someone spread a lie about you, Dare. You can't let them win like this. Perhaps this is what they want, for you to give up."

"Why?"

"I don't know. The man in the first dance. The officer. Do you know him?"

"I can't remember. . . ."

"Think!"

"Mara . . ." His legs buckled, so he slid to sit on the ground. "I can hardly breathe."

She sank down with him and gathered

him into her arms, discovering the faint tremble that ran through his entire body, and a cold sweat that had soaked the back of his clothes. By instinct, she held him as tightly as she could, rocking him as she might a child. "I love you. I believe in you. You're everything that is fine and admirable. . . ."

He shook his head against her shoulder, but his hands clutched on to her like those of a drowning man.

"Yes," she said. "Whoever did this cruel thing will live to regret it, word of a St. Bride."

He mumbled something about devil's hair.

"Exactly. I know now why Simon fought a duel. If I find out who did this, I'll . . . I'll do something violent."

He laughed, she thought, but the trembling hadn't stopped.

"You must come, Dare. To Salter and Feng Ruyuan, the ones who know what to do to help." She grasped his arm and rose, doing her best to force him to his feet. He made it with help from the wall, breathing in sharp gasps.

"Are you in pain?"

"Of various sorts," he breathed. "The mind is the worst. Nothing is right. Nothing is ever right."

"Come," she urged, trying to take his weight, though she had no hope of supporting him if he truly needed it. They made it to the door.

"Come," she said again, steering him toward the stairs. She talked him down them, Dare balancing himself with a hand on the wall. "We'll get you to bed."

At the bottom, they met Salter and Feng Ruyuan, probably summoned by the sound of her voice. Salter looked as if he'd take Dare in his arms, but Feng Ruyuan said, "You are late, Darius. Come."

The words were quiet, but seemed to snap Dare out of a haze. He cast Mara an anguished look that might have been a plea for help, but then staggered after the Chinese man.

Mara followed, but Salter grabbed her arm. "Begging your pardon, my lady, but you can't go there."

She twitched free. "Oh, yes, I can."

The ballroom doors were already closed when she reached them. She opened them and went in.

Dare was standing in that prayerful pose even though he swayed and trembled. Feng Ruyuan was speaking to him in a voice so soft that Mara could only catch words. Mind. Body. Control. Fear.

Then they began to move in synchrony, in flowing patterns. At first Dare moved like a broken toy and Mara wanted to protest. She fumbled her way to one of the upholstered chairs against the wall and sat, trying to lend Dare her strength.

In time something mended and he began to move almost as smoothly as Feng Ruyuan. There was a kind of sinuous beauty that reminded her of the most courtly dance, though it was like no dance she knew. She could tell that each slow step took strength, balance, and focus, especially as everything became more complex, involving turns and swoops.

Then Mr. Feng looked at her, even as he continued the patterns. He spoke to Dare, and while Dare continued, Mr. Feng beckoned her.

Mara felt a stupid urge to say, "Me?" But she stood and walked to the man.

"Like this," he said, and demonstrated movements of the hands that swept them outward, one high, one low, then back around themselves and together again. When she had it, he nodded, and turned to match Dare's patterns.

Mara continued the movement, feeling a little silly, but eased by doing something.

Feng Ruyuan returned to her and showed

her some steps. Forward, backward, and a turn. Mara found it difficult, especially in her long robe, but she would master this.

She tried to put the movements to music, but they fit no music she knew. She realized she needed to break free of her usual world in order to do this — and then it made sense. She slid into the flow and glanced at Feng Ruyuan. He smiled and showed her an additional step that formed a cycle so she could continue without pause.

It pleased. It soothed her mind, but not in the way of blanking it. More by elevating it like the best sort of prayer. She could see why this might help Dare to rise above torment and survive the night.

Then noises brought her back to earth and she stopped.

The men were fighting now as she'd seen them fight before. She recognized the patterns turned to violent force.

No, not violent. Just intense. The purpose was not to hit or hurt. That only happened if either made a mistake. The mistakes were always Dare's. When it happened, he paused, focused, and then picked up the patterns again.

Sweat poured off him now and his chest heaved so that Mara longed to cry halt, but she knew evil was pouring out of him with that sweat, and tormented thoughts were being vanquished. She simply sat again and tried to join her strength with his as he fought for his life.

They came to the point she'd witnessed before, when Feng Ruyuan called a halt and produced temptation. From her place, she could smell the opium, slightly sweet, slightly musty. Such a blessing when people were in pain, but such an evil when uncontrolled.

Dare was quivering, tension in every line of him, anguish in his face, and Mara longed to go to him. She understood that he had to fight this battle alone. He would always have to do this alone.

When the opium was brought close, his tremors became a violent shaking and his hands pushed together as if they'd break through each other. Mara bit her lips so as not to beg for him to take it, to find the peace it would bring. She closed her eyes and prayed that God give him strength and victory.

She heard the slight sound and opened her eyes. Feng Ruyuan had stepped back and was slipping the opium box out of sight. Dare still shook. Feng Ruyuan moved behind as he had before, and she could see now that he was massaging Dare's shoulders, hear that he was murmuring in a singsong that might be Chinese.

Then he led Dare stumbling away.

Mara was left sitting in the empty ballroom, surrounded by ghosts of labor and pain, but also by victory. *Thank you, God.* She rose, finding herself stiff, and left the room. She considered, but not for long, before going to Mr. Feng's room.

She knocked, marveling at herself, but sure of what she must do. There was no response, but she could hear something from inside. Music. Flowing flute music that matched the flowing patterns.

She opened the door.

Dare was lying on a narrow, high bed, his head turned away from her. He was naked. Feng Ruyuan was pummeling his oiled body in a way that looked painful, but Dare didn't complain. A woman sat nearby playing the flute.

Mara simply stood, at a loss, especially as everyone ignored her. It was as if Feng Ruyuan was saying, "Do as you think best."

She stepped in and closed the door behind her. She was intruding. Dare had no idea she was here, but she wasn't sure he'd been aware of her in the ballroom and she simply couldn't go elsewhere.

She watched the work of strong hands,

which meant she watched Dare's perfect body. Perfect except for scars — down one thigh, across his side. They were evidence of suffering as his lean, hard muscles were evidence of strength, of a battle won, of mind as well as body. *I am dangerous,* he'd said, and she saw the truth.

Every breath brought her subtle perfumes — cedar, perhaps, and incense, sandalwood and rosemary. But other perfumes, too, sweet and strange, all playing on her senses. She walked closer until she stood by the bed.

Feng Ruyuan put a cloth over Dare's body and worked his hands down Dare's legs to his feet, then sat on a stool to concentrate on ankle, instep, and toes. He gestured Mara to his side. Without being told, she knew she was being instructed again.

Could she? Should she?

She paid attention to the way he dug his thumbs strongly into Dare's sole and up around the base of his toes, then pulled and squeezed the toes. Then he rose and worked back up the legs as the encircling music wove on.

Mara sat, heart thundering. Her hands hovered but didn't touch, but then she made herself grasp Dare's right foot as the man had and rub firmly with her thumbs.

Dare stirred, doubtless recognizing an extra pair of hands, but Feng Ruyuan said something and he settled again. Mara focused, wondering if he would recognize her touch, whether she wanted him to.

She'd never touched anyone in such a way before, and this was Dare. It made her light-headed enough to faint, but it also made her strong. She poured strength through her hands because she knew that was what he needed, and tried to pour pleasure, too, for she was drowning in it. Every push, every stroke, every pull swept sweetness of the purest kind through her. There was nothing in this of carnal ecstasy. It was sublime.

She moved to the other foot, then worked her hands higher, rising to work up his leg to the jagged, sunken scar that marred one thigh. She could imagine the work and pain required to overcome that and still move well.

"He sleeps, milady."

Feng Ruyuan's soft voice pulled Mara out of another land. She straightened, feeling a sharp loss when her hands separated from Dare's body, and then a sharp twinge from her back. The music continued.

Feng spread the quilted cover entirely over Dare, then moved away from the bed. Mara followed. "Will he sleep through the night now?"

"No, but long enough to face another day. He sent you the gift?"

After a puzzled moment, she remembered the silk. "No."

"Then you must be wary of the one who did."

"I am."

"I wish to give you something if you will accept it, my lady."

"Of course," Mara said, but she felt uncomfortable.

He gestured her through a door into an adjoining room. The light of two branches of candles made Mara blink, and her discomfort increased. This was a normal bedchamber apart from various Oriental artifacts.

He picked up something and offered her a disk about the size of a crown coin, with a strange swirling design of black and white.

"We call this yin-yang, Lady Mara. It represents the balance of the universe, but also the balance we must all seek inside ourselves."

"Good and bad?" she asked as she took it. The disk was smooth beneath her finger and was made, she thought, of ebony and white enamel. In each swirl, there was a dot of the other color.

"Of light and dark," he said, "but dark is no more bad than nighttime is. Light and dark also represent the masculine and feminine in each of us."

"Dark being masculine and light feminine?"

He smiled and shook his head. "Your traditions do not appreciate the feminine. Dark is the female side — cool, contemplative, and healing. Light is the male side — hot, energetic, and mobile. In relationships, the woman is the rock around which the man flows. You are strong in yin, Lady Mara."

She laughed slightly. "I always thought myself an energetic, mobile sort."

"Remember, in each of us the two should balance. And also" — he touched one of the dots — "each should be balanced by a little of the other. You are balanced for one so young, and will become more so as you continue along the path."

Mara looked up from the fascinating pattern. "Thank you."

"You are an excellent match for Darius, my lady, but you need rest. You, too, must face tomorrow."

Mara turned to go, but then turned back. "Please, would you call me Mara?"

He bowed, hands together. "I am honored, Mara, and even more so if you would call me Ruyuan."

Mara repeated his bow. "I, too, would be honored, Ruyuan."

Mara returned to her room, the disk in her hand, and fell instantly asleep. She awoke brightly to the first light coming through the gap in the curtains. Ruth would be pleased.

But then she realized that her room reeked of Oriental magic. She leapt out of bed and opened the window, but realized the oil had smeared from her hands to the sheets. There was no water to wash in, so she found a bottle of perfume and spilled some on herself and the bed. It earned her a scolding for carelessness, but Ruth seemed more relieved than anything to see her lively and troublesome.

What to do today?

She and Dare had agreed to ride.

After last night, it seemed ridiculous, but she understood many things now. The ordinary days were as important to Dare as the extraordinary nights.

She wrote a note to remind him. When Ruth brought the reply, she also brought a pink rose, turning Mara almost dizzy with bliss. The note, however, said: *Alas, my love,*

Godiva must ride another day. A council of war has been convened.

My love.

The first time he'd written such a thing. It and the rose were affirmations of their love, despite anything the world could hurl at them. Inhaling the fragrance of the flower, Mara wondered if Dare realized what she'd done last night and what he thought about it.

"When you've finished sighing over that rose, milady, *what* do you want to wear?"

"Armor," Mara said. "I'm going to a council of war."

CHAPTER 24

Mara wore the rose between her breasts in a bud pin when she went downstairs, where she had to fight a preliminary skirmish. Simon was completely opposed to her attending the meeting, but Mara recruited Dare, who smiled at the rose, even though he looked strained.

"Of course she should attend, Simon. She's closely affected."

She linked arms with him to go into the library, where she found all the Rogues who were in Town, plus Lord Vandeimen and Major Hawkinville.

"Because of their military expertise and connections," Dare said, as he escorted her to a sofa.

"And they're friends of Lord Amleigh's, I gather."

"Like peas in a pod."

That seemed a strange thing to say, for the two men before her were not at all alike, but she let it pass.

"We all shared a billet in Brussels," Dare said.

"So they know you well."

"For their sins." He spoke lightly, but a deeper meaning lay beneath. With a shiver, Mara remembered Jancy's fortune-telling. An unexpected disaster. Here it was, but not disaster. Major Hawkinville had already eased matters.

Nicholas ceded control of this meeting to Sir Stephen Ball, saying, "I'm sure we need a legal mind."

Stephen sent him a look that showed it wasn't entirely a compliment, but he laid out the situation with crisp clarity. "The story was probably begun at Almack's," Stephen continued.

"Why do you say that?" Vandeimen asked. "It could simply have arrived there as the tidbit of the day."

"Because it wasn't there at the beginning of the evening," Leander said. "Judith and I arrived early and there was no hint of it."

Mara decided to speak. "I think I felt it begin."

Everyone looked at her. "When?" Stephen asked.

"During the second set. Could it have been sparked by seeing Dare there?"

"Perhaps because Dare seemed popular and apparently unharmed? But who would resent that?"

Berkstead? The name popped into Mara's mind, but he hadn't been there and she couldn't bear to expose her foolish behavior to all these men.

"I don't understand why it was believed," she said.

Stephen spoke without a trace of emotion. "Because the story presented to explain Dare's absence and recovery was always suspect. It sufficed as long as it was unchallenged, but it was always a cracked pot."

"They could have the whole truth and be damned," said Nicholas, "but it's an overblown tale without evidence to give it credibility."

"It doesn't address the current problem anyway," Stephen pointed out. "The only relevance is that if Dare had been discovered on the battlefield and cared for in the normal manner, this story would be toothless, even though it could as easily be true."

"Indeed," Hawkinville said. "Anyone in battle can receive wounds in an ignoble way, but especially men like the couriers, not attached to any body of soldiers."

Stephen nodded. "The peculiarities in Dare's story mean that the balance tips the other way. There's a danger the story will be accepted unless there is proof to the opposite."

"Which doesn't exist," Dare said. "Even I can't remember."

"We could advertise for witnesses," Francis suggested.

"Judging from the success at finding the children's parents," Dare said dryly, "that's a waste of time."

"And such an advertisement implies uncertainty," Stephen pointed out. "Never imply uncertainty. The first action we take is to present complete conviction. The story is too ridiculous even to be discussed."

Everyone nodded — except Dare, Mara noticed. No one was likely to confront him with the charge, but she wondered what he would say if that happened.

"Our next step," Stephen said, "is to find the originator of the story."

"Question everyone who was at Almack's?" Leander queried in mild alarm.

"Question those we know well enough," Stephen said. "It might show a flow of information from one particular point."

Mara knew she had to speak. She swallowed and said, "I'm wondering if it might be something to do with me. There's a Major Berkstead —"

"That poor fellow," Dare interrupted. "Mara might be right. He deluded himself that they were Romeo and Juliet and attacked me yesterday out of jealousy. But I doubt he was at Almack's. I broke his nose and possibly some ribs."

There was a murmur of approval.

Nicholas said, "Where do we find him?"

Dare supplied the address. "It's close by. Salter could go and check his present state."

That was agreed and arranged.

"He could have sent a deputy," Mara said. "Dare, do you remember in our first dance, an officer who seemed angry?"

He smiled at her. "I was dancing with you. How could I be aware of others?"

Mara blushed, but ignored it to address the men. "I thought at first the man was angry with me, and I wondered if it was something to do with Simon, because he said he'd been in Canada at the time of Waterloo. We were talking lightly about military matters when we met in the dance — you know how it is. But then I saw him look at Dare with such . . . anger."

It had really been disgust, but she couldn't bring herself to say that.

"Name?" Nicholas demanded.

"I'm sorry. I don't know."

"Was he in uniform?" Hawkinville asked.

"Yes."

"Describe it, please."

Mara did her best, but she hadn't paid much attention.

"Sounds like the West Middlesex. I can find him." He sounded astonishingly sure.

"If it is him," Mara asked, "what can we do?"

"Discover the basis for his anger," Nicholas said. "He looks like our first evidence of ill will."

"But why?" Mara demanded. "He wasn't at Waterloo. He said so."

"Perhaps he heard the story from someone who was," Dare said wearily.

Mara turned to him. "The story is not true."

Before he could protest, Hawkinville said, "It's certainly highly unlikely. I didn't lie about Wellington's approval of your work."

"I appreciate the endorsement but that doesn't mean I didn't lose my courage later. God knows, I can understand how that could be."

"As can any who've been in battle. I doubt you have that nature, however."

"And what nature is that?"

"In my experience," Hawkinville said, his voice calm in the face of Dare's rising temper, "the brave man who breaks has been fighting his fears all along. More credit to him for holding on. There's little glory in heroics without fear. Were you afraid?"

Dare suddenly laughed. "No. I have always been known to be mad."

"Thus the story is untrue."

Stephen spoke. "We need proof, however. And witnesses."

"Where were you when you were hit, Dare?" Vandeimen asked.

Dare grimaced. "Somewhere in the battle."

Hawkinville pulled out a notebook and pencil. "Tell me any detail you remember."

Under taut questioning, Dare produced fragmentary memories of uniforms, and then the important details of where he'd started out and where he'd been heading.

Major Hawkinville consulted some distant vision. "That gives me angles of inquiry," he said at last, "but it might take time. I suspect this battle will have to be fought in the air."

"What?" Nicholas asked, clearly puzzled.

"Among the *haut volée*."

Mara glanced at Dare and saw he, too, remembered joking about fine feathers and country nests. But the high-flying birds of society could have sharp beaks and talons. She took comfort from the fact that some of the eagles and hawks would be Rogues.

"Our greatest weapon, then," said Nicholas, "is the ball."

"Swung mightily?" queried Dare.

Everyone chuckled, and it was partly because Dare retained his sense of humor.

"Crushingly," Nicholas agreed with a smile. "Your formal betrothal would add weight and force to it."

Silence fell.

"We already spread the word," Mara said, "so why not?"

Dare said, "A rumor at Almack's is one thing. A formal announcement quite another. Simon doesn't want you jilted."

"I don't want me jilted, either." She met his eyes relentlessly and eventually he looked down at his laced fingers.

Simon objected. "We can hardly have a betrothal ball without Father's permission. Without his presence, in fact."

That crushed the idea, but then Mara straightened. "So we go to Brideswell now! Dare and I, at least." Above all, she wanted to get him to her healing home.

"Why not?" Nicholas said. "An extra advantage is that it removes you from society, Dare, with no hint of skulking."

Mara sensed that Dare was about to object, so she turned to him. "You won't nobly escape me, so there's no point in delaying the announcement. And our betrothal ball, blessed by many notable people, will smash any mere rumor to smithereens."

"Good God," Hawkinville said, "how many of you St. Brides are there?"

"Hundreds," Mara told him cheerfully, "but only two of us with the hair."

"Very well," Dare said.

She couldn't hold back surprise. "You'll do it?"

He glanced at the rose between her breasts. "I will do almost anything you command, as well you know, my lady. But this plan makes sense."

Simon rose. "If we're to reach Brideswell ahead of the news, we'd better leave now."

"The sooner the better," Mara agreed, "but you have a ball to plan, and rapid travel wouldn't be good for Jancy."

"She's right, Simon," Dare said, rising. "Jancy's already trembling at the thought of organizing and being hostess at any kind of ball, never mind the scandal of the season. In fact, I'm going to usurp you. We'll have it here. The staff can do it blindfolded, but my parents returned home last night. I'm sure Mama will be delighted."

Mara almost choked. His parents had been here while she was sharing Dare's nightly battle? Massaging his naked body?

Simon was protesting, but Dare was suddenly immovable. Jancy would definitely be grateful but Mara saw another problem.

"The original purpose of the ball was to launch Blanche into respectability," she pointed out. "We can't muddle the two."

"Ah, yes," Dare said. "My dirt would soil her."

"That's not what I meant, idiot!"

Nicholas's voice overrode hers. "Don't be an ass, Dare. In fact, combining the events should work perfectly. A ball at Yeovil House will challenge the ton to endorse you or offend your parents, who are well liked and respected. We let it be known that your betrothal will be announced at the event, making the situation clear."

"And if the ton stays away?" Dare asked.

"It's a gamble, true, but we hold many court cards."

"We can't gamble with Blanche's life."

Hal Beaumont had been silent up till now. "If it comes to a choice, she'll insist that our problems be put aside. They won't grow worse."

"In fact," Leander said, "the blend could work to her advantage. Her minor indiscretions . . ."

Mara felt her eyes widen at that diplomatic

description.

". . . will be overshadowed by Dare's dark dramas. She'll play a minor part."

"I'm not sure she'll care for that," Hal said, but it was a joke.

"I'll go and speak to my parents," Dare said and left.

"This could all go disastrously wrong," Leander pointed out.

"Will it?" Nicholas asked. It was a serious question, posed to an expert.

The diplomat considered matters. "If one influential person stands firm against us, we're sunk."

"Then we make sure none does. Your job."

Charrington laughed, shaking his head. "If you can guarantee the dukes and the Countess of Cawle, it would have to be a very influential person to capsize us." He looked at Hawkinville. "What of Wellington? I heard he was in Town."

"Briefly and unofficially."

"Even so," Charrington pointed out, "his failure to attend could be misconstrued."

Mara couldn't believe that such a mischance could explode their campaign.

"I can hardly drag him to the ball," Hawkinville said, "but I doubt he'd want to support this lie. Unless, of course, there is strong evidence."

"There can't be," Mara said, wanting to shoot the man.

But Nicholas said, "We'll make sure there isn't any."

Dare returned to hear this. "If there is any real evidence, let it out."

Mara wanted to shoot *him.*

"My parents are rising," he said. "They'll be down soon. Salter's returned. Berkstead's gone. His landlord said he'd been brought home injured, claiming to have been set upon by me without rhyme or reason, and he left the next day for parts unknown, fearing further attack."

"Would be nice if parts unknown were hell," Nicholas said.

"As it is," Stephen said, "he's probably showing his wounds to his friends as proof of Dare's efforts to silence him."

Mara felt furious and horribly guilty. "There were witnesses," she said. "Men who came into the lane from the street who could know nothing of the cause. This is all my fault!"

Dare took her hand. "Of course it isn't."

They searched each other's eyes and might even have kissed if Major Hawkinville hadn't spoken.

"If the bastard's spreading stories, he can't have gone far. I'll start a search for Berkstead and the angry dancing officer as well as for witnesses to Dare's fall in battle."

He left, and Mara said. "Can he do that?"

"If anyone can," Dare said. "He was one of those chiefly involved in organizing the movements of the army and he did seem able to keep it all in his head like a giant chessboard. As for Berkstead and the West Middlesex officer, what Hawk seeks, he finds."

"Well, good then. But if we're going to Brideswell and returning for the ball, we must be off."

But the Duchess of Yeovil came in then. She took Mara's hands. "My dear, we're delighted! I never would have believed the scamp could make such a perfect choice. Simon's sister!"

She was a sturdy woman with a kind face and brown hair beginning to be touched by gray. In a simple rust brown dress, she could have been anyone.

Mara tried to curtsy, but was warmly embraced. She wondered how much of the warmth was acting. But then, the duchess didn't yet know that Dare's recent problems were all her fault.

"And you're rushing away immediately," the duchess said, "before we have a chance to talk. But don't concern yourself about the ball. All will be perfect." She looked around the room. "Despite Rogues," she said. "I do hope you all will behave."

When she'd left, Nicholas said, "I feel delightfully sixteen." There was a bittersweet tone to it, for much indeed had happened in the past decade.

CHAPTER 25

It was an hour before Mara and Dare climbed into the duchess's traveling chariot, with Ruth as chaperone. Part of the delay was because of the children, who had become distraught at the idea of Dare leaving them for days.

Mara had loved the patience with which he'd reassured them, explaining that he needed to go to speak to Mara's father about marrying her. And that, no, they couldn't come this time.

Eventually, Delphie had slid over to Mara. "You are to marry Papa?"

"I am. And I will try to be the best mama in the world."

Delphie's solemn eyes hadn't changed. "You will be kind to him?"

Mara drew the child into her arms. "I love him, sweetling, perhaps as much as you do. I promise I will never hurt him or let anyone else hurt him."

Delphie suddenly hugged her back. "Why can't we come with you? We'll be good."

Mara looked at Dare, willing to give in, but he said, "You would slow us down, Delphie, and we must be back for the ball. We'll be back soon."

Delphie had let go, with a pout suggesting that she'd hoped to get her own way. The more confident she became, the more trouble she'd be, but delightfully so.

Now, in the speeding coach, Mara glanced at Dare beside her. It must have been very hard to be firm with the children he only wanted to protect and make joyous, but he'd done it.

He was a good father. As for Mara's own father, she had no idea how he would take their arrival and announcement. Simon was sending a courier ahead to give some warning, but still, Sim St. Bride didn't like sudden fits and starts, and he might not want his daughter involved with opium and scandal.

And how, she wondered, was Dare to manage his opium on this journey? Salter was with them, of course, riding alongside the chaise, and it was none of Ruth's business what Dare did or how he behaved, but even so, it could be difficult, and this nasty rumor had to be making his control harder.

Mara took Dare's hand. His fingers moved within hers in a gentle stroke that caught her breath and curled her toes. If only Ruth wasn't with them. But this was why Ruth was with them.

Their eyes met, and she was sure he was sharing her thoughts, but she saw the shadows and longed to chase them away. Perhaps she had the means. She picked up her carriage bag and took out some papers.

"This is an excellent opportunity to work on our novel."

Ruth snorted, but Dare laughed. "By all means. What further adventures have you devised for Anne and Canute?"

Mara wished she still had the excellent plan of Castle Cruel she'd impetuously burned, but she still had her notes. He applauded the addition of Ethel the Unready and the midget Halfacanute, and suggested that the castle cook be Alfred, because King Alfred had been the one to burn the cakes.

Their discussion came nowhere close to the sparkling fun at the Yeoman's Arms, but it was a candle flame against the dark, and passed the time.

They traveled at speed, but Mara insisted on a midday break, knowing Dare would need to take opium around then, and she demanded that they stop for the night when the light went.

Mara and Ruth shared one bedroom and Dare and Salter took another. They all four ate dinner together in a private parlor, but it was a quiet meal with servants present. Dare would have taken his evening dose but he still seemed shadowed.

Those foul rumors weighed on him, and she suspected that he couldn't rid himself of a splinter of belief that they were true. She needed to take him in her arms. She longed to at least be alone with him.

"Why don't we take a stroll?" he said when the meal was over, as if picking up her thoughts.

Ruth pursed her lips, but she could hardly forbid it.

"We'll be back soon," Mara assured her, but then hurried into her cloak, bonnet, and gloves before the maid could try. She and Dare were soon walking down the evening-quiet street, with moon and planets gleaming in a slate blue sky.

"This is the first time we've done this," she said, linking arms.

"Done what?"

"Strolled in the dark with no purpose in mind."

"The purpose, I thought, is to be together."

She smiled back at him. "Yes."

They could have talked, perhaps should have talked. Of the rumors, and of the ball and of all the ways it might go wrong. Of her parents. Of opium, even.

Instead, they walked the length of the street, sharing good evenings with the few people they met along the way. They paused to look in the window of a bookseller's shop, then to watch a mail coach rattle by, outside passengers clinging to the rail on top.

A glossy curricle tooled past under the control of a very young buck. He called a good evening, then tried to impress them with a tight turn around a corner. Mara winced when he almost tipped the sporting vehicle over.

"Young fool," Dare said. "But I remember doing the same."

As they turned back toward the inn, Mara said, "His generation won't have to go to war. I'm glad."

"Indeed, though there is the saying about the devil finding work. Some young men burn to take risks."

"Like you?"

"Not really. I met some officers who only seemed to come alive when in battle. Lacking that, they tended to stupefy themselves with drink, or seek danger in high-stakes gaming."

"Perhaps we need a gladiatorial system, so they can fight anytime they wish."

He laughed. "I know some men who would benefit from that."

"Does the sort of fighting you do with Ruyuan serve the same purpose?"

He considered it. "Mainly it teaches control, but yes. It burns off that urge toward physical challenge and drama."

They were nearing the inn, and Mara had to ask, "How will you manage the night here?"

"I'll take an extra dose."

She turned to him, knowing what that meant. "Oh, Dare."

He smiled wryly. "Apparently it's my next lesson. I have proved I can stand like a wall, Ruyuan says, and must now prove that I can bend like the willow. Or something like that. He becomes metaphorical." His voice had taken on a bitter edge and he added, "Rules are easier."

"I think that was his point."

He took out a finger-sized vial of deep blue glass with gold Chinese lettering. "I am even in charge of my destiny."

He was carrying the opium with him?

"May I see?"

He passed her the bottle and she saw that on the top of the cap was an etching of an Oriental warrior wielding a sword. "Laudanum?" she asked, trying to keep her tone mundane.

"Of a sort. Strong and without sugar. I prefer it bitter. I would prefer it to be in an ugly container, but there is some other lesson in that, I gather."

"That opium is not itself evil. It saves lives and eases so much suffering." Mara touched the picture of the warrior. "Do you still have my favor?"

"Always." He took back the vial and put it away, then took her hand to lead her down a lane between a house and a cobbler's shop.

There he drew her into his arms and pressed his lips to hers. She sensed he meant the kiss to be brief and decorous but tender need swept through them. She cradled his face and parted her lips to join with him in the only way allowed.

And such a blessedly complete way it was, as if hot mouths became the whole of them in everlasting connection. Rough wall pressed at her back, and Dare's strong body enfolded her. Mara lost all sense of reality other than him, and pleasure, and a building desire that could drive her mad.

They pulled apart, staring into each

other's eyes, only to press together again, this time bodily, with Mara's head on his chest, within which his heart pounded frantically just like hers.

"Oh, but I want you so much, Dare. I want to be yours completely. I don't know why! We'll be married soon. But I wish it were now."

"My adored, beloved Mara," he whispered into her hair. "Thank God for control, or I'd take you here against the wall."

A part of Mara leapt at that, but she too had control. He would hate himself after.

Reluctantly, they separated but held hands all the way, only breaking that contact at Mara's bedroom door, when they had to go to their separate beds.

They arrived at Brideswell the next afternoon and nothing could have been warmer than Mara's parents' welcome. She wished she'd seen their first reaction to the news.

"You look so well!" her buxom mother exclaimed to Dare, hugging him. "At Simon's wedding, it was all I could do not to coddle you and feed you nourishing food."

"I might have liked that," he said, smiling.

"Not at the time, you wouldn't." Amy St. Bride took both of their arms. "Come inside, come inside. It will be so wonderful to have another wedding!"

Over tea and cakes with most of the family present, the talk was all about the lighter aspects of London and weddings, but in the end, Mara and Dare were alone with her parents.

"I gather there's a bit of trouble," her father said, mostly to Dare. He was a trim, healthy man who looked younger than his fifty-two years, but he was every inch a country gentleman.

"Apart from the opium, you mean, sir?"

Sim St. Bride waved that away. "These nasty rumors, I mean. I'm sure they're not true, but I don't like to see Mara upset."

"I'm not upset," Mara protested.

But her father pulled a face. "I always knew letting you go off to London was unwise."

Mara took Dare's hand. "At least I'm not marrying away, Papa. Dare wants to find a home nearby."

"Ah," her father said, relaxing. "Well, then, there's a place coming up for sale not five miles away. But," he added, with a searching look at Mara, "I'll be surprised if your exploits didn't play a part in these troubles. Black Ademar's hair."

Dare intervened. "It's entirely my fault, sir. If this story was set about by this

Captain Berkstead, it's because of a disagreement between us. It ended in blows."

"That won't lead to a duel, will it?" Mara's mother asked, suddenly pale.

"No," Mara said.

"I doubt it," Dare said.

She turned to him. "It will *not*. No matter what Berkstead's done, it can't be worth calling him out."

"What if he calls me out?"

"On what grounds?"

"I did break his nose."

"After he attacked you!"

"You were there?" Her father's astonished question snapped Mara back into her situation.

Knowing she was blushing, she said, "I was visiting the mews to see Dare's new horse, Papa."

"And this scoundrel attacked Dare in the Yeovil House mews? Sounds like a madman. I assume the grooms dealt with him."

Mara struggled not to look harried. "Dare and I strolled back to the house down the mews lane, Papa. It happened there."

"Nothing wrong with that," her mother said. "I'm sure you and I strolled many a lane when we were courting, Sim."

"Not in London, we didn't," he grumbled. "A wicked, disorderly place it is, and you're

431

expecting your mother and me to rattle all that way for this ball. Better to hold it here, and in less of a rush."

He'd turned to Mara again, but Amy St. Bride responded. "You know why it has to be in Town, Sim. And only think, you'll be able to attend some votes in the Lords. You know you've been feeling guilty over not doing so."

If anything, that made the reluctant Earl of Marlowe's gloom deeper. "It's a busy time on the land. . . ."

"Which Rupert can manage very well. What about the meetings of the Agricultural Society in London?"

That proved to be more successful temptation.

"Oh, very well," Mara's father sighed. "If you will have it, you'll have it. We'll head off on Monday."

"Monday!" Mara gasped. "But, Papa, the ball is set for Tuesday."

He stared at her. "What madness is that? We cannot be there, then, and neither can you. What a heedless child you are, arriving on Friday with this news, knowing we can't travel on Sunday."

It was a disaster, but then Dare said, "With an early start tomorrow, we can make the journey in one day, sir."

"Travel *post.*" Her father stared as if Dare had suggested them flying to the moon. On his rare visits out of Lincolnshire, he had always used his own carriage and horses and taken the journey slowly.

Even Mara's mother was looking a bit short of air, but she managed a smile. "Won't that be exciting, dear? Come along, Sim. We'll grow old before our time if we avoid adventures."

"We'll die before our time if we go hurtling about. It's all Marlowe's fault," he complained. "Why he couldn't have sired a bunch of sons, I'll never know. And kept them in the country. It's London that sickens people. Austrey would have been all right if he'd not spent so much time in London."

"He'd have been better off living at Marlowe?" his wife asked.

He shot her a frustrated look and left, muttering about so much to do.

Amy St. Bride smiled at them. "He'll do it, dears, and it will be an adventure." But then she turned flustered. "How exactly does one travel post? We need to order a post chaise to come here for us, don't we? How do we pay the postillions at the changes?"

"Will you allow me to make the arrangements?" Dare said. "Two post chaises, I assume, even if Salter rides. Unless any other of the family would like to come?"

"Not the girls. Not to London. And the boys are at school. Rupert and Mary will be needed here. But servants. We will want our own servants."

Mara had to fight laughter at her mother's increasingly frantic tone.

"I suggest your servants travel in the family coach," Dare said soothingly. "In fact, if they start out soon and travel well into the night, they could be in London not long after us, and the coach will be available to bring you home."

"Oh, that would be nice. How efficient you are, dear. Then I'd best go and make arrangements. So much to do." But she paused to give Dare a hearty hug. "I am very pleased about this, my dear boy. I can imagine no one better for Mara."

When she'd left, Dare laughed softly. "That did sound as if you need a lord and master of extraordinary endurance."

"It's the hair. It's such a worry to them, the poor dears."

Dare took her hand and kissed it. "This journey does feel like taking innocents into the wicked world."

She moved closer to kiss. "They're not innocents at all and you know it."

"Yes." He nuzzled her hair and sweetness flowed through her.

Reluctantly, she stepped away. "I'd better go and help Mama with the arrangements."

"And I'd better command the post chaises."

They moved back to kiss. "This feels sweet, doesn't it?" Mara said. "Almost as if we're already married."

He raised a brow. "You expect our marriage to be sweet?"

She kissed him again, playfully. "Sugar and spice, and all things nice."

"That's what little girls are made of. I'm to find frogs and snails and puppy dog tails?"

"No," she said, with a firm, warning look.

"It would be a novel way of decorating a bridal bed."

"No," she repeated, laughing, and escaped, rejoicing at another glimpse of the old Dare.

Arranging for the post chaises took only a moment. Dare sent a groom to Louth with precise instructions, knowing the Brideswell name would be credit enough. Then he was at a loose end.

He spent a little time simply sitting in the

well-worn parlor in company with four dogs and three cats, aware of a kind of peace he could hardly remember. Brideswell was extraordinary, and he didn't know if it was simply the effects of the family or something more metaphysical.

One of the setters stirred and moved to flop at his feet; then a marmalade cat leapt up into his lap, circled, and settled to be stroked.

Doing so, he considered that before — before Waterloo — he'd not been much interested in peace and quiet. Since, it had become his precious jewel, but one impossible to find except in opium.

Until recently.

Until Mara.

Until here.

What if he'd not gone to London and Mara had been there without him? She might have fallen into terrible danger after that tryst with Berkstead. Even without that, she would have met many men. Might have chosen another man. The thought could shrivel his soul.

But what if some other man would be better for her?

He reined in his frantic thoughts and stroked the soothing cat, using breathing and relaxation skills so painfully acquired.

The clock struck five. At least an hour before he should take his next allowance. The damnable freedom of choice made everything harder.

Routine, that was the thing. Routine days. Routine seasons.

Why would anyone with a tranquil, useful life seek diversity? Didn't only the dissatisfied seek novelty? Or was that terror speaking? Was life only lived through excitement and challenge?

He inhaled and exhaled again, sought his faltering core of serenity and stroked the cat.

Amy St. Bride saw the man he used to be. Everyone wanted the person he'd been before. The Dare Debenham who didn't exist anymore except as a mask. Why didn't they realize no one could emerge unchanged from torture?

Inhale, exhale, stroke.

Even Mara wanted the old Dare. She glowed when he amused or came up with some idiotic novelty. Could he be the man she thought she was marrying? Or was he the monster of his worst nightmares?

God. He rose sharply, settled the cat back with its companions by the fire and headed for the door. The setter rose and looked up at him expectantly.

"Want a walk?" he asked.

As if summoned, the three other dogs romped to his side, changed from somnolent to lively in a moment. He shook his head and headed for the back of the house.

He'd had the run of Brideswell so often in his youth that he made his way easily through tangled corridors — until he became lost. The dogs waited patiently, tails wagging. The problem, he realized, was that a new extension had been added to the house, probably for Simon's brother Rupert, who was married now and lived here, acting as his father's estate steward.

He found a door to the outside and began a circuit of the house, noting the changes. The dogs kept him company, exploring new scents and flushing the occasional affronted bird. More blessed peace seeped into him. How long was it since he'd done a simple thing like this?

He paused on a path between flower beds to look at the rambling house. If it had beauty, it was the beauty of a wildflower meadow. Some of the alterations of the centuries looked more like motley patches on old clothing. It was a mongrel of a house and its magic, if it existed, did not come from good looks.

No wonder the family had been horrified

at the idea of moving to the designed perfection of Marlowe, even for part of the year. No wonder Simon had taken the burden from them. The magic of the St. Brides would wither there, like plants set in dry sand.

Simon had proved that he could flourish elsewhere — no doubt another inheritance from Black Ademar, a rootless mercenary until he finally settled in England. Simon loved Brideswell and wanted it alive and welcoming, but had never intended to live here until his father died. Hopefully in thirty or forty years.

Mara was different, however, despite the hair. She wouldn't flourish far from here. There was a house for sale nearby, but how could he commit so far until he'd fought free of the beast that coiled purring in the vial in his pocket, whispering to him now that there was no real need to wait? Peace could be his in a moment.

His hand was sliding into his pocket when the setter romped up, tail wagging, with a stick in its mouth.

Rescue. "Thank you," Dare murmured as he took the stick and hurled it as far as he could. The pack raced after it and he followed, meeting the victor partway and throwing the stick forward again. *Thus, with help, I progress.*

From the east side of the house, he looked over flat fields dotted white with sheep toward the invisible sea. What fun they'd had, Simon, he, and a gaggle of cousins and neighbors out on the sea in boats. He'd liked his home and loved his parents, but life at Long Chart had never contained the sort of joyous freedom that was taken for granted at Brideswell.

He continued on, progressing by stick throws as they skirted the walled kitchen garden. A gardener passed, pushing a wheelbarrow of manure and offering a cheerful "Good afternoon, sir."

But then the dogs ignored the stick and raced straight down the path. At the corner, they met a plump, running girl, an ear-flapping spaniel at her side. "Don't get in my way," she shouted at the dogs, booted feet flying beneath grubby skirts that ended inches above her ankles.

Then she saw Dare and skidded to a halt. "Who are you?"

It was a challenge, but she showed no fear. Why should she? This was Brideswell, and Dare had no doubt that the dogs would tear him to bits if he hurt her.

"Dare Debenham. I'm a friend of Simon's."

Despite plain clothes showing evidence of a day pleasurably spent, this must be one of Simon's young sisters. Her short hair was the family's typical brown and she had a distinct look of her mother.

"You were at the wedding," she said, turning friendly. "You weren't well. I'm Lucy. Lady Lucianne St. Bride," she amended, rolling her eyes and grinning at the absurdity of it.

Dare laughed and captured a grubby hand to kiss it. "Lord Darius Debenham, at your service, my lady."

She chuckled with delight.

Suddenly, stealing his breath, he remembered his first meeting with Mara. He'd been fourteen, so Mara had been about Lucy's age, and just as much of a free spirit. She, too, had worn her hair in a practical short crop of curls, and her skirts short. She'd had similar, sensible shoes. She hadn't been Lady Mara then, and had no expectation of ever being that, but she'd called him "my lord" simply to annoy.

"Are you all right?"

The child's voice recalled him. "Completely. I'm here with your sister Mara because we're going to be married."

"Lovely! I'll be a bridesmaid again. But I have to go. I'm late." She raced away, swift and agile in her liberating clothes, and all the dogs raced with her, forgetting Dare.

She'd been coming from the stables, so he went that way and found, as expected, a pony being rubbed down. Dare almost questioned the wisdom of letting a girl of what — seven? — ride around the area with only a spaniel for guardian, but Mara had done the same. He didn't think his sister Thea had ever left the house, never mind the estate, in her life without an adult.

But this was Brideswell.

The young groom nodded, clearly noting Dare as a stranger and becoming just a little watchful. Brideswell didn't preserve its idyll through carelessness.

Dare offered his credentials. "I'm Lord Darius Debenham. I'm to marry Lady Mara."

Concern vanished. "Many best wishes, sir." The groom turned back to the pony.

Dare strolled along the boxes greeting some of the horses, then headed back to the house. It was probably close to suppertime if Brideswell still kept country hours, as he was sure they did. Now, because he was far from his midday dose, the thought of a noisy St. Bride meal brought out a sweat, but he'd be able to take the next dose before he had to face it.

He realized he was fingering the vial in his pocket again and took out his hand. Damn Ruyuan. Salter could have the supplies and everything would be much easier.

To delay having to deal with people he took the long way back, along a wildflower-edged lane beside the paddocks, then through the orchard, where fruit was in its early swell. He touched a gnarled old tree, realizing that he'd never tasted a fresh apple from here. By harvesttime he'd been at school, and Christmas had always been spent at Long Chart.

The kitchen garden sprouted leafy greens, and frames supporting vigorous peas and beans. Everything was in order, but nothing felt regimented. Like the children of Brideswell, the plants grew best freely, but weeds and pests were dealt with ruthlessly. He sent a prayer that he not prove to be a pest.

"Dare?"

He looked up to see Mara coming down the path, a simple shawl around her shoulders. He smiled at how natural she looked here, so different from her London elegance.

"Are you all right?" she asked, concern in her eyes.

"Of course," he lied, for he was better for seeing her. "I met Lucy."

"That scamp. She got a scold for being late. Do you want to go and look at Derebourne Manor later?"

After food and opium all would be right with the world for a while. "Why not?" he said, and drew her into his arms.

He'd meant to kiss her, and to keep it decorous, but instead, he clung and she held him. And it was, for the moment, enough.

CHAPTER 26

After the noisy family meal at a table holding fourteen, Dare let Mara drive the gig to Derebourne Manor, a pleasant double-gabled house built in the reign of Queen Anne. They were taken around by the housekeeper and found the rooms to be adequate and everything in good repair. There was nothing wrong with it, but it held no magic.

"It will come to life when a family lives here," Mara said.

He heard the same doubts in her.

"We can do better," he said, and saw her relief even as she warned, "Not many houses come available nearby."

"If necessary, we can build."

"That will take time."

"And patience isn't your virtue," he said with a smile as they returned to the gig.

She glanced at him, laughter in her eyes. "You know me too well." There was love in her eyes, too, so they had to kiss, right there, in front of the house, where anyone could see them.

"One of the many advantages of being betrothed," he said, reluctantly easing out of her arms. "We are being outrageous, but not scandalous."

He took the reins for the drive back to Brideswell, saying, "We could perhaps rent Derebourne while a house was building. Is there land available?"

"I'm sure there must be. We don't want an estate, do we?"

"Not of any size."

They drove along a winding road talking comfortably of their ideal home, evening softness settling around them marked by the jangle of a cow bell heading for milking, and the first song of a nightingale.

An intense tranquillity enveloped Dare, such as he couldn't remember experiencing in his life before.

"Are we going to the village?"

Mara's question startled him back to life. "Damn. I've taken the wrong turn again."

"You always did that," she said with a chuckle. "Simon used to tease that you had a homing instinct for the ale at the Drunken Monk."

"Excellent ale, as I remember. Pity it's too

446

late to stop."

"We could," she said, as they entered the village and the ancient inn came into view, clearly in full use.

"You'd upset the locals."

The road followed the churchyard wall and they heard a different kind of singing: Evensong.

"We'll soon be married there," Mara said softly, then added, "I wish it could be now."

Dare halted the gig. "So do I."

"Alas that even Uncle Scipio wouldn't agree to marry us without a license."

Dare kissed her fingers. "We could attend the end of the service. Give thanks for the day."

And beg God's mercy for the night.

He tethered the horse and they walked up the path between gravestones and spring flowers. When they pushed open the heavy old doors, the hymn grew in volume, and when they opened the next doors to enter the body of the church, the rough but hearty singing filled the space.

St. Bride's was no more a great church than Brideswell was a great house, but it had the same comfortable rightness. The church was older than the house, having been part of the monastery of St. Bride, founded long before the Conquest. It was said that the church foundations went back that far.

They slipped into a back pew and joined in as the service was completed. When the congregation filed out, everyone said a good evening to Mara, many of them including Dare by name, remembering him from the past and from the wedding.

Then they rose to greet the vicar, Mara's uncle, a rotund, hearty man.

"A wedding here soon, I gather. Excellent, excellent. Everyone should be married in their home church. I don't hold with these London weddings."

"Some people do live in London," Dare pointed out, amused.

The round eyes widened. "Do they? Oh, dear, I suppose they must. And you're dragging poor Sim off there, I hear. Duty must, I suppose. Did you wish to talk to me about the service?"

"Not now, Uncle," Mara said. "We're just visiting the church."

"Excellent, excellent. Commune with the Lord! You must excuse me, then. My supper awaits." He strode off toward his vestry and Dare walked down the aisle, over flagstones and brasses marking the passing of illustrious St. Brides toward the altar and the stone cross beyond it.

Commune with the Lord. Here it seemed possible to an extraordinary degree. Something was humming in Dare's mind, something that reminded him of tai-chi and the hard-won peace he could find in discipline and meditation. Here it simply floated in the air, like music, like a blessing, available on a breath.

"Why was the monastery built here?" he asked, quiet in the sacred space.

"Good land," Mara said. "A river nearby. The monks needed to support themselves as well as pray."

Dare tested the air again. "I think it's more than that. Why have people traveled to sacred sites for centuries? To Compostella and Canterbury. To Stonehenge, even, and Egeria's Grotto. There are places that seem special."

She took his hand. "It will provide a blessing for our wedding."

He kissed that hand, but was assailed by an uneasy premonition. He tried to grasp the threat. It was as ethereal as fog and as unpleasant. He took Mara's other hand, weaving their fingers. "Do you know that the couple marry each other? The minister merely blesses the union."

"I don't think the law quite looks at it like that."

"It used to. That's why a Gretna marriage works. Will you pledge to me, Mara, here and now? I shouldn't do this, but I could not bear to lose you."

"You won't," she said, but smiling, a smile as sweet as evening light. "It's a lovely idea, but I can't remember the right words."

"Does it matter?" He raised her hands and kissed each. "I promise that if you are willing to entrust yourself to me, Mara St. Bride, I will be faithful to that trust. I will be a loving companion through life. I will cherish, protect, and respect you, and put your welfare first in all I do." He kissed her hands again. "Till death and beyond."

"I can't match that," she said, tears shining in her eyes.

"Of course you can. What do you promise?"

She looked up at the shadowy arches, then back at him, drawing their hands together, hers encompassing his.

"I promise to love you. I will always love you, Darius Debenham, and I will be faithful to you in every way. I will work always for joy — for us, for all around us, and for our future family. I will be your true companion in this life and beyond. This I promise."

They came together then to kiss, a deep

and tender kiss in the rosy light of the setting sun, and then simply rested there together. The peace of mind and heart was so profound that Dare lacked the strength to break it. Even the beast had been cowed in the church. Its snarls had been muted since arriving at Brideswell.

"They'll find us here turned to stone," he murmured.

Mara laughed and then moved gently away to take his hand and lead him out of the church, out into a beautiful evening crowned by a blessed, pearlescent sky and pure birdsong.

As he drove the gig toward the Brideswell stables, Dare said, "Is there room for us to live at Brideswell until we find the right place?"

"What an excellent idea. Grandfather Baddersley's rooms are still vacant — a bedchamber, dressing room, and parlor."

"Why isn't Rupert using them?"

"He and Mary did for a while, but there's no room for a nursery nearby. That's why Father built on. They would do for us, however, for a while."

A blush showed she'd thought about their children.

"There's Delphie and Pierre as well."

"They'll want to be in the children's

quarters with Lucy and Jenny."

"Yes, I think they will. But there'll have to be a dolls' house of some sort."

"And a toy boat," she said, but then smiled. "Perhaps not, for here Pierre can have a real one."

Mara hugged their private wedding to herself through a family evening that was blessedly short because of the next day's travel. She loved her family dearly, but at the moment, they interfered with blissful dreams.

Mara settled into her old bed at ten o'clock and snuggled under the familiar patchwork coverlet, amazed at the changes in her world since she'd slept there last and savoring all the wonders to come.

She couldn't sleep and began to worry about Dare.

He'd said he'd take an extra dose to get him through the night peacefully, but she knew how hard it would be for him. Would he do it? Or would he try to endure without disturbing the household?

He had Salter with him. But not exactly. Dare was in Simon's old room, and Salter had a room in the menservants' quarters.

When the downstairs clock chimed eleven, Mara sighed and sat up in bed. She knew what she had to do.

She climbed out of bed, reaching for her silk robe, the one Mary had given her. But then she changed her mind and dug into drawers in search of her old one. It was four years old and the bright blue wool had faded to gray, but it felt more comfortable.

She went to the door, remembering thinking that no one could creep around Brideswell undetected. She was about to find out if that belief was true.

She opened the door and listened, hearing all the familiar sounds — four discordantly ticking clocks and her father's intermittent snore. At least he was asleep. Jenny and Lucy were in the schoolroom on the next floor up. Rupert and Mary were in their own quarters in the extension to the house.

That left only her Baddersley great-uncle and -aunt, and her St. Bride grandmother in this part of the house. Did any of them suffer from insomnia? She had no idea. Then there were the dogs and cats. If they heard her, they might come in search of nighttime amusement.

At the moment there was no sign of life. The corridor was lit only by moonlight, but Mara could find her way around Brideswell blindfolded. She'd done just that many times in mischief and games.

She crept barefoot past the room that had been Ella's, then around the stairwell past her parents' room to where the boys' rooms lay. A hand run lightly along the wall discovered one doorway — Rupert's old room — then the next, Simon's.

Heart pattering, she listened and heard movement. Perhaps a chair pushed back when someone stood. Dare wasn't asleep, then.

Or Salter was keeping watch?

Ah, well. She turned the knob and eased open the door, praying the hinges didn't squeak. They didn't, and she saw Dare by firelight, standing at the window looking out at the sea. She slipped in and closed the door.

It made a little click and he turned, but not sharply. As if he'd expected her. As if he'd been waiting for her?

"I always thought it unfair that the boys got to look toward the sea," she said, intending to speak softly, but not quite so breathily.

He was in a dark banjan robe and held a glass of dark liquid in his hand.

"Is that . . . ?"

He started and looked down. "Laudanum? No." He put it aside. "You shouldn't be here."

"Why not?" she said, walking toward him. "We've taken our vows."

"Mara . . ."

But he didn't resist when she went into his arms, when she drew his head down for a kiss. She'd expected to have to fight honorable reluctance, but it was as if she'd flung a door open to release a torrent.

He ravished her mouth with a ferocious hunger that weakened her knees, so she clung as she ravished him back, senses rioting and exploding all civilized restraint. The touch, the heat, the smell of him swept through her, creating such need that she'd have clawed her way through walls to get to him.

She was tearing at his clothes when he swept her up and carried her to the bed, laid her there, collapsed over her — sweet, potent weight — and kissed her again. His hand gripped her thigh, her hip and she pushed against him, wanting more, fighting to get at his skin beneath heavy silk, longing for his skin on every inch of hers.

Panting, Mara heaved him off her, but only so she could strip for him; then she grabbed his garment.

He escaped, laughing, but only to strip it off, then to drag down the bedcovers. But then he took his shirt off a chair and flung it over the sheets before picking her up again and laying her on it, more gently this time, but his eyes burning with passion.

Fearing the pause, Mara raised her hand. "Come."

He took her hand, kissed it, but then settled at her side. When she protested, wriggled closer, he said, "Slowly, slowly, love, testing though it is. This is not a wine to be gulped."

He began to kiss and tongue all over her body.

Mara lay there, heart pounding, stroking whatever part of him came beneath her hands, trying to match him for control despite a passion that felt as if it would explode. She recognized a dim echo of the pleasure he'd given her last time, but this was torrent to stream. Her body would not stay still. It responded to his every ministration with shiver or stirring or sometimes an arch of need.

As when his mouth settled around one nipple, to tongue and suck. A cry escaped her.

"Hush," he murmured, and she heard the beloved laughter in it. So she hushed, even when he worked the same magic on her other breast, and when his hand slid into the folds between her spread thighs, finding the pleasure places there with a gentle, almost teasing touch.

She moved hungrily against him and tangled fingers in his hair to make him look at her. "This time I want you inside me. Promise me, Dare. I must be yours completely."

"Oh, yes."

His agreement soothed her mind but not her urgent body.

"Now." She spread her thighs wider and moved against him. He settled there, breathing hard, nudging her wider still, pressing closer still. Mara sucked in breaths as if the air was thin as his hardness began to fill her hot ache. Then it hurt, and she couldn't help a caught breath.

He sealed her mouth with a kiss, then thrust, so her short cry was caught there. Then he stilled and smothered any memory of pain in a searing kiss, one hand pleasuring her breast until she thrust up against him, wanting more. Wanting everything.

He met her, then slid in and out. "Yes," she gasped. This was what she wanted, had wanted in her secret knowing places for so long. With Dare. With Dare. With Dare.

She was thrusting against him now, as fiercely as he thrust into her, trying to hold back cries of effort and mindless pleasure, vaguely praying their exertions couldn't be heard, as her heart thundered in her chest and then her mind spun wildly into blank brilliance.

Still locked, Mara grabbed Dare to her and kissed him, heart still hammering, fire still pulsing through her veins. Then hard mouths turned soft to trail over sweaty skin, to suck, to lick, to love, and the world steadied around them.

A different world.

A better, more perfect world.

"Forever and ever. Amen," she murmured against his chest.

Then later: "You finally showed me a volcanic eruption."

He laughed, rather helplessly and rolled to lie on his back.

She coiled into him, hooking a leg over a strong thigh, running a hand over his hard abdomen. "That was perfect."

His hand cherished her hair. "With daylight and sanity, we may regret it."

"No, we won't. What does it matter? We're to marry in weeks."

Silence reminded her that he'd intended to wait until he'd won his battle, but then he kissed her hair. "You are truly precious to me, my dearest lady and I won't betray this trust."

They slid into comfortable talk of their future, then made love again, slowly, gently, but no less volcanically, before Mara had to slip back to her bed to catch a few hours' sleep.

Alone, Dare lay facedown where Mara had lain, inhaling her smell, absorbing her warmth, of spirit as much as flesh. Their lovemaking should not have happened, but he couldn't regret it.

How could he regret heaven? He gathered up his shirt, now marked with a streak of blood. He'd meant to burn it, but he couldn't. He folded it and packed it carefully away.

Then he picked up his glass, shivered, and drank.

CHAPTER 27

They arrived back in London after dark. Everyone was exhausted, but they had made it in one day. Mara was as relieved as her parents to arrive, for she'd not anticipated being separated from Dare nearly the whole way. It had simply been taken for granted that Dare would travel with her father in one chaise, and Mara with her mother in the other. There'd been no rational argument to make, so they'd met only for meals.

At those meals her parents had insisted on a half hour to digest their food before "rattling off again," as her disgruntled father put it. But Dare needed most of that time for opium, and though Mara wished he'd let her be with him then, she knew he'd hate it.

Thirteen hours apart had hurt as much as torn skin, especially after the wonder of the previous night, but when the post chaises entered the walled courtyard of Marlowe

House, Mara realized that torment wasn't over.

Simon and Jancy came out to greet them. They'd already moved here, and so, therefore, had she. In any case, with her parents here she'd have to live with them. How could she have been blind to that?

She climbed down close to tears. Dare had left the other chaise with her father and was talking to Simon, but in moments that chaise would take him on to Yeovil House.

He looked unhappy about it, too. But then she realized it must be something else. He looked as if he'd received news of a death. She hurried over. "What is it?"

Simon answered her. "A woman's turned up who claims to be Delphie's mother."

"No."

"Unfortunately, yes. She presented herself only hours ago at Yeovil House."

"I must go there," Dare said and walked rapidly to the waiting chaise.

Mara pursued, ignoring her family. She dashed in before the steps were raised, and then they were off. "It won't be true," she said, gripping his hand. "It's probably someone trying to get a reward."

"What reward?" He was looking forward as if that could force the carriage to make better speed through the London streets.

"You'd pay her to go away, wouldn't you?"

He turned to face her. "How could I do that if she truly is Delphie's mother? I've always known Thérèse would have snatched the children without care for other people's suffering."

Mara chose silence and prayer. When they arrived, she wanted to race into Yeovil House, but Dare was superficially composed, so she matched him.

When had he last taken opium? He'd need it for this. Probably when they'd stopped for dinner two hours ago. Not too bad a time of day for disaster, if that made any sense.

They were directed to the library by a footman, who looked upset despite his training. There they found the duke and duchess, and a young woman in shabby black sitting on a sofa looking both terrified and belligerent.

Delphie's mother? There was no obvious resemblance, but a white cap beneath a black straw bonnet concealed the woman's hair. She couldn't be Delphie's mother. To lose the girl would destroy Dare.

Dare's parents rose to stand with him as his father said, "This is Madame Clermont. She claims to be Delphie's mother."

"Annette!" the woman protested. *"Elle*

s'appelle Annette!"

The Duchess of Yeovil spoke soothingly to her in French. "She has been known as Delphie for some years now, madam. It is how she thinks of herself."

"But she is my daughter, madam. Mine. My Annette. She was stolen from me after the battle, when there were so many soldiers, so much death and dying." She began to rock herself, moaning. "I hear of her, and I know it is she. A pretty child with dark curls, yes?"

Mara was devastated by that detail, but then realized the woman could be repeating the description in the advertisement.

Would Delphie recognize her mother? She'd been so young when taken, but surely a well-loved child would.

"Has madam met the child?" she asked in English.

"Not yet," the duke said.

Mara turned to Dare, aware of the poor woman following their unintelligible conversation with frantic eyes. "You have to bring Delphie down, or take Madame Clermont up."

"She's in black," he said. "Delphie will be terrified."

She touched his arm. "Go. We'll see what we can do."

463

Dare left and Mara considered the woman. She was probably only in her twenties, but aged by gaunt distress. Understandable if she'd been seeking a missing child for two years, but she would frighten any child.

Mara went to sit by the woman. "Madame Clermont," she said in French, "the little girl is afraid of women in black. It is to do with the woman who stole her. You don't want to frighten her. Let us replace your outer clothing with something brighter."

But the woman shrank away. "No, no. You are trying to trick me."

"No, truly . . ."

But the woman pushed at her, so Mara gave up.

The duchess left and returned with a huge silk shawl in shades of blue. She put it around the woman's shoulders and it was not rejected. Madame Clermont's whole attention was fixed on the door.

It opened, but only to let in Mara's parents and Simon and Jancy. Mara quickly explained. Then they all waited in silence.

At last, Dare came in, carrying Delphie, who was clutching Mariette. Pierre marched alongside, fiercely on guard. That was another problem. How could the two children be separated?

Madame Clermont stared. She seemed stunned for a moment and Mara hoped, but then she leapt up and rushed to grab Delphie, crying, "Annette, Annette! I knew you were not dead. I knew it!"

Delphie shrieked and clung to Dare and all three ended up in a tangle, with the woman flailing at him. "Give her to me! Give her to me! *Give me my child.*"

Dare thrust Delphie into Madame Clermont's arms and everyone suddenly went silent. Delphie looked at Dare with such shocked betrayal that Mara covered her mouth with her hand. Huge, silent tears swelled in the girl's eyes and began to slide down her cheeks, but she made not a sound.

Madame Clermont began to moan, rocking the child. "Annette, Annette, Annette . . ."

Pierre stepped forward, lower lip thrust forward. "Her name is Delphine," he said in French.

Madame Clermont backed away from him. "Who are you?"

"I am Delphie's brother."

"No, you're not. You are not my child!"

"I am her brother and I must protect her."

"No. Go away! You are trying to steal her again!" She clutched Delphie even tighter. A squeak escaped the girl, but only a squeak. Mara recognized a child who had learned the hard way to be very, very quiet.

Everyone seemed frozen, not knowing what to do, but then Amy St. Bride went to the woman.

"You must sit down, ma'am," she said in English, for she'd learned little French, and that long ago. With a gentle hand, she steered the Belgian woman back to the sofa. "All will be well, but there's no point in upsetting the children. We'll all have a nice cup of tea and decide what to do for the best."

The flow of words and her innate kindness got the Belgian woman back on the sofa, arms still tight around the silent, weeping Delphie. Face set, Pierre marched to stand beside them and took Delphie's hand. She clutched his, and the tears stopped.

The duchess stepped outside and ordered tea.

Mara could laugh at her mother's solution to every woe, but a nice cup of tea could not solve this. If Delphie truly was this woman's lost child, she must be returned to her, even though Dare loved Delphie and Delphie loved Dare.

Had loved. Would the child recover from this betrayal?

Mara went to stand by Dare, taking his

hand as Pierre had taken Delphie's. Delphie clearly did not remember this woman, however. Wouldn't a child of five have some memory of a loving mother from two years ago? Or did terrible events wipe out memory?

She broke the silence, speaking in French. "The child doesn't seem to recognize you, Madame Clermont, and you have offered no proof."

The woman's glare was almost feral in her fear, but she scrabbled with one hand for a pocket and produced a paper. The duke took it and read it. "A birth record for Annette Marie Clermont, dated August twenty-fourth, 1812, in Halle."

For a moment, it exploded hope, but Simon said, "So she had a child. That doesn't prove that Delphie is that child."

"How many stolen girls of that age and appearance could there be?" Dare asked.

"What of your family, madam?" the duke demanded of the woman. "Surely you have not come to England alone, not speaking the language? There must be others who know your child."

She glowered at him. In her arm, Delphie could as well have been a wax doll. "Back in Halle, yes. There, everyone knows my Annette. I read the paper, the advertisement. I

467

travel to England, to London. It is not hard. I ask directions to the office given. A man brings me here." She rose, Delphie tight in her arms. "Now I will leave."

"Non." It was the tiniest plea from Delphie, but she directed it at Dare.

"No," he said. "My apologies, madam, but I cannot permit you to leave this house with Delphie until there is proof. You may stay here and be with her, but you may not take her away."

Madame Clermont looked as if she would argue, but servants entered then with tea, creating a bizarre interlude with the prosaic ritual of setting out pots, china, and plates of small cakes. The servants left and Mara's mother somehow got Madame Clermont back on the sofa. The duchess, looking dazed, poured tea.

Mara took a cup to the Belgian woman, but it was rejected. Perhaps she feared it was poisoned. Mara did feel sorry for her, for she was alone in the company of enemies, but she felt sorrier for the children and Dare.

She sat on the sofa and offered Delphie a cake. The child shook her head, looking at Mara as if saying, *Won't you stop this horrible situation?*

Mara couldn't resist the silent plea.

"Madam, the child is frightened. She will become sick with it. Please let me hold her for a while. I won't move from this spot, but she will be a little less upset as we all discuss this."

She hoped the fact that she wasn't Dare might help, and perhaps that she was young and female. The woman searched her eyes, sighed, and passed over the little girl.

Delphie clutched Mara, burrowing her damp face into Mara's neck, trembling all over. "Papa?" she whispered.

"Papa is near," Mara murmured in English, rocking the child, "but he cannot hold you just now." She wanted to tell Delphie that all would be well, but she didn't believe in lying to children. "He loves you very much, but this lady seems to love you, too. It is very difficult, but we will do our best to keep you safe."

Delphie sniffed and whispered, "Mariette?"

Mara hadn't noticed the doll's absence. She saw it on the floor by Madame Clermont's soiled dark skirts. "Pierre, could you give Mariette to Delphie, please?"

The boy picked up the stick doll, straightened the rag skirts, and put it in Delphie's hands. She clutched the doll close. "It's all right, Mariette," she whispered in French so softly Mara could hardly hear. "Papa is here."

Mara fought tears herself.

The duke and Dare had been talking together, and now the duke said, "Madam, we must send to Halle for witnesses. Whom should we send for? Your husband? A priest?"

"My husband is dead. But send for whom you will. Anyone will tell you this is my daughter. My Annette."

"Your parents?" the duke asked stonily. "They, too, are dead?"

"No."

"Their names and direction?"

"Lameule. They have a farm outside Halle. They will tell you. The priest will tell you. Everyone will tell you that this is my Annette."

Mara saw Dare whiten. The woman's firmness was terrifying. But even if she was Delphie's true mother, would it be right to force the devastated child to go with her?

"I will arrange for messages to Halle," the duke said. "My dear," he said to his wife, "perhaps a room could be prepared for the lady. She will probably prefer to be close to the child in the nursery area. Dare."

Dare left with his father. Delphie twitched, but then settled back, a limp weight in Mara's arms. Mara would like to think the child felt safe, but was sure Delphie was limp with misery. She stroked the girl's hair, desperately seeking a solution.

Soon they made their way upstairs, led by the duchess, with Mara still carrying Delphie, but Madame Clermont almost glued to her side. Dare came behind with Pierre.

A bed had been made up in the nursery, next door to the children's bedroom.

"Madam," Dare said, "please be comfortable here. Ask for anything you need, and spend time with Delphie as you wish during the day. Do not disturb her in the night. You may not take her away. You may not be alone with her. I'm sorry, but you could be a madwoman intending her harm."

"You will see. Now, my little one," she said coaxingly to Delphie, "come to your mother."

Delphie tensed and her hands clutched into Mara like claws.

Dare raised a hand. "First, I must try to explain to her, to both of them." He took Delphie in one arm, and knelt, putting the other around Pierre.

Mara sighed for love of him. It would be so easy for him to take the children apart for this, to exclude this intrusive stranger, but he wouldn't do that. He even spoke to them in French.

"I love you both as you know," he said, "but you know it is possible that you have parents who love you just as much, and who have been searching for you ever since you disappeared. That must be very hard to bear."

"You are our papa," Pierre stated, not giving an inch.

"In so many ways, but not by blood. If Delphie really is Madame Clermont's daughter, there are laws about these things, and good laws overall. If you were my true children and had been taken from me, it wouldn't matter that years had gone by and you might have forgotten me. I would find you, and bring you home. You see?"

The children nodded, but uncertainly.

"It will not matter what we want?" Pierre challenged.

"It may not. But whatever happens, I will not lose you. We will not be truly apart."

Mara wanted to protest a promise that could not be kept.

Dare put Delphie on her feet and stood. "You are both to try to be kind to Madame Clermont, but one of the footmen will be nearby at all times, and he will find me if you need me. Now it is time for bed, I think. Say good night to madam."

They did so, resentfully, and then he led them into their bedroom. When he emerged, he and Mara followed the silent duchess downstairs.

Dare let his mother get ahead, however, and took Mara into his bedroom. She wrapped her arms around him, remembering that first night here, when he'd rescued her. Her predicament had seemed so serious then. It had been nothing.

He sighed and moved away. "I think she's telling the truth."

"There's no evidence but her word," Mara protested.

"But her word is convincing, and she passed Solomon's test."

"What?"

"She surrendered the child to you because Delphie was suffering."

Mara sat on a chair. "It can't be true."

"Why would she come so far and at such effort to tell a lie that will explode as soon as it's investigated?"

Mara had no answer to that.

"One solution occurs to me," Dare said, turning to look into the fire.

"What?"

When he didn't answer, she repeated, "What, Dare?"

He turned to face her. "I could marry

her." Before Mara could protest, he said, "Then I will be able to care for Delphie and she and Pierre would not be separated."

Mara couldn't find words, but then she exploded to her feet. "What about me?"

He closed his eyes. "I must protect the child first."

"Then what about another child?" Mara protested. "Our child? I could be carrying one now — you know I could."

He covered his face with his hands. "Don't."

She dragged his hands down. "I must. What am I to do if I'm carrying your child? Marry someone else and live on dry bread all my days? Bear a bastard and try to explain to him one day that you put another child first, a child not even your own?"

He stared at her. "You are cruel."

"We took vows, Dare. Did you not mean them?"

"I took vows to the children, too. That I would never let anything harm them again."

Mara swallowed over an agonizing lump in her throat and enclosed his hands in her own. "That was a vow you could never keep, my dearest love. I would give you up, I would, if I thought it right. But what sort of husband will you be to that woman, all the rest of your life? How will it help Delphie to see you suffer? She's a caring, sensitive child, and as she grows, she will understand. And how will this affect your addiction?"

He tore away from her and turned to brace himself against the window frame. "I cannot betray Delphie by letting her be taken away. I simply cannot. You saw how she looked at me. She's suffered so much." He turned, haggard. "Do you know how long it took to persuade her to cry aloud like a normal child? To laugh? To complain or object?"

Mara remembered the child's total silence in the midst of terror and betrayal. Then something else made her gasp. "Our betrothal ball!"

"Cancel it," he said.

"We can't."

"What does my reputation matter?"

"Blanche's does."

He turned away again, gripping the curtain so hard, Mara feared he'd rip it down. She ran to find Ruyuan. Only when he and Salter were with Dare did she feel able to leave Yeovil House.

She wished desperately that she could stay.

CHAPTER 28

The next day was Sunday. Mara attended service at St. George's in Hanover Square with her family and didn't think she'd ever prayed so fervently in her life. Her prayers were entirely for a solution to the dilemma that seemed to have no happy ending.

Afterward, she, Simon, and Jancy went to Yeovil House to see how things were. They learned that Madame Clermont had insisted on taking Delphie to a Catholic mass. It had been allowed, but Dare had escorted them and Pierre had gone, too. He refused to let Delphie out of his sight.

Dare looked fine-drawn and pale, but his voice was even when he said, "The mass stirred some memories in Pierre, but nothing to identify his family or home."

"What about Delphie?" Mara asked.

"No, but that doesn't prove anything. She was young."

Not that young, Mara thought, but time

would reveal the truth.

She went up to the schoolroom with Dare, to find a chilly atmosphere. Madame Clermont was attempting to play with Delphie, offering the pretty dolls. Delphie was clutching Mariette and pretending the woman didn't exist. Pierre stood on guard. He even, Mara noticed, wore a wooden sword on a belt.

The Belgian woman was quietly angry, but much improved in appearance. She had been persuaded to wear brighter clothes, and the yellow-striped cream suited her. Perhaps she had eaten and slept well for the first time in ages, for her skin and eyes seemed more alive. She still wore her white close cap with its strings beneath her chin, but wisps of hair that escaped were dark and curly. Perhaps not so dark as Delphie's but dark.

Delphie looked instantly at Dare, but she didn't run to him. Something flickered on her face that might have been hope, but clearly the child was terrified of doing the wrong thing and being punished — the worst punishment being loss of Dare.

Mara ignored the tense atmosphere and any rules and swept Delphie up into a hug. "Hello, my precious," she said in French, so as not to upset Madame Clermont. "Here it is the day of rest and you are working so hard at dressing dolls." It was nonsense, but the best she could do. "And poor Mariette never has new clothes."

"Mariette likes her clothes," Delphie said.

"That thing," Madame Clermont spat. "It is ugly and dirty. It should be thrown on the fire."

She was correct, but oh so wrong.

"Children's tastes are unpredictable, madam. If you wish Delphie to be happy, you must permit her Mariette." She spoke to the doll. "Would you permit me to give you some jewelry, Mariette?"

After a moment, Delphie replied in the squeaky voice. "Yes, please."

Mara casually passed Delphie to Dare. "Hold her as I take out my earrings." She took off the pearl earrings, then used the wires to attach them to Mariette's cloth head, watching to be sure that the bit of necessary puncturing didn't upset Delphie.

Then she took Delphie back, gave her Mariette, and carried her to the mirror. "There, Mariette. Are they not pretty?"

"Very pretty," Delphie squeaked. "You are most kind, Milady Mara."

"May I give you something, Mariette?" Dare asked, coming over.

Mara turned child and doll to him. He

took out the golden pin that fixed his cravat and carefully set it into the doll's rag clothing.

Mariette thanked him. Then Delphie added, "Mariette would like to kiss you in thanks, Papa, and so would I."

It broke Mara's heart that the child thought she had to ask permission, but both Dare and Delphie needed the hug.

Mara glanced at Madame Clermont and caught a strange expression. The woman's lips were tight, but sadness accompanied fear and irritation. She, too, understood how impossible a happy ending might be.

Everyone had decided that the ball must go on, for to abandon it might confirm the stories about Dare and possibly harm Mara's reputation. The story of the woman who claimed to be Delphie's mother had already escaped, but no one would think that sufficient reason to cancel a hastily arranged important event.

Eventually they had to leave the children, but Mara stayed at Yeovil House, trying to help, but even if she had the power to bring sunshine into people's lives, the shadows here were too dense. Dare evaded her most of the day. Would he really marry the woman to save Delphie?

Yes, he would, and Mara might permit it.

Both she and he were strong and would survive. Delphie might not.

She returned to Marlowe House to sleep, but took a coach to Yeovil House after breakfast the next day. She couldn't stay away. She arrived at the door at the same time as Major Hawkinville. "Berkstead's back," he said.

"Where?"

"Let's find Dare."

Dare hurried downstairs and they all went into the library.

"He claims to know nothing of the story," Hawkinville reported. "He's probably lying, but there's no way to force him to admit it short of torture. He's blinded by jealous hate to such an extent that he probably believes the story himself. Still seems convinced that Mara's being compelled to marry you against her wishes. Even came up with Madame Clermont as a new attack on you."

"How?" Dare asked.

"She was your mistress in Brussels. Then you abandoned her and stole the child you'd made together."

"Delphie's five. The man's fit for Bedlam."

"Probably, but he's not frothing at the mouth yet, so he can sound quite plausible, and he does have friends. He was a good soldier and a good officer. What do you want us to do with him?"

Dare rubbed his head. "Oh, leave him be. He's spread his poison and we've applied an antidote, which will work or not as fate disposes. But, Mara," he added, "don't go anywhere alone."

She nodded. "This is my fault."

"You had no reason to think that a flirtation would be taken to this extreme."

He was not mentioning her true folly, and she supposed there was no benefit from confessing it here.

"This woman who claims to be your child's mother? Is it true?" Hawkinville asked.

"Probably."

"Easy enough to settle the truth, I'd think."

"Not before tomorrow night," Dare said, "which is when Mara and I announce our betrothal to the ton."

"I don't see the connection."

Dare glanced at Mara. "One way to unravel the Gordian knot would be for me to marry the woman. Delphie would still have me."

"Gordian knots are usually cut," the major said. "Pay the woman off."

"It's been tried," Dare said, shocking

Mara. "No amount of money will suffice. You see," Dare said to her. "Solomon, again. Her sole desire is to take her daughter back to Halle."

Mara could almost hear Major Hawkinville's brain clicking like a rapid machine. Could he actually come up with a solution?

"Compromise," he said at last. "She can live as the child's mother as long as she lives with you and Mara. Uncomfortable all around, but it's the best balance."

Mara was gaping, but she looked at Dare.

He met her eyes. "I can bear that, if you can."

"Given the alternative, of course I can."

She thought they both sighed with immense relief. It was not the life they'd planned, but it would be life together.

"We must put it to her, then."

At the door, they met a footman. "Major Beaumont wishes to speak with you, milord."

"Of course."

Hal came in looking rueful. "I come bearing a summons from my godmother, Lady Cawle."

Dare swore.

"She's on her high horse, claiming she agreed to give the nod to Blanche for my sake, and was willing to turn a blind eye to opium eating, but — sorry, Dare — won't be used as a cover for cowardice. I'll tell her to go to the devil if you want."

Mara longed to do just that. How many more burdens would be tossed onto Dare? But they didn't need more trouble. "You should go," she said to Dare, "but I'm coming with you. It might as well be now. Madame Clermont will wait."

The Dowager Countess of Cawle received them in her Albemarle Street house, enthroned on a sofa, crimson skirts spread. Seen up close, she was still handsome with excellent skin and sharp, clear eyes that assessed Dare coldly.

Dare bowed. "May I present my bride, Lady Cawle. Lady Mara St. Bride."

"Don't see why not," the lady said, assessing Mara. "I know nothing to *her* discredit."

"Then you don't know as much as you think, Lady Cawle," Mara said, dipping a curtsy but speaking plainly. If the woman was going to be unpleasant, she might as well know it wouldn't all go her way.

A hint of humor showed. "I've heard about your family's hair. There was one like you when I was a girl. A terror."

"That must have been Great-uncle Frederick. Fortunately he was able to enter the army and become a hero."

"I hope you don't intend any heroics here." Lady Cawle's gaze moved back to Dare. "And your army career, Debenham?"

"I was never precisely in the army, Lady Cawle, but I believe I acquitted myself well."

Mara hoped she'd suppressed a start of surprise. She hadn't known he'd come to be sure of that, but he wouldn't have said it otherwise.

"I agreed to attend the forthcoming ball to add some little support to my godson's wife. An actress, and not of spotless reputation, but it won't do to have Mrs. Hal Beaumont excluded. I did not agree to endorse you, sir."

"You have been put in an unfortunate position, Lady Cawle, and I apologize for it."

The apology seemed to disconcert her. They were waved to seats, which Mara assumed meant they'd passed the first tests. She was struggling against rebellion even so. What right had this woman to judge either of them?

"You need to be careful, gel," Lady Cawle drawled. "Your every emotion shows on your face and a warrior needs a shield."

Mara colored. "I'd prefer not to have battles to fight."

"Then you should have chosen your future husband more carefully, shouldn't you?"

"Does one get to choose?" Mara challenged.

"A believer in Cupid's arrow, are you? Would you have fallen in love with a pig herder if the arrow had commanded?"

Mara smiled. "I did once think myself in love with one of the gardeners."

"But did not marry him," Lady Cawle pointed out.

Dare said, "I thought you wished to joust with me, Lady Cawle."

The dark eyes moved back to him. "It's useful to see how a gentleman will protect his lady. You were somewhat laggard."

"Mara can fight her own battles. I was merely feeling neglected."

Lady Cawle's lips twitched, but Mara couldn't decide if it was with amusement or irritation. "You were always a rogue — and I don't mean that ridiculous schoolboy association. Mischievous, and at times silly. I assume the silliness has been knocked out of you."

"You tempt me to gibber like a monkey and throw fruit around the room."

"Wouldn't do you any good," Lady Cawle said, glancing at a bowl of plums and pears. "It's all wax."

"Thus I am disarmed." Dare smiled.

This time, the twitch was definitely an attempt to conceal amusement. "You are attempting to *be* disarming. What is this nonsense about you turning coward, and who is behind it?"

Mara relaxed a little.

"We suspect it was spread by a Major Berkstead," Dare said. "He is understandably in love with Mara and resents the fact that she has chosen me. He seems willing to believe any evil of me. My friends have countered the story, but we have not yet found the best defense — someone who actually saw me shot down in action."

"How likely is it that such a person will be found?"

"By tonight? Slight."

"So you intend to force the ton to choose without evidence. Including me."

"We see no other choice."

"And if we all stay away?" the woman challenged.

"That is why we're putting up with your foibles, my lady. Where you go, all will go."

Lady Cawle's eyes narrowed. "You plan to spread the word that I will attend?"

"No one would so presume. But if you do intend to be at the ball, it would be pleasant if you would inform some others."

The woman's lips gathered in what could almost be a pout. "I have little choice. Hal's wife needs my support, and Arabella Hurstman insists."

"Arabella Hurstman?" Mara asked, searching her memory.

Dare laughed. "Francis's aunt and doting godmother to Nicholas's Arabel. Miss Hurstman is a warrior for the welfare of women and has decided to keep a particularly keen eye on the Rogues' wives. She carries such weight with you, Lady Cawle?"

"We've been friends for forty years, and if I'd listened to her about marriage, my life would have been better. Apparently you cared for little Arabel when she was kidnapped."

Dare's face tightened. "I did little, being weak and in violent need of opium at the time."

"You did enough to make the child regard you as some sort of angel. To achieve that when weak and in violent need of opium is most telling." She seemed to brace herself. "My late husband was an addict. I know the nature of its hold. It tests a person like acid, eating away all but truth. It revealed him to be weak, but you seem not to be. Nor do you seem dishonorable or a coward. I will attend the ball."

After a moment, Dare stirred. "Thank you."

Mara thought it was more for the assessment of his character than the attendance.

They rose to go, but Lady Cawle said, "What of this woman who claims your adopted daughter? Arabella is concerned for the child."

"We're seeking evidence," Dare said.

"And if the evidence proves her story true?"

"Then I cannot deprive a mother of the child."

"Nonsense. You have the power to do anything, and the child must come first."

As soon as they were outside, Mara asked, "What did she mean? What could you do?"

"Ruthless, isn't she? I assume she meant that it would be simple to make Madame Clermont disappear."

"Kill her? You wouldn't do that."

"Thank you. It would certainly be possible, however. More subtly, I could refuse her access to Delphie while I draw the issue out in the courts until Delphie's of age. Any money Madame Clermont had would dry up long before mine."

"Instead you're bending backward to make everything easy for her." His behavior was exasperating, but she'd expect nothing less.

"I'm doing what's right, Mara. What I hope is right. But Lady Cawle is correct. Delphie's welfare must trump legal rights."

"So we use Major Hawkinville's solution."

"Yes."

They walked back to Yeovil House, discussing the implications. It would not be pleasant to share their home with Madame Clermont, but it would be better than any alternative. It would probably be a hardship for her to live in England, but everyone was going to have to make sacrifices.

Turning into Great Charles Street, they encountered Nicholas Delaney. "I was coming to see if there was anything I could do."

"Gorgons on one side," Dare said, "krakens on the other. I'm seeking smooth water between, but damned if I can see any."

They entered the house to find Delphie sitting on the bottom step of the grand staircase, clutching Mariette. Pierre stood on guard, wearing his sword and looking fierce. One of the nursery maids hovered, wringing her hands.

At sight of Dare, Delphie launched herself at him. When he picked her up, she clutched him tight.

"What happened?" Dare asked Pierre,

while soothing the little girl.

"That woman hit her, Papa."

"Where is Madame Clermont now?" Dare's voice was cold with fury.

"Lying on her bed," Pierre said with satisfaction.

"One could ask," Nicholas said, "why madam hit Delphie." He directed it at Pierre.

The boy stuck out his chin, but then muttered, "Delphie didn't want to play with her, Uncle Nicholas." After a moment, he added, "Delphie kicked her."

Dare looked at the boy. "War, is it?"

Pierre looked worried, but he nodded, mouth set.

Dare kissed Delphie's hair and looked at her face, which showed no marks except those of tears. "Perhaps if you kicked Madame Clermont it was not so wicked of her to hit you?"

"I hate her."

"I will not let her take you away from me, but you must try to be kinder to her."

"I must?" Delphie asked.

"You must, or I will be disappointed in you."

She sighed. "Then I will try, Papa. But it will be very hard."

He put her down. "We will go back up-stairs."

A child took each of his hands. "May we not go out, Papa?" Pierre whined.

"Not yet," Dare said as they went up the stairs, the banisters of which where already circled by ribbon and artificial flowers. "Some of Madame Clermont's family might be out there, and they might try to steal you away."

"Then we will definitely not go out," said Delphie. "And anyway, the ball is *amusant.*" The child's spirits were returning.

Dare left the children in the schoolroom and knocked on the door to the nursery. When given permission, he went in and closed the door. Voices soon rose, and then Madame Clermont could be heard weeping.

Dare came out, his face carefully blank, and spoke to Mara. "I have explained Hawkinville's solution to her, and that I will use the legal stratagem if she refuses. And, of course, that she is never to hit Delphie again."

"A middle way of sorts, but stormy waters."

"There are no calm seas and pleasant breezes. I must go." He touched Mara's arm as he passed, but that was all.

"He suggested marrying her," Mara said to Nicholas after Dare had left.

"Marrying Madame Clermont?" Nicholas asked. "That wouldn't serve."

"No."

"Let's find somewhere to talk."

Mara took Nicholas to the small drawing room, but nervously. She sensed an energy in him and wasn't sure it promised well.

"I have a strange notion," he said when the door was closed. "It offers hope, but rather uselessly, and some unpleasantness. It may not suit Dare, or it might help —"

"Talk sense," Mara interrupted.

He smiled. "You are *very* like Simon. The sense is this: On seeing little Delphie look so defiant, I saw a distinct resemblance to Thérèse Bellaire."

Mara stared. "She could be that woman's true daughter?"

"It's a raw idea I'm still digesting — what a horrible concept. But I'm becoming more convinced by the moment. I've glimpsed the resemblance before, but assumed she'd picked up some of Thérèse's mannerisms. If Thérèse allowed a child to grow inside her — and that's hard to believe — she would never have cared for it herself. She certainly had no infant with her in 1814. But she might have placed it with a family, then retrieved it for this purpose."

"Placed it with Madame Clermont's family? That doesn't help. In all ways that matter, she would be madam's daughter."

"The child would no more be a Clermont than a Debenham, but I don't think that's it. Before the run up to Waterloo, I doubt Thérèse had anything to do with a backwater like Halle. Her orbit was around Napoleon. When he abdicated to Elba in 1814, she was desperate enough to come to England and plan a move to America, but as soon as he resumed power, she returned to his circle. I wonder . . ."

"What?" Mara felt as if her head was spinning.

Nicholas slowly smiled. "Sheer speculation, but the only reason I can imagine Thérèse bearing a child and paying it any heed at all is that she thought it could be useful. What," he asked, eyes brilliant, "if Delphie's father was Napoleon himself?"

Mara sat down. "This is fantastical. But even if true, what use is that?"

"I did say it was useless," he pointed out. "But if we were completely certain that Madame Clermont is not the child's mother, it would alter things, would it not?"

"Yes. Yes, it would. But how can we be certain?"

"We can't yet, but there is a look of Thérèse, and Delphie has that cleft in her chin like Napoleon."

Mara exhaled. "So when we hear from Halle, it now seems possible it will be news that Madame Clermont is an impostor. I must tell Dare." But then she bit her lip. "How will he feel if Delphie is the daughter of that vile woman? And of Napoleon!"

"Certainly an extraordinary mix. He need never know."

"I couldn't keep something like that from him," Mara protested. "But things are so difficult at the moment and it might not be true."

"I leave it up to you," Nicholas said.

Mara almost protested, but she would trust this sword to no one else. "Do you know Feng Ruyuan?" she asked.

"Very well."

"I thought so. Sometimes it would be pleasant to be the river rather than the rock."

He smiled and it turned into a laugh. "Eleanor has said the same thing. I rather think, however, that if you are a rock, Mara St. Bride, it's a volcanic one."

Mara's face burned and she rose. "I think you're amber," she said, and had the satisfaction of seeing him take a moment to understand.

"Eternal imprisoner of insects?" he asked.

She'd meant simply from his amber-colored eyes.

"Make me coral," he said. "Built of tiny bits and pieces, but occasionally sharp. Do you return to Marlowe House?"

"Soon," Mara said. "But first I need to speak with Ruyuan."

Nicholas didn't try to stop her and the Chinese man was available. Mara sat with him for two hours learning about opium and what would happen when Dare fought the final battle.

She returned to Marlowe House, her mind swirling with problems but giving thanks because they'd avoided the worst.

That night, however, when Mara was about to prepare for bed, someone knocked at her door. Ruth opened it and admitted Jancy. A pale, stark-eyed Jancy.

"What is it?" Mara asked, turning cold.

Jancy took her hands. "Dare's been challenged to a duel."

"What?"

CHAPTER 29

Jancy drew Mara to the sofa, or Mara drew Jancy, but they ended up there, holding hands.

"Who?" Mara asked.

"Berkstead."

"What?" Mara exclaimed again. "Oh, the . . . rat! Dare's not going to accept, is he?"

"Simon's gone to Yeovil House to talk to him. Would you believe it's over Madame Clermont?"

"What?"

"I know. It's insanity. But apparently Berkstead's decided that Dare is Delphie's father and must do the honorable thing by Delphie's mother — Madame Clermont. What's more, he's posted the challenge all over Town. You must know the whole question about Delphie has become a matter for public excitement, and some are saying that rank and privilege are persecuting a poor woman deprived of her child."

"Oh, no. I had no idea. What do we do?"

"I don't know. Dare could refuse to meet him, but then it might revive the idea that he's a coward."

Mara stood. "I have to go to him."

"It's half past ten."

"What does that matter? Ruth, my cloak and bonnet."

"Milady —"

"Do *not* argue. Jancy, can you order a carriage, please?"

Jancy stood. "Of course, and I'll come, too."

They were soon rattling through the streets, a footman with them as protection, though Mara didn't think any of this directly threatened either of them. At Yeovil House they threw the attending footman into confusion. Lord Austrey was in the house, yes. With Lord Darius, yes. But in Lord Darius's bedroom.

"That doesn't matter," Mara declared and hurried upstairs.

She knocked and Simon opened the door. His brows rose, but he let them in.

Dare was pacing, and Mara could see how bad a time it was for him to face something like this. She went and took his hands. "The man's a rat. No, a scorpion."

It summoned a slight laugh. "And God

knows where the why is in this. I can't think straight. He's not entitled to demand that I meet him tomorrow, but if I don't . . ."

"He'll make it look like cowardice. I think we should go and sort this out, face-to-face."

"How?"

"I can try again to convince him that I would not marry him with a pistol to my head. We can possibly appeal to whatever vestiges of sanity remain in his thick skull." She turned to speak to the others. "He's not bad or mad. Not long ago he was a rational man and I enjoyed his company. I can't believe that's all been eroded away."

"It's worth a try," said Simon, looking at Dare. "He's at the Golden Cross, which is nearby."

Dare nodded. "If you'll excuse me."

Mara realized what he needed and left with the others. He would take some opium in order to cope. When would they ever have peace?

When they were in a reception room, waiting, she said, "I wish I'd never met Berkstead."

"It's not your fault," Simon said, putting an arm around her. "You didn't do anything to give him this mad illusion."

Mara burst into tears and confessed.

Simon and Jancy stared at her. "How could you?" Jancy asked.

"I don't know. It is so obviously insane now, but at the time it was simply a game. It was very, very stupid, but it's still no reason to persecute me like this. He sent me that awful silk, Jancy, with a note about our wedding night. I should have burned it, but I told Ruth she could sell it." She shuddered. "He was following me. Spying on me."

"You should have told me," Simon said.

"I never imagined . . . If anything terrible happens, this will all be my fault."

Jancy hugged her. "No, it won't, and it won't."

Mara heard footsteps and sprang away to attempt a bright smile for Dare as he came in.

He wasn't fooled. He took her in his arms. "Somehow, we'll sail through these storms to calm waters. Neither kraken, nor Gorgon, nor beast will consume us. Come, let's deal with Berkstead."

The Golden Cross was a busy place, even close to midnight, and their arrival didn't cause surprise. The request for Major Berkstead did, but a coin got the room number and a general direction. Simon knocked and, on demand, gave his name.

The door was flung open by a haughty Berkstead, but then he gaped. They all went in. Someone else was there — the chunky-faced officer from Almack's. He glared at them all and announced his name. "Lowestoft. Berkstead's second."

Berkstead's eyes were fixed on Mara and she saw in them a warped kind of devotion. She stepped forward to attempt reason.

"Major Berkstead, you are suffering under a dreadful error. I know I may have misled you, but I don't love you. I have never loved you or wanted to marry you. You must believe me." Seeing no reaction in his fixed expression, Mara added, "I'm not being forced to say this!"

"Yet you come under guard."

She turned to the men. "Please leave us."

"No," Dare said.

Berkstead came to life. "See! Why can't you see? If you're not being compelled by force, you must be under some sort of dementia. I cannot let you plunge into the hell of marriage to a despicable man like Debenham."

Mara hit him. She'd not intended to — her hand whipped out and did it all of its own. Her leather gloves must have softened the blow, but he staggered back in shock as much as anything, then surged forward, fury in his eyes.

Dare was between them. Berkstead froze, in part perhaps because Lowestoft had taken his arm.

"You started that rumor about me," Dare said.

"What rumor?" But his eyes flickered.

"That I fled the field at Waterloo. Fortunately for you, we have a witness to correct that mistake."

Mara worked at not showing surprised relief and saw confusion on Lowestoft's face.

"Fortunately?" Berkstead's chin went up. "Why should I be pleased by that?"

"Because I won't have to take steps to make you admit to the world that you spread an invention out of pure malice."

"Threatening me from your eminence?" Berkstead sneered, but he'd backed up a step. He recovered like a toy on a spring, however, making Mara despair.

"You can't force lies down people's throats with a title these days," the major blustered. "Or steal children and abuse defenseless women." He pushed his head forward to glare. "Are you going to marry the woman you wronged?"

"Have you even met Madame Clermont?"

Dare asked. Opium must give immense patience.

"Do you deny she's at your house and claims to be the true mother of your daughter?"

"No."

"And a duke's house takes in any raggle tail who turns up with a pretty story?"

"Major Berkstead," Dare said, "I have been advertising for the children's parents for nearly a year. Of course I'm interested in any claimant. I'm investigating the woman's story, but as she's alone in a foreign land, my parents have kindly given her lodging. She's a complete stranger to me, and when she conceived Delphie, I was at Cambridge. I have never claimed that Delphie is my true child."

Facts and Dare's almost eerie calm were having a strong effect on Captain Lowestoft and seemed to deflate the major. Berkstead turned to Mara.

"I must protect you, my darling. Debenham's an opium eater! I know what that means. It doesn't matter what he says. He'll always put the poppy first. You'll never be able to rely on him. You'd be able to rely on me. I'd never hurt you."

Mara suddenly saw a possible way.

"Yes, I probably would be able to rely on

you," she said gently. "That's why I've always thought of you as an uncle, Major Berkstead. You are, I believe, forty-one, and I am but eighteen. How can you ever have thought us suited to marriage?"

His jaw dropped.

"As an older friend," Mara continued, "of course you are concerned about my future, but if my loving family approves, how can I be wrong? Lord Darius has been almost a part of my family since I was a child. That's why we all know he will win free of the drug. But it's also why I know that if he didn't, he would still be a loving, trustworthy husband."

Dare took her hand.

Mara squeezed it, but kept her attention on Berkstead. "That's also why I know without proof that he didn't turn coward and flee the battle. It was very wrong of you, a soldier, to plant that unjust accusation."

She heard a mutter of agreement from the captain, who said, "What's the truth, old fellow?"

Berkstead's mouth shuddered as if he might be fighting tears. "I . . . I might have been mistaken. I only wanted to protect her," he said to his friend. "She's so young, so innocent. A sprite." He turned back to Mara. "You need a shield from the harshness of life. You don't know. You can't know what's best for yourself!"

Before Mara could protest, Simon did it for her. "Stop that infernal drivel, man. Mara has more sense and wisdom in her little finger than you have in your whole body."

Berkstead turned on him. "Then why did she slip out at night to romp around with me?"

Mara thanked heaven that she'd confessed.

"Because, as she said, she saw you as an uncle and trusted you."

Berkstead collapsed into a chair. "You see me as an uncle?" he asked Mara.

For a moment, pity almost softened her, but she met his eyes. "Yes," she affirmed.

"Are we done with this idiocy?" Dare asked. "No one is going to meet you at pistol point, Berkstead, but if you create any more trouble, we will call up some very big battalions and crush you into the mud."

The flat statement seemed to ring in the room. Berkstead licked his lips. "I see. You'll tell lies. Destroy my reputation. . . . I have only done what I thought was right. What I still think right. She is too good for you!"

"That, we can agree on," Dare said. "No one need tell lies about you. If you persist,

504

however, some will tell the truth. The terms are these," Dare said. "You cease to meddle in our lives. You scrupulously avoid Mara, which includes avoiding her sister and Sir George. We will have to tell the Verneys about your behavior, but if you keep your side of this bargain, no one will let the wider world know of your malice and folly."

"Because you don't want the world to know how shamelessly she behaved."

Mara felt Dare tense and braced to prevent attack.

But Dare said, "If you care for Mara at all, you do not want the world to know of her innocent follies."

"Innocent —" But Berkstead swallowed any further words. Mara wasn't surprised.

After a moment, Dare added, "I do have some sympathy, sir. Mara is wondrous and she has become your addiction. The better part of you is doubtless crying for you to be sane, but the baser part howls that life is not worth living without her, that it is your sacred duty to protect her. The beast can be defeated. You are reputed to be a brave man and you have friends. Fight."

He looked at the shaken Captain Lowestoft. "Will you assist him, sir, and also keep these matters private?"

"Yes, of course. Of course." The man

braced himself. "It was I who spread the story at Almack's. I believed it. His wounds gave weight to his story. If you want satisfaction."

"Heavens, no," Dare said. "Let's put it behind us, like, please God, the war."

He took Mara's hand and led her out of the room, down the stairs, and out of the inn.

"Will it work?" Simon asked as they walked along the street.

"I pray so," Dare said. "Lowestoft seems to be a decent man."

"What of the witness to counter his rumor?" Mara asked. "Who is it?"

"I lied," Dare said. "One effect of opium at its height is that it makes it so very easy to lie."

Mara returned to her bedroom in Marlowe House in no state to rest. When Ruth offered her laudanum, she dashed the bottle from her hand.

"But you must sleep, Miss Mara!"

"So must you, Ruth. Go away, please. I'll be all right."

Solitude felt like a blessing, but Dare's presence would be a greater one. Mara leaned by the window, looking in the direction of Great Charles Street, trying to send her love and strength. In some ways this would be an easier night for him because he'd taken extra opium, but that would make it a worse one, too.

Mara found the disk that Ruyuan had given her, then worked on the patterns Ruyuan had taught her. They came back to her and she went through them again and again, visualizing Dare doing the same thing at Yeovil House. Slowly her mind cleared, and she hoped it meant his had, too. When she went to bed, she slept.

The next morning, Jancy came to take breakfast with her. "What are we going to do?"

Mara buttered bread and spread jam on it. "Prepare for the ball."

"You know what I mean. Everything is in disorder."

"It could be worse," Mara pointed out. "Madame Clermont is not dragging a terrified Delphie off to Belgium. Dare isn't facing Berkstead at pistol point. Tonight, the ton will swarm into Yeovil House, thus attesting that they believe Dare to be brave, honorable, and true."

"You're sure of that?"

"I met Lady Cawle. I'm sure."

"I don't know how you can be so calm!" Jancy exploded. "You know how rumors stick. People will have written letters, spreading the story, but they won't bother to write a retraction. Especially if there isn't one."

Mara covered Jancy's anxious hands. "They'll write about the ball, too. Jancy, I'm trying to look on the bright side."

"Oh, sorry."

Jancy left and Mara remembered she'd been promised a ride.

She wrote a note to Dare and summoned Ruth to find her habit. Poor Godiva hadn't had a ride for a week or more. Mara was only just ready when Dare was announced, and she ran down, truly feeling full of bright spirits.

Instead of going outside immediately, however, he drew her into a reception room.

Her bright spirits fled. "What? What's happened now?"

"Nothing bad. I'm sorry for frightening you. I wanted to give you this." He produced a ring — a clear, faceted topaz circled by small cabochon rubies, then by tiny diamonds, and slid it onto her finger.

"It's perfect. How did you find it?"

"I commissioned it last week, before we left Town. The rubies protect the topaz," he said, tracing the stones, "and the diamonds protect both."

She searched his eyes. "No lingering thought of marrying Madame Clermont?"

"None." He brushed her cheek with his knuckles. "What good would a dead husband do her or Delphie, and how could I live without you?"

Mara went into his arms and simply held him, encircled him, never wanting to let go. She felt him kiss her hair and was complete, as she was now only when with him.

"We should go," he said reluctantly. "The horses are waiting."

So they kissed, left the house, and rode to Hyde Park. They talked, but only of tranquil plans, and they didn't talk much. In the park, they cantered and then indulged in a galloping race in the wilder areas, deliberately bringing it to a dead heat. It was good. It was normal. It was a pattern for their life together.

CHAPTER 30

Mara took lunch with Jancy and knew how she should spend the rest of the day. A young lady planning to attend a ball, especially one at which she would be a center of attention, should rest, then spend hours in preparation.

She, however, had something to do.

She summoned a carriage and, accompanied by Ruth and an armed footman, went to the jeweler's in Bond Street. The young man recognized her. "You require more beads, ma'am?"

"No," Mara said. "I wish to commission a ring. Can it possibly be made for tonight?"

The clerk's brows rose, but he summoned the master jeweler. The square-jawed, sharp-eyed man emerged in a working apron and was immediately intrigued by the challenge. He studied Mara's ring. "You want the same but with a ruby at the center, ma'am, surrounded by topaz? But gentlemen do not wear such rings these days. A cravat pin, perhaps?"

"It must be a ring," Mara said, "but I see what you mean."

"Perhaps, we could adapt a gentleman's ring?" He produced a heavy gold one with a smooth oval top ready for engraving. "The stones could be inset in one corner — very small — and the rest engraved."

Mara considered, then nodded. "Yes, that would be best. It can be done for tonight?" She gave him her best and brightest smile. "For my betrothal ball, you see."

His eyes twinkled. "It will be done for tonight, ma'am, but I will need the gentleman's size."

Mara hadn't thought of that, but said, "You shall have it within the hour, sir."

Once back at Marlowe House, she sent a message to Salter, instructing him to send Dare's ring size to the jeweler. Then she tried to do the expected things, but even the choice of gown fretted her. She summoned Jancy to help.

"They're all lovely," Jancy said. "I can't believe you're in such a twitch over it."

"I'm going to be the center of attention. And it's so important!"

"Whether you wear white, blue, or yellow will hardly affect anything."

"I know, but I need to do something to shape fate. Will you read the cards again?"

"No. They're not to be consulted again and again, and what they told you was good."

"More or less."

"None of us can expect a completely smooth path."

"We can wish for it, though. Work for it."

Then Jancy noticed the ring. "Mara, it's lovely! So unusual."

"It's Dare, protected by me, and by the Rogues. There are twelve small diamonds, see? I've ordered something similar for him, but it hasn't arrived yet."

Jancy was summoned to her bath and Mara studied the gowns again. Yellow would catch the color of the topaz.

How was Dare passing the time before this important event? Would the plan work, or would people stay away? What if Berkstead appeared in the ballroom to tell the sorry saga of her foolish adventure?

No. He was stopped. She truly believed that.

For the first time she worried that one of the men at the ball might recognize her from that gambling hell. She didn't think the patrons had been aristocratic, but it hadn't been a low dive, either. She studied herself in the mirror, remembering the mask and the turban-style headdress that had concealed her hair. The room had been dim and fogged with pipe smoke. Surely no one would know.

Then, as she sank into her bath, she was assailed by images of empty rooms, of the ton simply staying away. How could they if Lady Cawle had let it be known she would attend? Who would want to offend the Yeovils? Apart from their high rank, people liked them, especially the duchess.

She made herself stop running round and round these things like a dog in a pit and applied creams and a hint of color to her lips and cheeks.

Then the coiffeur arrived to begin his endless fiddling with her hair, chattering all the time. It gave her a headache, but the effect was lovely, she admitted, and exactly as innocent as she'd wanted. She was crowned with a mass of curls in a bandeau of yellow roses.

She put on the gown, which had a yellow satin underdress and an overlay of white spider net set with tiny crystals. The bodice was very low. She remembered Almack's, when Dare had admired her breasts. And Brideswell, where he'd worshipped them.

"What are you blushing for?" Ruth demanded. "Shocking, those bodices are, but you've worn them for years without a tremor."

"I'm nervous," Mara said, and Ruth seemed to believe her.

With the addition of pearls, she was ready. They would dine here, including the Yeovils and their family, then all go on to the ball at nine.

But where was Dare's ring? It would be his talisman. He must have it!

"Sit down, milady," Ruth said, "before you wear yourself out."

"I'm expecting something."

"What?"

"Never mind."

Ruth tidied up, muttering.

But then there was a knock at the door, and a footman presented a small box. Mara thanked him, opened it, and there was the ring, exactly as she'd hoped with the circles of jewels set in one corner, and an engraved entwined *D* and *M*. She'd decided on Mara, not Ademara.

The bell sounded, and Mara went down with the ring in her hand. Dare was waiting for her at the bottom of the stairs. Sudden awareness of the body beneath dark evening clothes flooded heat and hunger through her. The look in his eyes as he kissed her hand echoed her thoughts. Their hands tightened one on the other, seeking.

"I have something for you," she said.

"Heaven." It was a statement.

"Something else for now." She slid the ring onto his right hand.

He looked at it, then smiled. "This is perfect."

"As everything will be."

Their shared smile was a kiss, and became a kiss.

"Now, now. None of that!"

She broke free to look up at her parents coming down the stairs. It was her father who had spoken, but his eyes twinkled.

"I never would have believed it possible," Dare murmured.

Nor would Mara. Her parents looked every inch the Earl and Countess of Marlowe. She hadn't known her father owned such elegant evening clothes, or her mother such a grand gown.

"Father looks so long-suffering," Mara said, "but I suspect Mother is rather enjoying herself."

"And why not? She's a beautiful woman, still."

He stepped forward to flatter Amy St. Bride and even steal a kiss.

Mara realized with surprise that he was

right. The sapphire blue suited her mother and the fashionably low bodice revealed the swell of generous breasts. The Marlowe diamonds, including a tiara, glittered in the candlelight, completing the effect. Amy St. Bride's eyes twinkled as she smiled at Mara.

"What will the world come to?" Mara said as she linked arms with Dare and took him to meet her uncle Sir Algernon St. Bride and his wife, and her godparents, the bishop and his lady. Dare introduced her to his brother Gravenham and his wife. They were just like their portraits, and seemed both dull and pleasant.

Lady Theodosia Debenham also looked like her portrait. Mara wondered if she had ever missed her worn slippers and old stockings. She was swept on to enormous Sir Randolph Dunpott-Ffyfe and Lord and Lady Verwood. Then she smiled with true delight to see Lord and Lady Vandeimen and Serena and Francis.

"Isn't the aristocracy a tangled web?" Serena said. "We're here to give Dare moral support, but we have credentials. Maria Vandeimen was a Dunpott-Ffyfe, and Francis is a twig on the Debenham family tree through his mother. She's not in Town, but her sister is."

"Miss Hurstman," said Dare, looking

across the room. "We'd better go to her, Mara, or she'll hit me with her umbrella."

"She can't have an umbrella here," Mara protested as they crossed the room.

"I wouldn't put it past her."

Nor would Mara. Plain-faced Miss Hurstman was only marginally dressed for this occasion and looked as if she thought all the finery ridiculous. Her gown was silk, but of a dull, dark brown fabric. It was high in the neck and long in the sleeves.

"This way I won't need to manage gloves and a shawl," she said to Mara, as if reading her mind. To Dare, she said, "Don't worry about that ridiculous story. Maud and I have put paid to that."

They moved on to greet other people, but Dare murmured, "That does seem to settle it. Miss Hurstman is not a power in society like Lady Cawle — she avoids society as assiduously as your father does — but she's connected to nearly everyone and knows everything that's going on."

Mara relaxed, for the atmosphere here was so pleasant that it was impossible that anything go wrong.

Nerves returned when they moved on to Yeovil House. The house was ready, decorated and beautiful, but only a few servants met them in the hall. The place felt so empty that it was possible to believe it would remain so. Music could be heard from the distant ballroom, but it played only for faery dancers.

"Let's slip up to the schoolroom," Dare said. "I promised Delphie that you'd show her your gown."

"Good, for I have something for her."

Delphie fluttered excitedly over Mara while Madame Clermont glowered. How was this going to work?

It wouldn't need to, Mara remembered, if Delphie wasn't the woman's child. Mara studied the girl's pretty face. She *did* have Napoleon's cleft chin.

"See, Mara," Delphie said. "Mariette is ready for the ball *aussi.*"

Indeed she was, in a new skirt of pink velvet and a sash of gold.

"How pretty," Mara said, looking a question at Dare.

"Thea provided some scraps."

Mara had brought a gilded belt for Pierre, complete with a proper hanger for his sword, and a bandeau of roses for Delphie, similar to the one in her own hair.

Delphie admired herself in the mirror in dazed delight and then kissed Mara so enthusiastically she almost undid all the lengthy preparations. Pierre marched around, drawing and sheathing his sword. Then the footman came to say guests were arriving and they raced down the stairs to see the Rogues coming in en masse.

"Dashing Deb," Nicholas said with a laugh.

Mara finally met Lord and Lady Arden — the glittering marquess flirted and his wife scolded him, a twinkle in her eye — and Lord and Lady Amleigh, who seemed sensible country people. But then other guests poured in, becoming a never-ending torrent. Some of the glittering throng were avid and probably hoping for a scandalous event, but most seemed truly warm and ready for a pleasant evening. Mara began to believe the ball would be a tremendous success. The crowd alone was a triumph.

But eventually Mara said to Dare, "No Lady Cawle."

"If she stays away, so be it."

"It matters, Dare."

"Only you matter," he said and she rolled her eyes even as she blushed.

Then, with the dancing about to begin, Lady Cawle made a grand entrance in golden satin and a tiara enhanced by her escort — the Duke of Wellington himself. Mara went breathless as all attention turned to the meeting between the duke and Dare.

The duke gave one of his rare smiles and shook Dare's hand. "Glad to see you recovered, Debenham. Fine job you did. Fine job."

Mara could almost have fainted with relief. When the duke bowed to her, she gave him her most brilliant smile. She could swear he blinked.

There was only one other missing person of significance, Blanche, but she'd been supposed to arrive late.

The Beaumonts arrived a moment later, Blanche looking stunning in a celestial blue gown to match her eyes, sewn with pearls to match her hair, which was mostly concealed by a swirling confection of blue, silver, and white fixed with a diamond pin.

Her training enabled her to move with sublime grace looking happy and at ease, but her eyes couldn't quite play their part.

"I'm shaking in my slippers," she whispered to Mara. "Stage fright. Me!"

"It's the first time you've played the part of Mrs. Hal Beaumont in such company."

"Do I look all right?"

Mara laughed. "You're stunning and you know it."

"But I'm not sure I should be. I wanted

to try mousy, but Hal would have none of it."

"He was right."

Hal interrupted. "Blanche, if we don't go to pay homage to my godmother, she'll leave in high dudgeon and wreck everything."

"Oh, Lord," Blanche muttered, but added, "At least Wellington's with her. He's an admirer of mine from back when he was Wellesley."

Mara felt rather faint at the implications of that, but the ball commenced then with the formal announcement of the betrothal, to universal applause. Then Mara and Dare walked out to begin the line for dancing.

"Not, alas, a waltz," she said.

"Later," he replied. "I promise."

As the music began, Mara glanced up and saw two excited pairs of eyes peeping over the balcony in front of the musicians. Two hands waved. She wanted to wave back, but all eyes were on her. She couldn't see Madame Clermont, but she would be there, the specter at the feast.

Mara lost herself in the pleasure of the dance, and then was partnered by three dukes in succession — Yeovil, St. Raven, and Wellington. Wellington said, "I understand you're responsible for this campaign on Blanche's behalf. Well done, my dear. She's a gallant lady."

Mara smiled at him with genuine warmth.

She was tired of dukes, however, and made sure to capture Dare for the next, but as they were waiting for the music to begin, Major Hawkinville came over to them.

"I have an interruption for you," he said softly, "but I think it's one you'll like."

"A witness from Waterloo?" Dare asked.

"No. Come."

They strolled smiling out of the room and along the corridor, but Mara was strung tight. She needed no surprises tonight, good or bad, and neither did Dare.

"What?" Dare asked, as soon as they were free of the crowd.

"Madame Clermont's family. In your father's office."

"And it's good?" Dare asked.

"Yes."

They hurried down back stairs to the businesslike room, where Mara had studied the miniatures of the family. There they found three sinewy, solemn men in country clothing — doubtless a father and two sons. Two footman formed a kind of guard.

"Where is my daughter?" the older man demanded in French as soon as Dare entered. "What have you done with her? He"

— he jerked his head toward Hawkinville — "said only she was here. Here? What place has she here?"

Dare raised a hand. "A moment, please, sir." He dismissed the fascinated footmen, then said, "You are Monsieur Lameule from Halle, and your daughter is Madame Clermont?"

"That is she. She is unwell. We must take her home."

Mara clutched Dare's arm with relief. The woman was mad. It was tragic, but wonderful.

"She did not lose a daughter?" Dare asked.

"But yes, sir, she did. That is what made her ill. First her husband, then her child. She took it into her head that this child found after the battle was her Annette, and she would not listen to reason. I'm sorry if she has done anything wrong, sir, but we have come to take her home."

He seemed to think his daughter was a prisoner here.

Dare pressed his hands together and raised them to his lips. Mara realized she'd not thought to ask what he was doing about the opium. The normal evening dose would be beginning to wear off even without these additional strains.

The silence stretched, but then he said, "Please, come with me. We will take you to her."

The three men rose uneasily. They were probably in their best clothes, but their country boots clumped as they all went up to the schoolroom. Dare had sent a footman to ask madam to meet them there, but clearly she had refused to leave Delphie. When they entered the schoolroom, she had Delphie by the hand and Pierre stood on guard, regarding the three strangers with deep suspicion.

Mara watched Madame Clermont as the men entered the room and saw no sign of dismay. Instead, the woman smiled in welcome. "Father! Giles, Antoine, see. I was right." She picked up Delphie. "Here is Annette!"

Mara's heart shriveled.

But the father sighed. "Francine, my dearest girl, that is not Annette. Annette is dead."

"No, no, look, Papa! This is she. Do I not know my own child?"

He went forward to put an arm around her. "Annette is dead, my dearest one. She is in heaven with the angels."

Francine Clermont pulled away. "No, no!" She clutched Delphie to her, but Dare stepped forward and chopped at the woman's shoulder. It seemed to only startle, but it loosened her grip and he snatched the weeping girl. When Francine Clermont tried to get to Delphie, her father stepped in her way.

"It's a lie, Papa! I have found my daughter. I know my daughter, but they steal her again. I want my daughter back!"

Her father had no hesitation about wrapping the distraught woman in strong arms, but he rocked her, murmuring as he might to an infant. "I know, I know. It's hard, my chick, so hard. But she is dead. She is dead."

Mara saw that Dare had taken the children away and she quickly followed into their bedroom. Delphie still clung to Dare, but the tears had stopped.

"What is happening, Papa?" Pierre demanded. "Who are those men? I do not like them."

"They are good men," Dare said, sitting in the rocking chair with Delphie, and gathering Pierre to his side. "They are Madame Clermont's family. She is not Delphie's mother, but we must be very sorry for her. She had a little girl just as precious and her Annette died. That was such a great sorrow that she won't believe it. She'd rather think that her child was taken from her, so she searches for her. Her family has come to take care of her and to take her home."

Delphie nodded. "That is good."

It could be an expression of sympathy, but Mara thought it was relief. And if Delphie was Thérèse Bellaire's child, she realized, there was no danger of more claimants.

"So you are our papa?" Pierre asked.

Dare hesitated, for there would always be a mystery about their origins, but he said, "Yes. And soon Mara will be your mother."

"C'est bon," Delphie said and wriggled off his lap. "May we return to watch the ball, Papa?"

Dare looked bemused, but he sent them off accompanied by one of their nursemaids.

Mara took his hands, smiling. "Such resilience, but that, too, is *bon.*"

"Yes. Am I dreaming, or are all our major problems dispelled?"

A witness to his fall in battle would make all perfect, but they were blessed. Mara sat on his lap. "All is well with the world," she said, and kissed him. But then she made a decision and said, "There is one very small thing, Dare."

He looked wary, but she carried on and told him what Nicholas suspected about Delphie's parentage.

"Dear God," he said, and she feared she'd made a mistake. But then he shook his head. "It's exactly what Thérèse would do, and in keeping that she had not a trace of love for Delphie."

"You don't mind? People tend to resemble their parents."

"There's nothing wrong with Delphie, while there was something very wrong with Thérèse Bellaire. She cared for nothing and no one but herself, but Delphie is a loving person."

"And Napoleon?"

He laughed. "Was a brilliant man. In twenty or so years the world may have to be on its toes as Delphine Debenham begins to make her mark, but I doubt anyone will be the worse for it, especially," he added, smiling into her eyes, "if she's been raised at Brideswell."

They stole time for another kiss, but they were both aware that they would be missed and must not return to the ball disheveled. They stopped by the schoolroom, where Madame Clermont was quiet, but not at all at ease. She was rocking herself and weeping, guarded by her two concerned brothers.

All three Lameule men looked at a loss.

"Does the child resemble her Annette?"

Dare asked softly.

"A little, sir, a very little," Monsieur Lameule said. "You will not seek to punish her?"

"No, heavens no. She has all my compassion. Her child did die?"

"Of a certainty." The man drew them out of the room. "It was most terrible, sir. After the battle, some French horseman fled through our village. Francine and Annette were in the street. They trampled the child before her mother's eyes. I think she cannot bear to remember, so of course Annette is not dead. Perhaps we should have made her see the child's body, but it was a horrible sight. I have never seen the like."

"Is her home the best place for her then?" Dare asked.

"Of course, sir. She is surrounded by those who love her."

"Then may I suggest something? Once she thought she had found Annette, your daughter became quite well. She was unhappy because Delphie didn't like her, but she did her best to tend to the child. There are many poor waifs who would be blessed by a good home among loving family."

The man nodded. "Such a child would be much loved by all of us, and watched over by all of us. We have tried and tried to make her see the truth, but perhaps it is not possible or kind."

"Perhaps not. We must return to our guests," Dare said. "Do you require any help to return home?"

"No, thank you, milord."

"All the same, I would like to give Madame Clermont a gift. For her future daughter, perhaps. And I fear it would be best to drug your daughter a little before trying to take her from this house. I can provide a little laudanum. It does ease the frantic mind, but should not be used for too long."

Dare summoned his father's competent secretary and put all the arrangements in his hands. Then he and Mara returned to the ball. They sought out Major Hawkinville first.

"Thank you, Hawk," Dare said.

"Mostly luck. I worked on the assumption that her family would set out to follow her. They would have to register with the alien office at their port of entry, so I sent men to check the most likely. Once I found their names, it was easy to trace them to London."

"I wouldn't have thought of that," Dare said.

"It's the sort of thing he's good at," Clarissa Hawkinville said. "You can't imagine how organized our homes are."

"No thanks to you," her husband said with a smile.

"Two neat people would be unbearable. I'm so happy the problem is solved," she said to Dare and Mara.

The word was spreading through the Rogues and they all came by to congratulate Dare. Then the duchess announced that as a great honor, Mrs. Beaumont, the famous actress, would perform a short piece for the company before supper.

Mara had forgotten Blanche and had no idea what sort of performance was to come. She took Dare's hand and prayed as they turned to look up at the balcony.

Blanche in some way looked taller as she addressed the room, and her trained voice reached every corner. "There are too few powerful parts in the theater for women," she said, "especially ones which show women in their full virtue and strength, but I have chosen one such for this short performance. From Portia, in Mr. Shakespeare's play *The Merchant of Venice*."

She managed in some way to soften her voice without becoming any the less easy to hear.

The quality of mercy is not strain'd,

It droppeth as the gentle rain from heaven
Upon the place beneath: it is twice blest;
It blesseth him that gives and him that
  takes:
'Tis mightiest in the mightiest: it becomes
The throned monarch better than his
  crown. . . .

She held the silent room in thrall, but perhaps also she was asking for mercy for herself and Dare. Blanche left off the ending, specific to the play, and concluded with the lines:

Consider this,
That, in the course of justice, none of us
Should see salvation: we do pray for
  mercy;
And that same prayer doth teach us all to
  render
The deeds of mercy.

She bowed her head, and the room broke into rapturous applause. Mara thought of the mercy offered Major Berkstead and poor Madame Clermont, and squeezed Dare's hand. Revenge and even justice were often poor coin.

Blanche retreated, soon to emerge back in the ballroom on a proud Hal's arm, and receive further accolades.

Mara said, "I wish . . ." but stopped her own words. Society had endorsed Dare by coming here tonight. If doubts lingered, there was nothing more to be done about it. Probably no one on the chaotic battlefield had clearly seen what happened to Dare anyway.

Dare led Mara out into a waltz just as clocks chimed midnight. It was as well that the dance didn't require any change of partners for they became lost in a world of their own, one populated by moonlight, faery dancers, and perhaps by Oriental arts.

When the music ended, he said, "The Rogues are to take supper together now," and they walked toward the ballroom door. Just outside it, they encountered a striking man with dark hair and eyes and an impressive aura of vigor. Mara tensed, for there was something antagonistic about him.

"Canem," Dare said, pleasantly enough but not as if addressing an old friend.

"It's Darien now," the man said with a smile that didn't show in his eyes.

Please God, Mara prayed, let nothing new go wrong.

"I'm sorry," Dare said. "Father and two brothers?"

"One by illness, two by lightning. Clearly the family motto should apply to us, not to our enemies."

Dare turned to Mara. "My dear, I present to you Lord Darien. Darien, my future bride, Lady Mara St. Bride."

Lord Darien bowed pleasantly enough, but there was still something amiss.

"Lord Darien and Lord Darius," Mara said. "Now there's a scene for confusion."

"Fortunate that I didn't have the title at Harrow," Lord Darien agreed. "I was plain Cahvay then."

A strange name. Mara tried to keep the tense conversation flowing. "What is the family motto, my lord?"

He repeated his name and then she realized. The family name and motto were both Cave, the Latin for "beware" and pronounced that way. Cahvay. She knew of the Warwickshire family who had a snarling dog on their crest and, she remembered, were known as troublemakers. They needed no more trouble.

"I have only recently arrived in Town, Debenham," Lord Darien said, "and didn't know about the rumor. It has shocked me. I saw you shot down at Waterloo."

It took a moment for the words to affect Mara, but then she laughed for joy. The faeries were smiling on them.

"Thank you," Dare said, but with reserve.

"I'm not making the story up," Darien said rather stiffly. "Justice must be done."

Dare smiled, and perhaps colored a little. "Yes, of course. I'm sorry. One doesn't expect so many blessings on one night."

Lord Darien's lips twisted slightly. "That's probably the first time in generations a Cave's been described as a blessing. I'll make sure people know," he said and walked into the ballroom.

Mara watched him go. "He's an enemy?" she asked.

"No, not that."

"Then this is wonderful!"

He suddenly smiled, eyes bright. "It is, isn't it? Come. The others will be at supper already."

As they went downstairs, she asked, "Why was Lord Darien snarling silently?"

"It's an old story, but old hurts can rankle, and I made it worse by carelessly calling him Canem."

"It's not his name?" But then she realized. "*Cave canem?* Beware of the dog?"

"Exactly." They threaded their way, smiling and bowing, through the crowded house toward the garden room, where supper was laid out. "Cave was a year younger than I at Harrow and arrived small for his age and ready to fight anyone over anything. He picked a fight with me and I tried to deflect it with humor, saying *cave canem.*"

"The phrase would come to mind," Mara said.

"Yes, but he'd already made enemies and boys began to call him Canem, and not in a kind way. The Rogues tried to help, but I think he resented that, too."

Mara paused outside the supper room. "I'm surprised you called him that when it would sting."

"I didn't think it would. He was generally known as Canem in the army. 'Canem Cave,' and with a blisteringly fine reputation as a cavalry officer. It's probably only me he resents it from now."

She touched him in comfort. "It could only be a fleeting irritation, and he is the witness you needed."

"Yes. It really does seem that the minor troubles are over."

She knew he didn't mean that they had been minor, especially the struggle over Delphie, but only that the final battle with opium loomed over all.

They continued into the room, where the Rogues and associates were gathered around a long table. When Dare told them the latest development everyone raised their glasses in a toast.

But Con said, "So Canem Cave's in the peerage. Beware, my friends, beware. He's the sort who needs a war to soak up his energy."

After supper, Mara and Dare explored the garden, made magical at night by lanterns and a concealed wind trio. Then they returned to the ballroom to dance until dawn.

When the final guests were drifting out, or in some cases being carried to their carriages, Dare took Mara into the library.

She knew before he spoke. "You're going to stop now."

"Yes." He unstoppered the blue bottle and upended it. A solitary drop fell and he watched it disappear into the carpet. "To have none, and no prospect of any feels like being naked in a winter storm. I have to leave London, or I'll crawl off to a shop for some."

"I want to go with you."

"No."

She took his hand, which still gripped the empty bottle. "I want to be with you and I want you to do this at Brideswell."

He laughed bitterly. "You don't understand."

"I do. I talked to Ruyuan. You can have the place almost to yourself. I can persuade my parents to stay here, and to have Jenny and Lucy join them. They'll enjoy the cork exhibition, and the monkeys at Astley's."

"What about the rest of your family?"

"Everyone else will be welcome in nearby houses. I gather a week will suffice, for the worst?"

He shook his head. "An eternity, but yes."

"Brideswell is special, Dare. You know it is. It's a sacred place and it will help you."

He pulled free of her and turned away. "But do I want a special place to bolster me? I need to do this on my own."

Mara kept her voice calm. "You will be on your own, because no one can take this journey for you. But if you need Brideswell you will always have it, because you will always have me."

He turned back and took her outstretched hands to kiss each and then draw her into his arms.

"And if I —" But he broke that off. "No, I will not fail."

"No," she said. "You will not."

CHAPTER 31

They left the next day. Mara was surprised at the lack of objection from her family, but they understood. Salter traveled in the coach with them. Ruyuan and his musician followed in one close behind.

Dare seemed tense but normal at the beginning of the journey, but then turned restless and abstracted. He said, rather too often, "It's not too bad at the beginning." She tried bright conversation, but even to herself it felt like a fork squealing on a plate. She suggested reading to him and he agreed, but she wasn't sure he heard her.

He ate at the first stop, but then vomited an hour later. Mara let Salter assist him. Perhaps she shouldn't be here. Perhaps she was useless, or even a burden. She stopped the reading and he didn't seem to notice. He was a constant restless fidget that made her want to scream, so she turned away. She'd danced late and they'd left early and she eventually fell into a doze. She woke when the coach stopped in front of Brideswell.

It was dark and only two lights showed in the windows. When they all entered, Mara wondered if she'd made another mistake, for the silent, deserted house didn't feel like Brideswell at all. What if the magic, if there was any, came only from the people who normally lived here?

She guided Dare up to Simon's room, then showed Ruyuan the one next door.

"What do we do now?" she asked him.

"You sleep, Mara. There will be plenty to do when you wake."

She had to ask. "Is Brideswell special?"

He smiled. "Very much so. The *chi* here is remarkable."

"Even without people?"

"People come here and stay here because of the *chi*. Good people enhance it, but the pure energy comes from elsewhere."

"It will help him?"

"Immeasurably."

That allowed Mara to go to bed. She'd deliberately dressed so she could manage for herself, but she missed Ruth's fussing as she tumbled into sleep. She woke to sullen light and heavy rain, which seemed an ill omen, but she dressed herself and hurried to Dare's room. He wasn't there.

The exercises. Where would he do those? There was no ballroom here. She ran around the house, discovering only the three servants in the kitchens, the ones who'd stayed to take care of them.

Growing frantic, she raced back up to Dare's room — still empty — but then she looked outside and saw him and Ruyuan on the lawn, drenched by pouring rain. Ruyuan flowed like water. Dare fought him with clumsy violence that achieved nothing.

Then Dare coiled in on himself and crumpled to the ground. Mara ran out of the room and down the stairs, feeling as if her feet hardly touched ground, and then she was at Dare's side, hearing his choked gasps of pain. She moved to hold him, but he began to beat his body on the ground as if he'd kill something, or himself.

Ruyuan hauled Dare to his feet. "We run!" he said, and dragged Dare off. After a few yards Dare was running on his own, or staggering, off into the pouring rain.

Mara sat and let rain wash over her. What was she doing here?

Eventually, she sloshed back to the house and up to change, then carried her soaking clothes down to the laundry, where she rinsed and wrung them herself before draping them over a rack by the fire to dry.

When she emerged into the kitchen, the cook asked, "Breakfast, milady?" Mrs. Keating was trying too hard to act as if nothing was unusual.

Mara's instinct was to say no, but she realized she ached with hunger, so she sat to eat eggs and bread and drink strong tea. She took her time because she couldn't imagine what use she was in this war. Then Salter came in and calmly began to draw hot water from the big cistern.

"What's that for?" Mara asked.

"A bath, my lady."

He went off with two buckets and Mara followed. A bath sounded normal.

Was everything all right now?

Salter had set up the big bathtub in Dare's room and lined it with cloths. He poured the hot water into it and then left to get more. By the time he returned for the third time and the bath was half full, Dare staggered in, mostly supported by Ruyuan, who stripped him and settled him into the tub like a child.

As soon as he was in the water, Dare stilled, though he still breathed in shallow gasps and his eyes were shut. Ruyuan poured some oil into the water and strange aromas rose. But then Dare began to twitch and gripped the sides of the tub to try to stay still.

Mara hovered, wondering what she could do. Ruyuan was massaging Dare's shoulders and chanting to him. It seemed to work and Dare yawned. Then he yawned again, and it wasn't sleepiness. The next time his mouth stretched, a cry of anguish escaped.

Mara backed out of the room and fled. She had nothing to offer in this battle, not even the courage to watch. She returned to the kitchens and poured her frantic fears into kneading bread. When the rain stopped she walked, almost ran, and her feet took her to St. Bride's. She fell to her knees in front of the altar and prayed.

She had no idea how long she stayed there, but Mrs. Ludlow came in to put flowers on the altar, which drove Mara out. What would the woman think of her there, bareheaded and in prayer?

The village would know, of course. They'd know everything. She took back paths to the house, but still met a half dozen people, who wished her a good morning but looked at her with concern. She prayed they wouldn't hold this against Dare. Perhaps she shouldn't have brought him here. But Ruyuan said the *chi* was strong.

She would be strong, too. She returned to

the house and tidied herself, and then went to Dare's room. Ruyuan met her outside the door.

"I ran away," she said.

"It is hard to see those we love suffer. It is better now."

"Already?"

"No, not in that way, but I have given him herbs to help him sleep for a little while."

"Is there anything I can do that will help?" she asked.

"To take away the struggle, no. But you help him fight. He will win this time, for you."

Mara realized she was crying again and brushed away tears. "I wish he didn't have to."

He led her gently into her room and to a chair. "That is foolish and you know it. You did not make his prison, but he is locked in it. If he does not fight he cannot escape. Would you condemn him to perpetual imprisonment for fear of pain?"

"I've heard people can die of it." She'd not realized she held that terror inside until it escaped.

"He will not die, Mara. Those who try to go from a great dose to nothing, they can die of it. But Darius has followed the difficult path almost to the door."

Mara looked down at her twisting hands. "What is it like? The pain?"

"I have never taken opium," Ruyuan said, "so I have never had to escape it. But they say it is like acid in the blood, and torment in the belly, along with the worst possible pain in joints and head. It comes in waves, and all the organs rebel."

She stared at him. "Dear God. And what can bring him ease?"

"Movement, sensation. Anything to distract or overwhelm, but it is little enough. The herbs help, but only to a point — crutches that let a man walk, but not without pain."

"Is there anything I can do?" she repeated.

"In a while, I will massage him. You will assist."

It was an order, but Mara welcomed it. If Dare had slept, it had been briefly, but he was still on the bed. His sheets were soaked with sweat and every muscle seemed tense. He saw her and closed his eyes.

"Not too bad," he gasped.

"Liar," she said, stroking wet hair off his face.

Ruyuan rolled him and began the pummeling massage. "Take up that switch and hit him with it," he instructed.

Mara looked at the twig doubtfully.

"It will not hurt him. It will distract his nerves."

So she began to tap the stick up and down Dare's body, working around Ruyuan's rapid hands, and Dare did seem to relax. Perhaps "become still" was a better term, for she knew pain still twisted through him. Just maybe it was submerged.

But then he choked and grabbed his belly, becoming a rigid ball.

Ruyuan said, "You had better go now, Mara."

Mara hesitated.

Dare screamed.

She fled, fled out of the house entirely, unable to block the screams even when they stopped. She ran the half mile back to St. Bride's and collapsed near the altar there, weeping and praying until she simply lay there, exhausted. Her uncle Scipio found her and took her into his arms.

"I'm so weak," she wept. "I ran away."

"It's hard to see those we love in pain."

The same words Ruyuan had used.

But then her uncle added, "Come and have a cup of tea, my dear."

Mara laughed at the St. Bride solution to everything, but a cup of tea in the sanity of the vicarage, which was almost as crowded, chaotic, and blessed as Brideswell, did set her straight again.

When she left, her uncle walked back with her. At the gates to Brideswell, she asked, "Could I bring Dare to the church when he's able, Uncle? It is a special place."

"Of course, my dear. You know that at night the key hangs under the sheelagh."

That made her laugh, for the sheelagh was the strange naked female figure carved into one of the massive stones to the right of the church doors. Typical of Brideswell to keep the key there.

Mara slipped back into the house, testing the atmosphere. At least all was quiet. She crept upstairs and again found only empty rooms. When she looked outside, she saw Dare running, oh so clumsily, but as if pursued by demons, and Ruyuan, fleet and tireless at his side.

That set a pattern that paid no heed to night or day. Dare ran outside or paced the house, sweating, trembling, often unaware of where he was or who was with him. Sometimes Salter had to stop him beating his head against the wall, or trying to pound or kick his way through it. Sometimes Dare simply screamed, a howl of agonized despair, and often, Mara knew, he didn't only because he knew she was somewhere nearby.

Mara forced herself not to run from the screams, but she huddled, hugging herself and crying, praying that his pain stop. How much torment could mind and body take before they shattered?

She saw no way to get Dare to the church yet, so she went herself each day. Ruyuan spoke of the *chi,* and if it existed, it was even stronger in St. Bride's than in Brideswell. So she prayed, holding on to the yin-yang disk, certain that these mystical matters crossed all religious boundaries, and tried to gather blessings in her heart.

She helped with the massage, trying to work blessings into Dare's shuddering muscles as she might work butter into bread dough, dizzy herself from incense and aromatic oils and floating flute music, saying over and over and over, "I love you, I love you, I love you."

And then the cramps would come and he'd try not to scream and she'd run away so that he could.

She slept whenever she could no longer stay awake, falling into bed dressed sometimes. Salter made her eat. She tidied herself only for her visits to the church so the villagers wouldn't think her mad or, worse, mistreated.

She walked into Brideswell one day and

halted, suddenly terrified. Something was missing in the house, like a rumble silenced. She raced upstairs, colliding with Ruyuan on the landing.

He caught her. "He sleeps, Mara."

She stared at him, still half thinking he meant that Dare was dead, but he smiled and said it again. "He sleeps."

She crept into the bedroom to confirm the miracle. The window stood open and country sounds drifted in. Dare was indeed in a true sleep. He was under the covers, so she could only see his lank hair, but she knew there was no knotted tension in him. No agony in the head and bones, no acid in the veins, no tortured rebellion of the organs.

"Praise heaven," she whispered. "The victory is won?"

"With another, I would say maybe, for the lure can linger powerfully in the mind, but not with Darius. His abhorrence is more powerful than any pleasure opium has to offer. But he will not be well for some days and not truly well for a month or so. His body must heal."

Mara looked at the clock, but it only told her that it was twenty minutes past three. "How long has it been?"

"Five and a half days."

"An aeon. May I sit with him?"

"Of course, but I hope he will not stir for many hours."

He left and Mara went to the bed, taking off her bonnet and gloves. She longed to slip under the covers and lie with Dare, but she mustn't wake him. Instead she quietly drew a chair up by the bed and sat to watch, guard, and pray.

It was evening when he stirred. He seemed to struggle to open his lids and then he winced.

"Does it hurt?" she asked.

He did open his eyes then, but she wasn't sure he saw her. "Not yet."

She placed her hand over his covered chest. "Ruyuan says it's over."

"He might be right." But then he said, "This is difficult." His voice was hoarse. From screaming, she realized.

"You're in pain? Where?"

"Can it really have stopped?" He couldn't hide the fear. "Forever?"

Mara realized she no longer had to worry about waking him and got into the bed, dressed as she was, to hold him as tightly as she could. "Ruyuan says so, and that you will not relapse. It's over, my love. It's over. You won."

He gripped her in turn, but she could feel

weakness beneath desperation, and that he'd lost weight. In less than a week he'd become frail, but oh so strong. She kissed his chest, which no longer ran with sweat, though he was, she admitted, rather pungent.

"I wasn't always brave," she confessed. "I couldn't bear to see you in such agony."

He stroked her back. "I knew you were near." He moved a little more, rolling his head and flexing his body, seeking pain, she knew, like someone probing a decayed tooth.

He wasn't decayed, however. He was whole, and soon he would be strong again.

She eased away. "I'm going to order you a bath."

He smiled, and now he did see her, with humor in his eyes. "Is that a complaint?"

"You'll feel better for it," she evaded with a grin and went to call for Salter. She would have stayed away, but Dare asked for her, so she washed his back and hair, and they kissed in the warm steam. But he'd had to be almost carried to the bath, and he needed Salter and Ruyuan to stagger back to the freshly made bed.

"I feel a strange kind of peace," he said.

The light was going, so Mara lit a candle. "Why strange?"

"Because I'd forgotten the taste of it. I thought I might miss the tranquillity that opium brings, but this is sweeter."

Someone knocked on the door. "Come," he said and Salter entered with a bowl. "Mr. Feng says you must eat, sir."

Dare eyed the bowl uneasily, but he struggled to a sitting position and Salter gave it to him. Dare stirred the soup with the spoon. Mara could tell it wasn't completely an English recipe.

He drank one spoonful. "Many parts of me are wondering what this strange activity is." After four spoonfuls, he said, "That will do for today."

Mara wondered if she should argue, but a few moments later, he vomited the soup back up into a bowl Salter had to hand. Dare fell back, clearly in pain again, and Mara went to complain to Ruyuan.

"He cannot eat yet," she said.

"His innards must learn anew, Mara. It will not take long. Dare took a bath. You should, too."

Mara blushed to think what she must smell like, and obeyed. It made her feel better altogether, and for the first time in days, she thought about what to wear. She sent for Abby, the kitchen maid, to help her into a corset and a pretty dress of sunshine yellow. When she returned to Dare's bedroom, she was rewarded by a smile that lit his eyes.

"Come here," he said.

So she went, and they kissed.

"You look better," she said.

"Ruyuan compelled me to eat more of his soup, and it stayed down. There's a battle going on inside me, but perhaps the forces of light are winning."

He looked exhausted still, but not ready for sleep, so she said, "Would you like me to read to you?"

"Having rescued me from durance vile, shouldn't we rescue poor Canute?"

That all seemed part of another world. "I didn't bring my notes, but we can re-create them."

By candlelight, they recalled Canute and Anne Whyte, Caspar and the eyeless monk. "Who must be named Samson," Dare said.

It was tentative, but the beginnings of creativity and humor that had nothing to do with opium.

He fell asleep, between one word and the next. Mara returned to her room and prepared for bed, but then went back to curl up against him, to comfort herself with his warmth and steady breathing, and to give him anything she could.

She woke to a kiss and his clear eyes, and

they kissed both slow and long, with sweetness but not with passion, yet. When he got out of bed, he swayed. When he tried to walk, he crumpled to the floor. "I seem to remember this feeling," he gasped, lying there. "After being run over by a cavalry brigade."

"At least you've no broken bones this time," Mara said and called for the men to help him back to bed.

She'd been too hasty to put on a pretty dress and changed back into an old one, for Dare still needed massage.

"His *chi* must be restored to its natural flow, Mara," Ruyuan said, "or he cannot heal. All healing comes from the rightness within. If you will permit, I will do this for you. You, too, have fought and exhausted yourself."

Mara was very startled by the idea but she let Ruyuan take her to her room, where she lay down on the bed. He began by running his hands over her body in a way that would have shocked her to death mere weeks ago. Then he said, "I will work through the hands and feet."

It was strange to have him pushing, pulling, and pressing at her feet, but it soon felt as if she could be floating up off the bed, every limb relaxed. When he began on her right hand, she asked, "Can I learn to do this?"

"Certainly. It is nothing magical. Merely a matter of allowing the *chi* to flow. When we are unwell, in pain, in distress, channels close, and if we leave it so, everything becomes worse."

"The exercises do the same thing, don't they?"

"The *tai-chi?* Yes. They are very beneficial, but especially for the mind."

Still floating, Mara asked, "Have you been to St. Bride's? To the church?"

"I am not a Christian, Mara."

"I think the *chi* is particularly strong there. I'd like to get Dare there as soon as possible."

"Then when he wakes, we will go."

When Dare next woke, he managed to walk across the room to a chair by the window. There he ate a whole bowl of beef soup. After a half hour they all agreed that it would stay down. When the expedition was explained, he quoted from the Bible: " 'The spirit indeed is willing, but the flesh is weak.' "

"Then we'll drive," Mara said.

While Salter and Ruyuan dressed him and carried him down, she ran to get the gig. She had it by the door when he staggered out, more or less on his feet.

Salter and Ruyuan walked beside the gig, and it was probably as well that it was dark as the strange procession passed through the village. When they made it up to the church door, Mara didn't need to find the key, for the church was unlocked, waiting for them.

She led the way in, finding the church eerie in the light of the one small lamp before the altar. Dare collapsed into the pew nearest to the door, looking exhausted.

Ruyuan said, "Ah, yes," and walked around the small church, then sat in the center of the aisle, cross-legged. He gave no instructions, but Dare struggled to his feet and leaned on Salter to walk down the aisle. He found a spot and sat, then lay down, spread-eagled on his back.

Salter took a seat in a nearby pew. Mara might like to lie on the flagstones, too, but it felt too much, here in the family church, so she sat beside Dare's patient guardian.

"Do you feel anything?" she asked quietly.

"Can't say as I do, milady, though I'm not one to deny what others find beneficial," Salter answered.

"Will you stay with Lord Darius?"

"No, milady, but I've found this satisfying work. I may try to find another with the same trouble, and perhaps persuade him or her to seek Mr. Feng's help, though people can be very fearful of anything that seems strange."

Mara tried to imagine how she would have reacted if presented with this situation without preparation. She might have rejected it, but no one with an open mind could deny that something special flowed around this site, or that Ruyuan's *chi* had spiritual power.

God worked in mysterious ways.

When Dare stirred, he struggled to get to his feet, but he seemed stronger and steadier. Ruyuan rose and took his hands. Then he beckoned Mara and Salter. They went, though Mara could sense Salter's uneasiness, as if a rope held him back.

"Stand to either side of Dare," Ruyuan said. "Take his hands and mine."

They obeyed, forming a circle, and Mara felt it. It was like a hum passing round and round, rippling through her body, strengthening her, raising her mind.

Salter broke the circle first. "Very interesting," he said gruffly, and Mara knew he, too, was fearful of something he found strange.

They all walked out of the church into a soft, peaceful night. "Sometimes the whole earth is sacred," Mara said.

Dare kissed her hair.

"There's a small field just beyond that hedge," she said, "that still has a line of foundation from the monastery. We could build a house there. It would be a modest one with a small garden, but that is all we'll need and I'm sure the *chi* runs strongly there."

"For we are commoners," he said, "not a real lord and lady, so a small piece of heaven will suffice."

They walked on in each other's arms, and if he leaned against her, she still sensed the new strength inside him. "Thank you, God," she said to the starry sky.

"Amen," he said.

"So when do we marry?"

"I believe we already did."

She elbowed him. "Our families will prefer that we legalize it."

He rubbed his face in her hair. "It's for the lady to set the date, but I'll do you more credit in a month or so. On midsummer's day perhaps?"

"Just after the summer solstice? Perfect."

"And my birthday. What better gift?"

CHAPTER 32

It rained on June twenty-fourth, but it was a soft rain that sparkled in fitful sunshine. Mara recited the old tradition: "Rain on midsummer day, the angels do pray."

She was with child. Eventually everyone who could count would know, but she hadn't told anyone except Dare. He'd suggested bringing forward the date, but she'd refused. "I like the idea of marrying on your birthday. At least you'll never forget the date. And I want you full of strength and vigor on our wedding night."

Tonight, she thought as she walked with her family to the church. The showers had stopped, and this would be a simple country wedding, so walking was the right thing to do. She wore a new dress of blue and a hat trimmed with flowers. Dare's family waited in the church along with most of the village, but there would be no other outsiders. There'd been talk of all the Rogues attending, but Dare had put them off. Instead, he and Mara had promised to join a gathering in a week at Marlowe.

"An exorcism," Simon had said. Of the cold house, but also, she knew, of the dark thread begun by Thérèse Bellaire in 1814.

Delphie walked beside Mara, holding her hand, with Mariette, in yet more new finery, in the other. For once, the two children had agreed to be apart, for Pierre was with Dare. Mara suspected this was a plan on the children's part to make sure nothing prevented the marriage.

Then she saw Dare and Pierre waiting by the well along with many villagers.

"You're supposed to be in church," she said.

His eyes twinkled. "I want to see if my bride is chaste."

"She was," Mara said softly as he scooped out well water and offered it to her to drink. She drained the scoop. When she didn't keel over dead, everyone cheered.

She linked arms with Dare, and they walked into the church with an escorting child on either side. They said their vows — the approved ones this time — but as they looked into each other's eyes, they knew that their real vows had been said weeks before.

They walked out to pealing bells and showers of petals and grain, and on to the village green, for their wedding feast would be the midsummer fair, with contests, feasting, and dancing. Though they longed to slip away, they waited until dark, when the traditional bonfire was set ablaze. They joined hands in the circle that danced around it and Mara giggled to see the duke and duchess taking part. Gravenham and his wife must have left, for she didn't see them, but Lady Thea seemed to be having a wonderful time.

Then Dare directed everyone's attention to a dark corner of the green. "As a special treat," he said, "I have persuaded Monsieur Dubourg of the famous cork exhibit to bring his model of the volcano Vesuvius here to demonstrate its wonders."

Mara looked at him. "You didn't!"

"I promised you would see it explode."

"Erupt," she corrected with a grin.

Two torchbearers illuminated the mound and Monsieur Dubourg gave a judiciously short lecture on the volcano, emphasizing the horrid nature of its eruption, which had caught the people of Pompeii in their sleep and killed them on the spot.

Then he applied a torch and the dark mound began to glow with heat. Amid gasps and oohs and ahhs, red appeared to bubble up and over to run down the sides into the buildings of the town.

When all went dark again, the audience applauded wildly and many of them wanted to poke around and see how it all worked, but guards had been provided, and they returned to the bonfire and more drinking and merriment.

Dare took Mara's hand and drew her away.

"So that's why you insisted on staying until dark," she said.

"And on one of the longest days of the year. Bad planning, but I hope it sets the tone."

"Eruption?" she asked, tingling.

"Precisely."

They didn't have far to go, for Mara's widowed aunt Phoebe had given them her village house for the week.

As she prepared for bed, Mara said to Ruth, "It's going to be quite strange doing that here."

"Never you mind with doing that where, Miss Mara, especially as you've been doing that before you should."

There'd never been any hope of keeping the secret from Ruth. Mara hugged her. "You find yourself a good man and do that, too, Ruth."

Ruth went red and left.

Mara climbed into bed and waited. Not long after, Dare came in, wearing a banjan she remembered, loosely tied, which showed that he wore nothing else. He was completely and splendidly recovered. He raised a brow at her prim nightgown.

"I thought I'd do this properly," she told him.

His eyes danced. "Should I extinguish the candle and fumble under layers of cloth?"

"Should you?" she teased.

He shrugged off his robe. "It shall be as you command, my lady, but I doubt a volcano can erupt with propriety."

Her mouth dried at his beauty and strength and a ripple of desire flowed through her. "Then I command you to ravish me, my lord."

He slowly drew the bedcovers down off her. "My beautiful lady. Exactly how ravished do you wish to be?"

Mara's heart was racing and her toes curled. "Utterly," she said.

EPILOGUE

The dinner table was set up in the marble hall of Marlowe, the heart of the chilly house. As Nicholas Delaney had remarked, "I doubt it has a soul."

Despite being enormous, much of Marlowe was for show. Simon and Jancy had struggled to house ten couples and their children, for all the children were present from the oldest — Bastian Rossiter, Leander's stepson, to the newest — Nicholas's Francis.

For this dinner, however, the children were settled in their quarters with servants and the ten couples sat around the table.

The round table. That had been Dare's mischievous idea and Simon's doing. At first seeing it, Nicholas had laughed. "I told you and told you we weren't King Arthur's knights, merely Rogues."

"Then you shouldn't have chosen twelve of us," Lucien said. "We're either King

Arthur's knights or the apostles."

Now, with the summer sun still shining in through the glass cupola, joining with dozens of candles to drive away any evil spirits, they talked and laughed and remembered. Ten men's memories went back to boyhood, but ten women's memories went back as far because of tales their husbands had told them. And some of these women had been deeply involved in the dark adventures that had finally ended.

Mara had completed her string of beads and purchased one for each couple, which she now passed around. In the center were the two pearls for the missing Rogues. On either side sat the topaz for Dare and the garnet for Simon. Completing the string were jasper, jade, blue agate, malachite, bloodstone, and coral. For the last two Mara had chosen moss agate for Con, a solid country man, and lapis lazuli for Lucien.

Mara was wearing a parure of faceted topaz, which had been Dare's wedding gift to her.

Nicholas rose to propose a toast. "There is no greater blessing than friendship, in life and, especially," he said to his wife, "in marriage. We have weathered storms and sailed between gorgons and krakens, and found at last smooth water and steady winds. May it remain so."

Everyone raised a glass to the toast, but Dare said, "For some reason, I doubt that. You gathered us together at school because we were all destined for trouble, and you were right."

"I was, wasn't I?" Nicholas said. "Sometimes I feel like Cassandra. But I brought in Con for stability, and you for lightheartedness, and neither of you let me down."

"Ballast and sails?" Dare asked. "We won't wallow in the doldrums, then. Set sail for the future, and let krakens and gorgons beware!"

AUTHOR'S NOTE

Writing a romance about a hero addicted to opium wasn't easy. I put Dare in this position for my own plot convenience, however, so I had to get him out of it.

I didn't know how this would happen or who his beloved would be until I wrote *The Rogue's Return.* Up till then I knew nothing about Simon St. Bride other than his name and that he'd been in Canada during the rest of the Company of Rogues books. As his story unfolded, however, Simon's family and his home, Brideswell, became important aspects of the book. Then Mara emerged, and without knowing much about her, I knew she was destined for Dare.

(Destined for Dare. That would have made a title, wouldn't it? It was so very hard to resist titles with Dare in them. Dare to Love. Dare to Believe. I was strong.)

I still wasn't sure how to approach Dare's story, however. It didn't feel right to start with the focus on him and his addiction. It didn't feel right for Mara to be simply a ministering angel. Then the opening scene popped into my head. There was Mara in trouble and Dare to the rescue. Even better, Mara's trouble was completely her own fault and an aspect of that devil's hair that caused most of Simon's problems. Without knowing anything else about how the book would develop, I knew I had Dare's story.

It may surprise you — it certainly surprises me whenever I think about it — but I set very little of my Regency fiction in London. I tend to use country houses with only dips into London's ton society. ("Ton" comes from *bon ton,* meaning "good tone" in French, which equates to "the elegant people." As you see in the book, I've become fond of another term found in Regency documents — the haut volée — the high-flyers.)

I've been writing Regency settings for decades now, so balls, routs, Bond Street, and Almack's are familiar, but Dare was avoiding the haut volée, so where could he and Mara go? To all the places tourists back then went.

There are records left by people who visited London and talked of the sights. One of them was a source I'd already used for

The Rogue's Return — The Ridout Letters. One of the Canadian Ridout sons went to London and wrote detailed letters home.

There's also a book called *A Visit to London,* written in 1817. It's for children and, like so many sources, doesn't give all the details I'd like, but it was still a useful glimpse into the time of my book. For example, the children go to the Tower of London but the book uses that mostly as an opportunity for lessons on history and on animals of the world.

But how tempting to slide in the Juvenile Library, where little Maria gasps in delight over books called *Mental Improvement* and *Rambles Through the Fields of Nature.*

The titles Mara buys are real. Yes, *Husband Hunters!!!* — three exclamation marks and all — was a new novel in 1817. Alongside Jane Austen, who was unfortunately to die later that year, readers had a wide choice of romance novels, usually with dramatic and gothic story lines. *The Ghastly Ghoul of Castle Cruel* might even find a publisher if Dare and Mara ever finish it.

But back to opium. The history of opium, its uses and abuses, is fascinating and complex. I recommend *Opium, a history* by Martin Booth for an overview. I also read many personal accounts of the struggle with the drug at around the time of this book including Thomas de Quincey's famous *Confessions of an Opium Eater,* which gives less useful information than you might expect. The extremes and incoherence are probably evidence of his extremely high dosage.

I also benefited from e-mail contact with someone who has gone through withdrawal from a modern drug derived from opium. I thank him.

At the time of this novel, opium hadn't been refined into morphine, codeine, heroin, etc. It came as a resin scraped off the seed pods of poppies and was usually taken as laudanum — that is dissolved in alcohol along with flavorings and sugar.

It's important to remember that in 1817 opium was as legal and cheap as aspirin, and thought of in much the same way. Most houses would have some on hand to ease pain, soothe distress, and even to calm a fretful baby.

People could buy the paste themselves and make up medicines, or they could buy some type of laudanum from a druggist. (The words "chemist" and "druggist" are both used in the period. These days the British get their prescriptions from a chemist and the North Americans from a drugstore. An example of how language splits.)

This accessibility made life both easier and more difficult for the addict. There was no need to seek out criminals to get a fix, or to do without food to afford the drug. On the other hand, there was little to dissuade a person from continuing to take it except that an addict tended to take more and more and reach a point where both mind and body began to fall apart.

Few people back then seem to have become addicted for "kicks." Some did, like Nicholas, seek the supposed mental brightness of the drug, but most took it for pain at a time when there was nothing else that could help. If the source of the pain was chronic, they kept taking it for years, possibly in larger and larger doses to get relief, and thus they became trapped, because opium changes the body. Stopping it wasn't simply a matter of willpower because the body, especially the internal organs, could no longer operate properly without it. The addict who went "cold turkey" (not a Regency term) might die. They would certainly endure extreme agony of mind and body.

Nowadays there are drugs to help the process, but in Dare's time, the only hope was to slowly wean the body off opium until the point was reached where it could be stopped entirely without death.

Even so, the end stage was horrible and it was often all for nothing. If the addict had started to take opium for chronic pain, the cause of pain could still be there. If they'd taken it for mental stress, their fragile minds would still torment them. Many experts did believe that it was wiser to use willpower to take a low maintenance dose of opium than endure the torment and hazard of withdrawal. Remember, it wasn't illegal or expensive.

What about Feng Ruyuan? There are many stories about people from China and other Oriental countries having greater understanding of the way of the drug, so I used that to ease Dare's road. It seemed likely that Nicholas would know such a person, even though China was mostly a closed-off country at the time.

In the mysterious way of creativity, in the middle of writing this book, I received an e-mail from a fan in China who had come across one of my books. She was very helpful in pinning down who this man I was seeing might be and giving him an appropriate name.

As for Brideswell, there I drew on another

mystical tradition — that of sacred spaces in Europe. It seemed to me that a place that made such a deep impression on people's minds had to have some special vibes.

I enjoyed a visit to England to refresh my memory of London and to explore Lincolnshire. You'll find photographs on my Web site, and also contemporary pictures of places like Dubourg's Cork Exhibit. I invent many little details in my books — for example, Great Charles Street is made up because real people were living in the houses of the real streets and I didn't want to disturb them — but I stick to reality as much as I can.

I found a marvelous book called *The Shows of London* by Richard B. Altick, which tempted me to send Dare and Mara to a whole range of amusements. They never did get to explore Westminster Abbey or St. Paul's, or to inspect Napoleon's carriage, which was still riotously popular. They could have marveled at the huge panoramas of famous places around the world, especially one set up in the circular Rotunda in Leicester Square. There were waxworks and effigies and enormous paintings of things like famous battles. And what about the Panharmonicon that reproduced the effect of a brass band, and for which Beethoven composed a piece?

But writing a novel is so much about what to include and what to leave out. I manage not to dump all my research into the story by writing these author notes.

I enjoy hearing from readers. Contact details are on my Web site, www.jobev.com. Or you can write to me c/o Margaret Ruley, The Rotrosen Agency, 318 East Fifty-first Street, New York, NY 10022. I appreciate a SASE if you would like a reply. I have a newsletter list that gets a monthly e-mail (most of the time) and I send out a postal newsletter once a year.

And last, no, this isn't the end of the Rogues. The Rogues' World will continue and I'm already working on a story about Dare's sister, Thea. You see, she had a strange encounter at the ball.

Having these characters come to life for me is so much fun.

All best wishes,
Jo

The employees of Thorndike Press hope you have enjoyed this Large Print book. All our Thorndike and Wheeler Large Print titles are designed for easy reading, and all our books are made to last. Other Thorndike Press Large Print books are available at your library, through selected bookstores, or directly from us.

For information about titles, please call:

(800) 223-1244

or visit our Web site at:

www.gale.com/thorndike
www.gale.com/wheeler

To share your comments, please write:

Publisher
Thorndike Press
295 Kennedy Memorial Drive
Waterville, ME 04901

DATE DUE   BS

MAR 0 8 2007			
JUN 1 8 2007			
OCT 0 1 2007			
OCT 1 7 2008			
NOV 0 9 2009			
JAN 0 5 2010			
JAN 2 9 2010			
	WITHDRAWN		
GAYLORD			PRINTED IN U.S.A.